Hugh Miller, Harriet Myrtle

Edinburgh and its Neighbourhood

Hugh Miller, Harriet Myrtle

Edinburgh and its Neighbourhood

ISBN/EAN: 9783337365431

Printed in Europe, USA, Canada, Australia, Japan

Cover: Foto ©Andreas Hilbeck / pixelio.de

More available books at **www.hansebooks.com**

EDINBURGH AND ITS NEIGHBOURHOOD

GEOLOGICAL AND HISTORICAL;

WITH THE

GEOLOGY OF THE BASS ROCK.

BY HUGH MILLER,

AUTHOR OF 'THE OLD RED SANDSTONE,' 'MY SCHOOLS AND SCHOOLMASTERS,'
'THE TESTIMONY OF THE ROCKS,' ETC.

EDINBURGH:
WILLIAM P. NIMMO.
1869.

DIRECTIONS FOR PLATES.

Edinburgh, to front the Title-Page.

Bass Rock, with Fortifications in 1691, to front page 223.

Bass Rock in 1847, to front page 257.

PREFACE.

I have at length the melancholy satisfaction of presenting to the reader the last of that series of works fit for publication left upon my hands by my beloved husband. Four of these, it will be remembered,—viz., "The Cruise of the Betsey," "The Headship of Christ," "Essays, Historical and Critical," with the last issued volume of "Tales and Sketches,"—were prepared for the press by his own hand, although not in a convenient or portable form, the first three having appeared in the columns of the "Witness" newspaper; the last, in "Wilson's Tales of the Borders."

The remaining two, which were left in manuscript,—" Lectures on Popular Geology," and a portion of the present work on the "Geology of Edinburgh and its Neighbourhood,"—I have made it a sacred duty to give to the world, according to the repeatedly expressed intention of their author ; and

I have had the less hesitation in fulfilling this task, because all his manuscripts, especially those prepared for delivery before a popular audience, were written with the utmost care, and required no revision or addition, unless in the shape of an occasional note, where any late discovery rendered a modification or explanation of the sense necessary or desirable. The proofs of the present manuscripts I have submitted to the Rev. W. S. Symonds, to whom, as on many former occasions, my warmest thanks are due.

The two lectures with which the volume commences were read by my husband before the Philosophical Institution; the papers on the Brick-Clays of Portobello, and the Raised Beach at Fillyside, before the Royal Physical Society.

The miscellaneous essays which follow the portion of the work treating of the Geology of Edinburgh and its Neighbourhood were written for the "Witness." They are chiefly descriptions of memorable incidents in the modern history of the city, which came under the author's own observation; and to many readers they will form not the least interesting portion of the volume.

"The Geology of the Bass" explains itself to be a contribution to a work published in 1847, devoted to the elucidation of the History, the Natural History, and all the other peculiarities, of the Bass Rock. The work was got up under the auspices of James Crawford, Esq., W.S., a native of North Berwick, in conjunction with Mr W. P. Kennedy, publisher, and Mr John Greig, printer. Hugh Miller reserved the copyright of his own contribution on its Geology, for the pur·pose of making it a constituent part of his "Geology of Scotland,"—a work long contemplated, and into which all these papers and lectures, as well as those on Popular Geology, would have been incorporated.

The writing of the manuscript papers now for the first time published formed in reality the latest labours of my husband's life, the preparation for the press of "The Testimony of the Rocks" being a work merely editorial, although requiring more thought, and an intenser application, than the state of his health at the time could safely permit. Whilst residing at Portobello for the last four years of his life, he frequently left home about mid-day, and spent his time until late in the evening in exploring the shores of Leith, and the nearer towns along the margin of the sea, giving his exclusive attention to the formation of the coast-lines, and endeavouring to extract the secrets of the boulder and brick clays. His success, at a much earlier period, in the region of the Old Red Sandstone, at a time when it was a *terra incognita* to geologists, is sufficiently well known. His researches in the boulder-clay department,—that dark and mysterious period which was long believed to be the epoch of the Flood, shutting out the present act in life's wonderful drama from all the other long-drawn scenes of the past,—are scarcely, however, known at all, because I believe their only very distinct record is to be found in the pages now given to the public. It is thus hoped that this little volume, not quite so bulky as some of its predecessors, may prove not unwelcome to geologists; while I most fondly trust,—having kept it to the last with that especial view,—that it will be accepted by the citizens of Edinburgh as an additional memorial of one who lived among them for the best years of his life, who had their interests warmly at heart, and to whom all that pertained to his country was intensely dear. He has been called the last of the Scotchmen,—in an exclusive sense, I presume,—as a well-known writer called Dr Chalmers the last of the Christians. We may hope, however, that God in his providence will yet raise up for our country other Christians like Dr Chalmers, and Scotchmen like Hugh Miller.

I consider my task as editor of these posthumous volumes to have ended. By some, perhaps, the series may have been regarded as too lengthened. Yet it appeared to me that one more abridged would not have done justice to my husband's life-work, or placed his varied toils in a position in which they could properly be appreciated.

If I am spared, and permitted health and strength suffi-cient for affording some little assistance in the preparation of a Memoir subsequent to his autobiography, I shall think that I have not lived these latter painful years quite in vain. At any rate, such materials as I have shall be placed in the hands of a literary gentleman whom I consider competent to the task.

I am the more particular in mentioning this, as I have had frequent applications from gentlemen, who felt there was a want which ought to be supplied, requesting what materials I could afford, and offering to undertake the work. I there-fore take this opportunity of stating, that the precious record of my husband's latest and busiest years will be my next care, believing, as I do, that it is a record not wholly without warning, yet full of interest and instruction, for more than one class of his fellow-men.

LYDIA MILLER.

November 1863.

E R R A T A.

7, line 3d from bottom, for *Lemnidæ* read *Limnæidæ*.

19, line 16th from top, for *Dentalium entalis* read *Dentalium entale ;* and line 24th, for *Pecten fusio* read *Pecten pusio*.

71, line 7th from bottom, for *Sphenopterus* read *Sphenopteris*.

74, line 3d from bottom, for *Cistracion* read *Cestracion ;* and line 4th, for *Cistraciont* read *Cestraciont*.

80, line 6th from top, for *Neuropterus* read *Neuropteris*.

131, line 5th from bottom, for *Eversham* read *Evesham*.

133, lines 8th, 10th, and 14th from bottom, for *planorbus* read *planorbis*.

144, line 1st, place a comma after *lymnea ;* and line 6th from bottom, for *lymneæ* read *lymneidæ*.

251, line 2d from bottom, for *Tubipora radiatus* read *Tubipora radiata*.

EDINBURGH AND ITS NEIGHBOURHOOD.

GEOLOGICAL FEATURES.

LECTURE I.

Natural Features of the City—Once a Scene of Lakes—Its Trap-Rock Hills and Precipices—The Deposits found in the Meadows or old Borough Loch—How produced—Ancient Picture of Watson's Hospital and the surrounding Locality—What is now the City once covered with Trees and Thickets, the abode of Wild Beasts—The Ancient and Existing Coast-Lines—Traces of the Sea having once flowed as far as Stockbridge on the West and Fillyside on the East —The Duke's Quarry at Granton situated between the two Coast-Lines—Its Littoral Remains—Four Belts or Areas of Sea-bottom, termed Zones—Their Deposits—Tract of Laminarian Sea-bottom near North Queensferry—The Appearances which it exhibits—The Sands, Gravels, and Brick-Clays around the City—Ancient Sea-bottom in Banffshire—The Geography of Scotland, when covered by the Tide, widely different from what it is now—The Site of Edinburgh then existing as a Scene of Islands of the Sea—The Shell Alphabet —The Boulder-Clay Deposit—Its Organisms—Most of the New Town built upon it—Conclusion.

THE Scottish capital is one of the few great cities of the empire that possesses natural features, and which, were the buildings away, would, while it ceased to be *town*, become very picturesque *country*. And hence one of the peculiar

A

characteristics of Edinburgh.   The natural features so overtop the artificial ones,—its hollow valleys are so much more
strongly marked than its streets, and its hills and precipices
than its buildings,—Arthur Seat and the Crags look so
proudly down on its towers and spires,—and so huge is the
mass and so bold the outline of its Castle rock and its Calton, compared with those of the buildings which overtop
them,—that intelligent visitors, with an eye for the prominent and distinctive in scenery, are led to conceive of it rather
as a great country place than as a great town.   It is a scene
of harmonious contrasts.   Not only does it present us with
a picturesque city of the gray, time-faded past, drawn out
side by side, as if for purposes of comparison, with a gay,
freshly-tinted city of the present, rich in all the elegancies
and amenities; but it exhibits also, in the same well-occupied
area, town and country; as if they, too, had been brought
together for purposes of comparison, and as if, instead of remaining in uncompromising opposition, as elsewhere, they
had resolved on showing how congruously, and how much to
their mutual advantage, they could unite and agree.   This
remarkable prominency of natural feature renders it comparatively easy for us to conceive of the aspect exhibited by
what is now Edinburgh, ere yet it had become a home of
man.   Hogg, in his "Queen's Wake," describes with a few
graphic strokes the Edinburgh of the times of Edward I. :—

> " See yon little hamlet, o'ershadow'd with smoke ;
> See yon hoary battlement throned on the rock ;
> Even there shall a city in splendour break forth,—
> The haughty Dun-Edin, the Queen of the North ;
> There learning shall flourish, and liberty smile,—
> The awe of the world, and the pride of the isle."

Let us, however, attempt conceiving of it at a greatly earlier time,—at a time when those leaf-shaped swords of bronze found a few years since in its neighbourhood, on the southern flanks of Arthur Seat, glittered at the sides of the old aboriginal warriors, to whom the antiquary has now restored them, and when the ancient fortress of the Maidens existed in its first form, like the rude hill-forts of New Zealand, as a few earthen heaps ranged mound beyond mound, with deep ditches between, and topped by lines of tall undressed palisades.

The scene consists, more immediately in the foreground, of a series of what seem nearly parallel valleys, with ridges between, steeper or more gentle of ascent, according to the disposition and form of the trap-rocks which protected them from the denuding agencies on the west, and which at this early period are bosky with bush and tree. Each of these valleys has its blue gleaming lake. There is the *Nor'* Loch, a sheet of water still remembered by some of our older citizens, but whose very name points to another sheet of water, the *South* Loch, of which tradition retains no recollection, but of which unequivocal remains have been found, in the form of beds of silt, impressions of aquatic plants, and layers of lacustrine shells, in the valley now occupied by the Cowgate and the Grassmarket. Beyond, in a flatter and tamer valley, there is a reed-encircled lake on the area now occupied by the Meadows, which, as indicated by the extent of its remains, must have existed as a piece of open water for many centuries. A smaller lake, also indicated by its shells, —Limnæa and Cyclas,—lies along the hollow valley which intervenes between the classic ridge of St Leonard's and the sloping talus of Salisbury Crags.   Yet another lochen occupies the valley between the grassy back of the Crags and the dizzy front of Arthur Seat, known as the Hunter's Bog. Dunsappy Loch has been of late restored; and that of Duddingston, though with lessened area and ever-shallowing depths, still exists.   And thus, in a tract of country little more than one and a half square miles in extent, at least seven lakes must have opened their blue eyes to the sky, and given in these early times lightness and beauty to the otherwise shaggy landscape.

Let us now mark a peculiarity in its bolder features.   All its steeper precipices present their iron fronts to the west, while towards the east its slopes are prolonged and gentle. The Castle and Calton rocks, the erect front of Salisbury Crags, the western flanks and dark brow of Arthur Seat, the trap precipices that rise over Lochend, the low trap precipices of Hawk Hill, all look to the west, as if watching the advance from that quarter of the enemy that had wasted them of old.   There is another peculiarity of the scene.   I have said that its valleys appear at first nearly parallel; but they in reality converge towards the east, and most of them unite in that quarter.   The valleys of the Nor' Loch and the Cowgate meet at Holyrood; the valley between St Leonard's and the Crags has nearly the same point of junction; and yet a little farther to the east still, we find the valley of the Hunter's Bog uniting with the others.   In short, these contiguous valleys find their point of union towards the east, just where a great current, flowing from the west, and broken up into separate streams by the trap eminences, would find *its* point of union.   Let us mark yet one peculiarity more.

Immediately in advance of the taller precipices we find deep pot-like hollows. There is such a hollow in advance of the Castle rock, towards the west. There is a corresponding

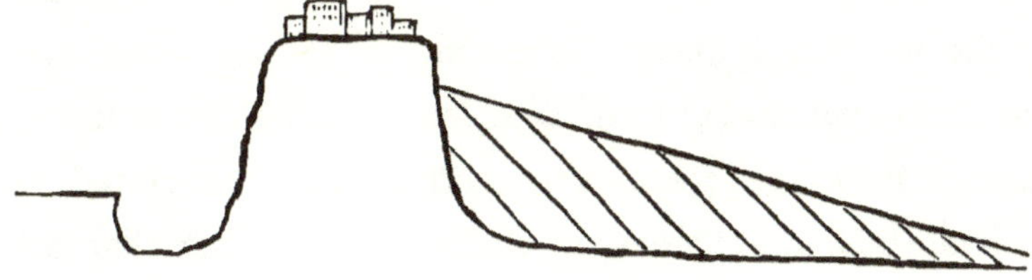

CRAG AND TAIL PHENOMENA.

hollow towards the west in advance of the precipices of the Calton. There is such a hollow in the valley in advance of Salisbury Crags. The hollow in advance of the precipices of Lochend is occupied by the waters of the loch. The restored loch of Dunsappy occupies the corresponding hollow to the west of that eminence. In fine, wherever the great current whose waters would have united where the valleys now unite would be beaten back by the bold cliffs, and form a scarping eddie, we find these excavated hollows.

Such seem to be the main features of the tract of country now occupied either by the Scottish capital, or in its immediate neighbourhood,—a tract which, if not appropriated by one of the most picturesque of cities, might be laid out into the most magnificent of landscape-gardens,—a garden with which Hagley, or Stowe, or the Leasowes, might compete in vain.

The most modern deposits in the neighbourhood of the city are those of its ancient lakes. And yet, as these hollows, surrounded by their natural barriers of rock or clay, must have been receptacles of water ever since the last upheaval of the land, their lower beds must represent what, in relation to human history, may be regarded as a very remote period. The Meadows,—the site of what was of old known as the Borough Loch,—were laid open in 1842 by a series of deep drains, which have converted into green sward what, previous to that time, used, in at least the winter months, to be unsightly morass; and the sections then exhibited bore inscribed along their sides, in easily decipherable characters, a history of the vanished lake. The lower and earlier deposits were formed of a fine gray silt, separated into lamina as thin as pasteboard, and that bore in its folds the partially carbonized impressions of what seemed to be the common water-flag and common reed. Immediately above the silt there occurred a bed of gray shell-marl, composed mainly of lacustrine shells, which thinned out towards the edges of the lake, but which near its centre had attained to the great depth of six feet. So light and small were these shelly coverings, that twenty, on the average, weighed only a grain; and yet every acre of the central portions of the Borough Loch had in the course of ages accumulated its many hundreds of cart-loads. They were, as I have said, chiefly lacustrine; but a few stragglers from the land,—helicidæ and bulimi,—might be found among them, washed, no doubt, into the lake by heavy rains; and in the middle of a thick bed the workmen came upon the wasted fragment of a deer's horn. Over this shell-marl there lay in some parts from two to three feet of peat-moss; and in one tangled mass I found embedded, in a state of wonderful preservation, the remains of the large evening beetle,—the insect so poetically described by Collins as winding

> " His small but sullen horn,
> As oft he rises, 'midst the twilight path,
> Against the Pilgrim borne with heedless hum."

The glossy elytra still preserved their prismatic tints of azure and green. But fragile as we may deem creatures of this division, the chitine or elytrine with which they are covered, and which form their strong wing-cases, is one of perhaps the most indestructible substances in nature. The chitine of dragon-flies of the Oolite, nay, of scorpions of the Coal Measures, has been detected, after the lapse of countless ages, lying unchanged in the rock. The characters in which, about twelve years ago, I found the history of the Borough Loch inscribed along the sides of the Meadow excavation, were, as I have said, easily decipherable. For many years there was a slow silty deposition taking place along its bottom. The soaking rains of winter and early spring, and the heavy thunder showers of summer and autumn, rendered it turbid, time after time, with the clay and soil of the surrounding grounds; each flood deposited its layer, which, though thin as the leaves of a book, gradually swelled by repetition into bulk and volume ; and now the leaf-like folds enclosed a reed, and now a flag, and now a rush, as if to tell that around the edges of this quiet lake there stood up a green rank hedge of aquatic plants, amid whose recesses the dragon-fly deposited its young, and the wild duck reared her brood. Anon the lake became a busy scene of life. Minute Cycladidæ crept by thousands over its bottom, each on its pale fleshy foot; while the air-breathing Lemnidæ walked along the under plane of its surface by hundreds, reversed, like flies along a ceiling, with their terminal whorls turned downwards. At length, after generation had succeeded generation for many ages, the exuviæ of the dead so filled the depths of the lake, that there was no longer space for the living; the water mosses began to spring up in its marly shallows, and gradually contracted its area, until what had been so long open water became unsightly morass, and the old Borough Loch was transformed into the Meadows. At least partially, however, it seems to have retained its character as a lake down to the middle of the last century.* In one of the larger rooms of Watson's Hospital, the plaster is occupied by a painting more than a hundred years old,—the work, says tradition, of a grateful pupil of the institution,—which represents the hospital itself as it appeared at the time from the part of the Meadows which lies immediately below. That portion of the central Meadow Walk which lies to the east of the building, and which is now overshadowed by a double row of trees, that exhibit in their gnarled trunks and stiff angular boughs an appearance of very considerable antiquity, is represented as a bare narrow pathway, unadorned by a single shrub. Instead of the closely-piled rows of houses at Lauriston, there is a tall narrow house, with sharp serrated gables, that peeps out from amid a clump of forest trees; and immediately in the foreground, in a locality now occupied by a piece of green sward, we see a quiet shaded corner of the Borough Loch, with a few drooping willows hanging their branches over it. I have said that in draining the Meadows the workmen found, at a considerable depth in

* This part of the subject is more fully treated of in a separate paper on the Meadows, which the reader will find in a subsequent part of the volume.

the marl, the fragment of a deer's horn.* Numerous deer-horns of great size were found embedded, about seventy years ago, in the marl of Duddingston Loch ; and you will remember that the old chapel of Holyrood was founded, in fulfilment of a vow, by David I., on the spot where he narrowly escaped being destroyed by a furious hart at bay. The arms of the ancient burgh of Canongate continue to exhibit the hart ; the head, with its branchy horns, still flares in gold from the walls of the gray, time-worn tolbooth : and I find it stated by Mr Daniel Wilson, so well known for his antiquarian researches, that the ancient service-book which records the incident relates that it took place in the fourth year of the reign of David, when he was residing in the neighbouring fortress,—then surrounded, it is added by the chronicler, "with ane gret forrest, full of hartis, hynds, toddis, and sic like manner of bestis." It costs an effort, amid the busy hum of a crowded and venerable city, to fall back in imagination upon a time ere the foundations of its gray antique buildings had yet been laid, and when the areas occupied by its tall tenements and narrow lanes were cumbered with great trees and dark thickets, and the fox crept stealthily through the bushes, and the red deer and the roe sheltered in its glades. And yet, both the history and the geology of the district testify of such a time, and tell that, amid the rocks, and trees, and blue gleaming lakes of what is now the busy Scottish capital, the huntsman might have pursued his sport amid the silence of shaggy solitudes,—a silence unbroken

* In the Museum of the Edinburgh Antiquarian Society there are the skull and horns of a large stag (*Cervus Elephas*), which were dug up at an earlier time in one of the parks of the Meadows.

save by the belling of the hart in its season, or the long howl
of the wolf in winter.

" Wolfs long howl when winter winds blow keen."

The geological deposit in our neighbourhood to which I
shall next refer, as next in age reckoning backwards, is that
which intervenes between the ancient and the existing coast-
lines.   It must have been formed, or rather must have received its latter modifications, when the sea at flood stood
against the grassy terrace which runs in a line nearly parallel
to that of the existing shore, round the larger part of Great
Britain and Ireland ; and which, in the near vicinity of
Edinburgh, has so often attracted the notice of geologists.

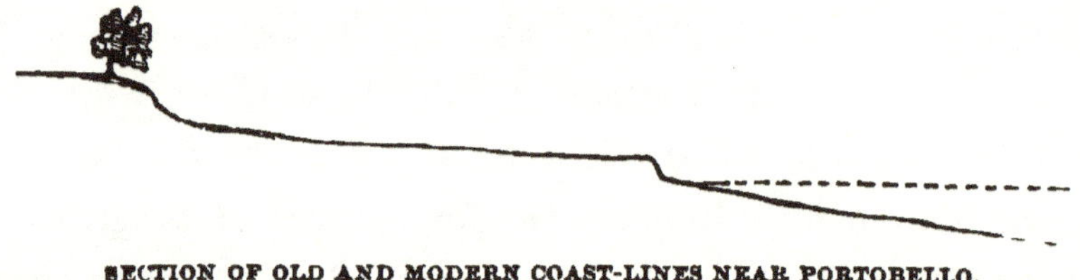

SECTION OF OLD AND MODERN COAST-LINES NEAR PORTOBELLO.

In this neighbourhood the old line seems to have had less of
that parallelism with the present one to which I have referred, than on most other parts of the coast, and its outline must have been, in consequence, greatly more picturesque
and varied than that of our existing sea-beach.   Besides the
nearly parallel valleys of the city and its suburbs, there is a
valley, well-nigh transverse in its direction, which opens upon
the sea towards the north.   The Water of Leith flows along
its bottom ; and its nether reaches, which are still occupied
at flood by the tide, formed the old harbour of Edinburgh.
Now, when the sea broke against the ancient coast-line, it

must have filled the bottom of this valley from its present opening to near Stockbridge, forming a quiet sheltered creek, fully two miles in length, by from nearly a half to a quarter of a mile in breadth. It must have also entered, though for a much shorter distance, along the flat valley near the old-fashioned farm-house of Fillyside Bank, once known as the Figget Whins; and thus a line of coast little more than a mile and a half in extent, which now presents a nearly recti-

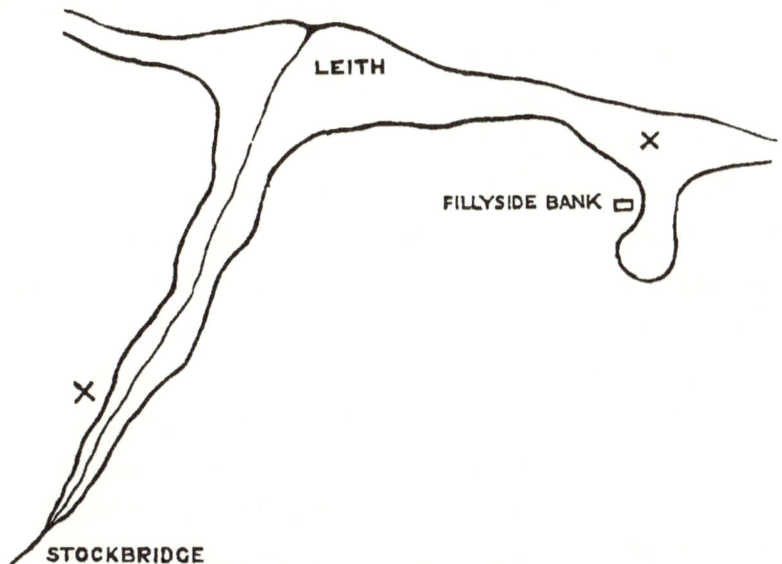

ANCIENT AND EXISTING COAST-LINES.

linear and somewhat tame outline, must have been then indented by two arms of the sea, on whose quiet waters the aboriginal huntsman of the stone period may have moored his primitive canoe, formed of a single log; or built, beside their forest-covered shores, his rude wigwam of turf and brushwood.

It is stated by Mr Maclaren, in his "Geology of Fife and the Lothians," that in 1834, in cutting the railway that runs between Portobello and Leith, the workmen found in the opening of what had been the smaller creek,—that of the Figget Whins,—an oyster-bed of considerable extent; and we know that the regular stratification of the sea-sand, which forms the subsoil in what had been the upper reaches of the larger creek or estuary,—that of Stockbridge,—attracted many years ago the attention of Playfair. We find it specially referred to in a work of classical beauty,—his well-known "Illustration of the Huttonian Theory." "The soil," he says, "after a thin covering is removed, consists entirely of sea-sand, regularly stratified, with layers of a black carbonaceous matter in their lamellæ interposed between them. Shells are, I believe, but rarely found in it; but it has every other appearance of a sea-beach." Mr Maclaren states, on the authority of Mr Jardine, civil engineer, that in the oyster-bed of the Fillyside or Figget estuary, most of the valves of the shells were separate, though in some few cases they occurred together,—a condition, of course, to be expected, if, as seems more than probable from the appearances, the land rose by fits and starts, during paroxysms of upheaval, with intervals of repose between. I cannot doubt that the oyster once lived on the spot. A few years ago, after a gale from the north-east, coincident with a very high tide, had swept the shores, and made several encroachments on the coast-line, I found, several hundred yards to the east of this old oyster-bed, numerous valves of oysters attached to a stratum of boulder stones, from which the overlying sward, with about three feet of laminated sand, had just been washed away. The nature of the evidence here could not be mistaken. The sedentary oyster, when living on a hard bottom, often solders itself by its lower valves to rocks or stones ; and many ages after death the valves remain, as in this instance, still attached to their ancient moorings ; but where the valves remain, the individuals to which they belong must have lived and died. It is, however, probable, that wherever we find great deposits of oysters, as at Fillyside Bank, between the ancient and modern coast-lines, they must have ceased to live in consequence of some previous upheaval of the sea-bottom ere the final recession of the sea to its present limits. The oyster-beds of the Frith of Forth are never *laid dry* by the fall of the ebb : they occur in what has been termed the Laminarian zone, in from four to seven fathoms water; whereas, when the *high-water* line rested along the base of the green escarpment at Granton and Portobello, the beds in question must have lain within, not the Laminarian, but the Littoral zone. And hence the displaced and scattered valves,—an effect, evidently, of the exposure of the shells after death to the waves of an open beach, subjected piecemeal to the action of the surf by the rise and fall of the tide. All the remains which I have found underlying, in this neighbourhood, the flat terrace that intervenes between the present and the ancient coast-lines, exhibit the Littoral character, though the original Laminarian character may, as in the adduced instance, be seen through it. There is no locality within a few miles of Edinburgh where these Littoral remains can be better studied than immediately over what is known as the Duke's Quarry at Granton. The whole of that huge excavation lies between the two coast-lines ; and we see everywhere in section, along the edge, in the overlying sand and gravel, the ancient shells which had strewed the old beach ere the last upheaval of the land. When I last passed that way, a series of excavations, apparently for drainage purposes, lay open in the lea field which lies between the quarry and the old ruinous mansion-house to the east. They were from about a hundred feet to a hundred yards distant from the present high-water line of stream tides ; and each excavation exhibited its layer of old shells, identical in character and disposition with those of the existing beach below,—such as single valves of the oyster and pecten, numerous specimens of the whelk, dog-whelk, and periwinkle ; specimens in less abundance of turritellæ and aporrhais ; and in the higher pits immediately under the grassy escarpment which had formed the margin of the old beach, I found numerous detached valves of a minute bivalve of the Laminarian zone,—Corbula nucleus. This last was the only shell of the *ancient* shore which I did not also detect on the *modern* one. I may mention, that among the old shells I found the wave-worn fragment of a horse's tooth. It was of small size, and must have belonged to some old aboriginal horse of the country, never broken in to the bridle, that had lived and died ere the last upheaval of the land.

As this mixture of Littoral and Laminarian characters has been misinterpreted by some of our geologists, and made the occasion of a good deal of controversy, you will, I trust, permit me to make it the subject of a few remarks. I need scarce remind you, that there are certain belts or areas of sea-bottom which usually maintain a degree of parallelism, more or less perfect, with the land, that, according to the depth of water by which they are overlaid, are occupied by certain species of plants and animals peculiar to themselves. These

belts or areas are termed zones, and may be regarded as four
in number.   There is first,—reckoning downwards from the

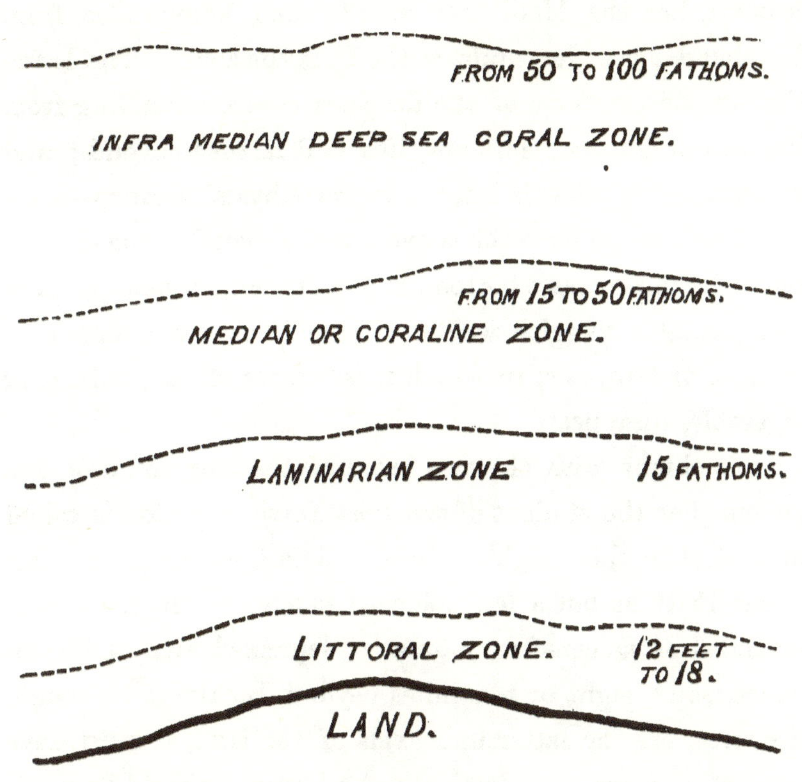

THE FOUR ZONES.

land,—the Littoral or shore zone, which comprises that strip
or belt of mingled beach and sea-bottom that intervenes between high and low water marks.   This zone has its own
peculiar plants and animals, such as the fucoids and the periwinkles.   Next comes the Laminarian zone, extending from
the line where the sea rests at the ebb of stream tides, to the
depth of fifteen fathoms.   As the name indicates, it is the
zone of the Laminaria or tangles.   In the Frith of Forth it is

that of the oysters and the common pecten,—Pecten opercularis ; and it is also that of most species of the genera Mac-
tra and Venus. Beyond, extending from fifteen to fifty
fathoms, lies the Median or middle zone, known also, from
the abundance of its corals, as the Coraline zone. The Infra-
Median zone, or zone of the deep-sea corals, extending from
fifty to one hundred fathoms, lies still farther beyond ; and
we then reach what is known as the Abyssal region,—a region in whose upper reaches even shell or coral becomes rare,
and over whose desert bottom, in the profounder depths, there
ever reposes a sluggish weight of ponderous water, unstirred
by tides or tempests, in which most traces of life, animal or
vegetable, disappear.

It is chiefly with the two inner of the four zones of sea-
bottom that the student of the Post-Tertiary period is called
on to deal in this neighbourhood. The Coraline zone exists
in our Frith as but a few detached patches (as in the neighbourhood of Queensferry), or as a depressed area in its entrance, some eight or ten miles beyond Inchkeith ; though,
of course, ere the latter upheavals of the land, it must have
been much more considerable. And what I would now call
your attention to is the fact, that with each of these upheavals
a change must have taken place in the zones of all the neighbouring seas. An upheaval which converted the Littoral
zone into dry land would have also the effect of elevating
the Laminarian zone into the levels which the Littoral one
had just occupied, and a portion of the Coraline zone into
the levels of the Laminarian one. And in course of time
these would assume respectively the Littoral and Laminarian
characters, and at the same time still retain, in at least their

dead shells, some of the characters which they had borne originally. What is now the Littoral zone of the neighbouring shore must have been its Laminarian zone when the waves broke against the grassy escarpment of Leith and Granton; and from the shells of the flat terrace on which, in this district, Portobello, Musselburgh, and the greater part of Leith and Newhaven are built, we find that, though it existed as a Littoral zone at the period of its upheaval, it had formed a portion of the Laminarian zone at a previous period, ere some earlier upheaval had taken place. We can still see in its organisms the Laminarian, if I may so express myself, through the Littoral zone. On the more exposed coasts in our immediate neighbourhood, the storms of many centuries have obliterated all mark of that previous Laminarian condition of what is now the Littoral zone, which must have obtained ere the last upheaval. In a sheltered bay, however, scarce half a mile distant from the village of North Queensferry, I was fortunate enough to discover this season a tract of the Laminarian sea-bottom belonging to the times of the old coast-line, raised far within the present Littoral level; so that I could look down, in the open air, on the remains of beds of shells which in ordinary circumstances can be swept by only the dredge and the trawl. It has assumed, however, since the period of upheaval, not a few of the Littoral characteristics; and, as being decidedly of the age of which I am now treating, and as its peculiar conditions throw light on those of the terrace of the old coast-line, I shall venture on a brief description of the appearances which it exhibits.

Opening among the trap-rocks of a precipitous shore in somewhat the form of a horse-shoe, it presents at its inner extremity the flat terrace of the old coast-line, which, when I was first introduced to the place this season, I found fra-

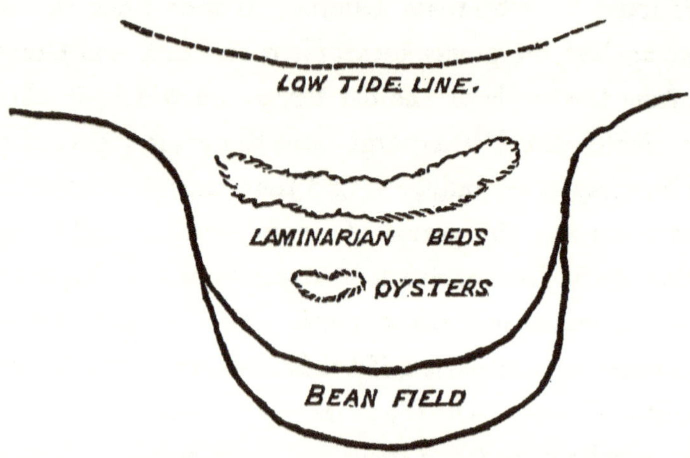

PORT LAING (NORTH QUEENSFERRY).

grant with a strip of rich bean-field, and the ancient escarpment, gorgeous with wild roses and the rock-geranium, rising steep and shaggy over the furrows. Beneath the field there is a broad sandy beach strewed with shells, along which the tide rises and falls; and observing, first, that most of its shells presented a worn and aged appearance, I next ascertained that there occurred among them in great abundance single valves of Corbula nucleus,—the single species which I found among the shells of the raised beach at Granton, but failed to detect on the neighbouring shore. As a beach shell, this Corbula is rare, but very common as a deep-sea one. "Whilst the naturalist," say the accomplished authors of the "History of the British Mollusca," "whose efforts at collecting are confined to the rocks, sands, and briny pools of our coast, is apt to regard this species as of unfrequent occurrence, its extreme prevalence is a subject of almost petulant complaint from the habitual dredger." I struck outwards along the sands, to ascertain whence the Corbula and the aged shells had been derived, and found, at the half-ebb line, a deposit of what is now a blue clay, but which had once evidently been a deep-sea mud, stretching from side to side of the little bay, and abounding in ancient deep-sea shells, evidently lying *in situ.* The remains of a great oyster-bed, some of the valves still united, and mottled with stones, to which groupes of single under-valves were still attached, might be traced to within twenty yards of high-water mark. As is common in such beds, numerous valves of Pecten opercularis mingled with those of the oyster. A bed of Corbula nucleus lay a little beyond, but still far above the line of low ebb ; and with these Corbulæ there occurred in considerable abundance specimens of Nucula nucleus, Saxicava rugosa, Anomia ephippium, Emarginula reticulata, Dentalium entalis, and Murex erenaceus. Specimens of Cyprina islandica and Cardium echinatum still lay fixed in the bed, with the two valves united, as when they had died. I found Turritella communis very abundant ; Modiola modiolus and Pecten maximus considerably less so ; and a few specimens of Pecten fusio, Lucinopsis undata, and Lucina borealis. Now, all these shells, though some of them are occasionally found alive at the ebb line of very low tides, are not Littoral, but Laminarian shells. They are exactly such shells as the dredge still brings up from such portions of the bottom of the Frith of Forth as are covered by from six to ten fathoms water. The oysters of the Frith are now dredged up from four to six or seven fathoms. But what had been in succession here a middle and upper belt of the Laminarian zone during the rise of the land, has now lain for many ages within the Littoral one, and it has assumed in the time not a few Littoral characters. We find the ancient clay perforated by borers that belong to the lower portion of the Littoral zone, such as Pholas candida and Pholas crispata, and by gapers, such as Mya truncata and Lutraria elliptica ; resting over it, we find the shells of periwinkles, the dog-whelk, and the edible cockle ; and by much the greater number of the deep-sea shells which cover it, washed, in their present exposed position, by the waves of ages, exist, on at least the surface, as detached valves.

There are just two circumstances that I would mention as curious in connection with this little bay. We find in the ancient clay, decayed fragments of wood, numerous cones of the Scotch fir, and occasionally, though more rarely, the shells of acorns and hazel-nuts,—all, apparently, from their state of keeping, and the manner in which we find them embedded, of the same age as the deep-sea shells. Such were some of the indigenous trees of the country ere the latter upheaval of the land. Swept down by the streams and rivers of the upper part of the Frith, these fruits and boughs, becoming at length weightier than the water which had sustained them, sank to the bottom, and became embedded in the mud ; and their existence in considerable quantity in this deposit throws light on the occurrence of vegetable remains of very different species, but corresponding character, among the Liassic shells of Eathie and Shandwick in the north of Scotland, and among those of the Mountain Limestone of Tweed Mill and Budle in the south. My other fact is a more curious one. The shells which belong to the time of the old coast-line have been found identical with those still living in our seas. I have been informed by Mr Smith of Jordan Hill, one of our highest authorities on the subject, that when he first set himself, many years ago, to compare the shells of the old coast terrace with those of the present coast, he found among the former three species which he had not at the time found living; but that subsequently he succeeded in dredging up all three in the neighbouring seas, and thus established the zoological identity of the Post-Tertiary periods with the existing one. I detected, however, in this little bay, existing as a fossil of the times of the raised beaches, a shell which has not yet been found living on our Scottish coasts, and which, though now an exceeding rare British shell, seems in those ancient times, when the Littoral clays of the bay existed as deep-sea mud, to have been a tolerably common one in the Frith of Forth. I refer to the Thracia convexa, "not yet found," say the authors of the "History of British Mollusca," "elsewhere than in the British islands, where it is reckoned one of our rarest species;" but of which I obtained here, in an area of less than an acre (though mostly in a very fragmentary state), portions of more than three dozen individuals. "The South Devonshire coast has produced," says Mr Hanley, "the greater part of the specimens of this shell existing in cabinets. In Torbay it is occasionally, though very rarely, brought in by the trawlers, who know it by the name of the *golden hen*,—possibly in allusion to the comparatively high price they obtain for it, or perhaps in consequence of its rich yellow colouring." It is surely curious enough to find, that what is now so rare in the southern locality, in which it is least so, should have been so abundant once in our own neighbourhood; and further, that the one shell which distinguished zoologically between the times of the old and those of the existing coast-line, should be a shell so interesting from its exclusively British character, and so highly valued by the collector.

Next in age in this vicinity, reckoning backwards to the terraces of the old coast-line, with their beds of existing shells, are those stratified sands, gravels, and brick-clays, which form the subsoil of so many of the richer fields that lie around the city.   In the sand, which usually contains a good deal of carbonaceous matter disposed in the laminæ, and curiously intercalates with the gravels, I have succeeded in finding in this neighbourhood no organism that properly belongs to itself. Carbonaceous matter, though originally organic, exists but as re-formations of culm and comminuted shales, derived from the Coal Measures.   But in the brick-clays a few organisms have been detected.   I have disinterred from out the brick-clays of Fife,—evidently of the same age as our own,—some of the lateral plates of Balanus communis, with fragments of Cyprina islandica ; and I have seen, with Mr William Rhind of this city, a specimen of what seemed to be a fresh-water shell, Cyclas cornea, derived from the brick-clays of Portobello.   But in order to find the stratified sands of apparently the same age as those of the neighbouring fields abundantly fossiliferous, the geologist would require to remove northwards to Banffshire, where a sea-bottom richly charged with shells may be found at a level considerably higher over the present sea-line than the higher parts of the New Town of Edinburgh, and which at one point lies from five to six miles inland.   When the tide covered that ancient sea-bottom, the geography of Scotland must have been widely different from what it is now. The great Caledonian Valley must have been an ocean-sound, open from sea to sea, bearing along its bottom, at its highest levels, near Loch Oich, twenty-five fathoms of water, and about thirty-seven fathoms where the town of Inverness now stands. A similar sound, broader but not so deep, would have connected what are now the Friths of Forth and Clyde. Scotland to the north would have consisted, *not* of one continuous land, but of two ; a third and larger division would have run far into England, and in our own immediate neighbourhood would present a striking scene of ocean channels and rocky islets. Over the spot where St Cuthbert's Church now stands there would rest twelve fathoms of water, and twenty-two fathoms over the spot now occupied by the Palace of Holyrood. The Calton Hill must have formed at that time an islet elevated, at its highest point, about a hundred and ten feet over the sea-level ; the ridge of the more ancient portion of the Old Town, with the Castle rock rising boldly at its western termination, an islet of an elevation of nearly two hundred feet. The elevated ground on which part of the southern portion of the Old Town is built would exist as a flatter and broader island, separated from the Castle Hill islet by a narrow channel occupying the valley of the Cowgate and the Grassmarket, and from the ridge of Bruntsfield and the Grange by a sea-channel occupying the flat hollow of the Meadows. A deep arm of the sea would run, amid the Arthur Seat group of hills, along the valley of the Hunter's Bog ; the group would itself form a picturesque island : and a wide and ample bay, traversed by the bold promontory of Craigmillar Castle, would cover the larger part of the Dalkeith coal-field, and submerge, to the depth of about seventeen fathoms, the site of the town of Dalkeith itself. When the curtain first rose upon us this evening, we saw what is now Edinburgh existing as a scene of lakes; we now see it existing as a scene of islands; and from the organisms of the raised sea-bottom of Banffshire, with those occasionally found in the brick-clays of the neighbourhood, and the more elevated Post-Pliocene deposits of the western coasts of Scotland, we can predicate the exact type of at least molluscan life which existed in its surrounding seas, and infer from that the character of the flora by which its islets were covered. Many of the Post-Pliocene shells are identical with those now found in our seas. I detected in abundance in the two hundred and thirty feet sea-bottom of Gamrie, the pretty little crimson-coloured bivalve of our sandy shores, Tellina solidula. I found also the common whelk, Buccinum undatum; the common edible cockle and mussel, Cardium and Mytilus edulis; the deep-sea cockle, Cardium echinatum; the horse mussel, Modiola modiolus; with Cyprina islandica, Turritella communis, Mangelia, and Fusus. But with these there mingled in great abundance shells whose proper haunts lie far to the north, such as Astarte arctica,—a northern form abundant on the shores of Greenland, but become so exceedingly rare in our seas, that the authors of the " British Mollusca," though indefatigable dredgers, had actually to borrow the British specimen which they figured for their work; and Tellina proxima. It is one of the peculiarities of this latter shell,—an exceedingly common one in the Banffshire beds,—that it receives its fullest development in point of size amid the intense cold of the higher latitudes. It thrives best in a wintry climate; and it is a curious fact, that while a specimen figured among the " British Mollusca," which, though not found alive, was dredged off the Isle of Skye in a state of great freshness, measured only about *half* an inch in length, and the larger specimens of the latter Post-Pliocene beds of the Clyde measure little more than *an inch* in length, the larger individuals of the two hundred and thirty feet sea-bottom of Banffshire measure nearly *two* inches in length.   The diminishing sizes indicate a gradually meliorating climate,—a climate, however, which, when the site of the Scottish capital formed a group of islands, and these large tellinidæ were living by millions in our seas, had not yet begun to improve.   The islands of the Castle rock and the Calton Hill must have been covered in these times by a subarctic vegetation, similar to that which we now find restricted to our higher hill-tops ; and the blue Pentlands must have borne, even at midsummer, their frequent streaks of snow.

Permit me here to call your attention to the pregnant meanings with which—regarded as the characters of a decipherable alphabet—the shells of a deposit such as that of the raised beaches of the neighbourhood, or of the elevated sea-bottom at Gamrie, may be found charged.   In several distinct aspects do shells—the testaceous coverings of the acephalous and gasteropodous molluscs—press themselves upon the notice of the human family.   In what may be termed the æsthetic point of view, we find them meetly associated with flowers.   When spending some quiet summer month with our children in some rural district washed by the sea, what do the little ones bring home to us in triumph, as the objects that most approve themselves to their native taste for the beautiful ?—what but flowers from the meadow and shells from the sea ?   We enter in our rambles some humble cottage, and, ranged over the chimney, we mark, as the results of a taste as unsophisticated, exactly the same combination,—a few freshly-pulled flowers, stuck into some glass or jug ; and, placed at equal distances, to satisfy the arranging faculty, a row of pretty shells.   Where the taste has been more highly educated, we find often the same combination : here, in a corner of some princely drawing-room, a splendid cabinet of exotic shells; and yonder, encased in glass, at the ample window, a luxuriant blow of exotic flowers.   And finally, in examining some ancient piece of sculpture, the product of an exquisitely refined age, or some specimen of the noble architecture of old Greece, we find, impressed by the classical stamp, the same combination still,—the wreathed shell blended with the opening blossom,—the curled ammonite existing as the volute of one classic order,—the still undeveloped circinate stems of the acanthus as the double volutes of another ; here a wreath of oak leaves ; there the elegant lamp-like nautilus, the acorn and the pecten, the murex and the laurel.   With flowers and foliage as the most obviously lovely of inanimate objects, the sense of the beautiful, alike in its most unsophisticated and its most highly cultivated state, has ever associated shells.   The honour of this companionship has been recently claimed for sea-weeds,—no doubt very beautiful objects when prepared by a careful hand.

> " O, call us not weeds ; we are flowers of the sea,
> For lovely, and bright, and gay-tinted are we :
> Our blush is as deep as the rose of the bowers ;
> Then call us not weeds ; we are ocean's gay flowers."

The claim is, however, a very recent one; nor has it its foundations in the æsthetic. Nearly two thousand years ago, when Virgil could refer to the "sea-weed cast out upon the shore" as "vile," and Horace as "useless," their contemporary, Vitruvius, was engaged, like the architects of a still older time, in uniting on frieze and pediment the shell and the flower; and the sculptor had given to Venus, as her pearly car, a vast conchifer, and to Triton, as "his many wreathed horn," a turreted univalve.

Still more interesting are shells when regarded, in the zoological view, as representatives of one of the four primary divisions into which, in all the successive creations, animal life has been separated. They exemplify one of the four great *ideas* of the Creator, as exhibited in succession in all the geological periods. Whatever has yet lived upon earth, if we except a few microscopic anomalies known as the Amorphoza, has lived in the vertebrate, molluscan, articulated, or radiated form. In these four assemblages the second place is usually assigned to the molluscs; and, from the great durability and simple forms of their shelly coverings, we find them much more entire in ancient rocks and deposits than the remains of animals of any of the other three divisions. Shells are peculiarly the medals of the geologist; and, thanks to our naturalists, we are *now* better able than in any former period to trace "the image" and read the "superscription" which they bear. The list of British shells, for instance, may now be regarded as complete. Though during the last few years the dredger has been busy around our coasts, and our beaches and shores have been well tried by the collector, scarce a single new shell has been added to the number previously known. The list of the British shells that live in our seas may be regarded as fairly and adequately taken ; "the number of our marine Acephala, or bivalve shell-fish, may be stated," say the authors of the "History of the British Mollusca," "at a hundred and sixty species ; the number of our testaceous marine Gasteropoda, or univalve shell-fish, at two hundred and thirty-two." We have thus three hundred and ninety-two British shells. Some of these the naturalist finds restricted to the Littoral zone, some to the Laminarian, some to the outer and inner Coraline zones ; some, again, belong to only the southern parts of the island ; some to only the north. Some few are found to be either peculiarly British, such as Pecten niveus and Thracia convexa ; or, like the common edible oyster, receive in the British seas their fullest development. Others, like the Haliotis tuberculata* of the Channel Islands, belong to a southern group that barely touches the southern extremity, not of Britain itself, but of its immediate dependencies ; while others belong to essentially northern groupes, and, like Astarte elliptica, are found in only the northern shores of Scotland. The proportion, too, in which certain shells appear on certain parts of the British coasts has been carefully noted. Some are exceedingly rare in the north, though abundant in the south ; and others unfrequent in the south, though common in the north. The various depths of water in which the various shells live,—the climatal belts in which they live,—the extreme limits which they barely reach, and then cease to appear, with reference both to zones of climate and zones of depth,—their range, too, of fullest development in relation to both,—have all been noted, with their peculiarities of habit

* The Haliotis abounds on the shores of the Channel Islands, and is called the Ormer. It adheres to the rock with its foot, like the limpet.

and structure, the various ties of relationship that run through their several families and genera, and the degree in which certain disturbing conditions serve to modify their form and size ; and these zoological facts, interesting to every student of natural history for their own sakes, borrow a new interest when we come to regard them as meanings attached to shells viewed as the characters of an alphabet by which the history of ancient deposits and bypast periods can be read. In this special point of view, shells become well-defined hieroglyphics, to which the naturalist furnishes the key.

This shell-alphabet consists in Britain, as has been shown, of three hundred and ninety-two several characters or words, —a large but still manageable number, compared at least with the alphabet of the Chinese, or the hieroglyphic symbols of the old Egyptian. Nor is it necessary to know all these (for some of them are of exceeding rarity, and may not be seen once in a lifetime), in order to be qualified adequately to read the inscriptions which they compose. I have already attempted reading the meanings of the mingled group of Laminarian and Littoral shells which we find buried beneath the grassy terrace of the old coast-line at Fillyside Bank and Granton. They tell that the level strip along our coasts which has been dry land ever since the historic ages began (mayhap long before), had at a previous period been covered during flood by the Littoral or shore strip of sea, and at a period still earlier by the Laminarian sea-strip, or strip of the tangles. In other words, they tell us that the land rose by paroxysms of upheaval, with periods of repose between. Even the single exceptional shell of the Granton old coast terrace to which I have referred (Corbula nucleus) as occurring in the excavations more than a hundred yards in-land, and which we do not now find, in at least aught approaching to similar abundance, on the neighbouring shores, gives evidence of the same fact. It tells that, when the spot where we now find it, immediately under the grassy escarpment, lay along the high-water line, a Laminarian strip, containing beds of the deep-sea shell Corbula nucleus, lay exposed beyond, in consequence of a previous upheaval, to the action of the surf. Mark, however, the further fact recorded by the various shells of the Granton terrace,—a fact equally borne out by the shells found at the same level all around our shores. Here, in the box before me, is a collection of these Granton shells. The group is as un-sightly a one as may be,—sorely decayed, for the sand and gravel amid which they lay freely admitted the percolating moisture, and did not wholly exclude the air. The mere lover of the æsthetic would find no charm in them; the mere zoolo-gist would seek to study the species which they exemplify in greatly fresher specimens ; the mere collector of the exotic and the rare would fail to find among them a single shell to which he would attach the slightest value. In what, then, does their interest consist, seeing that they are identical, not only in species, but also in the proportions in which they occur, and the degree of size to which they have attained, with the commonest living shells of the neighbouring frith ? Their interest mainly consists in the fact which they record in their character as an alphabet. They clearly and une-quivocally tell, that when the sea beat against the old coast-line, and covered the site of fully two-thirds of the sea-port towns of Scotland, the country had exactly the same climate as it has now.   It may have been somewhat modified by the wide-spreading forests of the time; but the average temperature of the Scottish seas must have been then just what it is now; the gulf-stream must have set in towards our shores just as now, giving to us a climate which scarce belongs to our latitudinal zone ; the cereals then, as now, could have been successfully reared upon our plains ; nor can we doubt that then, as now, the Germanic flora flourished in our sheltered valleys and on our lower hill-sides.   And such is the curious story with which, in their character as the letters of an alphabet, these decayed Granton shells of the common type are charged.

Very different is the piece of narrative which we find shell-inscribed upon the brick-clays and the stratified sands of the higher levels.   As shown by the shells of the raised sea-bottom of Banffshire, elevated about twenty-five feet above the level of the building in which we are now assembled [the Music Hall, George Street, Edinburgh], a subarctic climate must have obtained, in the age in which they lived, in what is now Scotland.   Such, in the case, is the testimony of the shell-alphabet.   Its group of shells is no longer British.   Its prevailing tellina,—the Tellina proxima,—occurs along the more northerly shores of Norway and Labrador, but is no longer found living in our seas.   Its prevailing astarte,— Astarte arctica,—belongs, as its name indicates, to a high arctic parallel, and, though very rarely seen on even the northern coasts of Scotland, is very abundant on those of Spitzbergen.   Its prevailing fusus,—Fusus propinquus,—is essentially a boreal species.   Its prevailing natica is Natica clausa,—also a shell of Spitzbergen and the North Cape.

Even such of its shells as are still not rare in our seas, such as Cyprina islandica, are northern shells, and occur in its beds and layers, not in the British, but in the Icelandic or Norwegian proportions. In short, the inscription written on these high-lying sea-bottoms and beaches in the old shell character, tell us that the climate of the period was subarctic; and as we find a certain well-marked subarctic flora on the northern coasts and islands around which these shells still continue to live, we infer—having the fixity of the conditions and constitution of animal species for our basis—that when they lived amid the deep retiring valleys of the Arthur Seat group of hills, or harboured around the submerged feet of the Calton and Castle rocks, the group of islands which now exist in their altered character as the site of Edinburgh must have been covered by a boreal vegetation, constituting what is now known as the Scandinavian flora. Further, associated with these shells, where they now live, we find in the iceberg and the glacier, powerful mechanical agents at work, grooving and furrowing the solid rocks, and transporting to great distances huge stones. And, detecting in our own neighbourhood the unequivocal marks of these agencies,—vast boulders of travelled rock, and dressed rock-surfaces,—we infer, that when Tellina proxima and Astarte arctica lived at the bottom of its seas, extensive floats of field-ice must have careered over its surface; and that, while the frequent iceberg grounded on its coasts, numerous glaciers must have descended along its hill-sides. When lately touching, in conversation, on some of these circumstances to Mr Ruskin, he exclaimed—"What a subject for a painter would not that wintry archipelago form!" The scene, if restored by the pencil of a Harvey or a Hill, would indeed be a striking one. In front, a solitary group of islets, familiar in their forms, but strange in all their adjuncts, would rise, shaggy with the Scandinavian flora, over an ice-speckled sea; in the background, the blue Pentlands, snow-streaked at midsummer, and with the glacier gleaming blue in their sloping hollows, would stretch along the horizon their undulating line; while in the submerged valleys of what is now the Scottish capital, the whale would blow, and the seal raise its round black head; and on some drifting sheet of ice the lazy morse would lie stretched in the sun, amid the screaming of a *scull* of subarctic birds,—the arctic skua, the snow-fowl, and the Icelandic gull.

Beneath the stratified sands and the brick-clays we find the boulder-clay,—in this part of the country the oldest of the superficial deposits. It occurs very extensively in this very neighbourhood, and by much the larger part of the New Town of Edinburgh is built on it. Like our stratified sands and gravels, it is unfossiliferous in this part of the country, but abounds in shells farther to the north, as in Caithness; and it has of late yielded shells to the south, in Wigtonshire; and in both ends of the kingdom we find these exhibiting exactly the same boreal character as those of the stratified sand in Banffshire. The deposit, however, is further remarkable for the strange mechanical phenomena which it exhibits. Most of the larger shells which it contains exist as but broken fragments; the stones which it encloses, from the largest boulders to the minutest pebbles, are mysteriously lined and grooved,—most frequently in the direction of their longer axes; and the rocks upon which it rests are almost invariably scratched and polished, as if worn down by the prolonged action of some such agency, on a great scale, as we see employed in the yard of the stone-cutter, in smoothing the surfaces of his pavement slabs and sepulchral tablets. It was evidently the same agent that grooved and dressed the rocks and scratched the pebbles, that broke the shells ; and, referring once more to our shell-alphabet, we know that, just as we find the Scandinavian flora associated with such a group of molluscs, we find also associated with them a sufficient agent for the production of the mechanical pheno- mena of the deposit, in icebergs and glaciers.   In formerly addressing you on this subject, I called your attention to some of the more striking characteristics of the boulder-clay deposits in the immediate vicinity of Edinburgh,—to its travelled rocks of huge size,—its great depths in hollows sheltered from the old denuding agencies,—its general cor- respondence in tint to the average colour of the rocks which it overlies,—to the heights, too, to which it ascends along our hill-sides, and which evidently testify of a time when the sea stood at least a thousand feet higher than it does now, and most of our mountain groupes existed as but clusters of islands.   Farther, I pointed out the several places in the neighbourhood where, as on the southern flank of Arthur Seat, and at St Margaret's Station on the North British Railway, the grooved and dressed rock-surfaces so generally associated with the formation may be most advantageously seen·*   I can at present add to the characteristics at that time adverted to, only one other striking feature of the

* Dressed surfaces are to be seen on the Calton Hill, on Salisbury Crags, near the quarry opened at Blackford Hill, and at Corstorphine.

boulder-clay,—a feature, however, still unrecorded, save very briefly by Mr Robert Chambers,—to whom I pointed it out, —in his able and interesting paper on the glacial phenomena of Scotland. There occurs deep in the clay, at two several points on our coast, what I have ventured to term *pavements*,—for such is their appearance,—composed of boulder-

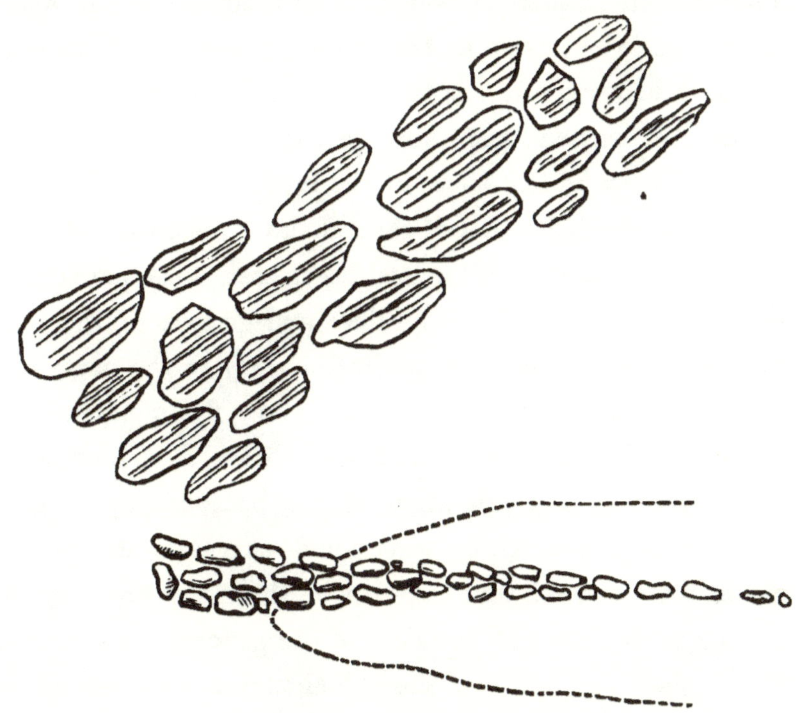

PAVEMENTS IN THE BOULDER-CLAY.

stones laid, as in a common pavement, with their smoother surfaces upwards. The ancient pavements of Pompeii and Herculaneum exhibit, when bared of the overlying ashes or lava, the marks of the old wheel-ruts into which they were grooved so many ages before. These pavements of the boulder-clay, when uncovered, as in this neighbourhood, by

the action of the waves, are found to be similarly grooved
and rutted. As decidedly as the greenstone causeways of
our streets bear evidence, in their scratched and furrowed
surfaces, of the heavily-laden carts and waggons that have
passed over them, are these pavements of the boulder-clay
charged with evidence that great moving masses had also
dragged their ponderous weight over them. But the agent
was evidently the same as that which grooved and polished
the rocks beneath : it was the ocean-borne icebergal cars of
winter that rutted these strange subterranean pavements,
compared with which, those of the buried cities of Vesuvius
are as of yesterday.   All of them I have yet observed have
their direction and striation east-north-east,—the general direction, in the district, of the lines and grooves of the rock
below ; almost all of them decline slightly to the east, and,
when relieved by the waves, resemble low flat moles stretching from the land into the sea. They indicate, I am inclined to
hold, pauses in the formation of the boulder-clay deposit,
during which, washed by waves and currents, its general
surface was lowered, and came to be thickly covered by the
disengaged pebbles and boulders of the general mass, ranged
in one place.   And then the old agency re-commenced its
operations ; and, pressing the stones down into the mass, so as
to imprint the pavement-like regularity on their upper surface, it grooved and striated them, as when acting at an
earlier period on the solid rock below. These curious pavements may be regarded as conclusive, in the proof they
furnish, that the boulder-clay was not, as some think, a
simultaneously formed deposit,—the product of some great
mud wave from the sea,—but of slow formation ; and, further,

that it presented surface after surface in succession to the great grooving and polishing agent to which it seems to have owed its origin. Two of these pavements may be found about a quarter of a mile apart, and at a half-way distance, on the line of coast between Leith and Portobello, and two others on the line of coast between Portobello and Musselburgh.

I have already referred to the subarctic character of the shells of the boulder-clay. Its other organisms are rare in Scotland. They are, however, quite sufficient to identify it as geologically of the same age as what is known as the Mammaliferous Crag of Norfolk, and to show how very strange the fauna which our island, or rather group of islands, at that time possessed. The nearest locality to Edinburgh in which mammaliferous remains of the boulder-clay have yet been found seems to be that clay deposit in the neighbourhood of Falkirk in which, in the year 1821, twenty feet from the surface, a tusk of the Elephas primigenius was found. Similar tusks, with fragments of the horns of reindeer, were detected in the same deposit about eight years later, in the immediate vicinity of Kilmarnock. And from the remains of the Mammaliferous Crag we know how very strange that fauna of our country was which was associated with the northern elephant and the reindeer. Many of my auditory must have seen the very extraordinary collection exhibited in Edinburgh rather more than a year ago by Mr Gordon Cumming,—a collection extraordinary in itself, but altogether unique regarded as the trophies of one bold hunter,—a genuine representative in these latter times of those mighty hunters of the mythologic ages who, warring on the wild beasts, the previous occupants of the soil, made way for its true possessors, the agriculturist and the shepherd.   It will be remembered, that what first struck the eye as peculiarly characteristic of that collection was the huge proportion borne to the whole by its pachydermous specimens.   Vast tusks of the African elephant, huge skulls of the hippopotamus, and still huger skulls of the rhinoceros, some of them bearing, according to their species, their single, and some their double horns, formed the prominent features through which the unique peculiarity of the collection was most readily appreciated, and by which it has been best remembered.   And, strange to relate, the fauna of the British islands during the ages of the boulder-clay and the Mammaliferous Crag was marked by exactly the same prominent traits.   At once the most striking and most abundant of its mammaliferous remains are the remains of its huge pachyderms.   Its elephants seem to have been greatly more abundant than their congeners in the African or Asiatic centre. It had, like Africa, its two species of rhinoceros, both, however, double-horned, and a large species of hippopotamus. And with these huge animals there were associated the great cave tiger, the great cave hyæna, the great cave bear, the Irish elk, the reindeer, and the gigantic ox.   The description given by an English naturalist of the group of animals which in this early age inhabited the south of England, would apply equally to the vicinity of the Scottish capital.   " Those who ramble," he says, " amid the beautiful scenery of Torquay, or gaze with admiration on the bold outlines of the Cheddar Cliffs, will find it difficult to believe that in former ages these spots were roamed over by bears, surpassing in size the grizzly bear of the Rocky Mountains or the polar bear of the arctic regions ; yet the abundant remains found in the neighbourhood incontestibly prove that such was the case. Grand indeed was the fauna of the British islands in those early days. Tigers as large again as the biggest Asiatic species lurked in the ancient thickets ; elephants of nearly twice the bulk of the largest individuals that now exist in Africa or Ceylon roamed here in herds ; at least two species of rhinoceros found their way through the primeval forest ; and the lakes and rivers were tenanted by hippopotami as bulky, and with as great tusks, as those of Africa." The immense size of some of our mammals of the Post-Pliocene period, regarded as the inhabitants of a northern latitude, and a climate greatly more severe than now, is one of not the least curious circumstances connected with the group. I found that the largest elephant-tusk in Mr Gordon Cumming's collection measured nine feet in length, and had a diameter at the base of six and a half inches. When passing my foot-rule over it, the person who showed the collection came up and said, "That tusk is the largest ever *seen* in Britain." "The largest," I remarked, correcting his statement, though the correction escaped notice, —"the largest ever *brought* to Britain." There was a very considerable difference in the case between the terms *brought* and *seen*. No tusks of our recent elephants, Asiatic or African, larger than Mr Gordon Cumming's splendid specimens, had ever been *brought* to England ; but greatly larger tusks of the old native species have been *found* and *seen* in England. A specimen found at Ilford, and which Professor Owen describes as the finest tusk of a British mammoth that has come under his observation, measured *twelve* feet six inches in length. Another tusk, dredged up from a tract of sea-bottom near Ramsgate, had its lower part awanting; but the fragment which remained was nine feet in length, and eight inches in diameter. The great size of the bones of this extinct species corresponds with that of the tusks. In the skeleton of the large Indian elephant which is preserved in the Museum of the London College of Surgeons, the humerus measures two feet eleven inches in length, and has a circumference in the middle of one foot one inch and six lines; whereas a humerus of the Elephas primigenius, found on the Norfolk coast, measures four feet five inches in length, and has a circumference in the middle of two feet two inches and six lines. The bone of the ancient British elephant is eighteen inches longer, and thirteen inches more in circumference, than the corresponding bone in what is deemed a large specimen of the Asiatic one. Of a surety "there were giants in those days." It is one of the strange circumstances connected with the extraordinary group of animals that lived in Britain during the ages of the boulder-clay, that some of the creatures their contemporaries still continue to survive. The skeleton of the badger of Kent's Hole cannot be distinguished from that of the species which still burrows in our hill-sides; nor the bones of its wild cat, from those of the existing wild cat of the less frequented jungles and ravines of the lower Highlands. The existing otter and fox, too, seem to be of equal antiquity. Again, many of the existing shells date their beginnings from a time greatly more ancient. Many of them, such as the common edible periwinkle and mussel, ascend to the ages of the Red Crag; and not a few more, such as the whelk and the edible oyster, to the more remote ages of the Coraline Crag.

But who shall attempt measuring off by seasons or centuries the duration of the more ancient families of our native mammals, or reckon up the years that have passed since the extinct elephant, the contemporary of their progenitors, found his way through the dense, low-stemmed forests of our country, or the reindeer browsed on the moss of its hill-sides? We know that for at least two thousand years, land and sea in our island have maintained, in relation to each other, the present levels,—that the Roman wall of Antoninus was made to terminate at the Friths of Forth and Clyde, with reference to the existing coast-line on both sides of the island,—and that, when Cæsar landed in Britain, St Michael's Mount was connected, as now, with the land, at low water, by a flat isthmus.*   We ascertain further, from the average depth of the caves of both the present and the old coast-line, that if the surf broke against the present shore for a period of but two thousand years, it must have broken for at least three thousand years more against the grassy escarpment of the old line. On the lowest calculation, then, we exhaust the five thousand years during which man has been a denizen of earth, ere we rise beyond the comparatively recent period in which the climatal conditions of our country were exactly what they are now,—in which the same shells lived around our coasts, and the same plants flourished on our plains and hill-sides,—in

* Diodorus Siculus refers to Julius Cæsar as having "*in our time*" conquered Britain ; and then describes the ten miners of Cornwall as conveying the smelted metal "to a British isle near at hand, called *Ictis*. For at low tide, all being dry," he adds, "between them and the island, they convey over in carts abundance of tin in the meantime."— Book V. chap. ii.

which our mountains rose over the sea-level only some thirty feet less than they do now, and our land possessed, with the exception of the old coast terrace, its present extent of area. Calculation loses footing in the vast void beyond. But the periods must have been very lengthened during which the subarctic molluscs flourished in our seas, and then gradually died out, and during which, stage after stage, the land rose, till what had been a scattered archipelago became the mountain groupes of our country, and the islets and ocean-sounds of what is now Edinburgh passed into a picturesque wilderness of hill, valley, and lake. Greatly more than ten thousand years may have elapsed since the last Scottish elephant ceased to live, or the last iceberg drifted along the submerged valleys of our country. But the eternity of the past furnishes ample room for vastly greater periods; nor must we forget, that with the Adorable Being who superintended and fore-ordained all the revolutions of our earth and its inhabitants, "one day is as a thousand years, and a thousand years as one day."

LECTURE II.

The Scenery of Edinburgh praised by Men of Genius: Burns, Hogg, Scott, Campbell—The various Subsoils of the District—Its Stratified Deposits: the Silurian, the Old Red, and the Carboniferous—The Arthur Seat Group of Trap-Rocks—The Huttonian Theory first suggested by their Appearances—The Maclaren Theory—Description of the other Trap-Rocks of Edinburgh and its Neighbourhood—Their Upheaval by Convulsions—Theory regarding their Formation—The Coal Measures—Their Extent—The Colliers once bound as Slaves to the Soil—Their final Emancipation in 1799—The Class still strongly marked by the Slave-Nature—The Coal-Seams of Mid-Lothian—Theory as to the Time required for their Formation—Visit to a Coal-Pit at Dryden—The Ancient Flora of the District—Animal Foot-prints on a Block of Sandstone—Other Foot-prints of Animals to be found—Distillation of Oils and Naphtha from the Coals and Shales of the Oolitic and Carboniferous Systems—Their Application to Economic Purposes—The Question, What is Coal? litigated—Marine Limestone, and the Shale Deposit beneath it—Most of the Old Town of Edinburgh built on the latter—Picturesque View of the successive Geological Periods.

IT is always in some degree perilous to attempt connecting new associations with old scenes. The process is ever exposed to the sort of criticism that consists in the drawing of disadvantageous contrasts, and of comparisons of the kind instituted in Holy Writ between the new wine and the old. And where the scenery is of so exquisite a cast as that which surrounds the Scottish capital, and the associations wedded to it for centuries of so high a character, the risk must of course be all the greater. It is not ordinary men that have been highest in their praise of the scenery of Edinburgh ; nor yet enthusiasts of the shallower kind that have been most powerfully moved by its varied beauties.   Lockhart tells us, in his "Life of Burns," that the "magnificent scenery of the Scottish capital filled the poet with extraordinary delight. In the spring mornings," it is added, "he walked very often to the top of Arthur Seat, and, lying prostrate on the turf, surveyed the rising of the sun out of the sea in silent admiration ; his chosen companion on such occasions being that learned artist and ardent lover of nature, Mr Alexander Naismith."   As shown by the magical snatches of description in the "Queen's Wake," the Ettrick Shepherd must have been scarce less deeply moved.   Amid the mountain tracts of that wonderful Park, so unlike any other piece of pleasure-ground attached to any other great European city, he found enough of the wild, and the stern, and the lonely, to awaken that peculiar genius for the supernatural in which he excelled all his poetical contemporaries ; and straightway its upland solitudes became, as the night fell, a haunt of spirits.

> " By mountain sheer and column tall,
> How solemn was that evening fall !
> The air was calm, the stars were bright,
> The hoar-frost flighter'd down the night.
> But oft the listening groupes stood still,
> For spirits talk'd along the hill ;
> Yes, all along, from cliff and tree,
> On Arthur Seat and Salisbury,
> Came voices floating down the air,
> From viewless shades that linger'd there.
> The words were fraught with mystery :
> Voices of men they could not be."

I need scarce refer to those descriptions given by Scott of

his "own romantic town," which have stamped its bold features on the world's literature ; nor, in especial, to that scene in which the picturesque walk under Salisbury Crags is described,—a walk to which I shall shortly have to advert, as scarce less classical to the geologist than to the poet. It may, however, not be so generally known, that Thomas Campbell, in his projected poem, "The Queen of the North," which unfortunately exists as but a mere fragment, describes himself as taking his stand for a general survey, amid the same mountain tract by which Burns was so powerfully impressed, and which Hogg and Sir Walter have so exquisitely described. We first find the poet apostrophizing the scene as a favourite haunt of his boyhood.

> " Ye mountain walks, Edina's green domain !
>   Haunts of my youth, where oft, by fancy drawn
>   At vermeil eve, still noon, or shady down,
>   My soul, secluded from the deafening throng,
>   Has woo'd the bosom-prompted power of song."

And then, standing on its rocky summit, we find him expatiating over the goodly prospect that opened around, and appealing to its associations of the gray, hoary past.

> " Ever musing here beside the Druid's stone,
>   Where British Arthur built his airy throne,
>   Far as my sight can travel o'er the scene,
>   From Lomond's height to Roslyn's lovely green,
>   On every moor, wild wood, and mountain side,
>   From Forth's fair wanderings to the ocean tide,—
>   On each the legendary loves to tell
>   Where chiefs encounter'd and the mighty fell ;
>   Each war-worn turret on the distant shore
>   Speaks, like a herald, of the feats of yore ;

> And, though the shades at dark oblivion frown
> On sacred scenes and deeds of high renown,
> Yet shall some oral tale, some chanted rhyme,
> Still mark the spot, and teach succeeding time
> How oft our fathers, to our country true,
> The glorious sword of independence drew,—
> How well the plaided clans, in battle-tread,
> Impenetrably stood or greatly died,—
> How long the genius of their rights delay'd,—
> How sternly guarded, and how late betrayed."

However perilous the attempt, I must cast myself full on associations of a widely different character; and in asking you to take your stand in fancy on the noble hill-top, with its cincture of dark precipice, where Campbell invoked the muse, and from which Burns, with the rapt feeling of the poet, watched the sun of early summer rise out of the Frith, it is less to survey the existing landscape, with its land and sea, or to trace the many links which unite its fair scenes with human history and the noblest trophies of the national literature, than to call up widely different lands and seas which once occupied the same area,—" even waters,"—to borrow the sublime language of Job,—" waters forgotten of the foot, and dried up and gone away from men; and paths which no fowl knoweth, and which the vulture's eye hath not seen."

Glancing for a moment at the smiling fertility of a prospect which the historian Macaulay selects as adequately representative of what can be effected in even unfavourable circumstances by the noble self-reyling genius of Protestantism, let us bare the soil of its vegetable mould, as the anatomist divests his subjects of the integuments, and then mark the formations which lie immediately beneath. The skin-deep beauty of the landscape has disappeared ; and we find almost all the lower grounds appropriated by the agriculturist covered over by the stratified sands and gravels, and the brick clays. We have already dealt with these and with their teachings ; but let us just remark in the passing, how wide the area which the looser subsoils occupy in the prospect,— subsoils that scarce at all differ in their materials from the sands and gravels of our sea-shores. Such also are the materials which the hot winds of the great rainless deserts heap up over the arid rocks that compose their nether framework. These deserts are simply, like the flatter tracts around us, old sea-bottoms, over which "hot and copper skies," like those sung by the poet, never suffered the vegetable crust to form. And hence mainly the difference that obtains between the dreary wastes of Sahara and the tracts of variegated verdure which surround the Scottish capital. It is to our ever-dropping climate, with its hundred and fifty-two days of annual rain, that we owe our vegetable mould, with its rich and beauteous mantle of sward and foliage. And next, stripping from off the landscape its sands and gravels, we see its underlying boulder-clays, dingy and gray, and here presenting their vast ice-borne stones, and there their iceberg pavements. And these clays in turn stripped away, the bare rocks appear, various in colour and uneven in surface, but everywhere grooved and polished, from the sea-level and beneath it, to the height of more than a thousand feet, by evidently the same agent that careered along the pavements, and transported the great stones. Let us attend first to the natural divisions through which this vast chaos of rocks may be converted into a scene of order, amid which we may be enabled to prosecute our researches without risk of losing our way.

Of the various stratified deposits laid open before us, the most modern is the Carboniferous system, which we find here consisting of two well-marked divisions,—the Coal Measures proper, in which all the workable coal-seams occur; and an underlying division of marine limestone and calciferous sandstone,—the analogues, apparently, of the Mountain Limestone and millstone grits of the English coal-fields. These two divisions occupy by much the larger portion of the fore and middle grounds of the prospect; but along the western flanks of the Pentlands and the northern slopes of the Lammermoor range we may catch a glimpse, on the skirts of the landscape, of an older system,—the Old Red Sandstone; and the Lammermoors themselves, with a minute though fundamental portion of the Pentland group, belong to the yet older Silurian system,—that emphatically ancient group of rocks during the deposition of which life, animal and vegetable, seems to have had its commencement on our planet. Our view from Arthur Seat thus includes at least representative members of the three prevailing systems of the great Palæozoic division,—the Silurian or Lower Palæozoic system, the Old Red or Middle Palæozoic system, and the Carboniferous or Upper Palæozoic system. It includes, however, yet another group of rocks,—rocks that occur in proportions so large, and present outlines so striking, that the scene possesses scarce a prominent feature which it does not owe to them. And these, not deposited, but erupted, belong, considered as a class, not to one, but to every geologic period in the world's history, and are, even in this neighbourhood, though they may not sweep across the entire chronological scale, of very various ages. I of course refer to the trap-rocks,—that picturesque family to which we owe, with the various islands of the Frith, the Castle, the Calton, and the Craiglockhart Hills, the noble Arthur Seat group, the wood-ed heights of Corstorphine, and the blue range of the Pent-lands.

Let us, in the first instance, deal very briefly with these trap-rocks. We stand on what may be well termed the clas-sical ground of geology. It was the appearances presented by this very group of hills which first suggested that theory of world-wide celebrity which Hutton originated and Play-fair illustrated, and which derived such solid support from the experiments of Sir James Hall. There is scarce a trap eminence around us for the possession of which the assert-ers of the antagonist schools of Scotland and of Germany have not contended. They have been all subjected to the rival claims of Neptune and of Pluto,—of water and of fire. Along that walk introduced by Scott into one of his happiest fictions, as the scene of the morning adventure of Reuben Butler, and which he so graphically describes, the hottest of the battle has lain. It formed one of the favourite walks of Hutton. An altered fragment of rock traversed by a vein of argillaceous hæmatite, which stands up in one of the cleared spaces, still bears his name, and was spared, it is said, when the quarrier was busy around it, at his request, as strik-ingly illustrative of his theory of mineral veins. A little lower down, towards the south, there occurs in the green-stone a few minute flags of indurated shale, to which the Wernerians have triumphantly referred in the controversy, as bearing out their hypothesis of stratification from above. A little farther up, in the opposite direction, an extraordinary mass of the same shale, torn from the sedimentary rocks below, has been hurled upwards into the greenstone, by the eruptive forces acting from beneath, and forms one of the most remarkable illustrations anywhere to be seen of the Huttonian theory. The neighbouring eminence has formed the subject of the careful descriptions and singularly ingenious hypothesis of Mr Maclaren,—a hypothesis which, though embodied in language severely simple, throws back the imagination upon a time when volcanic fires vexed the bowels of the mountain, and a wide-spread sea dashed against its summit, and when what eruptions extruded, and the heat and pressure consolidated, the slow wear of the surf wasted away. In the overhanging precipice to the south we are presented, in what is known as Samson's Ribs, with one of the finest specimens of basaltic columns on the east coast of Scotland, and of which the general aspect has been made widely known by the print given in the section devoted to volcanoes, in the great Physical Atlas, edited by Mr Alexander Keith Johnston of this city,—a work of more than European reputation, which reflects honour on the science of Scotland. I need refer to but a few of the other names associated with the singularly instructive phenomena of this trappean group of hills,—to that of an accomplished mineralogist, the late Mr Thomas Allan of Edinburgh,—to that of the late Mr Hay Cunningham,—and to those of Mr Townson, Mr Milne Home, Dr Fleming, and Professor Jamieson. In closing my reference to that contest so long maintained between the schools of Hutton and of Werner, and of which the Arthur Seat group formed for a series of years one of the pitched battle-fields, it will, I trust, not be deemed disrespectful to any veteran of science, honourably worn in the service, if I express my satisfaction, that the victory should now be all but universally recognised as resting with our countrymen. Not indifferent, I trust, as a geologist, to the claims of scientific truth, nor wholly insensible, as a Scotchman, to the honour of my country, I must be permitted to congratulate a Scotch audience on the fact that the Scottish school of Geology, originated by a native of Edinburgh, in this neighbourhood, bids fair, in its own province, like the Scottish school of Metaphysics, to give law to the world.

The trap-rocks of Edinburgh and its neighbourhood consist of vast beds, such as that of Salisbury Crags, injected, apparently, among the sedimentary strata,—of huge masses, like that which forms the Castle rock, and which are in all probability the upper portions of tower-like columns protruded from below, and descending to very profound depths,—and, further, of long-extending dikes, like those which traverse the Water of Leith in the immediate vicinity of St Bernard's Well, and which may be regarded as the mere fillings-up of cracks in the earth's crust by the protrusion of molten matter from the reservoir beneath. The trap-tuffs constitute yet a fourth form, and combine, as in the tuff-beds of the Calton Hill, sedimentary arrangement with trappean materials. It seems not improbable that, in the production of many of these beds or strata, an union of the two great forces took place, and that components furnished originally by the Plutonic agencies were ultimately consigned to the stratifying operations of the aqueous ones. Let us in especial mark the trap-dikes that seam the stratified rocks all around. They are very numerous in this neighbourhood; and it has been remarked, that when they cut the sedimentary strata at nearly right angles with the plane of deposition, they have usually their direction and bearing on some great trap eminence in the neighbourhood. Thus, the two trap-dikes of the Water of Leith, near Stockbridge, bear direct on Arthur Seat; and a broad trap-dike at Niddry, about equally distant from that hill on the opposite side, also bears direct on the Seat; and, could we but actually see the landscape as I have asked you to conceive of it,—stripped of the superficial deposits,—I entertain little doubt that we would see these dikes radiating from the mountain as their centre, like the spokes of a wheel from its nave,—or rather like those glistening lines of light that radiate in every direction from the crater-formed mountains of the moon, and which have been so admirably illustrated both by the pencil and the experiments of a distinguished native of Edinburgh,—Mr James Naismith, the inventor of the steam-hammer. Very terrible convulsions must have accompanied the protrusion of those immense prominences. They seem to have everywhere broken and shattered the shell of sedimentary rock, as an unannealed pipkin is broken by a sudden change of temperature; or rather starred and cracked it where they came through, as a pane of glass is starred and cracked by the passage of a stone or bullet. Unlike, however, the fracturing force in the pipkin, or the blow dealt to the pane, the disturbing agent here, with its fine flood of molten matter, again cemented, in most instances, what it broke; and our trap-dikes may be regarded as the edges of the cement lines. In other instances, however, the cement is wanting, and the unfilled cracks are accompanied usually by great misplacements of the strata, known technically as faults or shifts. You may receive as a familiar but not inadequate illustration of these, what sometimes takes place in an arch with an ill-fitted together keystone. The keystone shifts by slipping downwards (till arrested at the point where its breadth fits the opening into which it had been thrust), and by its partial fall gets out of the line of the other ring-stones;

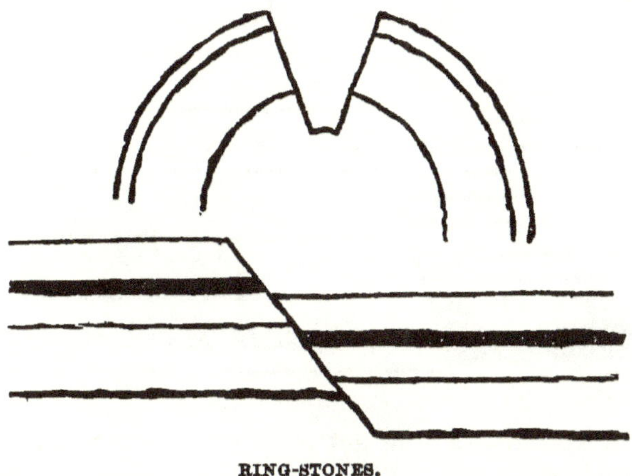

RING-STONES.

and very enormous, in the Mid-Lothian coal-fields, some of these shifts are. At Sheriff-hall, near Dalkeith, there is a slip of eighty fathoms. The strata on the one side of the crack, which is about nine feet in width, have fallen down four hundred and eighty feet below the strata on the other side,—a height about equal to that of the lower summit of Arthur Seat over the Hunter's Bog; and at Loanhead there is a fault of sixty fathoms: the downcast is more than equal to the height of Salisbury Crags over the valley of St Leonard's. Even between the tract of carboniferous rocks over which the New

Town of Edinburgh is built, and the tract of greatly older carboniferous rocks on which the Old Town is situated, there is a fault at which a downcast of several hundred feet must have taken place. The New Town rises, if I may so speak, on the slipped key-stone. The underlying strata, though geologically, and in their original position, several hundred feet *higher* than those which underlie the Castle esplanade, are

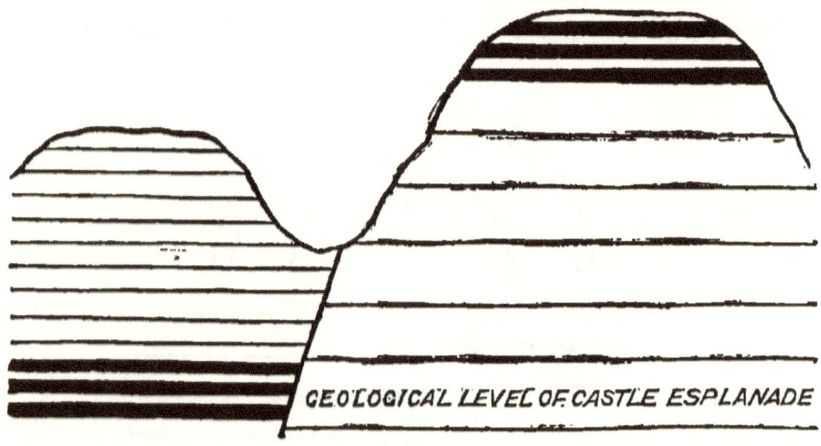

now, with respect to the actual level, nearly two hundred feet lower. In a lecture on what may be termed the geology of the moon, delivered in the October of last year before her Majesty the Queen and Prince Albert, by Mr Naismith, he referred to certain appearances on the surface of that satellite, that seemed to be the results, in some very ancient time, of the sudden falling in of portions of an unsupported crust, or a retreating nucleus of molten matter; and took occasion to suggest that some of the great slips and shifts on the surface of our own planet, with their huge downcasts, may have had a similar origin. The suggestion is at once bold and ingenious. The displaced keystone of our illustration would certainly not have slipped had there not been an empty space below ; nor does it seem improbable that the lowered platform on which the New Town of Edinburgh now stands may, at some incalculably remote period, have settled downwards, amid earthquake convulsion, through some intersticial space (an effect of the refrigerating influences), on the molten nucleus beneath. These faults and slips would have left to our earth, save for another great force, less potent but greatly more persistent in its operations than the Plutonic one, a surface as uneven and abrupt as that of the moon itself. But the denuding agencies, prolonged through unreckoned ages, planed down the surface, as a house-carpenter planes off what he terms the over-wood of his flooring ; and across the lines of faults, the opposite sides of which must have originally shown a difference of level to the extent of hundreds of feet, the plough can now be driven. Throughout the Mid-Lothian coal-field the *over-wood* has all been ploughed down.

The Coal Measures themselves fill a great basin, which occupies the comparatively level space between the western slopes of the Garelton Hills near Haddington, and the eastern slopes of Arthur Seat and the Pentlands. The surface is comparatively level, because *the basin is full;* but were these Coal Measures to be removed from it, that plain now laid out into the rich corn-fields of Mid-Lothian would exist as by far the profoundest valley in Scotland,—a valley greatly more profound than Corrisk, or Glen-Nevis, or Glencoe. Were Ben-Lomond, with its three thousand two hundred feet of altitude, to be set down in the middle of this valley or basin, it would be so nearly submerged, that its summit would scarce rise to the level of the Queen's Drive. We find this enormous basin filled with about a hundred and seventy beds of shale, clay, coal, sandstone, and ironstone, ranged, layer above layer, in long irregular curves, much broken by

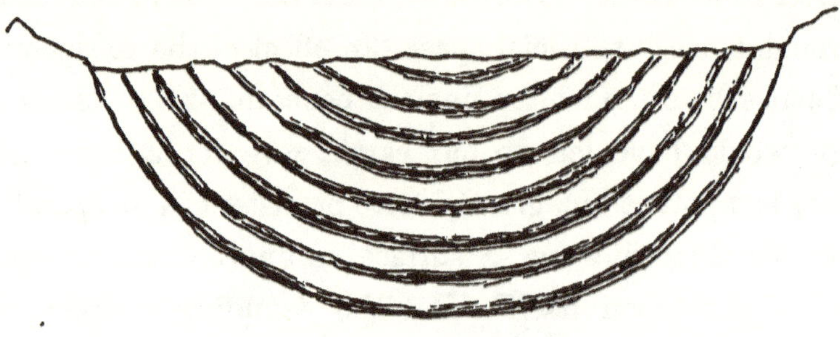

CLAY-BEDS.

the faults and shifts to which I have already made reference, but, save for these breaks, of greatly later date than their deposition, continuous over wide areas; and of these hundred and seventy beds, rather more than thirty consist of workable seams of coal. One of the most distinctive characters of the flat tract which overlies the basin,—the feature that strikes the eye of the traveller who hurries along its lines of railway as peculiarly its own,—consists in its numerous coal-works and collier cottages,—in its narrow-gabled engine-houses, with their ever-smoking chimneys and their huge outstretched arms, that are seen on the verge of the horizon, ever rising and falling as the mighty moving power expands and condenses,—and in its lines of low-roofed huts, uniform, in their humble mediocrity, as those of slave-villages. The dwellers in these low huts have a very singular history, regarded as that of Scotchmen. It is not yet fully eighty years since they were slaves, as firmly bound to the soil as the serfs of Russia, and transferable, like the huts in which they dwelt, or the minerals amid which they burrowed, from the hands of one proprietor to another.

In conversing not long since with a distinguished foreigner, better acquainted than almost any one else with the history of the Sclavonic races, he informed me that serfship in some of the Russian provinces is by no means of high antiquity. It is not derived, as might be supposed, from the barbarism of an ancient time, but introduced as one of the encroachments of modern despotism on the wild freedom of tribes, weak because they were ignorant and their numbers few. And such seems to be the history of our Scottish colliers. Profoundly ignorant,—kept apart, by their underground profession and their peculiar habits, from the other people of the country,—and, withal, not very formidable from their numbers, —their liberty seems to have been taken piecemeal from them mainly during the seventeenth century, by the acts of a Parliament in which they were of course wholly unrepresented, and by the decisions of a court in which no one ever appeared for their interests. It was the old Scottish Parliament and our present Court of Session that made the colliers slaves ; and the *salters* or salt-makers of the north-eastern shores of Mid-Lothian were associated with them in bondage. The coal and salt masters (as they were termed) of this part of the country were powerful proprietors, possessed of great political influence ; and they seem to have been virtually the authors of the acts and the prompters of the decisions. The greatest of their number in this locality were the ancient Seatons of Winton, a very influential family during the reigns of the latter Stuarts. Old Professor George Sinclair, the author of a curious volume on ghosts and witches, entitled

"Satan's Invisible World Displayed," of which some of our grandmothers knew a good deal, dedicates one of his works to the Earl of Winton, who flourished immediately previous to the Revolution; and, after expatiating on what he quaintly enough terms his "Lordship's virtues anent the coal and the salt," he goes on to urge upon all, with a curious eloquence, that his titled patron was "the greatest nobleman who was a coal and salt master, and the greatest coal and salt master that was a nobleman." I fear the "virtues anent the coal and the salt" of this distinguished family, with those of the other great mineral proprietors, their contemporaries, were mainly of the kind rendered too palpable in the Scottish acts anent colliers and salters; the earliest of which of any mark or importance dates no farther back than the year 1606. It was then statute and ordained, under a penalty of a hundred pounds, that no person within the realm should hire or employ colliers, coal-bearers, or salters, unless furnished with a sufficient testimonial from the master whom they had last served; and further, "that sae mony colliers, coal-bearers, and salters," as without such testimonial received such "fore-wages and fees, should be esteemed, repute, and holden *as thieves*, and *punished in their bodies*." Pretty well, methinks, as a specimen of the class-legislation of the good old times! This act, however, stringent as it may seem, was found insufficient: there was a class of persons employed in the pits whom it did not include; and in 1661 it was further enacted, "that because watermen, who lave and draw water in the coal-heugh heads, and gatesmen, who work the wayes and passages in the said heughs, *are as necessary to the owners and masters of the said coal-heughs* as the coal-hewers and coal-bearers, it is therefore statute and ordained, that they should come under exactly the same penalties as the others, in the event of quitting their masters without certificate ; and that it should be equally illegal, in the lack of such a document, for any persons to employ them." There was still, however, a certain degree of incompleteness in these slave-making acts. The coal-workers unreasonably demanded wages; and, to put down claims which were found troublesome, it was further enacted, in a specific clause, that it should " not be lawful for any coal-master in the kingdom to give any greater fee than the sum of twenty merks in fee or bountith,"—a clause which, according to the interpretation of Lord Kames, fixed the large sum of one pound two shillings sterling as the yearly wages of colliers and salters. It was, however, found, that at times the poor subterranean men became restive, or, breaking out into wild licence, refused to work ; and so there was a further clause devised to deal with the difficulty, and in which the "virtues anent the coal and salt" became more than usually palpable. "Because"—so runs the reason given" —"coal-hewers within the kingdom, and other workers within coal-heughs, with salters, do ly from their work at Pasche, Yule, Whitsunday, and certain other times of the year, which times they employ in drinking and debauching, to the *great offence of God*, and *prejudice of their masters*, it is therefore statute and ordained, that the said coal-hewers and salters, and other workmen in coal-heughs in the kingdom, work all the six days of the week, except the time of Christmas." The slavery of the colliers and salters was now fully completed by act of Parliament ; the Supreme Court gave effect, by its decisions, to the imposed law ; the Habeas Corpus Act, introduced into Scotland in 1701, expressly declared in one of its clauses, that its provisions were not to be extended to workers in coal or makers of salt; and for a hundred and fourteen years, men and women born within four miles of the Scottish capital were held as strictly in thrall by their masters as the negroes of Cuba or Carolina are held at the present day.   The letters of Junius had appeared, rousing the English people to resist even the slightest encroachment on their liberties; the War of Independence in the American colonies had begun; Robert Burns was cherishing, as a peasant lad in Ayrshire, those sentiments of a generous freedom which breathe from every stanza of his noble and manly verse; nay, Granville Sharp had obtained his act, through which slavery, if that of the negro or the foreigner, could not come into contact with the soil of Britain without ceasing to be slavery; and yet the poor Scotch collier, buried in that very soil, and bearing about with him its stains, still remained a slave.   Not until the year 1775 did the law which had so insidiously bound him set him even nominally free; and certainly very strange, regarded as a British law of the latter half of the eighteenth century, is the preamble of that act which extended to him, in the first instance, a verbal freedom.   "Whereas,"— it runs,—"by the statute law of Scotland, as explained by the judges of the courts of law there, many colliers, coal-bearers, and salters, are in a state of slavery or boudage, bound to the collieries and salt-works, *where they work for life, transferable with the collieries and salt-works;* and whereas, the emancipating," &c. &c.   This Emancipatory Act failed, however, virtually to emancipate, in consequence of certain conditions attached to it, which the poor workers underground were too improvident and too little ingenious to implement ; and their actual emancipation did not take place until the year 1799, when it was effected by a second act, which stated in its preamble that, notwithstanding the former enactment, "many colliers and coal-bearers still continued in a state of bondage" in Scotland. When residing in a village on the neighbouring coal-field, nearly thirty years ago, I had many opportunities of conversing with Scotchmen, the colliers of a neighbouring hamlet, who had been born slaves ; and at that time found the class still strongly marked by the slave-nature. Though legally only transferable, in the earlier time, with the works and the minerals to which they were attached, cases occasionally occurred in which they were actually transferred by sale from one part of the country to another. During the lapse of the present century, the son of an extensive coal-proprietor was engaged in examining, with a friend, the pits of a proprietor in another part of the field ; and, finding a collier the tones of whose speech resembled those of the colliers of his own district, he inquired of him whether originally he had not belonged to it ?   " Oh !" exclaimed the man, with apparent surprise, "d'ye no ken me ?   Do ye no ken that your faither sold me for a pony ?"   I owe the anecdote to Mr Robert Chambers.

I trust this digression will not be regarded as standing greatly in need of an apology. There are few things more interesting in geological science than those snatches of human history, or those peculiarities of human condition, which we find associated, necessarily often, but usually very unexpectedly, with certain formations and groupes of rocks. Dr Buckland has shown, in his "Bridgewater Treatise," that the various branches of industry prosecuted in the various districts of England,—pastoral, agricultural, manufacturing,— are regulated almost exclusively by the development of the several geologic systems which form the framework of the special tracts in which they are pursued. I have been told by the late Dr Malcolmson of Madras,—a man who stood high both in medical and geologic science,—that he found the diseases of India vary according to the formation of the country. I attempted showing on a former occasion, that a large proportion of the world's wars of independence have been prosecuted in its primary and its trap districts. And we now see how in Scotland even, a subterranean life, spent amid the Coal Measures, separated in destiny and standing one portion of the people as widely from all the others as the Russian serf is separated at the present time from the free-born Englishman. Nor is this curious passage in our domestic history without its lesson. The poor colliers had become very ignorant and very improvident ere the law-enacting and law-administrating powers of the kingdom metamorphosed them into slaves. May we not safely infer from such instances,— and they are very many,—that intelligence and morals form the true defences of a people's liberties in even comparatively civilized times,—that he who would connive at the popular ignorance is indifferent to the popular freedom,—and that the truest patriot is the man who, by extending to his humbler countrymen the blessings of a solid education,—an education both of the head and heart,—would impart to them at once the discernment to detect and the moral courage to repel every aggression, whether open or insidious, of unprincipled power ?

But let us pass from the colliers of our Mid-Lothian coal-field, to the coal-seams amid which they labour. I have said that rather more than thirty of these seams are workable; and the number of the unworkable seams, varying from a few inches to about a foot and a half in thickness, amounts to at least as many more. In the comparatively small section of the Carboniferous strata presented in the Joppa Quarry, near Portobello, we find no fewer than seven coal-seams, four of them unworkable, and three of them wrought out. By much the larger portion of the coal in this Mid-Lothian field seems to have been elaborated *in situ*, where we now find it. Under at least three-fourths of the seams, the original soil that produced the vegetable matter which composed them may be detected existing as a stratum of grayish-coloured clay, much traversed by roots that pass upward into the overlying coal. And, when sauntering along some vertical section of the Coal Measures, we see, for hundreds of yards together, bed succeeding bed, and, with deposits of clay, or shale, or sandstone between, seam succeeding seam; when we remark that many of these beds, as shown by the extreme thinness and great number of their laminæ, must have been of very slow deposition,—that the formation of each layer of soil below the coal-seams must have been the work of years,—for in no circumstances do soils form rapidly; and further, when we reflect that most of the seams themselves,—some of them from four to six feet in thickness,—were elaborated from air and water by these underlying soils in the vegetable form,—can we avoid coming to the conclusion that enormous periods of time must have elapsed ere the *three thousand* feet of the Mid-Lothian Coal Measures could have been formed or deposited?

It has been estimated by Mr Maclaren, on the data of Macculloch, that this coal-field alone could not have been produced
in less than six hundred thousand years.   The estimate may
seem extravagantly high, regarded even as an estimate of the
duration of the Carboniferous period anywhere ; and yet we
find that, however correct an approximation it may be with
reference to our own coal-field, it fails adequately to represent the amazingly prolonged *eons* of the Carboniferous stage,
in the general history of the globe.   Sir Charles Lyell, in his
recent visit to America, examined the Nova Scotia coal-fields,
and found, from one uninterrupted section on the shores of
the Bay of Fundy, that the thickness of its strata amounts
to fourteen thousand five hundred and seventy feet.   And
amid these strata, as amid those of Mid-Lothian, there are
beds of ancient soil, each of which must have taken many
years to form, and numerous seams of coal, that must have
been elaborated on the spot which they continue to occupy ;
but even casting out of the calculation the long periods of
elaboration by vegetable growth, and regarding the whole
field as a result of simple deposition, Sir Charles succeeds in
showing, that at the rate of deposition now going on in the
Delta of the Mississippi, it would take *two millions* of years
to form the Nova Scotia coal-field.   Well may geology and
astronomy be regarded as peculiarly the sister sciences.   If
the one enables us more worthily to conceive of the sublime
vastness of that space in which God dwells, not less does the
other heighten our conceptions of the awful eternity during
which he has existed.

There is not much of the geological to be seen in the coal-
pits of Mid-Lothian ; and a visit to their gloomy recesses is

always disagreeable, and sometimes attended with danger. As not, however, without a special interest in their way, I shall give you the details, as I recorded them at the time, of a visit which I paid nearly twelve years ago to a pit at Dryden,—more, however, in connection with the movement of that period for meliorating the condition of the collier women, which terminated in the act abolishing female labour in the pits, than with any geologic object. Previous experience had taught me that a single section opened up along some coast-line by the sea, or along the sides of some ravine by a streamlet, was worth, for purely geologic purposes, all the coal-pits in the country.

There is not a prettier dell in the south of Scotland than that of Dryden,—rendered classic by the allusion of Sir Walter Scott, in his ballad of Rosabella. We are told there that the wondrous blaze which gleamed from above the sepulchral vault of Roslyn,—some sign that disaster impended over the line of high St Clare,—

> " Was seen from Dryden's groves of oak,
> And seen from classic Hawthorn-den."

Dryden is a winding valley, overhung by precipitous banks and stately wood, that opens into the wider valley of the Esk, and exposes, in its course, a series of strata singularly interesting to the geologist. Passing fresh over the shales, sandstones, and unprofitable coal-seams that in this part of the country underlie the Mountain Limestone, we *rise*, in our downhill progress, to the limestone itself,—here very amply developed, and rich in its peculiar fossils. Then passing over a series of overlying sandstone and gray shale, with here and there a layer of coal, and here and there a belt of ironstone, we at length arrive at a workable coal-seam. We see a few cottages overhung by trees, and with these, an engine-house rising beside a low precipice on the one side of the dell; and the huge square wall of coal which blocks up the level spot on the other side shows the nature of the working. The strata along which we have been pass-ing lie at an angle of about forty; and the seam, in conse-quence, is one of the kind most difficult to the collier, and known as an edge-coal. At a little distance farther down the dell there is a perpendicular shaft, adown which we de-scend by a wooden staircase of six flights. The steps are slippery and covered with mud, and the land-springs descend along the sides in a perpetual shower. At the bottom of the shaft we see an opening about four feet in height, into which we grope our way; and, as the daylight has wholly failed, we strike a light, and then descend for some fifteen or twenty feet along a sloping plane cut into steps. We next enter a narrow gallery, ankle-deep in mud, and pass on till we reach another opening, lower even than the first, adown which we descend by a second flight of steps, and arrive at a second gallery. The floor is drier, and we find we are treading on a pavement of coal, and that the roof overhead is also coal. We reach yet another opening, but the gallery stretches past it; and, ere turning aside to de-scend to a lower level, we force our way forward into what, from the untrodden appearance of the floor, and the mould on the roof and walls, seems to be an old deserted work-ing. Here and there, too, a mouldy wooden prop supports the insecurer portions of the roof. But our light warns us to return. It sinks into sudden dimness, and, assuming the form and size of a pistol-bullet, seems stuck on the top of the wick, like the ball of a discharging rod on the wire. It brightens up again as we approach the opening. We have got into the fresh current; and the glow of unwholesome perspiration which came so suddenly upon us scarce a minute since is as suddenly checked. We descend yet a third flight, and reach the lowest gallery to which the workmen have yet descended. The atmosphere is close and heavy, charged, apparently, with the smoke of the miners' lamps, and rendered still more oppressive by a strong smell of train oil. There is a heap of tools lying on the floor; and immediately before us we see the coal projecting, in partially loosened blocks, undermined by the pick, and which a few blows of the wedge will entirely separate from their place in the seam. But the uncouth chamber into which we have penetrated is a place rather for the coal-hewer than the geologist. The black cubical coal stretches over and under us, and the dark walls on either side are composed, the one of a gray arenaceous clay, the other of barren shale.

The time chosen for our exploratory descent is that when the workmen are absent at their mid-day meal; nor would it be very convenient to thread a passage so narrow and long, so broken by descents, and perplexed by turnings, when the bearers are passing out and in, either laden with coal, or carrying on their shoulders the bulky basket. Here the miners come, however, each furnished with his lamp. They squat themselves down in a reclining posture, which only habit could have rendered bearable; and, striking out the projecting masses of coal, roll them over into the gallery. And now come the bearers with their baskets, to carry up to the surface the coal thus disengaged. But what work for women ! Each bears a lamp fastened to her head, to light the long upward ascent; and, laden with more than a hundredweight of coal, and bent forward at nearly a right angle, to avoid coming in contact with the low roof, they ascend slowly along the flights of steps, and through the narrow galleries, and, lastly, up the long stair of the shaft; and when they have reached the surface, they unload at the coal-heap, and return. And such is the employment of females for twelve, and sometimes fifteen hours together. It has been estimated by Mr Robert Bald, the distinguished mining engineer, that one of their ordinary day's work is equal to the carrying of a hundredweight from the level of the sea to the top of Ben-Lomond. These poor collier women—the coal-bearers of the old Scotch acts—were even more strongly marked by the slave nature, at the time they first came under my observation in this part of the country, nearly thirty years ago, than the men. I have seen them crying like children, when toiling, nearly exhausted under the load, along the steep upper stages of their journeys to the surface, and then returning with the empty creel, scarce a minute after, singing with glee. They were marked, too, by a peculiar type of mouth : both the upper and under lip drooped forward, swollen, meaningless, void of all mark indicative of the compressive control of mind. It was the mouth of the savage in that humblest and least developed condition of which the great weakness is an even more deplorable trait than the prevailing rudeness and barbarism. I describe, however, a state of things which has already become obsolete in the district. Women are no longer employed as animals of burden in our Scottish coal-pits. The drooping, degraded type of mouth seems already to have disappeared from among our collier population ; and when I visited Dryden a few years ago, I found the galleries of this last of the pits that had been wrought in the ancient style of the times of the slave-colliers, lying vacant and deserted. My description, were it to survive, might be well regarded as one of the fossils of the Coal Measures,—a memorial of a condition of things become extinct. And such is the character borne by even the comparatively recent history of our Scottish colliers in general. It bears upon its front the stamp of obsolete ages, and of states of society long gone by.

From the gloom of this coal-pit, with its carbonaceous ceiling and floor, and its dingy walls of shale and fire-clay, would that I could transport you to the deep forests which furnished of old the materials of the seam! I remember that, in emerging to the light of the wooded dell above, I was at first dazzled by the bright sunshine ; but the soft green foliage of the noble trees that rose along the steep sides of the valley, and of the brake and lady-fern that shot up tall and luxuriant in the shaded recesses below, fell soothingly on the eye, and the entire scene contrasted very agreeably with the more than dungeon darkness of the excavations beneath. And not less, but more marked, would have been the contrast, had it been from the coal-pit into the forest which had resolved into the coal, that I had emerged. Noble trees of the araucarian type, a hundred and fifty feet in height, would have taken the place of the oaks and elms of the dell ; the lepidodendron, an enormous club-moss, tall as a ship's mast, and covered with spiky leaves, and with seed-bearing receptacles light as the cuttings of the willow, would have been substituted for its ashes ; for its birch and hazel we would have seen the ornately fluted sigilaria, and the ulodendron with its scaly trunk and its rectilinear rows of sessile cones ; while for its plants of a humbler order,—— the bracken, and the sweetly-scented woodroof, and the mare's-tail,——we would have found numerous somewhat resembling families,——tall calamites, the asterophyllites, with their many-rayed, verticillate leaves, and more than two hundred species of ferns, some of them slim and graceful, like the delicate sphenopteris, and some of them rising into the arboraceous form, and assuming the dignity of trees.

Some of the remains of this gorgeous flora which have been detected in the immediate neighbourhood of Edinburgh are remarkable for their great size and fine state of preservation. I have seen in Joppa Quarry, as completely relieved from the general strata as a column from the mass of stone out of which it had been cut by the workmen, a considerable portion of a lepidodendron, thicker than the body of a man, and which must have belonged to a plant fully seventy feet in height. Some of the finest specimens of ulodendron ever found have been furnished by Craigleith Quarry, and the bed of the Water of Leith, near Colinton. One very fine specimen from the quarry, figured and described by Dr Buckland in his " Bridgewater Treatise," may be seen in the Museum of the Royal Society of Edinburgh ; another specimen of great beauty, which I disinterred from the bed of the stream, may be seen on the table before us. The ulodendron must have been a very remarkable plant. The late Captain Basil Hall describes, in his notice of the island of Java, a singular tree called familiarly the "travellers' friend," *urania* being its botanic name. "We found it to differ," he says, "from most other trees, in having all its branches in one place, like the sticks of a fan, or the feathers of a peacock's tail." The ulodendron seems also to have had its branches all in one place; but, besides this peculiarity, there ran along its trunk and its greater boughs straight continuous lines of stemless cones, like rows of buttons on the dress of a boy, that left impressed on the bark, when they dropped off, lines of beautifully sculptured scars. The general surface, too, was delicately fretted by obovate scales; and, bearing each an apparent mid-rib, they may serve to remind the architect of that style of sculpture adopted by Palladio from his master Vetruvius, when, in ornamenting the Corinthian or composite torus, he fretted it into closely imbricated leaves. The sigillaria, of which frequent specimens occur in the Mid-Lothian coal-field, with its carved and fluted column-like stem, must also have been an extraordinary, and, in its more ornate species, a very fine plant, or rather tree; and nothing can well be more graceful than the sphenopteri of Burdiehouse, and the neuropteri and pecopteri of Preston and Dalkeith. I set myself nearly a twelvemonth ago to restore, from a series of specimens, the frond of Sphenopterus affinis, one of the most abundant of the Burdiehouse ferns. I drew it slowly and laboriously, piecemeal, from my authorities the fossils, without drawing on imagination for a single pinnæ or leaflet; but greatly more graceful and elegant than if I had set myself to design something I deemed pretty, it grew up under my hands. The *rachis* or stem somewhat resembled that of the common hill-side bracken, Pteris aquilina, but—a peculiarity without example in the ferns of the present day—it divided, not into three, but into two parts; and then a series of alternate pinnæ and alternate leaflets completed the frond. This ancient fern must have imparted lightness and beauty to many a dank meadow and sloping hill-side during the times of the Lower Coal Measures, and waved its slim pinnæ and minute leaflets with a billowy motion over wide areas, to the hot breezes that shook the old Carboniferous forests. The fossils, however, for which this neighbourhood is most remarkable are its gigantic trees. The fossilized araucarians of Craigleith, when first found in 1826, were wholly unique in the geologic world; nor has anything equal to the arau-carians of the ·Granton Quarry yet been found. In exa-

ARAUCARIANS OF THE GRANTON QUARRY.

mining these last, two in number, which the Granton Rail-way brings within less than a mile of Edinburgh, and which, while those of the other quarry have been removed through the operations of the quarrier, have been spared through the good taste of the noble proprietor, his Grace the Duke of Buccleuch, I would urge the visitor to observe the angle at which they both lie;—the one raised on its rocky pedestal; the other laterally exposed in the precipitous side of the quarry. The angle of inclination is the same in both,—both lie the same way,—in both the nether and weightier portion.

of the ponderous bole is turned downwards; they are both evidently what an American would term the *snags* of some river of the Carboniferous period, that flowed in what is now, in reference to the existing arrangement of the land, an up-hill direction. Neither of them is complete,—they are but mere fragments of trees; and yet the smaller of the two is about four feet in diameter by seventy feet in length; while the larger, still more a fragment, has a length of sixty-one feet, but then it has a diameter at the lower end of about six feet, and a diameter at the upper end of two. The height of the latter, when it existed entire as a living tree, could not have fallen short of a hundred feet. And of this vast tree, which must have rivalled in bulk and size that sung by Milton, as

> " Hewn on Norwegian hills, to be the mast
> Of some great ammiral,"

the larger and massier part survives within a short distance of Edinburgh, in the character of one of the hugest fossils in the world.

I have little to add to my former description of the shells and fishes of the neighbouring coal-field. The little is, however, of interest. I was shown last winter by Mr Cadell, the scientific and accomplished mineral surveyor of the Duke of Buccleuch, the foot-prints of some large animal impressed on a block of sandstone which had formed part of the roof of one of the coal-seams wrought in the immediate vicinity of Dalkeith. The block, little more than three feet either way, bore only six of the prints, or rather of the casts of the prints; but I was informed by Mr Cadell that they could be traced continuously for several yards, as they crossed diagonally one

of the excavated passages.   They stood up in bold relief on
the stone.   Apparently some animal of the great reptilian class
had trodden heavily across the upper surface of what is now
the coal-seam, when it existed as a black carbonaceous mud
or moss, sinking deep at every step; but the semi-elastic
matter received the impressions only indifferently well : it
received them much as a foot-print would be received by our
existing mosses; and so the sand afterwards cast down upon
it, and now existing as stone, though it presents casts of the
prints in regular sequence, does not exhibit that sharpness of
outline in each print necessary to the determination of the
order of reptiles to which the creature belonged.   We only
know from these strongly but not sharply marked impressions
on the rock, that over that portion of the earth's surface now
occupied by the rich fields of Mid-Lothian, and the noble
parks of Dalhousie and Dalkeith, huge reptiles strode heavily
in the ages of the Carboniferous era,—monsters, mayhap, as
strangely aberrant of type, compared with the existing denizens of the animal world, as the great plants ulodendron,
calamites, and sigillaria, under which they passed, seem ano-
malous and aberrant, compared with the existing denizens of
the vegetable one.   To the gigantic ganoidal fishes of Gilmerton and Burdiehouse,—fishes that bore in their jaws reptilian teeth thrice bulkier than those of the largest crocodile,
and formidable in proportion to their bulk,—the course of discovery has recently added a huge placoid from the Dalkeith
coal-field, of the Cistraciont family; but we know little else
of this ancient shark than that, where the Port-Jackson Cistracion bears a defensive spine of one and a half inch long,
it bore one about fifteen inches in length, and more than

equally stout in proportion. And that is just all. In these recent additions to our Carboniferous fauna we have but the track of the reptile and the spine of the shark. In, however, what must be regarded as originally a part of the same coal-field as that of Mid-Lothian,—the coal-field in the neighbourhood of Carluke,—there have been recently discovered fragments of the osseous skeleton of a reptile closely allied to the archigosaurus of the Carboniferous deposits of Germany. Besides the bearing of such discoveries on the world's history, they show, among other things, with what equal progress, in at least those highly civilized parts of the world in which science is cultivated, the course of geologic discovery is going on. In writing no farther back than in the year 1846 on the first appearance of the reptile in creation, I stated that, so far as was known, it had taken place during the times of the Magnesian Limestone,—a member of that Permian system which immediately overlies the coal, and forms the most modern of the great Palæozoic deposits. Since that time, however, either the remains or foot-prints of reptiles have been discovered in the coal-fields of Rhenish Bavaria, in the coal-field of Pennsylvania in the United States, in the coal-field of Nova Scotia, and now in the Carluke and Mid-Lothian coal-fields. But then, on the other hand, the fact that in a system so extensively wrought as the Coal Measures, reptilian remains should not have been sooner detected, and that they should still be so very rare, must serve to show how very inconspicuous the place which was occupied by the reptile during the old Carboniferous ages. The great prevailing vertebrates of the period were not its reptiles, but its sauroid fishes.

I had purposed adducing in my address a few curious facts

regarding the coal-fields in our neighbourhood, mainly economic in their bearing; but my narrow limits forbid. Permit me, however, just to advert to a natural process of distillation, of which we are presented with an instance to the west of Edinburgh. It is comparatively of late that the chemist has set himself to distil, for economic purposes, the coals and shales of the Oolitic and Carboniferous systems. A recently established work among the Kimmeridge shales yields in abundance valuable oils and naphthas, from what, in the times of the Upper Oolite, had formed the fleshy framework of innumerable ammonites and belemnites; and to what is known as the Torbanehill mineral, the Carboniferous vegetation has imparted so inflammable a character, that there can be extracted from every ton of the substance not less than twelve gallons of naphtha and twenty-six gallons of parafine oil. Nature, however, had her distillations in this neighbourhood long ere patents or chemists, or even the human family, existed. In what is known as the Binny Quarry,—a quarry of a white building sandstone which occurs in the tract of lower Carboniferous rocks that intervenes between the Mid-Lothian and Falkirk coal-fields,—a highly inflammable substance has been found, which the quarriers have been in the practice of converting into candles of a consistency resembling that of bee's wax, but not altogether so white. This substance occurs in the fissures of the rock; and I lately paid the quarry a visit, in order to ascertain whence it had been derived. I found the district much overflown by trap. The Binny Crags,—a greenstone eminence lofty enough to form a feature, though a remote one, in the prospect from our Castle Hill,—is in the immediate neighbourhood of the quarry ; and its erupted traps seem to have come in contact with a thick bed of shale which overlies the sandstone bed in which the quarry has been opened. A sort of natural distillation took place. The bitumen or parafine, freed from the shale by the heat, forced its way downwards into the vertical cracks and fissures of the stone ; and in these, and these only, not in the interstices of the stratification, is the substance found. It has been used for many years in lighting, in the long winter nights, the neighbouring cottages ; but it is only now that the chemist is learning to employ one of the substances extracted in his distillations from coal and shale, to a similar purpose, by making it assume the form of parafine candles. There might be also some interest in referring to the fact, had we but the necessary time, that during the present year, three great legal cases have arisen,—one on the Continent, another in America, the third in our own country,—all hinging on the one question, What is coal ? Without in the least challenging the opposite judgments which the various courts have pronounced, but rather, on the contrary, holding that, whether they determine black to be black, or black to be white, or black to be black in one place and white in another, they are all equally legal and in the right, I must be permitted to say, the simultaneous existence of such cases in localities so widely separated as Prussia, Scotland, and the United States, must be regarded as an evidence of the existence of thought and inquiry in unwonted directions over no small portion of the civilized world. The American case, tried before a special jury, was made to hinge on the question whether a certain inflammable substance, dug out of the earth, and occasionally employed in tarring the bottoms of boats, was an asphalt or a coal; and the jury decided it to be a coal. In our own country, where the issues were also subjected to a jury, the decision on a very different substance,—the Torbanehill mineral,—was the same. Whatever makes money and gas is coal to a coal-master; and whatever comes out of the ground and burns is coal to most jurymen. In Germany the question was subjected, not to a jury, but to an association of scientific men; and they, sitting in judgment on this same Torbanehill mineral, and in direct opposition to the interests of their employer, the State, decided that to be merely a singularly inflammable shale which our Scotch jury had pronounced to be a true coal. I, of course, refer to the subject as merely a curious one. It certainly *is* a curious fact, and strikingly illustrative of what has been termed the glorious uncertainty of the law, that a certain mining firm or company should be permitted to work in this country a certain mineral substance because it is here legally determined to be a coal, which they are permitted to export duty free into Prussia because it is there legally held *not* to be a coal, and to supply with it, in the city of Frankfort, in its character as a resinoed shale, an oil and resin gas company; while a coal-gas company in the same city is inhibited, on the plea that it is not a coal, from dealing with them.

But I must hasten to a conclusion. At the base of the Coal Measures proper, we find the Marine Limestones, with their remains, representative of a period when seas of moderate depth, and abounding in molluscs, placoid fishes, corals, and whole forests of encrinites, stretched out for ages over the area subsequently occupied by the coal. I have already referred to the Marine Limestones of Dryden,—one of the best sections of the formation as developed in Scotland which I have yet anywhere seen; and we find it exhibited in this neighbourhood in several other localities, as at Liberton, at Gilmerton, and very interestingly near that ancient castle of Crichton rendered classic by the well-known description in "Marmion." The time seems to have been one of vicissitude and revolution,—land and sea not unfrequently changed places: and so, intercalated with the limestones that in almost every fragment bear some organism of the sea, we find beds of shale containing only terrestrial and fresh-water plants, and thin unworkable seams of coal. Beneath the Marine Limestones, and representative of a still older period, there occurs a largely developed formation of red or pale-coloured shales, that alternates with sandstone beds of the same hue, and exhibits in its upper portions occasional seams of limestone, that seem to have been formed in lakes or estuaries. On this nether formation, which in this part of the kingdom forms the base of the Carboniferous system, the larger part of the Old Town of Edinburgh is built; and the far-famed limestone of Burdiehouse, specimens of whose fishes and plants may be found in almost every geologic museum in the world, composes one of its higher beds. Still descending in the scale, we pass into another and more ancient system,—the Old Red Sandstone,— a system whose upper members are largely developed, in this vicinity, in the western portion of the Pentland range, and in a considerable tract of country, flanking the Lammermoors, that extends from beyond Fala to Dunbar. I am not aware, however, that it has produced any fossils in the neighbourhood of Edinburgh, at least nearer than the interesting section extending on the sea-shore from Sellar Point to Dunglass

Burn, where it is found to contain scales of Holoptychius, and plates of its characteristic genus Pterichthys. In the same tract, in the neighbourhood of Dunse, it has yielded, though decidedly a marine formation, terrestrial plants, calamites apparently, and a fern that very much resembles the Neuropterus gigantea of the Coal Measures. It is generally held, from the manner in which the Old Red strata are deposited, that the grauwackes of the Lammermoors existed at the time as a sub-aerial tract or island; and it seems not improbable that these plants of the sandstone may have been drifted from its shores, and that they formed on its slopes and planes part of a flora greatly less rich than that of the Coal Measures, but, generally at least, of the same character.

The grauwackes themselves, or, as they are now termed, the Lower Silurians, belong to a greatly more ancient period still,—to a period so vastly more ancient, that when the seas of the Upper Old Red Sandstone spread out around them, they existed as a series of old-looking rocks,—rocks every whit as old-looking as they are now, and uptilted in a position so directly vertical in many instances, that their upper could not be distinguished from their under beds, or the ascending line determined from the descending one; and yet they too had their period of slow deposition in an ocean in which we find no trace of land. It was tenanted by the trilobite, the orthoceratite, numerous brachipods, and, as in the long posterior seas of the Mountain Limestone, with numbers innumerable of crinodea. In its lower depths we find little else than graptolites, with occasional beds of an impure anthracite, composed, it is not improbable, of the sea-weeds of the period : and then the record closes; and, as is fabled of ancient voyagers, such as the wanderer of Ithaca, we cross the line where the precincts of the cheerful day terminate, and a curtain of thick darkness drops down upon the deep.

Let us cast a glance, ere this curtain ultimately falls, along the various succeeding scenes of our long upward passage. The Silurians, at which we have just arrived, present us with but a shoreless ocean, which, though the light falls, through the transparent water in the middle spaces, on pearly shell, and stony flower, and snow-white coral, we see encircled all around the horizon with a thick fog, like that which rested on either hand of the great bridge seen in vision by Mirza. The curtain falls and rises, and a wide sea still spreads out around; but, unlike the other, it is a sea much vexed by waves and currents, whose vast shallows of water-rolled pebbles rise to the action of the surf, and abounding in uncouth ganoidal fishes,—Holoptychii, and Pterichthyes, and the sculptured Asterolepis. And in the midst, encircled with its snow-white line of breakers, there lies, inlaid in the blue, a flat green island. We have looked abroad on the times of the Old Red Sandstone. And then the curtain again falls, to rise over an ever-changing landscape of fern-covered plain, and reed-bearing "marish," and bright coraline sea, and boundless forests, spread on and away to the far horizon, tangled, and dark, and dank, and inhabited by doleful creatures; their deep still lakes travelled by the reptile fish, and their gloomier shades the haunt of the scorpion and the salamander. And then the curtain again descends, and ere it yet again rises, ages and systems pass away; but we see dimly through its folds the gleam of erupted fire, and a submarine volcano flares fiercely on the dark horizon; and, blent with the deep

groan of earthquakes, we hear the loud rush of denuding currents, and the ceaseless dash of waves. And slowly as the
curtain once more ascends, we see a boreal scene of islands :
the bolder features of the landscape have become familiar ; but
a subarctic sea breaks high against the hill-sides, and the
whale blows in our submerged valleys ; and where street or
ample square now extends, the morse floats past on his raft
of field-ice, and the seal raises its round black head ; and,
though summer has risen on the scene, the brow of the distant Pentlands gleams white with snow, and along the hollow
dells of the hills the glacier descends. And yet once more
the scene changes. The climate has softened, and the sea
receded, and the rich Germanic flora gives its flowers to the
meadows, and its tall forest-trees to the woods ; and amid a
tract of shaggy hills and blue gleaming lakes, David of Scotland has gone forth from the Maiden fortress, perched high
on its rock, to hunt the deer and the roe amid the bosky
thickets that rise thick and tangled around the precipices of
the Calton. I have performed my task hastily and inade-
quately : I have drawn but a few thin and meagre lines ; but
they at least touch some of the bolder features of what, in a
more skilful hand, would worthily fill a noble breadth of can-
vas ; and I leave it to some happier pencil to lay in the colours, and to supply the lights and the shading.

BRICK-CLAYS OF PORTOBELLO,

WITH THEIR

ORGANISMS, VEGETABLE AND ANIMAL.

WHAT are known as the Portobello brick-clays occupy a considerable tract of comparatively level country, which intervenes between the eastern slopes of the Arthur Seat group of hills and the sea. The covering of rich vegetable mould which forms the upper stratum of the tract,—so valuable to the agriculturist, that it still lets for about six pounds per acre,—precludes any very exact survey of their limits; but we know from occasional excavations in the tract, and at least one natural section, that they extend over an area of at least a square mile. A well sunk a few years ago at Abercorn Place, one hundred and ten yards on the upper or Edinburgh side of the first milestone from Portobello, passed through a stratum of the brick-clays six feet in thickness; and several excavations made in the immediate neighbourhood, on the farm of Mr Scott of Northfield, laid open the continuous bed which they form at various points, fully a mile distant from the sea, where they averaged in thickness from five to seven feet. In all probability, judging from the

general level, and their gradual thinning out, they terminate
in this direction about the middle of the field which extends
to the house of Willow Bank; while more to the south they
appear about sixty yards below the mill of Easter Duddingston, in the section formed by the Figget Burn, whence they
stretch eastwards to near Joppa Quarry.   They acquire their
greatest elevation at Stuart Street and its neighbourhood,
where they rise about eighty feet over the high-water line;
and attain to their greatest known depth in the town of Portobello, at the paper-works of the Messrs Craig, where, at one
point, immediately beside the burn, they were perforated several years ago, in sinking a well, to the depth of not less than
a hundred feet.   Their extent along the shore to the west
has not been very definitély traced, but from their eastern
extremity near Joppa, to where they terminate beyond the
brick-works of Mr Ingram, cannot greatly exceed a mile.
The boulder-clay appears all around the edges of the area
which they occupy, and forms, I cannot doubt, the basin in
which they rest.   It appears in a characteristic section a little
above Duddingston Mill, charged with its grooved and polished boulders; it was cut through to a considerable depth
by the excavations for the North British Railway, in the vicinity of Stuart Street and Abercorn Place, and there found
underlying the brick-clays; and it appears along the shore,
accompaniéd by some of its most striking phenomena, both
to the east and west of Portobello, a little beyond the limits
of the basin.   In short, the Portobello brick-clays may be
regarded as occupying a boulder-clay basin or valley about a
mile in length and breadth, not reckoning on their unknown
portion, which seems to extend outwards under the sea; and,

thinning out all around the edges of the hollow, they attain, where deepest in the lower reaches of the Figget Burn, a thickness, as I have already said, of at least a hundred feet.

Their colour is very much that, on the average, of the boulder-clay of the district : they bear a deep leaden hue ; nor can I doubt that their materials were originally derived from it. But they must have been deposited at a somewhat later time, and under different conditions. They are finely laminated throughout : even their most compact beds, when exposed edgewise for a few weeks to the weather, are found to consist of hundreds of layers, thin as sheets of pasteboard ; and there run throughout the deposit thin strata of silt or sand, that, unlike the arenaceous intercalations of the boulder-clay, preserve for many yards the same thickness, and maintain in many cases nearly the same level. The brick-clays in this locality must have been slowly deposited in comparatively tranquil waters, undisturbed, apparently, by the restless agencies which, during the boulder-clay period, grooved and furrowed the solid rocks of the country, and transported and left their strange marks on the great stones to which the boulder formation owes its name. Up till a comparatively late period it was not known that the Portobello brick-clays enclosed their organisms,—the remains of plants and animals that had existed during their deposition. I was informed, however, several years ago, by Mr Allan Livingston, senior, the intelligent proprietor of one of the Portobello brick-works, that his workmen, many years before, had cut, at a considerable depth, through a scattered layer of shells, and found a stump of a doddered tree ; and a respected member of our society, Mr William Rhind, produced, at one of our meetings of the session of 1852-53, a sorely-decayed shell which he had found in the deposit, and which, so far as could be judged in its state of extreme decomposition, was a fresh-water bivalve, —Cyclas cornea.   All my own attempts to find organisms in the deposit were unsuccessful.   I was informed, however, in January last, by the younger Mr Livingston,—whose kindness, both in tendering me the information, and in affording me every facility at his works in following it up, I must here be permitted to acknowledge,—that his brick-clays were again furnishing their shells in considerable abundance ; and accordingly, shortly after our January meeting, I visited the deposit, and I have, as leisure served, been working it out ever since.   I found the bed of shells to which he referred in the upper part of his brick-field, a few yards from the road which passes between the Portobello railway station and the old Roman way familiarly known as the Fishwives' Causeway.   It occurs at the depth of from three to five feet from the surface of the brick-clay, and from about six to eight feet from the surface of the soil; and when I last examined it, it measured, from where it first appears in the section, to the point where the excavation terminates and it disappears in the bank, exactly fifty yards.   The level of the bed is from fourteen to fifteen feet above the high-water line, from which it (the bed) is rather more than a quarter of a mile distant. Where thickest, the bed is about eighteen inches in depth. All the shells which I at first detected were of one species. And as most of the specimens were in a bad state of keeping, and associated exclusively with what seemed to be fresh-water remains, some time elapsed ere I could determine what that species really was.   It was, I saw, a bivalve varying from an inch to an inch and half in length and breadth ; and as it was not until my third visit that I succeeded in detecting the hinge, and as I found it occupying evidently the place in which it had lived and died, among roots of the common reed (Arundo phragmites), and apparently those of the water-flag, I too hastily leaped to the conclusion that it could not be other than a fresh-water shell, though of a kind which I could not identify as still native to the country. On finding the hinge, however, though in but an indifferent state of pre-servation, I was struck by the resemblance of the obliquely triangular fulcrum in either valve to that of Scrobicularia ; but finding it associated with not only the reeds and flags, but with also the trunks of sorely-decayed oak trees, and fre-quent branches of alder and birch, I still hesitated; and it was not until I had submitted my specimens to Mr Gray of the British Museum, and to perhaps the highest conchologi-cal authority in the world, M. G. P. Deshayes, whom I was fortunate enough to meet in the Museum, that I was content to yield to the evidence, and to recognise a shell associated, so far as I had at the time ascertained, with no marine pro-duction, as a marine shell. Since my return from London, however, the same deposit has yielded me, from a lower and more arenaceous stratum, scattered specimens of the common periwinkle (Littorina littorea), and a few much-wasted valves of the crimson tellina (Tellina solidula). It has also yielded me, washed, apparently, from the bed, a specimen of Helix nemoralis. The large shell-bed, notwithstanding the asso-ciated reeds and branches of trees, must be recognised as a bed of Scrobicularia piperata, still occupying the place, as the position of the shells indicate, where the individuals which compose it had lived and died. "Scrobicularia piperata," as Montagu remarks, "is chiefly found at the mouths of rivers or inlets, not remote from fresh water ; and, though never beyond the flux of the tide, yet it delights in situations where fresh water is occasionally flowing over. It principally inhabits sludge or muddy places, buried to the depth of five or six inches." "It is from the comparative inaccessibility of such spots," add the Messrs Forbes and Hanley, in their " British Mollusca," "that the species, though abundant, is not frequently taken alive, and that cabinets are usually only furnished with dead valves, washed on shore after rough weather." I may mention, that I was informed, when last in London, that in the lower reaches of the Thames, near Gravesend, miniature forests of reeds and rushes stand out at the river edge in the brackish water, and that whole beds of Scrobicularia piperata burrow at their roots.

The oak trunks which I found associated with the shells were, with one exception, rather of small size, varying from about six inches to a foot in diameter. The larger trunk was, however, that of a pretty considerable tree, measuring twenty-seven feet from the root, at which it was nearly two feet in diameter, to the fork of its first large bough, where it measured about sixteen inches across. Both the larger and smaller trees had all the appearance of being drifted to the spot where they lay, and had apparently been in a state of decay, and half-sunk in the mud, when the shells were living around them. They were deeply cracked in the line of the medullary rays ; and the flags and reeds had in not a few instances insinuated themselves into the cracks. One curious specimen,—a branch of Scotch fir,—had been in such a state of decay when the aquatic vegetation flourished over and around it, that the underground stems seemed to have found a scarce less ready passage through its substance than through that of the clay itself; and it appeared, in consequence, as if literally sewed by them to the stratum in which it lay. From the peculiar appearance of this specimen, it struck me that the question might be fairly raised, whether the vegetation, chiefly subterranean in its character, that thus perforated the wood, might not have existed at a considerably later period than the shells with which we find it associated. Certainly, the mere contiguity of shells *in situ*, and of decayed underground stems also *in situ*, gives no evidence whatever of the contemporaneity of the shells and stems. Purely marine shells might be found occupying the spot in which they had lived and died, associated with purely lacustrine stems similarly circumstanced; but as the special stems and shells of the brick-clays, here at least, *could* have lived together, there of course attaches less interest to the solution of the question in this particular instance. Over the brick-clays at the eastern extremity of the shell-bed, and, in the average, about four feet higher in the section, there rests detached beds of fine yellow sand, a foot in thickness or so, which, however, in two several places thin out and disappear; over the sand there lies a thinner but more continuous stratum of moss; over the moss about a foot more of gray silt; and the vegetable mould overtops the whole. The greater part of a fir tree, about ten inches in diameter, still lies in the sand; but, as shown by its under side, which is in contact with the underlying clay, the sand must have been merely deposited around it; and in the stratum of moss above, there occurred several trunks, of small

size, of birch, alder, hawthorn, and what seems to be ash.   All
the deeper lying oaks and firs were in such a state of decay,
that they offered scarce more resistance to the labourer's spade
than the surrounding clay ; the upper-lying birch, hawthorn,
and alder, were also much decayed ; but a portion of the fir
tree in the sand still retains its turpentine ; and the heart of
the large oak to which I have referred preserves a considerable degree of toughness of fibre.   The shells, even the best
preserved individuals among them, are in such a state of extreme fragility, that it was my first work, on getting home,
after every visit to the deposit, to steep my specimens in a
solution of gelatine, which seems to have restored to them a
portion of their original solidity.   It may be mentioned as
a curious circumstance, suggestive, mayhap, of the unsalutary
character of the salt-water marsh, that the brick-clay, in its
upper beds, in this place, where most thickly traversed by the
roots of the reed and water-flag, diffused, when first laid open
by the workmen, a peculiarly heavy odour.

In referring somewhat more in detail to the remains, plant
and animal, of this interesting deposit, permit me first to make
a few remarks regarding its vegetable organisms.   In the
overlying silt I found no other remains than those of recent
roots, shot downwards from the soil above ; on the other
hand, at about from eight to ten feet beneath the surface of
the clay, the vegetable remains disappear.   The lowest lying
organism which I detected,—a sorely decayed twig of oak,
—did not exceed the ten feet ; and downwards for about
thirty feet more,—for such is the depth of the formation at
this place,—the stiff and finely laminated clay has hitherto
not been found to yield a single plant or shell.   A little above

the place of the oak twig, nine feet or so from the surface, there occurs a thin dark-coloured stratum of vegetable matter, traversed nearly horizontally by pointed stems, much flattened, and in a bad state of keeping, but apparently those of Arundo. Above this stratum the stems become very abundant, maintaining mostly the erect position, and presenting, when first laid open,—though they shrivel up, when dried, into mere films,—the original character very distinctly. When preserved in water, they might pass for the remains of plants that had lived only a few seasons ago. Still higher up in the bed, however, where the specimens must be by many years more modern than those beneath, they are greatly more indistinct and antique-looking; while higher up still in the sand, where they must be still more modern, they exist as mere encrustations of ferruginous stone, that, if one judged merely from their mineral appearance, might be deemed as old as the times of the Coal Measures. The instance is a curious one of the inadequacy of the test furnished by the mere state of keeping of a fossil to determine its age. Nor is it uninteresting to observe how, in comparatively recent times, a nucleus of vegetable matter attracted around it, as similar nucleii used to do in the times of the Carboniferous system and the Lias, the iron previously existing as a disseminated oxide in the stratum in which it lay. The trees of the deposit, from its demonstrably great antiquity, in relation at least to human history, must be regarded as in every instance indigenous to the country. The oak, birch, alder, hawthorn, and Scotch fir, have long been recognised as indisputably native to Scotland. I am not sure, however, that the ash has been generally regarded as one of our indigenous trees. I find Gardiner, in his "Flora of Forfarshire," referring to it as probably introduced into at least that part of the kingdom; and doubts also rest on the indigenousness of the yew.   I am mistaken, however, if this Portobello deposit does not furnish specimens of both species. A slender trunk in the thin stratum of moss lying immediately beneath the upper stratum of silt exhibits exactly the appearance and grain of a young ash, though, from its extreme state of decay, I have been unable to subject it in transparent slips to the microscope; and a trunk, also of small size, lodged in the stratum occupied by the shells, presents, so far as I have been able to test it, all the peculiarities of the yew.   It is exceedingly close of grain; its zones of yearly growth lie in as little space as sheets of pasteboard ; the longitudinal sections of sufficient thinness, which I have succeeded in detaching from it, show the coniferous disks existing, as in Taxus baccata; and the external surface of the stem has the twisted appearance so common in our yews, and so uncommon in any of our other conifers.   From the brittleness of the specimen, however, I have been unable to procure a transverse section. One of the trunks of birch which lay in the same stratum as the shells, though sorely decayed in its ligneous interior, still retained the bark in a state of great entireness.   The tough outer integument continued to bear its silvery hue, just a little tarnished; and in a specimen now on the table, I found it perforated by a series of circular borings, the work, evidently, of some worm or grub that had lived in the Scottish forests of perhaps some three or four thousand years ago.

The animal organisms of the deposit we find charged with an evidence still more curious than its vegetable remains.

Its few fresh-water shells, Helix and Cyclas, must have been washed into it by the stream. Its scattered periwinkles and Tellinidæ were probably carried dead into it by the waves; at least, all the Tellinidæ which I detected existed as single valves; nor, though the stratum to which I found the periwinkles restricted was greatly more arenaceous than the strata above and below, could I find any evidence that they had lived on it. Though the periwinkles occasionally occur in small numbers on muddy shores, they usually prefer a harder bottom than they could have found in the estuary of the Figget Burn. The evidence furnished by the Scrobicularia bed is, however, of a very different kind. It cannot *rationally* be doubted, that on the spot where we now find them, the individual shells which compose it once lived and died. Let me run briefly over the various points which bear upon the fact. In the first place, the clay in which they occur must have formed exactly such a mud as that in which the living shell still loves to burrow. Farther, we find them associated, in the stratum which they occupy, with no other shell: the only exceptional instances occurred at just a single point, where I found two detached valves of Tellina solidula, and the specimen of Helix nemoralis. Farther, in the great majority of cases, the Scrobicularia of this bed exist as double valves, retaining, in some instances, even the ligament. And it is surely not in the least probable, that a shell so inaccessible in its oozy haunts as to be usually found, according to the Messrs Forbes and Hanley, represented in collections by but single valves washed ashore by storms, should be found in the bed, existing as complete shells, by hundreds and thousands, and this, too, without the companionship of other shells, as if it had been merely washed to the spot by some great wave, like that which accompanied the earthquakes of Lisbon or Calabria. But yet farther, the position in which almost all the fresher specimens occur is wholly irreconcileable with the supposition that they could have been *transported* to the spot on which we now find them. Scrobicularia, when living, stands erect in the mud on one of its ends,—an end which furnishes, in proportion to the general mass of the shell, a base scarce so large as that furnished by the edge of a shilling or sovereign; and it would be no more irrational to suppose that, of a heap of gold or silver coin swept hurriedly along a floor, greatly more than the half would erect themselves on their edges, than that, of many thousand flat bivalves similarly swept, and left to rest in the position natural to them on the ordinary mechanical principles, *greatly* more than the one half should erect themselves on *their* edges. But I still very considerably understate the argument furnished by the position of the shells. When in their proper habitat, burrowing in the mud, they cannot present either end indiscriminately as the upper one. It is indispensable to their wellbeing that the rounded end should be the lower end, and the sub-triangular end, from which the long siphonal tubes project, should be the upper one;—a reverse position would be quite as unnatural to the animal as it would be for a man to stand upon his head; and the question, of course, comes to be an important one,—viz., what end of the shells do we find sticking downwards in the clay, and what upwards ? What first struck me in my earlier visits to the deposit, was the *upright* position of the shells. I found, on my first visit, seven standing upright in the clay in the space of eighteen inches; and on the second, five in the space of six inches. But their state of preservation was scarce perfect enough to enable me conclusively to determine their subtriangular from their rounded end. Since that time, however, I have, in all my visits to the deposit, kept the point in view; and I have now disinterred from the bed, at various times, no fewer than sixty-three specimens standing erect, or but slightly inclined from the perpendicular, all in such a state of keeping, that their anterior could be distinguished from their posterior ends. And mark the result. In every one of the sixty-three examples, the subtriangular end, from which the siphuncular tubes had once protruded, was placed uppermost; the rounded end below. All these shells occupied the position proper to the living animal. Nothing, save the vital principle once operative within them in exactly the place where we now find their remains could have produced such a result. That it could have been the result of any mere chance arrangement, is greatly more improbable than that sixty-three halfpennies thrown up into the air should all turn up heads on their descent; seeing that in the case of the shells there would be not only the chances against their all presenting the same end upwards, but also the chances against their standing up on a sharp edge, instead of resting, as would be natural for them on mere mechanical principles, on one of their flat sides.

All the shells of the deposit, however, do not stand erect. Occasionally a fallen shell may be found tolerably entire, though in most instances they are very much broken, and exist not unfrequently as single valves, divested of the thin yellowish-coloured epidermis. And fallen shells in a detach-

ed fragmentary state are by no means rare.   But let it be
remarked, that the negative evidence which these furnish in
no degree militates against the positive evidence furnished by
the erect ones.   Exposed to accident, and under the influence
of the ordinary mechanical laws, it is natural for the erect
to fall; but all the more, not the less, distinctly and conclusively on that account do the ones that still remain erect
and unfallen testify to the influence of laws *not* mechanical.
The law of gravitation so certainly stretches a dead man along
the ground, that we at once infer that the man who stands
erect owes his erectness to a vital principle operative in de-
fiance of the law.   But it is unnecessary to contend for what
cannot be disputed.   Let me next remark, that where we
now find the shells of Scrobicularia, as in this bed, in their
natural position, the sea must once have been; nay, that
they must have been washed twice in the twenty-four hours
by even the lower neap-tides,—a condition necessary to their
existence as shells not *lacustrine*, but *marine*.   And that
such must have been their level in relation to that of the sea
at the time, we find borne out by the circumstance that the
thick stratum of clay which rests over them,—a stratum varying, as I have said, from three to five feet,—seems to have
been deposited in conditions similar to those of the stratum
beneath.   The estuary in which they lay seems to have been
gradually silted up after their death ; but we can scarce suppose that it could have been so silted to a higher level than
that of stream-tides, without some change taking place in the
character of the deposit.   The shells, then, when living, must
have been covered at spring-tides, in the place where they
now lie, by from four to six feet of salt or brackish water ;

and so the sea at flood must have stood, in that remote age, at a level about twenty feet higher than it does now, or the land at a level about twenty feet lower. The thin beds of sand which in several places overtop the brick-clays in the Figget valley may have been either deposited by the waters of the stream during land-floods, and, of consequence, ere the upheaval of the old coast-line ; or they may have been drifted by storms from the sea during unusually high tides, or wafted by the winds from the beach; and the overlying strata of moss and silt are the deposits of a still later time, when what had been previously in succession a quiet muddy arm of the sea, and next a brackish reed-bearing estuary, had probably existed alternately as swamp and lake,—a lake dammed up, it is probable, by a sand-bar or storm-beach, raised by the waves along the line of the shore. But even the last of these strata must have been deposited ere the upheaval of the old coast terrace—estimated here, I find, by our respected president, Mr Robert Chambers, in his "Ancient Sea Margins," at twenty feet—gave to the spot its present free drainage and its thoroughly subaerial character. And the old Scrobicularia bed must have been covered up ere that remote event,—an event removed far beyond the historic period,—by from six to eight feet of clay, sand, silt, and moss. Thus, then, the bed, besides its other points of geologic interest just enumerated, is of yet farther interest as an example of what is rare in Scotland,—a deposit intermediate in age between the old glacial deposits, which we find charged, like those of Gamrie and the boulder-clays of Caithness, with shells similar to those which now occur on the coasts of subarctic Norway and Greenland, and the deposits which occupy the flat terrace immediately beneath the old coast-line.

The place held by the brick-clays of the entire Portobello deposit, in their relation to the Arthur Seat group of hills, and their probable derivation from the boulder-clays of the district, is not unworthy of being noted. Sheltered by the hills,—when these must have existed, during the glacial ages, as a group of islands,—from that easterly flowing current of whose existence we have so many evidences in the form and direction of our valleys, of denudation and the aspect of our trap-rocks, they occupy exactly the position in which, under the condition of a partially submerged land swept by such a current, such a deposition might be expected. The water, charged with the washings of the boulder-clays, would throw down its sediment in the calm and shelter of the spot where we now find the brick-clay deposit. It may be stated, in connection with this suggestion, that boulders do occur at times, though very rarely, in what seem the older brick-clays, and that such of their number as were not too hard to receive the glacial markings, or too coarse-grained or friable to retain them, exhibit the workings still. There lies at the brick-work of Mr Ingram, who has kindly afforded me every facility in examining the deposit on his grounds, and given me much valuable information regarding it, a sandstone boulder of nearly a ton weight, which was dug out of the brick-clay a considerable time since; and of several smaller boulders recently found about seven feet from its surface, there is a specimen now on the Society's table, on which the characteristic grooves and scratches are as distinctly marked as on any similar block the product of the boulder-clay. The uppermost or last deposited stratum of the older brick-clays,—a stratum about six feet in thickness,—is much mixed with streaks and lines of a fine yellow sand, in some places curiously disturbed and contorted ; and as it is easily distinguishable in consequence, its relation to the newer brick-clays—those in which the shells occur—we find traceable without difficulty.   The newer, apparently a re-formation of the older, as the older themselves are a re-formation of the boulder-clay, occupy an oblong basin in the general deposit, which runs to a hitherto unascertained extent inwards along the valley of the Figget Burn.   They are evidently, as satisfactorily shown by one of the sections now open, the fillings up of an estuary by which the old brick-clay was traversed, many ages, mayhap, after the deposit itself had been formed, but which, silted up by the disintegrated clays, had ceased to exist, save as a mere swamp, ere the last upheaval of the land.   In the section referred to,—that furnished by an excavation at present in the course of being hollowed by Mr Livingston's labourers,—the line between the newer and older clays is distinctly traceable, shelving outwards from the centre of the valley, to what must have been the western shore of this ancient estuary.   The entire deposit, older and newer, furnishes us with two little bits of picture. We are first presented with a scene of islands,—the hills which overlook the Scottish capital, or on which it is built,—half-sunk in a glacial sea.   A powerful current from the west, occasionally charged with icebergs, sweeps past them, turbid with the washings of the raw, recently-formed boulder-clays of the great flat valley which stretches between the Friths of Forth and Clyde ; and in the sheltered tract of sea to the east of the islets, amid slowly revolving eddies, the sediment is cast slowly down, and, layer after layer, the brick-clays are formed along the bottom. And then, in long posterior ages, after the land has risen,—all save its last formed terrace,—and the subarctic rigour of its climate has softened, we mark a long withdrawing estuary running along what is now the valley of the Figget Burn. It is skirted by the aboriginal trees of the country,—oak, and birch, and alder, and the Scotch fir ; and, save where a sluggish stream creeps through the midst, we see it thickly occupied by miniature forests of reeds and rushes, amid the intricacies of whose roots the mud-loving Scrobicularia breed by thousands.

RAISED SEA-BOTTOM NEAR FILLYSIDE BANK

BETWEEN LEITH AND PORTOBELLO.

IT is stated by Mr Charles Maclaren, in his "Geology of Fife and the Lothians," that his attention was called in 1834, by Mr Jardine, civil engineer, to a bed of oyster-shells which had been laid open by the labourers engaged in cutting the line of railway which extends between Leith and Portobello. "The shells," says Mr Maclaren, "lay about a foot, or a little more, under the vegetable soil, in a fine gravel, and extended over a considerable space along the railway, but were in greatest abundance near the mouth of the Foul Burn, about half a mile east of Seafield Baths. They lay, he adds, pretty close together; were so numerous, that probably a thousand might be found within a space three or four yards square; were in general much decomposed; and existed as but detached valves, though in a few instances the valves still occurred unseparated. The oyster greatly predominated in the bed; but it contained a mixture of other shells, such as Buccinum, Pecten, Patella, and Cardium edule. And further, the level of the stratum in which they lay embedded was, he found, from six to eight feet above that of the highest stream-tides, and about twenty-six or twenty-eight feet above the lowest level of low water." So far Mr Maclaren. He adds, however, in a note, that he recorded his observations on this deposit in the "Scotsman" newspaper of November 1, 1834, unaware at the time that the shells had been exposed many years before, and described by Professor Jamieson to his class.

In the immediate locality where Mr Maclaren found the shells lying most thickly, the land is protected against the encroachments of the sea by a bulwark of rude masonry, and so cannot be seen in section. To the east, however, about one hundred and sixty yards from the Foul Burn, the bulwark terminates; and the higher stream-tides of winter and spring, when urged upwards by gales from the sea, wash the bank, which presents, in consequence, a low abrupt front, consisting of two several deposits. The lowermost of these is composed of the ordinary boulder-clay of the district; the uppermost, of a stratified sand and gravel, which forms here the immediate subsoil of the thin layer of vegetable mould that rests over all. I observed many years ago, in this sand and gravel, an interrupted layer of partially decomposed shells, chiefly oysters, but mingled with occasional specimens of Buccinum, Littorina, Cardium, and Patella, which occurs from fourteen to eighteen inches from the surface, in the line of the stratification; and identified it, from its character and position, as the stratum of shells described by Mr Maclaren. A few years later, however, after a great tide, which had encroached very considerably on the bank, I marked, in the neighbourhood of the shells, another appearance, to which I attached even more importance in its bearing on the question of upheaval. Immediately on the top of the underlying clay, and in some instances partially embedded in it, there is an irregular layer, at this spot, of boulder-stones, from some of which the stratified sand and gravel had now been washed for the first time. And to not a few of these newly-uncovered stones I found the under valves of oysters still firmly attached. Unless the stones had been carried there previous to the formation of the bed of stratified sand and gravel, by some enormous wave of translation, an oyster-scalp must have existed on that very spot; and the appearance certainly did not favour the notion of a wave of translation. The oyster-valves occupied the sides and upper portions of all the boulders to which I saw them fixed : a wave of translation would surely have reversed some of them ! The stones bearing the shells lay contiguous, not scattered : a wave of translation would surely have scattered some of them ! And though none of them were of great size, at least one of their number,—a block of greenstone,—contained from four to five cubic feet of ponderous stone ; and even the least massive of the others would have demanded for their transport from the existing oyster-grounds of the Frith, to their present place above the level of stream-tides, the agency of a very formidable wave. Further, they occupied exactly the position, with relation to the boulder-clay, in which we usually find such groupes of boulders in the instances—as along shores and river-banks— in which there has been a partial denudation of the deposit. Some of the limestone boulders, their neighbours, I found perforated by the cells of Pholas and Saxicava ; and in some cases the decayed shells of Saxicava rugosa, and of that dwarf variety of Tapes pullastra which, though unable to scoop out a house for itself, finds at once a refuge and a prison in hollows excavated by the boring molluscs. Such were the appearances which I remarked at this time. I had, unluckily, not visited the spot immediately after the storm which had laid it bare ; and a talus of loose sand and gravel, which had fallen from the upper deposit, had in the interval formed over the clay, and lay scattered amid the stones, and thus prevented me from detecting those further particulars of the deposit to which I would now call the attention of the Society.

In the latter part of last month, a heavy gale from the sea, coincident with a high stream-tide, again swept the lower margin of the land at this point, and, encroaching on the double deposit of boulder-clay and stratified sand, opened up a fresh section. I visited the spot immediately after the storm had blown over, and found the talus which had covered the surface of the clay washed away, and a second bed of shells, which underlies the bed described by Mr Maclaren by about two feet and a half, laid bare. It lies at the base of the stratified deposit, and consists, in large part, of oyster-shells, existing, however, almost exclusively as single valves, and largely mingled, especially in the upper part of the bed, with the more common littoral shells, such as the periwinkles, Littorina littorea, and Littorina littoralis, with Patella vulgata, Purpura lapillus, Cardium edule, and Tellina solidula. It contains also shells of a lower level, which are, however, frequent on our beaches, such as Cardium echinatum, Pecten opercularis, Turritella communis, and Anomia ephippium ;

with shells which might have belonged to either the Littoral or the Laminarian zone, such as Buccinum undatum, Solen siliqua, Trochus cinerarius, and Tapes pullastra. In some of the specimens of Tapes I found the valves still united by the sorely-decayed ligament, as also in a solitary specimen of oyster, and in a single entire specimen of a shell comparatively unfrequent on our shores, though once very abundant in what are now the brick-clays of Portobello,—Scrobicularia piperata. "Of this shell, though not absolutely rare," say the authors of the "British Mollusca," "cabinets, from the inaccessibility of its habitat, are usually only furnished with dead valves washed on shore after rough weather." My collection contains not a few specimens of Scrobicularia from the Portobello clays, with their valves still united ; but my best and least decayed specimen is that which I derived a few weeks ago from this comparatively modern, but absolutely ancient, bed.

Immediately below this stratum of shells, which extends, so far as I could trace it in the section, about a hundred and thirty feet, the layer of boulders occurs which rests upon the boulder-clay. I found fewer of their number exhibiting the attached oyster-valves than on the former occasion. At one spot, however, within the compass of about three yards, and only a few inches beneath the level of the shell-bed, I reckoned five to which these sedentary molluscs had been fast anchored by their nether valves,—one of them a block of about half a ton weight; and from the deeply hollowed cells of several of the limestone boulders immediately beside them I extracted shells of Saxicava rugosa, and of the distorted variety of Tapes pullastra already referred to, and which was known to the conchologists as Venus perforans.* Under the sloping edges of three of these stones, and protected by a re-formation of the clay which had wrapped them round till washed off by the previous tide, I found three oysters,—one in each instance, —still existing as double valves; one of them still sticking fast to its stone,—the other two still in junction with theirs, but with their hold loosened, apparently, by the rotting percolation of fresh water from above. In the flattened portions of the valves that had furnished the area of connection there were Balani embedded, which had been sticking to the stones previous to the attachment and growth of the shells, and which had been grown around and enveloped in their substance. In the individual which had still retained its hold of the rock I found a delicate Lepralia thus enclosed. Another patch of Lepralia, so perfect in its state of keeping that, for aught which appeared, it might have been living only a few weeks ago, occurred in the interior of one of the three oysters, immediately over the muscular impression,— of course showing, that while still in its deep-water habitat, the original possessor of the shell had died, and had left an empty apartment to the occupancy of the little Lepralia. The surface of the boulder-clay was in many places thickly covered with shells, some of them minute and much broken, others of larger size, and, when of the bivalve division, with the valves still attached. Of these last, large well-preserved specimens of Tapes pullastra were most numerous. Pecten

---

* "The length of our largest specimen is about two inches, and its breadth about an inch and a quarter. These dimensions, however, are but rarely attained to, the majority of examples being about an inch and a half only in length, and of proportionate width."—*British Mollusca.*

pusio also occurred, though, in all the instances save one, as single valves only; with large specimens of Anomia ephippium. The prevailing univalve of this layer was the common Trochus cinerarius, still bearing very freshly, in most of the specimens, its native colours. Nassa incrassata and Turritella communis were not unfrequent; Murex erinaceus and Nuclea nucleus were present, but comparatively rare; and I found only a few specimens of Patella pellucida. Specimens also occurred of Purpura lapillus, which seemed, however, to belong to a thin, higher-lying layer than that to which Pecten pusio, Murex erinaceus,' and Anomia ephippium, belonged, and which was evidently littoral in its character. Many of the minuter stones on this lower bottom I found encrusted with serpulæ, and lepraliæ, and exactly resembling in their appearance the smaller stones brought to the surface by the dredge from the inner bands of the Laminarian zone. Several of its larger boulders had also their serpulæ, though in a state of greater decay. It had also its darkly-tinged oyster-shells,—the dead shells, evidently, of a Laminarian sea-bottom,—similarly encrusted. More importance, however, must be attached to my remaining fact. On the surface of the boulder-clay, and perforating it to the depth of from three to four inches, I found well-grown specimens of Mya truncata, evidently occupying the places in which they had lived and died. The firm boulder-clay lay in most of the cases undisturbed around them. Their open siphuncular ends were turned upwards; their rounded ends downwards. In one instance, the ruins of the tubular membrane which had protected the siphons lay inside the opening, just where they had fallen during the process of decay.

The shells were still covered—such was their state of keeping —by the yellowish-brown epidermis, and were as solid and en- tire as if they had lived only a few years ago. The area of clay-surface laid bare was comparatively small, and much cumbered by boulders. It furnished me, however, with twelve (now nineteen) specimens of Mya in the state and position described, and with several others in a similar state of keeping, but detached from their original places by the surf. But to these last, of course, I attach no importance in the argument which I would derive from the position of the other. In laminarian deposits of this character, whether merely raised within the Littoral zone, or to a higher level, altogether beyond the reach of the tide, sorely decayed twigs of weeds, fir cones, and hazel nuts, are of not unfrequent occurrence. I found in this deposit a few dark-coloured twigs, existing—such was the state of decay—as mere vege- table pulp; and a single hazel-nut.

I have referred to a thin, higher-lying, layer of littoral shells which rested immediately over this laminarian layer, and was in some places much mixed with it. I found it composed chiefly of the shells of Patella vulgata, Purpura lapillus, Trochus cinerarius, and the periwinkles. The spe- cimens were usually much broken, tinged in many places with a ferruginous stain, which the laminarian shells wanted, and collected in considerable quantities round the looser stones and boulders. Similar accumulations of the same shells, in the same broken state, may be seen among the stones and boulders of the middle and lower zones of shore laid bare by the larger ebb-tides; and are characteristic of a littoral, but not of a beach, deposit. The various appearances of the entire section here, with its several beds, I read as follows.

In some dateless and undateable period, very remote in its relation to human history, but geologically recent,—for exactly the same shells as now existed on our shores,—the surface of the boulder-clay at this spot formed, with its groupes of boulders, a sea-bottom of the Laminarian zone, occupied by an oyster-bed.   Mya truncata burrowed in the stiff fundamental clay, and Saxicava rugosa and Venus perforans, in the calcareous blocks which lay scattered over it ; its pebbles were encrusted by Serpulæ and Lepraliæ ; it was traversed by Nassa, Turritella, and Trochus ; Pecten pusio found its home in its crevices, and in the hollows of its decayed shells ; and Patella pellucida and Anomia ephippium attached themselves to its tangles and pebbles.   The depth of water which rested over it I cannot determine other than approximately. " The oysters of the Frith of Forth," say the authors of the " British Mollusca," " are dredged in from four to six or seven fathoms water."   In some instances, however, in very sheltered localities, they approach almost to the line of low ebb : I have seen the inner edge of an oyster-bed laid dry at Flowerdale, in Gairloch, during stream-tides ; but the individual oysters, in all such cases, are of small size ; and as the shells of this elevated oyster-bed of the ancient coast attained to the average proportions common in the Frith beyond, we may, I think, safely assume for it at least the minimum, if not, indeed, the average, depth of our oyster-beds of the present day, viz, from four to five fathoms. Either from an upheaval of the land or recession of the sea, a change in the level of the bed took place : it was elevated within reach of the surf; its oysters, unfitted for such a habitat, died; and, save where sheltered amid the crevices of the boulders, or attached to them by their under valves, were washed upwards, to form a littoral deposit. This I take to be the origin of the thick bed of shells at the base of the stratified sand and gravel; and its numerous mingled molluscs that select the space between low and high water as their proper haunts, —such as the periwinkles, with Patella vulgata, Purpura lapillus, and Tellina solidula,—testify to the nature of the change. The thin irregular stratum of shell, much broken, and bearing a ferruginous tinge, that lies between this mixed shelly stratum and the fundamental Mya bed, indicates, I must hold, a transition period which intervened between the upheaval of the deposit to the level of the *lower* Littoral zone, and its yet further upheaval to the level of the beach proper, or *upper* Littoral zone. Over the mixed shell-bed there took place an accumulation of common beach deposits, chiefly sand and gravel, to the depth of nearly three feet, and then the uppermost shell-layer was formed. Though composed mainly of oyster-shells, I cannot regard it as marking the site of a *second* oyster-bed. Though not without its mixture of other laminarian shells besides the oyster, such as Cardium echinatum and Pecten opercularis, it has its shells of the Littoral zone, such as Patella vulgata and Cardium edule; and the mingled sand and gravel in which it occurs bears entirely the beach character and aspect. I regard it simply as indicating that a farther upheaval of the land had brought some oyster-bed in the sea beyond from the laminarian to the littoral level, and that the shells, driven upwards by the surf, and mingled with other shells, littoral and laminarian, thickly strewed the beach at this line.   From about fourteen to eighteen inches of yet farther beach deposits took place, covering up all ; and then a final elevation of the land raised not only the upper sand and gravel strata, but even the underlying argillaceous sea-bottom, with its Mya, Anomia, and attached oysters, above the level of ordinary stream-tides. Such I take to be the history of the deposit.

The escarpment so generally recognised as the old coast-line, though of no great height in this neighbourhood, is well marked, and, from its rampart-like continuity, and the line of willows which runs along its summit, forms a conspicuous feature in the prospect. Its sloping base, against which the waves must have broken at the full of the tide for ages, lies two hundred and fifty-four yards inland from this ancient sea-bottom, and at an elevation over it of about sixteen feet. Our stream-tides of March and September fall rather more than eighteen feet ; and so, when the high-water line reached to but the base of the escarpment, the deposit must have been already a littoral one. The some fourteen or eighteen feet more necessary to furnish depth enough of water for its oysters, would have very considerably affected the outline of the coast here. As Mr Maclaren well remarks, a change in the level of the land of little more than thirty feet beneath the existing one would cover the greater part of the site of the town of Leith, and fill the lower reaches of the valley into which the harbour of that place opens with an arm of the sea about two miles long and a quarter of a mile broad; and the flat winding valley of the Figget Burn, immediately behind Portobello, so remarkable for its Scrobicularia bed, would be similarly occupied for about three quarters of a mile.

The old coast-line between Leith and Portobello is of a more picturesque character than the present. It advances on the green gently sloping terrace at its base, in the form of low promontories, or recedes into shallow bays; and one of the largest and deepest of these occurs so nearly opposite the oyster-deposits here, that the deposit described by Mr Maclaren as occurring at the Foul Burn occupies about the same place at its mouth, on the western side, as the one just described does on its eastern one. The old solitary farm-house of Fillyside Bank, with its drooping willows and dank meadows, occupies the inner part of this ancient bay, long deserted by the sea; and beside and behind the building there are hollow swamps, which existed, in all probability, when the land stood some eighteen or twenty feet lower than at present, as muddy lagoons. Scrobicularia find meet habitats in such localities; and it seems not unlikely, that from some of these hollows, when occupied, during flood, by every tide, the specimens of this shell furnished by the lower-beach bed of the deposit may have been derived. Though it supplied me with but one entire specimen of the shell, I detected in it, when first laid bare, several broken valves.

It is not always safe to estimate the age of a shell-bed by the state of keeping in which its shells occur. The freshness of the various strata of shells in the very deposit I describe seems in an inverse proportion to their age; the uppermost, and, of course, newest stratum, being in a state of sore decay; the second, and considerably older stratum, if not absolutely fresh, at least tolerably so; the third, or last littoral stratum, though broken by the mechanical action of the waves, in the main fresher still; and the fourth, and oldest of all, that of the underlying sea-bottom, existing in a state of preservation wonderfully good. Its Mya, and not a few of its oysters, might, for aught that appears in their state of keeping, have been living, as I have already said, only a few years ago. The nature of the matrix in which shells lie determines their condition much more influentially than the number of years during which they may have lain in it. But in matrices of an equally conservative quality, the comparative states of keeping ought surely to furnish approximate tests of age ; and the sorely-decayed condition of the Scrobicularia of Portobello, though enclosed in a stiff clay, compared with the freshness of the Scrobicularia of this deposit, seems to indicate that they belong to ages pretty widely separated. The Scrobicularia of the muddy wood-skirted estuary which is now the Figget Burn must have been dead and silted over for many years ere those of the Fillyside deposit had come into existence. Geologically the recent period is one ; but from the first appearance of its group of shells, as preserved in old upheaved estuaries, such as that of the Figget valley at Portobello, and that of the Lones of Fearn in Ross-shire, and the period of that last elevation of the land which gave to our country its present coast-line, thousands of years may have elapsed ; and of even the later period, we know that it lies beyond the first beginnings of the national history. It is a curious fact, but not the less a real one, that some of these fresh-looking shells on the Society's table had ceased to live, and were locked up in their matrices of sand or clay, long ere the battles of Largs or Luncarty had been stricken, or the names of Wallace and the Bruce had become watch-words in Scotland. If man lived at all in our island previous to the last general upheaval of the land, it must have been as an uncultured savage, unacquainted with the metals, and ignorant of all save the most rudimentary arts.   But there is no fact oftener denoted by our science than the very curious one, that the *recent* of the geologist and the *remote* of the antiquary are convertible terms; and that what we describe without hesitation as a modern shell may be older than the times of Homer or of Hesiod, or than even the first beginnings of human history.

ANCIENT SEA-MARGINS.

SHOULD the Edinburgh reader, in availing himself of the present long evenings for the purposes of exercise or recreation, extend his walk along the coast-road which connects Portobello with Leith, he will perceive, when the tide is out, that the portions of dry land and sea-beach immediately under his eye consist of two belts of sloping plain,—an upper belt covered with long luxuriant herbage, and a lower belt composed of bare sea-sand and gravel. With this difference,—purely a result of their present difference of level, which imparts to the one a sub-aerial, and to the other a sub-aqueous character,—the two belts present a wonderful identity of character. They slope transversely at nearly the same low angle, and spread out laterally in nearly the same flat line. Were we to dig into the soil a little below the rank grass of the upper plain, we would find that it is formed of materials exactly resembling those of the lower, *i. e.,* 'stratified sea-sand and gravel, mixed with marine shells of the existing species ; and that in both, the sand, shells, and gravel rest on a subsoil of the boulder-clay. From this clay those numerous boulders that stud the lower platform have been derived. They seem to have existed on the upper platform also, and may still be detected along one of the water-courses; but a careful husbandry has long since cleared them from off the surface. What, however, most strongly marks the resemblance of the two plains are the continuous escarpments which bound their upper sides.   The one, lashed by the surf during the frequent storms of winter, runs, irregular and broken, along the coast at the stream-tide line of high water ; the other, so smooth and comparatively regular as to resemble a very flat rampart, bounds the view on the upper side of the road, and bears atop a long line of willows.   More varied in outline than the lower escarpment, this upper line presents, in succession, its two grassy bays that retire towards the interior, and an angular willow-crowned promontory that projects between.   In the eastern extremity of the western bay, just where the old-fashioned farm-house of Fillyside Bank is situated, there must have existed in ancient times a sort of muddy lagoon, that ran upwards for several hundred yards along the flat valley through which the small stream that drained the hollow now occupied by the Cowgate and the eastern and northern ravines of Arthur Seat, found its way to the sea.   On the western side of this rural grass-bearing bay, the escarpment is considerably higher than on its eastern side ; and on the corresponding escarpment of the lower platform, directly opposite, there is a similar rise.   Save that the upper escarpment is the more undulating and graceful of the two, there is as thorough an identity between them as between the contiguous steps of a stair ; but while the lower escarpment forms the present coast-line, and is an effect of the encroachments, during stream-tides, of the sea at the existing level, the upper escarpment formed the coast-line thousands of years ago, when the sea stood higher than now, or the land lower, and when, though the country seems to have had its human inhabitants, the art of communicating with posterity by alphabet or symbol was an art either very partially developed, or, what seems more probable, altogether unknown. When this green winding bank, topped with willows (the most modern of the " ancient sea-margins "), was washed by the waves at full and new moon, like the bare broken escarpment below, the inhabitants of the country were rude savages, who dwelt in wigwams formed of green branches, or in cave-like subterranean dens of undressed stone,—who employed in war and the chase weapons of flint and jasper,—and who navigated their rivers and estuaries in canoes hollowed by fire out of single logs of wood.

Now, this lower and most modern of the old coast-lines may be traced along the greater part of both the eastern and western shores of Scotland. The level platform which it overtops forms a broken selvage of irregular breadth all around the island, extending outwards on shallow coasts, as on the coast of Forfarshire, between Arbroath and Dundee, for several miles, but restricted where the water is deep, as along the southern coasts of Aberdeen, to a narrow belt a few yards in breadth ; or, where lines of precipices rise abruptly out of the sea, wanting altogether. Not a few of our seaports and watering towns, such as the greater part of Leith, Portobello, Fisherrow, Kirkaldy, Dundee, Dingwall, Invergordon, and Cromarty, are built upon it ; and it furnishes in various localities extensive ranges of sandy links, and large tracts of valuable gardens and fields. It is strongly marked on the southern side of the Dornoch Frith, immediately below and a little to the east of the town of Tain, where it attains a breadth of from one to two miles, and where the coast sea-margin, rising over the cottage-mottled plain below in a series of alternate bays and headlands, strikes even the least practised eye as

possessed of all the characteristic peculiarities of a true coast-
line.   It is scarce less marked in the neighbourhood of Cromarty, and on the opposite shores of the Frith, in the parish
of Nigg.   It runs along by much the greater portion of the
eastern coast of Sutherland ; and forms, at the head of Loch
Fleet, in the neighbourhood of Dornoch, a long withdrawing
frith, bounded by picturesque shores, and covered by a short
green sward, level as the sea in a calm, on which groupes of
willow and alder trees take the place of busy fleets, and the
hare and partridge that of the coot and the porpoise.   It is
not improbable that canoes may have floated on this frith,
now an extended plain, grazed by herds of cattle ; and that
the dwellings of the rude fishers by whom they were navigated may have arisen among the woods on its shores.   At
a not later period the estuary of the Clyde must have extended at least six or eight miles higher than Glasgow ; and
on three several occasions ancient vessels have been dug out
of the silt which underlies some of the busiest streets of the
city, that must have tilted high over the area now occupied
by squares and public buildings, ere this last of the ancient
beaches was deserted by the sea.   But though man had entered upon the scene, it was in an age anterior to human history, in at least this island.   "Mr Smith of Jordan Hill,"
says Mr Robert Chambers, in his "Ancient Sea-Margins as
Memorials of Changes in the Relative Levels of Sea and
Land," "has pointed out that the Roman wall, at its termi-
nations on the Friths of Forth and Clyde, appears to have
been formed with respect to the present relative level of sea
and land.   He also quotes the description of St Michael's
Mount in Cornwall, which Diodorus Siculus gives in the time

of Augustus, showing it to have been then, as now, connected with the main land at ebb-tide."

Could we fix with any certainty the time when the last change of level took place, and the platform of the lower coast-line was gained from the sea, there might be an approximation made to the anterior space of time during which the sea continued standing against it, and the line of high water had been the willow-crowned escarpment at Portobello. There are portions of the coast that at this early period presented lines of precipices to the waves, which are now fringed at their bases by strips of verdure, and removed beyond their reach. There are other portions of coast in the immediate neighbourhood of these, where similar lines of precipices, identical in their powers of resistance, were brought by the same movement, whether of elevation of the land or of recession of the sea, within that very influence of the waves beyond which the others were raised. And each line bears, in the caves with which it is fretted,—caves hollowed by the attrition of the surf in the direction of faults, or where masses of yielding texture had been included in the more solid rock,—indices to mark, proportionally at least, the respective periods during which they were exposed to the excavating agent. Thus the average depth of the ancient caves in an exposed line of coast, as ascertained by dividing the aggregate sum of their depths by their number, and the average depth, ascertained by the same process, of the recent caves equally exposed on the same coast, and hollowed in the same variety of rock, could scarce fail to represent their respective periods of exposure, had we but a given number of years, historically determined, to set off against the average measurement of the

recent excavations.   Even wanting this, however, it is something to know the fact generally, but absolutely, that though
the sea has stood at the existing sea-margin in this country
since at least the closing days of the Roman Commonwealth,
it stood for a considerably longer period at the last of the old
sea-margins.   The rock of which those remarkable promontories, the Sutors of Cromarty, are composed, is a granitic
gneiss, much traversed by faults, and enclosing occasional
masses of a soft chloritic schist, that yields to the waves;
while the surrounding gneiss, hard enough to strike fire with
steel, remains little affected by the attrition of centuries.   It
has, in consequence, along these promontories its numerous
caves, ranged in a double row,—the lower row that of the existing coast, the upper that of the old coast-line ; and we have
examined them with some little degree of care.   The deepest
of the recent caves measures, from the opening to its inner
extremity, where the rock closes, exactly a hundred feet ; the
deepest of the ancient ones, now so completely raised above
the surf, that in the severest storms and highest tides the
wave never reaches its mouth, is exactly a hundred and fifty
feet ; and these respective depths, though much beyond the
average of their several rows, bear, so far as we could ascertain the point, the proportion to each other borne by these
averages.   If the excavation of the recent caves be the work
of two thousand years, the excavation of the ancient ones
must have occupied three thousand.

Above this lowest and most modern of the ancient sea-
margins there is no other coast-line at all to be compared
with it in continuity of extent, or the distinctness with
which it is marked.   There are detached sets of terraces in

various localities, in some instances widely separated, that wonderfully correspond in height; and to demonstrate that correspondence over extensive areas, and to show that each set, according to its height, must have owed its origin to the sea when the sea stood at the analogous line of level, forms a portion of the plan of the singularly interesting and meritorious work of Mr Robert Chambers to which we have already referred. It is of course to be expected that, the higher and more ancient the beach, the more must it be worn down by the action of the elements, especially by the descent of water-courses; and as the beaches intermediate between that of the strongly marked line to which we have adverted, and the upper lines traceable in detached fragments in the moorland districts of the country, occur in an agricultural region, the obliterating wear of the plough has been added to that of the elements. Still, after all fair allowances have been made, there remain great difficulties in the way. We have been puzzled, for instance, by the fact, that Scotland presents us with but two lines of water-worn caves,—that of the recent coast-line, and that of the old line immediately above it. Mr Chambers enumerates no fewer than fifteen lines intermediate between the twenty-feet line and a line at three hundred and six feet; and in the range of granite rocks already referred to, that skirts the Sutors, there are precipices fully a hundred yards in height, and broadly exposed to the stormy north-east, whose bases bear their double line of deeply hollowed caverns. But they exhibit no third, or fourth, or fifth line. Equally impressible throughout their entire extent of front, and with their enclosed masses of chloritic schist, and their lines of fault as

thickly set in their brows as in their bases, they yet present
no upper storeys of caves.   Had the sea stood at the fifteen
intermediate lines for periods at all equal in duration to those
in which it has stood at the lower ancient or at the existing
coast-line, the taller precipices of the Sutors would present
their seventeen storeys of excavations ; and excavations in a
hard granitic gneiss, that varied from twenty to a hundred
feet in depth, would form marks at least as indelible as parallel roads on the mountain sides, or mounds of gravel and
debris rising over the course of rivers.   The want of lines of
caves higher than those of the second coast-line would seem
to indicate, that though the sea may have remained long
enough at the various upper levels to leave its mark on soft
impressible materials, it did not remain long enough to ex-
cavate into caverns the solid rocks.

What forms the prominent feature of Mr Chambers' work,
already referred to, is the decided leaning which it exhibits
on the part of the writer to the old geological theory of the
recession of the sea, rather than to the more modern one of
a comparatively partial elevation of the land.   According
to the modern view, the line of the sea-level is regarded as
one of the most fixed in nature, while that of the land, subject to elevations and depressions, is laid down as an arbi-
trary and fluctuating line ; whereas, according to the ancient
view, it was the sea-line that was regarded as fluctuating,
and that of the land as stable and immoveable.   It has been
demonstrated by very ample experience, that the land-line is
not stable: in the Old World there are at least five localities,
—Scandinavia, the west coast of Italy, the coasts of Cutch and
of Aracan, and part of the kingdom of Luzon,—where the

land is rising at the present time; and in the New World there are vast districts in which it suddenly changed its level for a higher, during the present century. But it by no means follows that, because the line of the land fluctuates, that of the sea is stable: exactly the reverse inference would, we should think, be the sounder one.

THE MEADOWS.

THE Town Council improvements in the large tract of flat marshy ground on the south side of Edinburgh so well known as "the Meadows," are progressing daily, and bid fair to be very decided improvements indeed.   The large boulder-stones which lined the edges of the tract in a broad belt of some sixty or eighty yards across, are in the course of being broken up by gunpowder and the hammer; several thousand yards of drains have been formed; and at present (1842) the surface of the entire area presents a broken scene of recently felled trees, loose heaps of newly fractured stone, pyramids of draining tiles, and large accumulations of soil, that vary in colour, according to the character of the bottom, from white to rusty brown, and from deep black to gray.   In a few weeks, however, the whole will be smoothed over; and if there be virtue in labour well directed, and tile-draining according to the most approved mode, we shall soon have a continuous sheet of green dry sward for an unwholesome marshy hollow; and the last vestiges of the ancient Borough Loch shall have disappeared.   All our readers have heard of the Borough Moor: it has been graphically described by Scott in "Marmion," as the site of the encampment of the unhappy James previous to his fatal march to Flodden.   Fields, and gardens, and tasteful villas, now cover it over: there remains not a vestige that maintains the ancient character: its very name has become a thing of tradition : but it still exists in the pages of Scott as a wild broken moor, partially covered by the remains of an ancient forest ; and we have but to give our imaginations up to the poet, in order to see it still, with the white tents shining from amid the mingling foliage,—the standard of Scotland rising tall in the midst,—groupes of a picturesque soldiery scattered over the sylvan area,—and the dusky town, strongly walled and jealously guarded, looming in the back-ground. But while the recollection of the Borough Moor has been thus preserved, the Borough Loch, its neighbour, has been less fortunate ; though, at the time when the poet represents Marmion as riding over Blackford, it must have formed as marked a feature in the landscape as the moor itself ;—it must have stretched a broad blue sheet of water between the half-felled forest and the city,—the home of the pike and the perch, and the occasional haunt of the coot and the sea-gull ; and its huge boulder-stones, one of which is even now yielding its ponderous bulk to the expansive force of gunpowder, and flinging up its fragments into the air, must have stood up along its sedgy shore, amid thickets of reeds and flags, and wide-spread shallows covered by the white flowering trefoil.

The Borough Loch seems to have been one of a chain of small shallow lakes, which, until a comparatively late period, studded the bottom of the long hollow valley, which extends onwards from Duddingston towards Falkirk, and which is bounded on the north by the ridge of low trap eminences to which Corstorphine Hill belongs, and on the south by the resembling ridge to which Blackford and Craiglockhart Hills belong. A loch in the neighbourhood of Corstorphine, now, like the Borough Loch, a green hollow, had its boat and its duck-shooting as late, it is said, as the middle of the last century. Edinburgh had a lake, it is evident, at one period, in each of its three nearly parallel hollows,—that to the north of the Castle, now occupied by the Prince's Street Gardens, —that through which the Cowgate runs,—and that more especially the subject of our present description, and of the Town Council improvements. Duddingston and Lochend still exist unchanged. The great extent of water exposed in the line of the valley had its marked effect on the atmosphere and the general health of the inhabitants ; the crops of the farmer suffered severely from cold fogs ; and diseases now scarce known in Scotland were comparatively common in the district. The records of the Medical Faculty in Edinburgh do not extend to a period by any means remote. We have been informed, however, by a medical friend, that among their earlier entries, agues and marsh fevers occur as usual diseases of the town and neighbourhood. The diseases of the Scottish capital in those days seem to have resembled the diseases of Canada and the Low Countries now. Combe adverts to the fact in one of his writings, but perhaps without taking sufficiently into account the numerous lakes of the district. In the causes to which he chiefly refers,—causes connected with an unskilful and slovenly style of husbandry, and the filth and moisture suffered to accumulate around the dwellings of the country people,—it resembled all the rest of Scotland at the period. "A gentleman who died about ten years ago, at an advanced period of life," says the writer, in a work now fourteen years before the public, "told me that six miles from Edinburgh the country was so unhealthy in his youth, that every spring the farmers and their servants were seized with fever and ague, and needed regularly to undergo bleeding and a course of medicine, to prevent attacks, or to restore them from their effects. After, however, an improved system of agriculture and draining was established, and vast pools of stagnant water, formerly left between the ridges of fields, were removed, dunghills carried to a distance from the door, and the houses themselves made more spacious and commodious, every symptom of ague and marsh-fever disappeared from the district." The fact is at once curious and instructive. Rousseau could describe the savage state as the state of nature; but facts such as these,—facts furnishing the true solution of the problem why, as established by our life-insurance tables, human life should be more extended now than in the days of our grandfathers,—unanswerably demonstrate the contrary. They show that, so natural is civilization to man, that he cannot live out his proper term without it.

It would be difficult for the young geologist to find a more instructive walk, or a walk in which he will find more that serves to connect the agency of existing causes with some of the earlier geological phenomena, than that along the open drains of the Meadows. He will detect in it a lacustrine deposit in the very act of passing into dry land, and find not a few of those appearances that seem so puzzling in the ancient formations, not yet dissociated from those every-day operations of nature through which they were produced. May we ask the reader to accompany us for just a few hundred yards along one of the deeper drains. And, first, let us mark the varieties of bottom. That leaden-coloured earth, which rose to the spade in large adhesive masses like clay, but which is

now falling asunder under the influence of the weather, and re-
solving itself into a mixture of fine sand and dried mud, is
the kind of subsoil known as silt, so common in the deltas of
rivers and the bottoms of lakes and estuaries.   The rains of
a thunder-storm in the gentler seasons of the year, or of a
tempestuous night in winter, wash away particles of the looser
and lighter soil from a thousand declivities, and every little
stream rushes down foul and turbid to the lake, river, or estuary, into which it disgorges its waters.   The lighter particles are carried farthest, and subside last.   We have seen a
northern frith many fathoms in depth, and with a surface of
many square miles, rendered turbid throughout its entire
extent by a thunder-shower of scarce an hour's continuance.
The process is repeated some sixty or eighty times every season ; layer subsides over layer ; the delta enlarges and gains
upon the sea ; the lake or estuary gradually shallows and con-
tracts its area ; and in many cases the soil formed is just such a
silt as that which we see thrown out of the ditch before us.
It must have formed very slowly in a piece of water that, like
the Borough Loch, had no considerable stream falling into
it ; but the stratification observable in the weathered masses
thrown out show that in this manner it must have been formed.
We see them splitting into crumbling layers as thin as paper.
Mark, further, that in one or two places the silt is of a lighter
tint than in the general mass, enclosing fragments of lacustrine
shells, and that it presents an iron-shot appearance, not at
all unlike what we often find in the older sandstones.   It is
thickly mottled by minute ferruginous spots, which seem, from
the vestiges of decayed plants which we can trace among them,
to have had a vegetable origin.   Had the ferruginous mark-

ings of the older standstones a vegetable origin too ? It is not uncommon to find what seem consolidated silts among almost all the formations. An ancient Danish ship has been found embedded in silt near the mouth of one of our English rivers. In the Coal Measures we find beds, composed, apparently, of the same substance, but hardened into stone, rich in remains of the ancient fish and strange flora of that remote period. In the Old Red Sandstone a resembling mixture of stratified sand and mud is found to contain the uncouth cephalaspides and gigantic crustacea of the cornstones. The creations were dissimilar in all their many productions; but in all alike, rains descended, and streams swollen and turbid discharged their waters into lakes and seas.

We pass onwards, and reach a different subsoil. The leaden-coloured tint has given place to one of deep black, with here and there a mingling band of brown. We have arrived at one of the beds of lacustrine peat in which the Meadows abound. The Irish labourers employed in the work of draining, reminded, apparently, of their green bogs, and their weeks of periodical summer-labour spent in re-stocking their turf-stacks, exhausted during the chills of winter, have been cutting the masses in the peat form, and placing them end-long, in pairs, all along the margin of the ditch. The bed out of which they have been cut seems here to cover about half an acre; and we see it composing the bottom of the ditch, which has failed to perforate it, and rising nearly two feet along its sides. When the Borough Loch began to shallow, it must have formed a swampy patch, whose surface, level with that of the water, would seem, in the drier seasons, a low island, and, after prolonged rains, would return to its original con-

dition of a dark tangled shoal.   The floating islands of our
old chroniclers were formed of patches of lacustrine moss, such
as the one at which we have arrived, removed from their
foundations by either their own buoyancy or the force of currents.   Sir Thomas Dick Lauder graphically describes one of
these patches, which had been torn up by the very roots in
a small Highland lake during the great Morayshire floods of
1829, and then stranded high on a neighbouring shore, as a
wrecked island.   Let us examine some of the masses thrown
out by the Irishmen.   This light spongy fragment seems composed almost exclusively of some species of aquatic moss: the
slim branching stems, covered by their minute silky leaves,
are well-nigh as distinct as when the plants to which they
belonged were vegetating amid the water.   In this other fragment we find what seems to be a moss of a different species :
the stems are harder and more slender, and the much minuter leaflets, less numerous and less silky, stand out as stiffly
as thorns or the shoots of the wild rose.   Occasionally we find
a minute twig, occasionally the remains of a beech leaf; and
these, it is probable, have been drifted from the shore.   There
occur in the more solid peat, circular spots of deep black, surrounded by a lighter-coloured ring, waved with such regularity as to remind one of the section of a fluted column.
These are the remains of the roots of aquatic plants : the
comparatively light-coloured ring is composed evidently of
woody tissue.   Not a few of the masses abound in minute
shining seeds, or rather the shells of seeds.   They cannot be
those of the chara, figured by Lyell as abundant in a fossil
state in the recent lacustrine deposits of Forfarshire, as, instead of the spirally-curved integument of the seed-vessel of

the chara, we are presented with an integument altogether smooth, and brightly japanned. In this pale marly mass we find the remains of a flattened reed : two of the joints are still discernible, with the minute striæ that run between them ; and the entire organism, both from its well-marked form and its deep black colour, contrasted with the pale tint of the surrounding mass, serves strongly to remind us of a calamite of the Coal Measures, enclosed in a smoke-coloured limestone. We have disinterred fossils in Burdiehouse,— slender calamites,—carbonized in the pale, splintery stone, that could scarce be distinguished from that recent reed in its matrix of marl.

But what have we here, in the centre of this fragment of peat ? The well-preserved remains of a beetle, apparently of the heavy rounded species, known as the twilight or dung beetle. The head, breast, and three of the legs, are distinctly traceable; and the elytra are as entire as when they covered the living insect. And yet, in all probability, several centuries have elapsed since the creature, struck down in its twilight course, perchance by some sudden breeze, found death and a tomb in that tuft of aquatic moss. But what are centuries, when associated with the highly-preserved remains of even much more fragile insects than the beetle ? Dr Buckland, in his recently published address to the Geological Society of London, states that in the course of last year there had been found in the Lias of Warwickshire, near Eversham, the fossil wing of a dragon fly, in such a state of perfect keeping, that the opaque spot usually found at the anterior margin of the wing in Libellulidæ is distinctly marked, and the branching nervures entire enough to show that they closely resemble those of recent species, "approaching most nearly to the genus Æshna." Even well-preserved insects and Arachnidans of the Coal Measures are not very uncommon. The remains of spiders, scorpions, flies even, that may possibly have enjoyed life for but a few days, have been found entire in the ironstone nodules and limestones of the Carboniferous period, or embedded in pieces of coal, or even enveloped in sandstone. The enduring nature of the peculiar substance chitine or elytrine, of which the elytra of beetles and the skin of scorpions are composed, says Dr Buckland in his address, explains the cause of their perfect preservation in rocks so ancient.

We have passed from the moss to a grayish-white subsoil, speckled by millions and tens of millions of minute shells. Every fragment thrown up is seeded over with them, some so very thickly, that the entire bulk is owing chiefly to their presence. That grayish-white subsoil is shell-marl, so valuable in some soils as a manure. The Meadows, if we may judge from the long lines of pale-coloured soil thrown up along the drains, and the apparent depth of the beds in some places, must contain many thousand loads of this substance. And yet, how very minute the shells of which it has been formed ! Twenty of them, of the average size, scarce weigh a grain. We see but the shells, entire, or existing as a chalky earth, and every trace of the animals which inhabited them has disappeared. Much of the animal matter, however, remains in that gray earth, in the form of ammonia. We brought home with us one of the richer masses, with the intention of preserving it in a tin box, and placed it beside a strong fire, to evaporate the moisture with which it was charged. As it heated, and the vapour arose in a stream, it began to yield a peculiar odour, at first of an undecided character, but which gradually waxed more powerful to the heat, and became ultimately very strong. It was that of animal matter in a state of decay. Some of the shales of our north-country Lias, quite as rich in organisms as the marl of the Meadows, yields a strong foetid odour when struck by the hammer; and the ammonia of the marl seems to illustrate the cause. At the first glance we detect three genera of lacustrine shells among the myriads strewed at our feet; the most abundant a lymnea, and the next most abundant a cyclas; the first a turbinated univalve, somewhat like the whelk; the other a cockle-like bivalve. As we examine, we find the genera increase, and with the genera the species also. We find at least two species of cyclas, and, if we mistake not, three species of lymnea; and with these shells of rarer form, two very deli cate species of planorbus, and more than one species of valvata. We saw a very pretty collection of these shells picked up among the drains of the Meadows within the last few weeks. Some of them were of great beauty : among these, two species of planorbus, which, if found in a fossil state, might readily be mistaken for ammonites of the secondary formation : there is the same discoid form. The planorbus, like the ammonite, is a regular volute. One species, too, like a numerous family of ammonites, has a delicate dorsal keel ; in another, the keel, as in a still more numerous family of ammonite, is wanting. All that seem lacking to restore the extinct Cornu ammonis in this existing shell are the numerous chambers and the siphuncle. The generations of the molluscous animals whose remains now whiten the Meadows

must have succeeded one another for many centuries, generation after generation, ere these rich accumulations of lime
and ammonia could have been formed.   It is not improbable
that in this green hollow a portion of the waters of the Noa-
chian deluge remained, what time the ebbing currents had
just ceased to roll over the higher grounds ; and that, from
that remote period until less than two centuries ago, the
boundaries then marked out in obedience to the natural law,
which fills the moist hollow, and leaves the height dry, continued to be occupied by that ancient lake.   The bittern has
boomed amid its reeds, and the stately swan skimmed over
its surface, when yonder castle-rock was a naked cliff, rising
amid an uninhabited country, and the gigantic elk and the
bear found shelter in the shaggy forest which waved on these
ridges, now crowded by their ten thousand human habitations,
and musical with the murmurous hum of a busy population.
What is recent to the geologist is remoteness to the antiquary.
It is not improbable that some of the shells in the lower portion of that marl bed were browsing, according to their nature, on aquatic plants, or alternately rising to the surface
to respire, and descending to feed, full four thousand years
ago.

We find no remains of birds along the open drains, nor
yet of fishes.   The Borough Loch, however, must have had
both its fish and its birds.   For the preservation of the fish,
the circumstances must have been unfavourable.   The great
paucity of the remains of birds in all the formations since the
creation of this class has often been remarked.   Lyell attri-
butes the paucity to their extreme lightness in proportion to
their volume.   "For, in consequence," he says, "of the hol-

low tubular structure of their bones, and the quantity of their feathers, they do not sink when they die on the water, but float on the surface until stranded on the shore or devoured by predaceous animals." "And to these causes," he adds, "we may ascribe the absence of any vestige of the bones of birds in the recent marl formations of Scotland; although these lakes, until the moment when they were artificially drained, were frequented by a great abundance of water fowl." But we have exhausted our space, and, we are afraid, the patience of some of our readers, without at all exhausting our subject. A good deal might be said in showing how recent lacustrine deposits, like the one described, illustrate some of the fresh-water deposits of the older formations,—the Wealden patches of Skye and Morayshire, for instance, or those lacustrine deposits of the Eocene, in the Paris basin, which furnished Cuvier with the strange quadrupedal remains of which he made so wonderful a use,—perhaps even of some of the beds of the Coal Measures in our own neighbourhood. We have been told by Dr Malcolmson of Madras, that for many thousand square miles in Hindustan, the whole geology of the country consists of detached lacustrine patches, apparently of some Tertiary period, and of immense tracts of an overlying basalt, which seems to have burst from the abyss, in the remote past, on a low district of lakes and marshes. On the whole, our visit to the Meadows has been a much quieter one than that described by poor Ferguson, on which it is comment enough to say, that the visitor died at the age of twenty-four, in the asylum that stands scarce four hundred yards from the northern edge of the hollow. Do our readers remember his description?

" Hear then, my bucks, how drunken fate decreed us
For a nocturnal visit to the *Meadows*,
And how we valorous champions durst engage—
O, deed unequalled—both the *Bridge* and *Cage*,
The rage of perilous winters which had stood,
This 'gainst the wind, and that against the flood ;
But what nor wind, nor flood, nor heaven could bend e'er,
We tumbled down, my bucks, and made surrender."

THE DROUGHTS OF 1842.

THE newspapers still bear occasional testimony to the extra-ordinary droughts of the autumn just gone by. One paragraph informs us that all the springs of a country-side have been dried up, and the farmers of the district compelled to send for the necessary supply of water, with cart and cask, to the deeper pools of some distant river. We are told by another of some extensive lake sunk so far beneath the ordinary level, that it no longer sends off its waters to the sea through the accustomed channel, but, like some of the lakes of the tropics, finds its diminished sources less than sufficient to supply the waste of evaporation. A third describes the condition of some Highland river sunk from a broad impetuous stream into a meagre runnel, that seems half-lost in a wilderness of whitened pebbles and gravel, with here and there a patch of aquatic weeds bleached in the sun to the semblance of tufts of flax, and here and there a bed of pearl-mussels, all gaping and dead, and prepared to yield the rich glossy seeds which they enclose, to the hand of the first shepherd or sportsman that visits the solitude where they lie. There was poetry, and something more, in the fact narrated in yet a fourth para-graph,—the one descriptive of the drying up of the Elbe near Pirna, and of the square sculptured stone discovered at the bottom. "When last men saw me, in August 1629," said the inscription, " they wept, and they who see me next shall weep too ;"—a curious memorial of sufferings forgotten for

more than two centuries,—of melancholy forebodings and
fears indulged amid fields and vineyards, leafless and brown,
on which the produce of the year had been parched into
ashes by the prolonged drought of an ungenial summer and
spring.   And something more, too, than merely a curious
memorial;—an eloquent voice from depths silent for ages, or
whose sounds had joined in but the general chorus of nature,
amid the roar of the floods and storms of winter, or the softer
murmurs of the sinking winds and lessening currents of spring;
—the voice of a preacher urging on all men, through the
medium of an argument of no common-place character, the
duty of thankfulness.   The Elbe was dried up in 1629, and
men wept;—it has been dried up in 1842, and the pheno-
menon is regarded without either fear or sorrow.   How has
the difference occurred ?   Simply from a transposition in the
periods during which the producing cause operated, of somewhat less than two months.   The droughts of the one year
were droughts in spring and early summer, and famine was
the consequence: the grapes hung blighted on the vines, in
sapless diminutive clusters; and the fields rustled light and
dry with unshot corn withered in the ear-blade.   The river
was dried up in August.   The droughts of the passing year,
on the contrary, were droughts in autumn, and the river was
not dried up before October.   And so men deciphered this interesting memorial of the remote predecessor of the present
season amid the gaiety of a corn-harvest of much more than
the usual plenty, and of a gay and glorious vintage.   We
are not sure that we have ever heard a better thanksgiving
sermon than the sermon read by the inscription of the Elbe.

Our old black-letter historians would have delighted to

record such an event. The effects of the late drought, even as shown in our own country, would have found a place in their dingy pages, amid narratives of state transactions, details of the huntings and journeyings of monarchs, and descriptions of treasons, executions, and wars. History has become a different sort of thing now from what it was in the hands of the chroniclers; and it is perhaps well that such should be the case. There has been a proper division of labour in the literary field; and the history of natural phenomena has come to be dissociated from that of human affairs, except in the instances in which they chance to be united in the relation of cause and effect. We, for instance, hear of a protracted drought from a modern historiographer, in the event of its producing a famine, and the famine an insurrection or poorlaw; but not otherwise. Most lovers of black-letter will, however, agree with us in thinking, that no slight share of the pleasure to be derived from the works of the old chroniclers arises from the curious glimpses of natural phenomena which they contain,—glimpses rendered in most cases all the more striking from the atmosphere of superstitious belief through which we are made to catch them. They form, as it were, a set of vignettes to the works in which they occur, —vignettes of no ordinary splendour. All of them have at least interest as pictures. The bloody battle fought at midnight in the northern sky, when the wild flash of artillery gleamed red and blue from the pole to the central heavens, and from the central heavens to the pole; and then, when all was over, the flush of deep crimson that remained behind, to tell how deadly the conflict had been! The wonder seen in the sun,—the flaming sword,—the double or treble moon,

—the bearded star,—the shower of blood,—the terrible hurricane,—the inundation,—the year of continued floods,—the drought prolonged till rivers and lakes disappeared, and the very earth seemed chopt and cracked for lack of moisture, like a kiln-burned pipkin too rudely exposed to the heat; nay, even the strange fish thrown ashore on some sea-coast, or dragged out of the mouth of some river,—or the worm found with a human face and a crown on its head,—or the preternatural birth, brute or human,—or the monster-savage caught in the woods;—all have their interest, as the figures of a sort of wild unintentional poetry, which only a dark age could have originated, and whose *beau ideal*, as a thing of art, we find embodied in Coleridge's "Rhyme of the Ancient Mariner." These chroniclers have a kind of successors in our own times,—not, as we have shown, in our historians properly so called, but in writers of a humbler class,—men who record the history of a day or week, or (as chances in our own case), of half a week, at a time. Theirs are the only histories that have at least all the breadth of the black-letter ones about them, however little they may possess of their interest; and we but availed ourselves of our privilege of late, when, in referring to the recent drought, we detailed a few of its most curious results,—the disappearance of the large artificial lake in the neighbourhood known by the rather prosaic name of the Compensation Pond, among the rest.

The name of this piece of water must have militated against it with our readers at a distance. They have conceived of it, in all probability, as a mere patch, with rectilinear sides and right angles,—a genuine pond, in short, just a very little superior to a tolerable horse one, with a submerged churchyard at its bottom, *infused* for the special benefit of our Edinburgh water-drinkers. The drying up of such an affair would be no event worthy the notice of an old chronicler. But not such the character of the Compensation Pond. Let the reader imagine of it as marked by all the better characteristics of a genuine Highland loch in a genuine Highland glen, surrounded by bold steep banks, embosomed by hills varying from a thousand to nineteen hundred feet in height, with water much more than enough, in its ordinary condition, to float the largest vessel in the navy, and almost roomy enough for her to tack in with a head wind. Were an ordinary-sized sloop to founder in some of the deeper parts of the Compensation Pond, the whole of the mainmast would disappear, and two-thirds of the topmast to boot. It is obvious that the drying up of so huge a reservoir, full for at least the last twenty years, must have presented appearances not unworthy the attention of the naturalist, and of interest, regarded as keys, if we may so speak, to geological phenomena. It is not every day that one can walk dry-shod over the bottom of a lake a full mile in length, and not less than ten fathoms in depth. The novelty of the occurrence renders us desirous of recording a few of such of the more striking appearances as seem to have escaped the notice of our contemporaries; and, should the reader indulge us with his company, we shall take just a few minutes' walk together over the brown surface of the uncovered area, and point out the various phenomena as we go along.

The artificial mound which confined the water in the valley is hid by yonder projecting point; and the aspect presented, in consequence, very much resembles that of a muddy estuary left by the tide.   But the vastness of the vacant depth interferes with the idea.   Not in even the Straits of Magellan does the tide fall so far ; and on the eastern coast of Scotland it would require the ebbs of four stream-tides united to uncover so profound a hollow.   The opposite bank rises at a steep angle to the top of the hill.   All above is brown with heath and withered fern ; all beneath is browner still with sludge, gravel, and mud ; but a rectilinear bar of lighter colour runs along the high-water line, where the light of day and the waters of the lake have been operating, during the last twenty years, in bleaching the various earths and stones on which for that period they have been beating together. What was a small island of about half an acre when we last visited the lake, and saw its waters gleaming blue along that light-coloured line, now presents the appearance of a bluff knoll, standing out at the foot of one of the hills, with a slight depression on the one side along the connecting neck, where the water could have stood only a foot or two at most, and with a sheer descent of at least fifty feet on the other.   The foundations of the ruined chapel of St Catherine of the Hopes occupy a lower eminence farther up the valley.   All around is brown with sludge : there are sludgy hollows and sludgy acclivities, that must have looked considerably better when covered by a carpeting of yellow springy moss, studded with flowers.   In the midst there rises a pyramid of hardened mud, piled over the tombstone of James Glendinning (1666), to protect it from the ravages of the class who entertain so thorough a regard for interesting monuments of antiquity, that they always carry them away piecemeal in their pockets, unless prevented per force.   On the ridge of the eminence we may see a low brown parallelogram, as if cast in clay, some forty feet by twenty or so. And these form the entire remains of the chapel of St Catherine of the Hopes and its burying-ground. One can say all of the building now, however, that George Chalmers ventured to say of it when he wrote his " Caledonia :"—"Its ruins may still be seen by those eyes that delight to dwell on what is old." Our readers are probably acquainted with the traditions associated with its origin ; but they may feel some further interest in it from its chance connection with one of the more important cases which have arisen out of our present ecclesiastical struggle. Originally the chapel belonged to the monks of Holyrood ; but it has been in the possession also of the Presbyterian Church, and has had its Reformed minister ; and he, though unprovided with a parish, had a seat, in virtue of his status *quoad sacra*, in the Presbytery of Edinburgh.

As we descend to the lower levels, every patch of vegetation disappears. Higher up, and where the water must have stood from perhaps twelve to twenty feet, we find bunches of weed, slimy and minute of leaf, that here and there lie studded over the brown sludge, like tufts of faded worsted, or the russet seats of skin described by Cowper. All marks of life, however, have not ceased. In even the lowest depths we find the surface studded over with minute, dark-coloured specks, like pin-heads, and perceive, on examination, that these minute specks are shell-fish. The surface is covered by millions, and thousands of millions, of that delicate bivalve the cyclas. All are dead. The mollusc within exists but as a minute-coloured blackish speck of decaying animal matter. Mark, further, that though we occasionally meet with the shell of a univalve,—a lymnea or valvata,—these are comparatively rare,—not in the proportion of one for every one thousand of the other class.   Let us not too hastily infer, however, that the bivalves were by much the more abundant inhabitants of the lake.   They were only worse fitted for retreat than their neighbours.   They were fixed by nature to the place which they now occupy, and, when left by the receding waters, they died ; whereas the univalves marched downwards as the waters fell, and may now be found by myriads, we doubt not, in the patch of a few acres into which the lake has contracted its limits.   What a puzzle for future geologists !   In this layer of shells they will find scarce any thing but bivalves ; in the layer that will be deposited above it, it is probable that univalves will be the more numerous. Or, suppose that the whole lake were to dry up, and that, with all the bivalves, all the univalves were to perish also.   How account for the vast accumulation of the latter in one spot, as opposed to the equal diffusion of the other class ?   How very difficult a riddle, and yet how easily read with the assistance of the key !   We understand that great numbers of the fish of the lake have already died.   The survivors shelter with the lymneæ and their congeners ; and, as in many deposits of ichthyolites, their remains, were the lake to dry up altogether, would lie in a dense shoal.   They would occur in a single stratum too ; and hence at least one mode of accounting for the frequent restrictions of ichthyolite bone-beds in quarries to a single layer in the strata.*

* The general appearance of the bottom of the Pond, with its footprints of men and animals still uneffaced, is described in the "Sketch-Book of Popular Geology," Lecture Fifth, p. 163, *et seq.*

The terraced beaches of the lake,—parallel roads, as they have been termed in other localities,—are in some places remarkably well defined. We walked for several hundred yards along one of its beaches, dug by the waves out of a steep slope of about thirty-five degrees, where the terrace was fully six feet in breadth, and declined at so low an angle that it made no unpleasant road. At another place we counted no fewer than eighteen of these terraces, varying from a few feet to a few inches in breadth, in a declivity of not more than fifty feet. Like those pencillings of the ventometer through which the winds are made to register their own power and direction, they served to indicate what gales had prevailed during the various stages when the waters were sinking, and with what force they had blown.

EDINBURGH.

EDINBURGH, one of the most picturesque of European capitals, has also one of the most picturesque of histories, and is scarce less fitted to form the subject of an amusing book than of a fine painting.   Most other cities have had but one historic nucleus or centre : Edinburgh had two, or, if we include Leith, more properly three.   Most other cities, though they have their older and newer portions,—their fashionable "west ends," and their ancient densely peopled east ones,—exist not in duplicate, but as one.   Edinburgh, though change has been unhappily busy during the last half-century amid its older streets and lanes, still exists as two cities, each representative of a different and strongly contrasted time.   Towns such as Glasgow, Aberdeen, Elgin, Dunblane, St Andrews, Arbroath,—some of them now very great, others mere skeletons,—had an ecclesiastical nucleus : they formed at first round their respective cathedrals, and began life as handmaidens to the clergy. Towns, again, such as Stirling and Dumbarton, with perhaps a majority of the more ancient villages of the kingdom, had a military origin : they congregated for protection around some strong castle or fortress : while yet a third class, comparatively rare in Scotland, though not without representatives on the north side of the Frith of Forth, and comparatively abundant in the sister kingdom, commenced their existence as traffickers and merchants.   But Edinburgh, if we include the port and town of Leith, first made parts of herself by Robert the Bruce; and so, old enough to rank, in point of antiquity, with at least our second-class towns, had all the three nucleii around which to form. She had her military centre in the grand old Castle, whose first ages are lost in the obscurity of the pre-historic periods; her ecclesiastical centre in Holyrood, with its attendant village of Abbey Hill and burgh of Canongate; and her commercial centre, of at least five centuries standing, in the port of Leith. And each centre has a peculiar interest of its own, more especially the military and ecclesiastical ones. Nothing, however, so adds to the effect of the earlier points of her history as the very striking scenery—unchanged and unchangeable in its main features—in which they were set. The early history of most other large towns is associated with but mere perished collections of old buildings, which can be but imperfectly restored in imagination from here and there a surviving fragment. American writers, such as Nathaniel Hawthorne and Washington Irving, in introducing into their works notices of the early history of their cities, derive no small advantage from the newness of their country in its relation to civilized man. They find it easy to represent their greatest towns as consisting of a few log shanties in the brown recesses of a forest, or of a few storehouses rising immediately over a rude quay, formed of turf and stakes, on the swampy edge of an estuary or river. Nor does it ask any great stretch of fancy on the part of the reader to conceive of even their largest and most densely-peopled cities as existing as the tracts of wild wood or dank meadow, which they actually constituted some two or three hundred years ago. It is greatly more difficult so to conceive of the ancient cities of Europe,

that were places of human dwelling ere the first beginnings
of history.   But great boldness of natural feature has in one
respect nearly the same effect as recentness of date ; and in
no European city ought this to be more strongly felt, or more
strikingly exemplified, than in Edinburgh.

It is stated by John Wesley, in referring to his early life,
that his history ought properly to be regarded as commen-
cing a very considerable time before he was born.   He then
goes on to relate a quarrel which took place between his father and mother on purely political grounds, and which led
for a time to their separation.   In like manner, the history
of most cities, especially such as have had a military or
commercial nucleus, ought to date a long time before they
were *born*.   For in most cases their future history was determined by some great operation of nature, ere even the
human species had any existence.   And Edinburgh forms a
striking illustration of this class.   It is situated in a great belt
of country that stretches across the island from sea to sea, in
which the strata, consisting of shales, stratified clays, and
sandstones, are comparatively soft and incoherent, but which
were injected and overflowed in many places, in a very early
age, by hard, stiff trap.   Long after, when, during a period of
submergence, the land sat low in the water, this tract was
washed for ages by a great easterly-flowing current, persistent in its direction as the great Gulf stream, and probably a
prolongation of it ; and under the incessant friction which it
induced, the shales, clays, and sandstones were denuded and
worn down, and the harder traps left standing up in high
relief over them.   The appearance produced was very much
on a large scale what we see on a small one along a steep road

roughened by stones and pebbles, and thick with dust, after it has been washed by a heavy thunder-shower. The stones stand up more prominently than before, and most of them bear a trail of sand and gravel behind them. And it is thus with the trap-rocks. They present bluff, bold faces to the west, where the wasting current had flowed; and bear to the east trails of the softer strata, which they shielded from denudation, as the pebbles of our illustration shield each its trail of sand and gravel. Such is the character of almost all the trap eminences around Edinburgh. Farther, such, with a few exceptions, is the character of all the insulated trap-hills which occur in the yielding Coal Measure belt, to which we have referred, in its course from sea to sea. And long ages after the excavation of these hills,—after the westerly current had ceased, and the land arisen, and trees had taken root in the gray and lichened fissures, once clothed with seaweed, man,—fallen and a wanderer, and at war with his neighbour, found in them places of strength on which he could build his hut in comparative safety, and defend himself against odds. One trap eminence he found peculiarly suited for this purpose. It was the head of a great column-like mass, from whose steep front and sides the current had washed away the softer rocks, leaving, though at a greatly lower level than that of its summit, a narrow trail of the incoherent strata behind. And thus, form elaborated by the joint agency of fire and water, long ages ere man had being, coupled with the evil nature which he manifested shortly after he began to be, and the necessities which arose out of that evil nature, determined that the insulated rock should in the first instance be the site of a fortress, and in the next the centre of a town.. Such was the origin of Edinburgh,—the deciding incident in its history that took place ere it was born. It is more than probable that the Castle Hill has formed the site of a stronghold ever since man took possession of the island. Its fortifications would have at first consisted of a few grassy mounds, topped, like the hill-forts of New Zealand only au age ago, by lines of palisades; it would then possibly take the second form of fortress, known iu Scotland as that of the vitrified fort; and then walls and towers would encircle it, and a town would grow up on the sloping talus, almost under its shadow, to share in the protection which it afforded. Every succeeding age would witness new changes; there would be changes in the towers and ramparts, and changes in the gradually growing city below. In the year 1600, Edinburgh was little more than half a mile in length, by little more than a quarter of a mile in breadth. It has since become what we now see it,— a great metropolis, for which man has done much, but nature more.

The ecclesiastical portion of the place grew up long after its military portion. At the distance of about three quarters of a mile from the hamlet under the battlements, there rose far adown the sloping talus, as early as the year 1200, a second hamlet, separated from the first by open fields and thickets of brushwood, and which had grown around the ecclesiastical centre of the place. The old chapel of Holyrood was founded, in fulfilment of a vow by David I., on the spot where he narrowly escaped being destroyed by a furious hart at bay.* On the third day after the celebration of the mass, the King, yield

* This incident is also alluded to in the first lecture, page 9.

ing to the solicitations of his young nobles, set forth from the Castle, it is said, to hunt, notwithstanding the earnest dissuasions of a holy canon. "At last, quhen he wos comyn threw the vail that lies to the eist fra the said Castell, quhere now lyes the Cannongait, the staill past threw the wood with sic noyis and dyn of buyillis, that all the bestes wer raisit fra their dennis." The King, separated from his train, was thrown from his horse, and about to be gored by a hart "with awful and braid tyndis," when a cross slipt into his hands, at the sight of which the hart fled away. And the King was thereafter admonished in a vision to build the Abbey on the spot. "The account is curious," remarks Mr Daniel Wilson, "as affording a glimpse of the city at that early period, contracted within its narrow limits, and encircled by a wild forest." Undoubtedly, from the character of the country around Edinburgh, and the remains found in its superficial deposits, it must have furnished a promising centre for the sportsman in the days of David, and long after. It was a scene of hills, valleys, precipices, and scraggy wood; and almost every valley had its lake. And in the deposits of these lakes no unequivocal traces of the early game of the district have been found. Occasional traces of the old woods have also been detected in similar formations. There are few of the aboriginal trees of the country of which specimens have not been found in an argillaceous deposit near Portobello; and from a print of the city, not older than the time of Charles II., we find that at least the lower slopes of the Arthur Seat group of hills were, in that comparatively recent age, covered with bushes and stunted wood.

Amid this picturesque landscape, with the ancient rock-

perched fortalice as its centre, were those scenes enacted which
occupy so prominent a place in the history of our country.
We have been pleasingly reminded both of their number and
variety by a goodly volume, entitled "A History of Edinburgh from the Earliest Period to the Completion of the
Half-Century 1850, by John Anderson." Mr Anderson
states, in his preface, that he has been engaged, more or less,
for the last ten years in procuring materials for this work;
and certainly, the result of his labours is a very curious and
interesting book. There is something fascinating to minds
that to an active imagination unite a taste for antiquarianism,
in the more ancient streets and lanes of an old town. "Walter
Scott," says Lockhart, in a passage quoted by Mr Anderson,
"delighted in passing through some of the quaint windings
of the ancient city, now deserted, except at mid-day, by the
upper world. How often have I seen him go a long way
round, rather than miss the opportunity of halting for a few
minutes on the vacant esplanade of Holyrood, or under the
darkest shadows of the Castle rock where it overhangs the
Grassmarket, and the huge slab that still marks where the
gibbet of Porteous and the Covenanters had its station! His
coachman knew him too well to move at a Jehu's pace amid
such scenes as these. No funeral hearse crept more leisurely
than did his landau up the Canongate or the Cowgate; and
not a queer tottering gable but recalled to him some long
buried memory of splendour or bloodshed, which, by a few
words, he set before the hearer in the reality of life." For
the poet Crabbe the Old Town had a similar fascination.
"As to the city itself," he said (see Lockhart's letter to the
son of the poet), "he soon got wearied of the New Town, but

could amuse himself for ever in the Old one. He was more than once detected rambling after nightfall by himself among some of the obscurest wynds and closes; and Sir Walter, fearing that at a time of such confusion [the time of the visit of George IV.] he might get into some scene of trouble, took the precaution of desiring a friendly *caddie* from the corner of Castle Street to follow him the next time he went out alone in the evening." A similar taste has been the origin of such works as Wilson's "Memorials," and the "Traditions" of Chambers. Mr Anderson's work is of a somewhat different cast from either of these last: it is a volume of annals, with numerous biographic sketches intermixed; but it ministers to the same feeling, and is suggestive of many a curious picture and practice. How suggestive, for instance, are notices like the following :—"The streets of Edinburgh were first lighted in 1555, when, on account of the frequent robberies, the Council ordered lanterns or *bowets* to be hung out in the streets and closes, to continue burning from five till *nine* o'clock in the evening." Hours wore later as the years passed; and in 1584 the Council gave one hour more to the decent citizen. For it was this year decreed that, in order to prevent broils and disorders in the streets, " there should be sounded every night at ten o'clock forty strokes on the great city bell, after which no person to be on the streets under the penalty of twenty shillings Scottish and imprisonment." The High Street, in the age when such laws were found necessary, must have been a rather indifferent promenade in the night-time. The various markets, as established by James III., indicate, by the sites to which they were restricted, the old localities of the city,—some of them, after the lapse of nearly four centuries, well-known localities still.   The " horse meat market" was held in the Cowgate,—the fish market, in that portion of the High Street which extended from Friar Wynd to the Netherbow,—the salt market, in Niddry's Wynd,—the " camp of chapmen" lay between the bell-house and the Tron,—the nolt market, about the Tron,—the shoe market, at Forrester's Wynd,—the meal and corn market at the Tolbooth and up Liberton's Wynd,—butter, cheese, and meal, were exhibited for sale at the Upper Bow,—cutler's and smith work beneath the Netherbow,—and all saddlery work in the Grassmarket.   There must have been curious grouping on fair-days in Edinburgh.   Down till the Reformation, the incidents connected with the city history are mainly of local and antiquarian interest ; with the rise of Protestantism they broaden in their consequences and bearings, and culminate in that famous riot in the High Church in which Jenny Geddes struck the first blow.   On the long war which began there and then, and which did not terminate until the Revolution of 1688, the liberties of Britain and America depended; nay, the future prospects of a world.[*]

* " Edinburgh an Age Ago," may be regarded as an appropriate sequel to the above.   It will be found in the volume of Hugh Miller's works entitled " Essays, Historical and Critical."

THE QUEEN'S VISIT TO SCOTLAND IN 1842.

EDINBURGH during the passing week has resembled one of those inland seas into which an hundred different streams disgorge their waters, but from which no great stream takes its rise in turn. It has formed a kind of reservoir, into which the living tide of our rural population has been flowing through all the many channels of conveyance which connect the capital with the provinces. Roads, railways, canals, the sea,—all in lesser or larger proportion,—have contributed to swell the general amount; and the place, now overflowing in its many streets and lanes, resembles an overcharged lake in an open winter, when broken by eddies and disturbed by antagonist currents. The occasion can be no uninteresting one, that has drawn to our city, at a season when the tide flows naturally in the opposite direction, at least an hundred thousand visitors, many of them from very considerable distances, and at no inconsiderable expense; and we think we can scarce do better than attempt setting before the portion of our readers that have been unable to join in the crowd, a few of the more striking scenes that so many have come so far to see. We shall rather delineate than narrate.

Wednesday last, in the southern and midland districts of Scotland, was one of those mild agreeable days of tempered sunshine and shadow of which our better tracts of autumn weather are mainly composed. It was what Gilbert White of Selborne would have termed a *delicate* day. There were a few white clouds high over head ; there rested on the outer skirts of the landscape a soft gray haze ; a slight breeze just served, by rippling the waters of the Frith, to give intensity to their tints of blue ; the distant heights, with their multitudinous squares of yellow, so significant of the decline of the season, looked soft and dim, as if sketched in an unfinished drawing ; the city itself, seated proudly amid its hills, raised its picturesque and close-piled masses through the thin haze, as if it were a thing half of earth, half of cloud,—its shadows softened into a bluish-gray,—its mingling lights sobered down into a pale and smoky amber.   One of our poets speaks of the *roar* sent by a great city "through all its many gates." One had but to stand and listen on this morning, to decide regarding the appropriateness of the phrase.   An infinity of blended tones,—the hum of eager and moving crowds,—the rattle of coaches,—the incessant strokes of workmen employed by hundreds in the erection of balconies and scaffolds,—a thousand nameless sounds, besides,—were all mingled into one mighty roar,—the voice of the city,—resembling at a distance the noise of a high wind in a leafless wood, or the murmur of the far-off ocean in a tempest.   The streets were early astir. There were, if we may so speak, main currents in the living tide, which continued to flow from long before noon till nightfall.   One main current had set in towards the shore ; others of lesser volume and momentum, and more broken by meeting tides, flowed full in the direction of the nearer heights which command a full view of the Frith.   The Calton, blackened by its moving thousands, resembled a huge ant-hill just stirred.   We could descry, too, in the distance, and but barely descry, that the upper outline of Arthur Seat was roughened by its anxious crowds. But in no locality was the appearance exhibited of a more animating or impressive character than in the immediate neighbourhood of Granton, the projected scene of her Majesty's landing. It was in this direction that the main current had set in. The green sloping bank which runs parallel to the shore, at the distance of less than half a field's breadth from the beach, and which at one period must have formed the coast-line, was literally blackened by spectators. The road below was more than equally crowded,—the broad strip of beach uncovered by the tide was mottled by its restless groupes. Nor was the Frith beyond less a scene of life and animation. Boats, and vessels of larger size, crowded by their pleasure parties, flitted around the huge mole which here projects its vast length into the sea,—now casting anchor, now again making sail, and turning their heads down the Frith, as if in eager anxiety to descry the expected flotilla. Steamboats, with their long evanescent trails of cloud, went gliding in every direction athwart the blue; ever and anon a larger vessel hove round, and, turning her side to the shore, saluted the harbour with a gun. The echoes rang merrily; the group of vessels laid along the mole, when some half-dozen steamers or so moored at once among them, seemed as if enveloped in cloud and darkness; and flag and pennon waved sullenly from amid the smoke, like the gauds and braveries of life when dimmed by its troubles. The day wore fast on : still no signal intimated from cliff or castle that the royal flotilla had entered the Frith. The tides and winds had been adverse : it was feared, too, that what had been but a thin fleecy haze ashore might have been a fog at sea. All expectation of the Queen's arrival before nightfall at length vanished, and about four o'clock the vast crowds began to break up and disperse.   We could mark not a few blank countenances among the humbler pedestrians,—many of them country people from the neighbouring counties, who had got just their single day to see the Queen, and who, disappointed once, could entertain no hope of enjoying a second opportunity.   We could sympathize in the vexation manifested by a stalwart shepherd in a gray maud, who had left his flock on the previous evening on a hill-side some thirty miles away, as, in turning from his conspicuous and well-chosen stand, he gave vent to his feelings of disappointment in a half-sad, half-humorous, "Dash it, and will I no see her after a' !"

The fall of evening was marked by a scene scarce less striking than that of the day, though of a character altogether different.   A brown haze hung over the skirts of the horizon, dense enough to blot out the whole opposite line of coast and the wide extent of Frith below, and yet not so dense but that the fires kindled up on all the more conspicuous heights shone through, each surrounded by its own dusky halo.   A dotted outline of red light served to restore well nigh all the bolder features of the vanished landscape.   The flames rose broad and high on the nearer heights.   A huge uneven pennon of fire flared on the summit of Arthur Seat, lighting up its own swart trail of smoke with an umbry red, and converting into a vast halo, of more than a thousand yards diameter, the mist-wreathes that brooded above.   The rugged outline of Salisbury Crags stood out distinctly visible in the foreground, like a sketch in black richly bronzed.   The ridge of the Pentlands had its three fires ; the Binny and Dalmahoy Crags, in the long retiring valley to the west, had each their beacon; and with these, many a solitary peak besides, where the unwonted light must have scared the fox in his lair and the hawk on her perch. The Calton Hill, even after the night had closed, was still crowded by its thousands of spectators, —its brown and sombre groupes, half-visible, and only half, by the red flickering light that streamed from the neighbouring hill. There was a charm to detain them in the scene itself,—well-nigh one of the most sublime of the kind we ever witnessed; and there was something for the imagination to lay hold of, in the circumstance that already must the expected flotilla have entered the Frith,—a long dim vista tracked in fire; and that all the flaming peaks which composed the line on either side must have addressed their welcome ere now to the gaze of the royal voyager. At length the flames began to sink, and the crowds to disperse.

The morning rose dull and drizzly, but it cleared up as the hours passed; and ere nine o'clock, though still somewhat gloomy, it had become at least dry overhead. The morning papers had intimated to the city the arrival of the royal squadron in the roads over night. And at seven o'clock a signal-gun had been fired from the Castle. We were fortunate enough not to know exactly what the latter had been intended to mean; and, inferring that it just intimated that the Queen was to be soon visible, we set out early, determined, at all events, to see the Queen. We found no such heady current in the greater thoroughfares as on the previous morning; and the few we spoke to on the subject seemed secure that, on some definite understanding at which her Majesty's Ministers and the city Magistracy had arrived, the royal progress through the city would not take place before noon. Perhaps, however, save for the disappointment of the previous day, there would have been somewhat less patience manifested by the inhabitants,—less of a disposition to wait for nearly the stipulated hour. We made our way to the Calton, where we found a few hundreds already assembled, and ensconced ourselves among the shrubbery on the edge of the low precipice that overhangs the road. The Castle guns began to fire, and we concluded that the Queen had just touched Scottish ground. There were a few open carriages drawn up on the road below ; and the one immediately under the place where we were stationed we found particularly worth looking into : it carried the noble Hindu, Baboo Dwarkanath. We were admiring his singularly expressive countenance,—one of the most intellectual in its cast we have almost ever seen, —his well-formed forehead, and dark bright eye,—and remarking how very handsome a man may be, maugre a brown skin, and features both a little touched by age, and of the decided Asiatic type, when the cry arose, " Here comes the military." We looked westward, and saw that Prince's Street, from the Mound to the North Bridge, had suddenly become one dense sea of moving heads, and that every cross street and opening was pouring in its thousands to swell the amount. There was a minute patch of scarlet inlaid in the mass ; all was dingy around it ; and it came moving steadily along in the midst, like a float of drift-wood falling down a river. This, thought we, must be the van of the procession,—the advanced guard, to reconnoitre and clear the way : the main body, with the Queen, must still be a considerable distance behind. The patch of scarlet came floating on. We could discern bright helmets and the glitter of steel; we could mark a sudden crowding to the windows,—a hasty rush to the overhanging galleries, more than two-thirds empty but a minute before,—a waving of handkerchiefs and of hats; and a cry, not loud, but deep, which we could scarce term a cheer, but which seemed to express a deeper feeling, ran along the line of spectators as the military passed. Could this be the Queen? It was. She sat in a low open carriage, with Prince Albert on her left,—clear-complexioned, but pale,—tastefully but plainly dressed,—one whom in private life we would perhaps describe as a pretty woman, very thoroughly the lady, but who, as the daughter of an hundred kings, and a monarch on whose vast dominions the sun never sets, seemed, of course, a great deal more. The presence of the learned Baboo Dwarkanath served to heighten our estimate of her greatness. The illustrious Hindu from the far east,—the representative of an hundred millions of the human species,—had been led to this spot to look upon one who was as certainly *his* Sovereign as our own.

Alas! how the ridiculous contrives to mingle itself with all human attempts at the sublime! The procession passed on; and, quitting our stand in the shrubbery on the Calton, we joined the thickening masses in Prince's Street, where all seemed disaffection and anger. Not one out of every four we met had seen the Queen; and the chagrin manifested at the disappointment seemed in due proportion to the previous enthusiasm. It was hard for men, some of whom had travelled from one to two hundred miles just to catch a glimpse of her, to be baulked so miserably; and they seemed in lack of an object on which to vent their spleen. "The Queen's Ministers have insulted the city Magistracy," said one. "We must have the illumination countermanded," exclaimed another. There was a gausey, buxom fishwife passing at the time on a cart. "Why," there is a Queen for us," shouted out a third ; and a thousand heads, at the hint, were bent in mock obeisance to the fishwife. There was more of bitterness than of sport in the incident,—not, however, on the part of the fishwife, apparently a person of humour enough to appreciate the kind of honour paid her, and who went on bowing right and left to her loving subjects,—not, indeed, with all the grace of monarchy, but with a degree of mock dignity that travestied it exceedingly well. We understand that in the untoward misarrangement which led to the disappointment of so many thousands the Queen herself had no share whatever, and that the city Magistrates shared in it quite as little. The odium,—and it is by no means slight,—is attached by the citizens to her Majesty's Ministers.—*September* 3.

LADY GLENORCHY'S CHAPEL.

*" Carry up my bones from hence."—*GENESIS, *i. 25.*

IN the lower and deeper part of the picturesque valley which separates the Old from the New Town of Edinburgh, there is a plain but massy and not unimposing structure, lately a place of worship, which a party of workmen are at present engaged in razing to the ground. It presented on the first day of the new year a singularly forlorn and desolate appearance. The rafters of the roof rose dark and bare over the dingy walls, like the ribs of a decaying carcase, from which the blackened integuments have dropped piecemeal away. The large windows, divested of the glass and the framing, revealed to the spectator outside, tottering columns, broken galleries, and ranges of dilapidated pews, with here and there a ragged gap in the plaster, from which some sepulchral marble had been recently torn. All around there lay huge heaps of stone, the debris of walls overturned to their foundations, blent with irregular piles of splintered trunks and torn branches of trees,—the sole remains of that old botanic garden of Edinburgh which was established about the middle of the seventeenth century, by one of the earliest cultivators of natural history in Scotland, Sir Andrew Balfour. Amid the desolation there rose, still entire, the single column of a gateway, which had given access to the building; and the iron gate itself swung unbroken on its hinges; but where the corresponding column had stood there yawned a deep and wide excavation, through which one might look down, as in some pictured section of the geologist, from the travelled soil of the surface, to a lightish strip of native mould beneath, thence to a belt of red sub-soil, and thence to a deep stratified bed of yellow fire-clay, alternating with bands of stone, which belong evidently to the base of the Coal Measures. The chasm had cut off the pathway on which, for full seventy years, a devout and numerous congregation had found access to the place of worship beyond; and all that remained to indicate its place was a line of hawthorn bushes, that projected, root and branch, over the steep broken edge, and the remaining column of the gateway, with its hanging gate. There lay around, amid the heaps of earth and stone, the remains of iron pipes, incrusted with rust; tubes of lead, the conductors of another element, projected into the excavation; and the foggy atmosphere was largely charged with escaping gas,—an unmistakeable evidence that some of these useful underground veins and arteries of the city, when severed, in the course of the operation which had cut among them so deeply, had, as surgeons express themselves, been too carelessly "taken up." Rarely have we looked upon a scene of greater desolation than that furnished on the opening day of the year by this ruined place of worship, whether we regarded the dilapidated building itself, with its yawning openings and naked rafters, through which the rising breeze whistled so drearily, or the rough scene of ruin that bristled all around it, or the dismal enveloping atmosphere of mingled fog and smoke, charged with the oppressive scent that, "smelling horrible in the nostril," suggested to the imagination one circumstance more of decomposition and decay.

The broken chapel of our sketch had presented, seven days before, a different but not less striking scene. Nine in the morning had struck on the clock of St Giles's; but a dense fog, accompanied by a thick drizzling rain, hung over the city, and the light of day seemed as if still engaged in an uncertain struggle with the darkness. The tall tenements of the Old Town rose over the valley, tier above tier; but the upper tiers on the hill-top, barely discernible amid the haze, seemed but the beginning of other and higher tiers; and the city,—a thing rather of shadow than of substance,—appeared, like the city of a fairy tale, as if rising to the clouds. The huge North Bridge loomed through the fog as but the mere spectre of a bridge,—as if a mere apparitional erection of gray cloud, with crowds of unsubstantial ghosts hurrying along its upper line; and inside the chapel below all was gloomy and brown, save where a few lights gleamed from the centre of the area, where a party of workmen were engaged in laying open an excavation in the floor. A hearse with its nodding plumes stood in waiting at the gate without. A few ponderous flags, one of which bore, inserted on its upper plane, a square plate of brass, were heaved warily aside with lever and bar, disclosing below a deep recess and a descending flight of steps; and in a narrow catacomb to which the steps led, the light flashed on the gilded studs of a solitary coffin, that for nearly sixty years had rested in the darkness. A line of coronets on the sides had borrowed from the close damps of the place a tinge of deep green; but the coal-black cloth seemed untarnished, and the gilding of the plates and nails atop were in some places scarce less fresh than when it had first passed from the burnisher of the workman. The years of more than half a century had, however, accomplished their work of decay. The coffin, in the first attempt of the labourers to remove it from its place, parted longitudinally atop; and as it was carried past us, to be deposited within a new shell prepared for the purpose, we could see through the opening a human skeleton,—tall for that of a female,—enveloped in brown dust, in which there mingled the remains of the cerements that had attired the body for the tomb. The plate above bore, in characters still distinctly legible, that the remains were those of Lady Glenorchy, the foundress of the chapel, and that she had departed in July 1786, in her forty-fourth year. The cover of the new shell was then screwed down over both the mouldering skeleton and the coffin to which it had been consigned so long before; and after it had been removed to its place in the hearse, the vehicle moved slowly away, followed by a few gentlemen, members of the Free Church, who, in accordance with the terms of her Ladyship's will, were the trustees of the building. The whole scene, singularly picturesque and deeply impressive, was of a kind which, once seen, can never be forgotten.

" Her Ladyship," says her excellent biographer, the late Dr Jones, " had expressed a wish to be buried in her chapel at Edinburgh. The persons who took the charge of her funeral accordingly ordered a vault or catacomb to be prepared to receive the body. On taking up the flooring, the ground was found to be solid rock; but with considerable difficulty an excavation was made, sufficient to contain the coffin. The head of the excavation lies directly under the middle of the communion-table; and a stone, with a brass-plate inserted in the centre, on which is deeply engraved her Ladyship's name, age, and time of death, closes the opening. On Monday the 24th,—fourteen days after her death,—the body was deposited in this place. The present [late] Earl of Breadalbane, who came from London for the purpose, attended as chief mourner; and her silent obsequies took place in the midst of a great multitude of weeping spectators, who on this occasion crowded the chapel." Such is the description given by Dr Jones, an eyewitness of the scene, and who, on the following Sabbath, preached her Ladyship's funeral sermon, to a congregation again moved to tears. The history of her deep interest in the chapel,—and it was but one of many which she had reared, some in England, some in the Highlands,—arose out of the protracted struggle and the many prayers which it cost her, ere she had succeeded in placing it on a foundation at once independent of the National Church, and yet in connection with the Church's better ministers. Lady Glenorchy was peculiarly one of the class who, conscious of their high destiny as heirs of immortality, live in the broad eye of eternity, and walk with God. " As an entire character," says her biographer, " she did not leave one behind her who might be compared with her." She had watched the struggle then going on between the two great parties in the Establishment; and seeing that Evangelism had the worse in the contest, and that it was still sinking, she had built her Edinburgh chapel in the hope of furnishing it with a lodging place, in which, in its time of depression and defeat, it might find shelter. She reckoned among her friends and counsellors some of the best and ablest men of the party,—old Dr John Erskine of the Greyfriars, Drs Webster, Walker, and Hunter, and Dr David Johnstone of Leith. She found, too, a singularly acute and disinterested adviser in the advocate Crosbie,—better known to the readers of " Guy Mannering" as the accomplished lawyer Pleydell ; and, with the assistance of these men, she at length succeeded in getting the chapel placed on such a footing, that it was at once in connection with the Establishment and independent of it. But a hard and protracted battle had first to be fought around its walls; and we recognise among the combatants on both sides the leading men of their respective parties at the time. Moderatism, regarding it as a suspicious outpost, from which the party might catch a mischief, fought hard to get its communication with the Establishment cut off: Evangelism struggled as hard to get it maintained. Dr Carlyle of Inveresk, Dr George Hill of St Andrew's, Dr Campbell of Aberdeen, and all the lower but not less zealous men of the party who made common cause with them, strove to fix upon it the brand of separatism and dissent; while Drs Erskine, Johnstone, Hunter, and Webster, strove as hard to extend to it the countenance and communion of the National Church. At times the one party had the advantage; at times the other. Dr Erskine gained his point in the Presbytery of Edinburgh ; but in the Synod of Lothian and Tweeddale he sustained a defeat, on the motion of Dr Carlyle, who succeeded in getting a sentence recorded, which discharged all ministers and probationers of the Church, within the bounds, from officiating in her Ladyship's chapel. And there was little expectation entertained that the General Assembly, constituted as it was in those days, would reverse the finding of the Synod. Moderatism mustered strong; and Lady Glenorchy gave up all hope in the matter, but, as her Diary shows us, not all prayer; for we find whole days set apart by her to earnest solicitation, in the solitude of her closet, that "God would overrule the counsel of the Assembly respecting her chapel." The day of conflict came; the lawyer-elders, including the officers of the crown for Scotland, stood inexplicably aloof on the occasion from their Moderate friends; nay, more, one of their number, Chief Baron Montgomery, spoke and voted against them; and, after a keen and protracted debate, Dr John Erskine and the Evangelists, to the astonishment of all men, carried the day. There was not a devout minister in the Establishment but was now at full liberty to preach in the chapel of Lady Glenorchy.

The principles and conditions of its constitution were laid down in the document which embodied them, with the most scrupulous care. "I am sure a' will gae right," says Dandie Dinmont, in the novel, in reference to the Ellangowan case, "if Mr Pleydell will take this bit job in hand." The original of Pleydell did not belie this character, in drawing up the constitution of Lady Glenorchy's chapel. So stringently was it framed, that it required an express act of Parliament to set it aside; and of its various clauses, there was at least one which looked so profoundly into Scottish law, that perhaps few living lawyers could have told three twelvemonths ago at what it really pointed. It strictly prohibited all and sundry from attaching to the chapel a territorial district; and it was not until our *quoad sacra* churches were cast as illegal by the civil courts, rather on the fact that they had assumed territorial districts, than on the fact that their ministers had sat in the ecclesiastical courts, that the occult meaning which Crosbie had no doubt intended the clause to embody was fully understood.   Moderatism, however, found various means of annoying Lady Glenorchy and her people, independently of law.   She had secured for her chapel the services of Mr, afterwards Dr, Balfour, so well known for many years in an after period as the venerable minister of the High Church of Glasgow, but who at this time was minister in the country parish of Lecropt.   On tendering his resignation to his Presbytery, however, they refused, contrary to all practice, to receive it; and so Mr Balfour, greatly to Lady Glenorchy's disappointment and his own, was prevented from entering on his engagement.   She met with various other studied annoyances of a similar kind; but her design, notwithstanding, proved eminently successful.   The congregation attached to her chapel ranked among the most numerous and select in the city; and for more than half a century they enjoyed the ministerial services of Dr Snell Jones, at once one of the most excellent men and useful ministers within the Church.   The reader may find a high, but not too high, appreciation of his character, religious and intellectual, in the form of a critique on his published sermons, among the writings of Dr Chalmers. Her Ladyship's many prayers for her chapel had not been unheard nor unanswered; and we have but to glance over the extracts from her Diary, as we have said, to see how many and how deeply earnest these prayers were.   The first minister appointed to the charge, a thoroughly good man, had died of consumption in the course of the first twelvemonth, and she had assiduously tended him in his last illness.   "For two months past," she says,—we extract from her Diary,—"I have been employed in attending the dying-bed of Mr Sheriff, who this day lies at the point of death.   He has borne a noble testimony to the power of faith in supporting and quieting the mind under bodily distress and the certain approach of death. For six weeks past, the Lord has given me much heartfelt submission to his will in this trial. He has shown me wherefore it was sent; convinced me of the expediency and necessity of it to subdue my will in those things I judged not only lawful, but in which I thought I might be zealous. He has brought me to give up the chapel wholly to Himself, being the Head, Governor, and Lawgiver of his Church; and last night and this day [June 7, 1778] he enabled me to surrender up myself and all my plans wholly to Him, without any known reserve. I got power to ask much for the chapel for ages to come, that it might be a lamp and a witness for the doctrines of the true Church in future generations,—a place where true vital religion might be taught, and where souls might daily be born again, and savingly united to Christ. I had some degree of faith for this, and that a proper pastor would be provided for it by the Lord in his own time; and I sought patience to wait upon Him for the answer of this prayer. And now, O my gracious Saviour, as I have devoted myself, and all that I am and have, unto Thee this day, upon my knees, and with my heart and tongue, I would now, in thy presence, confirm it with my hand, and, with all sincerity of heart, solemnly give up and commit to Thee my soul, body, and spirit, my life, reputation, goods, friends, relations, health, and outward comforts, my understanding, will, and affections, in short, all that I am and have, to be disposed of as shall be most for the glory of thy name, and for the eternal good of my soul. Guide and conduct me through life; be with me, to support and comfort me, in death; and receive me at last into thy kingdom and glory, to be ever with Thee throughout eternity.   And the whole glory and praise shall be ascribed unto the Father, Son, and Holy Ghost, one God, for ever and ever."

Such were the aspirations and prayers, and such the covenants with her God, of Lady Glenorchy.   For full fifty-seven years after her death, her chapel continued to form one of the strongholds of Evangelism in Edinburgh.   It had furnished during the reign of Moderatism, when the city churches were under Moderate control, a ready place of meeting for all evangelistic purposes of a public nature ; and as our ecclesiastical struggle drew towards a close, and interdicts and inhibitions were shutting churches against the principles, as they had been shut at the earlier period, though in a different way, it again became a place of resort for it, which no interdict or inhibition could shut.   The public meetings for prayer which immediately succeeded the Convocation were held in Lady Glenorchy's.   The Disruption ensued : the Residuary Presbytery of Edinburgh, after hesitating nearly three quarters of a year, as well they might, at length determined to act in the matter agreeably to their character ; and, turning out into the streets, at the commencement, if we remember aright, of a snow-storm, her Ladyship's congregation, they seized upon the building.   Moderate clergymen preached in it by turns, and saw skeleton congregations of some six or eight persons scattered over pews in which from sixteen to eighteen hundred had wont to assemble ; and, in holding their miserable mockery of a communion, they witnessed some three or four poor creatures sitting at the table at which from eight hundred to a thousand of the excellent of the city had used to communicate. This sad residuum sat down over the dust of Lady Glenorchy, amid the dreary vacuity of her chapel ; and good people, cognizant of the fact that the dust did rest below, and familiar with her Ladyship's character and prayers, had strange thoughts and misgivings on the subject, which they knew not how to express, and termed the providence a mysterious one. And so it perhaps was. But it seems a not less wonderful providence that the mockery of the sacrament was not permitted to be repeated. At the very time when the excluded people were engaged in contributing funds and taking measures for erecting for themselves a place of worship, which they purposed should bear the name of the respected lady to whom they had owed their existence as a congregation, but which would have been merely one of *two* Lady Glenorchy's chapels in the city, an event, all unforeseen and unthought of, was preparing to dash into the dust the desecrated structure, and to raze not only the building itself to its foundations, but even to annihilate, for fathoms down, the very soil upon which it had stood. The North British Railway passes over the site of Lady Glenorchy's chapel, at a considerably lower level than that which had been occupied by the chapel's lowest foundation-stone ; and the revered dust of her Ladyship will now rest, in consequence, in the building occupied by the descendants of her people,—men who continue to hold, as she held, by Christ the Head. Once more, say we, a curious, and surely not uninstructive story. Many a strange event had to take place ere the bones of Joseph could be carried by the Israelites from their Egyptian place of sepulture to the Land of Promise. It would have been no easy task ten short months ago to have predicated the kind of event through which the bones of Lady Glenorchy were to be removed up from the place which had been so miserably diverted from the purpose for which she had reared it, and which she had given up in covenant to her God, as the " Head, Governor, and Lawgiver of his Church."

More than fifty-eight years have elapsed since a weeping assembly witnessed the burial of Lady Glenorchy.   Many a change since that period has come over the affairs of men. America had just closed its struggle of independence at the time.   The dissolute French Court was engaged in sowing the seeds of the Revolution.   Napoleon was a nameless boy. And while belief in the truth of revelation appeared as if dying out among men, what seemed the dawn of a political millennium was rising on the horizon.   The buds of promise have been blasted, and buds that seemed withering have freshened and blown.   Dynasties, since the death of her Ladyship, have sunk and disappeared,—kingdoms have changed their Governments, their boundaries, and their names,—aristocracies have gone down,—royal blood has flowed on scaffolds,— heroes have arisen to accomplish missions of vengeance, the purport of which they knew not, and then, their work done, have been laid ignobly by.   The political dawn proved a mere electric flush in the heavens, that broke in lightning and tempest ; and after the lapse of more than half a century, the kingdoms of the earth, with not more to enjoy than they then possessed, seem less inclined to hope.   They have seen reform, heroship, revolution, all on the largest and sublimest scale, and are yet none the better for having seen them.   But what seemed the dying belief,—the belief of struggling minorities every day becoming weaker, and of the lamented good passing prematurely away,—still lives on, vigorous and effective, as in its early youth, while all of earth that promised to live and occupy its room is dying or dead. All has changed except that faith held so firmly by Lady Glenorchy, and the God on whom that faith reposed ; and if there be a voice to the Free Church of Scotland from her Ladyship's tomb, is it not a voice that tells of an overruling Providence, who, amid scenes of evil, works out his own good purposes, and makes every event, however seemingly untoward, fulfil the counsel of his will ? —*January 4, 1845.*

A VOICE FROM THE GREYFRIARS.

" Our holy and beautiful house is burnt with fire."—ISAIAH, xliii. 2.

THERE were two churches in Edinburgh a very few weeks ago, which were more specially connected than any other churches in the kingdom, the one with a personal, the other with a great National Covenant. These covenants bore, in both cases alike, that Christ Jesus, the adorable Son of God, and not any secular court or earthly potentate, is the sole King and Head of the Church. Both buildings had alike passed into the hands of the Establishment,—an institution that, rather less than two years before, had practically repudiated the grand doctrine which the documents had been framed with the express purpose of maintaining,—the one, as we have said, in a personal, the other in a national relation. Both alike, from the durability of their materials, and the rock-like solidity of their masonry, bade fair to endure for centuries. And both alike, at the present moment, lie in dreary desolation and ruin, open to the wild winds of heaven and the bleak wintry showers. We state but the facts, and leave others to draw from them what inferences they may. The one building,— the chapel which Lady Glenorchy gave up in covenant to her God, " as the Head, Governor, and Lawgiver of his Church," —exists as but a group of broken walls, that totter to the stroke of the workman. The other,—that venerable church of the Greyfriars in which, two hundred and seven years ago, the best and noblest of Scotland assembled to swear fealty to the Divine King and Lawgiver, and not a few of them to subscribe the binding instrument with their blood,—that church which, in the seventeenth century, was the church of Alexander Henderson,—which in the eighteenth was the church of Dr John Erskine,—which in the nineteenth was all but the church of Dr Andrew Thomson, for he held his first Edinburgh charge under a prolongation of its roof,—that venerable building exists now as a mass of scathed and blackened ruins, its huge beams and timbers dissipated into thin air, and many of its very stones calcined into a ferruginous sand.

We passed the Greyfriars on our road churchwards on Sabbath last, a little before ten o'clock, and saw, through the trees of Heriot's, its huge length of roof stretching entire from gable to gable, but covered with what seemed a dense white vapour, that appeared as if issuing from every joint in the slating, and that rose slantways in a broad many-volumed column into the clear morning air. A circular opening in the apex of the gable was meanwhile belching out smoke of a darker hue, like some vast cannon to which the lint-stock had just been applied. A minute jet of intensely red light, the first fire visible from the outside, rose for a moment from beside the ridge, immediately beneath the pinnacle on the eastern end; the white thick vapour caught the flame sudden as a train of gunpowder or a jet of coal-gas; and what had been vapour but a moment before became at once a continuous stratum of fire, that, without touching, played over the slates, and, after disappearing for a moment, as a light breeze from the west passed over the roof, kindled again, and was again extinguished. The great eastern window, which was still unbroken, glared with a deep fiery red, shaded with umber, that gave an idea of the thickest darkness of cloud struggling, imprisoned, with the intensest light of fire ; a tongue of flame came dashing outwards, crashing through the glass ; and in a moment's space the mass of red bronze within had kindled into intense brightness.   A broad pennon of fire came rushing through the whole breadth of the arched window, waving and cracking like a whip-thong over the graves below, many of which now lie scorched and blackened ; and a still huger volume of flame rose through the roof, and curled and roared for full thirty feet over the ridge, hurling high into the smoke, ashes and flaming embers, that, again descending, twinkled among the tombs in a shower of fire.   The pinnacle on the eastern gable, —a pyramidal mass of stone,—whitened and cracked amid the flames, and, throwing off splinter after splinter into the fiery area below, assumed a striking resemblance to a human figure, that, standing unmoved where the conflagration raged most fiercely, seemed the very genius of the scene.   In rather less than twenty minutes from the first appearance of the flames, every window of the church was vomiting fire ; and all that remained of the roof on the main body of the building,—for on the aisles it had disappeared even sooner,—was merely the large skeleton beams, which, though all gilded with flame, continued for a few minutes longer to stride from wall to wall.   The roaring of the flames,—the crackling of the calcining stones, that threw out all around them from the columns their red-hot fragments,—the crashing of the beams, as they parted and came rushing down,—the duller patter of the broken slates, as they fell from above in showers,—all made up a fearful concert, which mingled in the silence of the

Sabbath morning with the low murmurs of the awe-struck crowd and the shouts of the firemen. A sea of fire continued to rage within the area of the building, after the beams had all parted from their places above ; but the gleam gradually sank lower. It had raged awhile along the roof,—awhile half-wall high along the galleries ; and now it rose but a few yards over the floor, wreathing its tongue-like flames around the columns, and playing amid the pointed arches. Such, however, was the intensity of the heat, that not a fragment of the charcoal has remained ; not even the butt-end of a beam in the wall. The last smouldering embers threw off their successive coats of white ashes ; and, floating away in light impalpable films, left not a vestige behind. The area of the Old Greyfriars,—an uneven waste of broken slate and stone,—lies as bare as the floor of a quarry.

It seemed at one time as if the adjoining church of the New Greyfriars,—a building which dates rather more than a century later than the perished erection,—might possibly be saved. The flames lingered for a few minutes at the dividing wall, as the light breeze from the west blew them backwards over the scorched ruins on which they had already wrought their worst. The illusion, however, was speedily dispelled : they rose fierce and high over the ridge ; and the central opening in the western gable, like that in the east so shortly before, began to belch forth into the air its thick column of fire. But the work of ruin went more slowly on : the flames had to travel against the wind, that ever and anon blew them away from the materials on which they fed. The firemen of Edinburgh, too, assisted by a party of soldiers from the Castle, were all on the ground ere now. They had opened up their

communications with the various reservoirs in the neighbourhood; and four engines were kept in full play, emptying their
contents on the ignited rafters and the galleries.   The hissing of the water on the glowing embers mingled with the
roar of the flames; and the clank of the engines, with the
crash of falling beams and the rattle of descending slates.
There mixed, too, in the vast volume of thick dingy smoke
that, blown aslant over the burying-ground, threw a more than
twilight shade on the graves, clouds of white steam; and the
fire glowed less brightly within the area of the building.   But
all that great daring and much exertion have accomplished
in the case merely amounts to this, that while the main body
of the more modern erection is roofless from end to end, the
entire roof of one of the side aisles, and a broken fragment of
the roof of the other, have been preserved; and the floor of
the building is strewn, not with fragments of calcined stone,
but with heaps of charred rafters, and the ruins of broken
galleries and pews.   It presents a more, not a less, melancholy
appearance than the church of the Old Greyfriars, apparently
on the principle that invests a mouldering carcase with more,
not less, circumstances of the horrible than a fleshless skeleton.   The fire originated, as almost all such fires do originate,
through the overheating of a stove, the flue of which passed
under a piece of panelling attached to the wall, and which
communicated with one of the galleries.   The person in at-
tendance, after lighting the fire about four o'clock in the morning, and then leaving it, returned just in time to see the piece
of panelling falling in red embers on the floor, and the flames
nimbly spreading from the portion of the gallery immediately
over it to the parts adjacent.

The ruins, during the whole of Monday, and the greater part of Tuesday,—until, in consequence of some new manifestation of insecurity in the walls of the old church, it was deemed necessary to shut them up,—were largely visited. And of the thousands who gazed upon them, and saw a work of decay such as it usually takes many centuries to accomplish, wrought by the havoc of one short hour, few have been unimpressed. What first strikes the eye, on entering, is the completeness of the ruin, and the raw colour imparted to the stone. The huge gaping window of the eastern gable, with its thick-set mullion, is bordered by a calcined frame; and the hewn work is chipped and flawed, as if Knox's "rascal multitude" had been hammering upon it for a week. The graves below, for several yards away, testify to the formidable body of flame to which the opening must have given vent. The long rank herbage that had sprung over them in the summer, and had faded and dried up in the autumn and winter, had caught fire, and they lie scorched and blackened, as if covered by a pall. On an ancient and very fantastic monument beside the window, there stands, in prominent relief, a tall figure of death, in the common skeleton form, and armed with the all-destroying scythe. The grim sentinel kept his place bravely. He has borrowed from the conflagration a darker grin; and the smoke seems to have circled thickly in the hollow of his open ribs; but he has caught no scathe from the fire; and when the vast bolt of flame roared from the opening beside him, and the graves were blazing at his feet, he must have furnished no inadequate resemblance to his prototype, the "goblin full of wrath," described by Milton, that took his stand by the infernal gates,

> " When wide they stood, and, like a furnace-mouth,
>   Cast forth redounding smoke and ruddy flame."

On entering the interior of the ruins, the utter desolation of the scene comes more fully in view. The double row of squat columns which divide the aisles from the body of the church, and support the side walls, seem wasted to half their former size : base and capital, the mouldings, and the octagonal angles, have all disappeared; and there remains but a rude irregular surface of calcined rock-work. They look less like columns than like bars of wasted iron worn almost to a point. The very ring-stones of the arches have lost their hewn faces in the fire, and present as broken and rubbly an appearance as the pillars on which they rest. Where two stone-stairs had led to the galleries, we see but a few minute fragments projecting from the wall : nor do even the detached steps appear in the rubbish below ;—they seem to have crackled away, in the intense heat, into minute fragments. The upper portions of the walls are less scathed ; but the pinnacle, so strangely chipped into a statue, looks fantastically down on the ruins ; and every breath of wind blows away the burnt and loosened mortar in clouds of dust. We saw, projecting from the walls, a wasted iron bolt, that had been fixed there ages before to support the magisterial mace ; and marked directly above, where the outer plaster had peeled away, a portion of the royal arms of Scotland, chiefly the mantlings around the crown, with the crown itself, and part of the rampant lion of the crest, bearing the sceptre in its one paw and the sword in the other. It seemed curious enough that these silent remembrancers of the splendour of the past should have thus contrived to peep out amid the utter desolation of the present.

They served to remind us that, let Moderatism build to itself whatever kind of church it may, it will not be the church of Alexander Henderson, nor of John Erskine, nor yet that in which the National Covenant was signed.

The building which, like an old martyr, closed its history on the morning of Sabbath last in smoke and fire, has wit-nessed some of the most striking scenes recorded in our ecclesiastical annals. It was erected after the accession of James to the throne of England, at a time when many of our better ministers were languishing in prison or in exile, and when the hirelings who had supplied their places made oath at their ordination, as a part of the ceremony, that they recognised the "King's Highness as the onlie supreme Governour of this realme, as weel in all spirituall or ecclesiasticall things or causes, as temporalL" But the spirit of the nation was not dead, nor could it be excluded from the Greyfriars. Baillie tells us that even prior to the famous scene in the High Church, which proved pregnant with two great revolutions, "on the Sunday morning, when the Bishop of Argyll, in the Greyfriars, began to officiate, incontinent the serving-maids began such a tumult as was never heard of in our nation since the Reformation." And the tumult which these Edinburgh serving-maids thus commenced,—for there chanced to be deep meaning in their quarrel with prelacy and the Bishop,—employed Leslie, Cromwell, and William III. completely to finish.

In the following year the Church of the Greyfriars witnessed the subscription of the National Covenant. " As the hour drew near," says Hetherington, in his singularly eloquent and graphic narrative, " the people from all quarters flocked to the spot, and before the Commissioner ap-

peared, the church and churchyard were densely filled with
the gravest, the wisest, and the best of Scotland's pious sons
and daughters.   The meeting was constituted by Henderson,
in a prayer of very remarkable power, earnestness, and spi-
rituality of tone and feeling.   The dense multitude listened
with breathless reverence and awe, as if each man felt himself alone in the presence of the Hearer of prayer.   When
he concluded, the Earl of Lauder stood forth, addressed the
meeting, and stated, explained, and vindicated the object for
which they were assembled.   He directed their attention to
the covenants of other days, when their venerated fathers had
publicly joined themselves to the Lord, and had obtained support under trials and deliverance from every danger ; pointed
out the similarity of their position, and the consequent propriety and duty of fleeing to the same high tower of Almighty strength ; and concluded by an appeal to the Searcher
of hearts, that nothing disloyal or treasonable was meant.
Johnston of Warriston then unrolled the vast sheet of parch-
ment, and, in a clear and steady voice, read the Covenant
aloud.   He finished and stood silent.   A solemn stillness
followed, deep, unbroken, sacred.   Men felt the near presence of that dread Majesty to whom they were about to vow
allegiance, and bowed their souls before Him, in the breathless awe of silent adoration.   *   *   Again a deep and solemn pause ensued,—not the pause of irresolution, but of modest diffidence, each thinking every other more worthy than
himself to place the first name upon this sacred bond.   An
aged nobleman, the venerable Earl of Sutherland, at last
stepped slowly and reverentially forward, and, with throbbing
heart and trembling hand, subscribed Scotland's Covenant

with God. All hesitation in a moment disappeared. Name followed name in swift succession, till all within the church had given their signatures. It was then removed into the churchyard, and spread out on a level grave-stone, to obtain the subscriptions of the assembled multitude. Here the scene became, if possible, still more impressive. The intense emotions of many became irrepressible. Some wept aloud; some burst into a shout of exultation; some after their names added the words *till death;* and some, opening a vein, subscribed with their own blood. As the space became filled, they wrote their names in a contracted form, limiting them at last to the initials, till not a spot remained on which another letter could be subscribed."

In the year succeeding the one in which this impressive scene took place, Alexander Henderson was appointed minister of the Greyfriars. To-day (the 22d January), making the necessary allowance for the change in the style, is the two hundred and sixth anniversary of his induction; and his tombstone may still be seen in the adjoining churchyard. He passed away, and a long and dreary period of persecution ensued; the echoes of the church of the Greyfriars were awakened day after day by the clank of hammers from the neighbouring street, busied in erecting gibbets for the martyrs of the Covenant so ominously subscribed in blood; and the venerated remains lie interred in the malefactor's corner, some half a stone-cast away, at the foot of the grave-covered slope over which the building rises. On the opposite side of the burying-ground there is a retired alley of tombs,—an Egyptian-looking street of the dead, in which the prisoners of Bothwell Bridge were cooped up by hundreds, and kept in the open air, exposed to every vicissitude of the seasons for nine months together. The Revolution came round; the principle of the Covenant triumphed; and the Greyfriars became once more a Presbyterian church. The second century after its erection wore on; Moderatism became potent in the Establishment; and, by one of those curious chances which occur so rarely in the history of institutions or states, if chance we may term it, the two great leaders of the antagonist parties,—Principal William Robertson and Dr John Erskine,—were associates in the collegiate charge of the Greyfriars. We need scarce remind the reader of the well-known anecdote associated with the place, and so characteristic of not only the men themselves, but of the opposite sets of principles which they represented. "If virtue," said the Principal,—full of confidence in man's natural love of the just and good,—"if virtue were to take to itself a human form, and visit our earth, all men would love, admire, and worship it." "Let it not be forgotten," remarked his venerable colleague, on referring to the sentiment in the after-service of the same day, "that virtue *did* once take to itself a human form, and *did* visit this earth, and that men, instead of loving it, admiring it, worshipping it, reviled, persecuted, and finally crucified it." The building, too, in reference to this middle period, has an interest reflected upon it by the charms of inventive genius expatiating on a solid substratum of truth. The church to which the lawyer Pleydell is represented as bringing Guy Mannering, when on his visit in Edinburgh, is the church of the Greyfriars; and the preacher whose appearance and manner are so graphically described in the novel was Sir Walter's own minister,—during at least his boyhead,—the venerable Dr

Erskine. It is further worthy of notice, that the last truly wise man of his party, Dr Inglis,—a man, however, who, as he advanced on eternity, receded from that party more and more,—who originated the Indian Mission,—and who, had his life been spared, might have prevented that suicidal course pursued in the late struggle by Moderatism which precipitated the Disruption,—was one of the ministers of the Greyfriars. His immediate successor, with the successor of his colleague the late Dr Anderson, were the last collegiate ministers of this church ; and they are now ministers of the Free Church. The last of the twain in charge,—for Mr Guthrie had been draughted to St John's a year or two previous,—the good and able man who laid down his living at the call of sacred principle when the hour of trial came, and quitted a pulpit rendered venerable by many a high and interesting association when he found it could no longer be usefully or honourably occupied,—was standing in the middle of the ruins as we entered, looking around him, as if striving to recall, in the utter desolation of the place, the features by which he had so long known it. The remark with which he greeted us was a very simple one, and yet it was fraught with meaning :—"I have not been here before," he said, "since the Disruption."

We suppose Moderatism will be by and by setting itself to repair the more modern church of the Greyfriars, and to erect a new building on the site of the more ancient one. It will matter little. There is abundance of room for half a dozen such congregations as the congregation of the one, in the neighbouring church of St John's, which, without loss to any party, might be erected into a collegiate charge ; and more than room for at least as many such congregations as that of the other, in the Assembly Hall, which might very safely be converted into a collegiate charge too. If the building scheme goes on, we shall have an uninteresting, useless new house substituted for some very interesting ruins, that, with the assistance of a few wallflower seeds, and a few ivy bushes, might be made to harmonise as finely in aspect as in reality with the antique monuments, classic names, and stirring associations, of the surrounding burying-ground. These classic names and stirring associations are many. In but one narrow corner of the erection which the fire has spared we see the tablets of Allan Ramsay, Colin Maclaren, and Hugh Blair, looking down from the wall. It may be remarked, in conclusion, that the history of the perished building strikingly illustrates the vicissitudes to which the principle of spiritual independence has been subjected in this country during the lapse of little more than two centuries. In the course of that period the church of the Greyfriars had been twice in the possession—at one time for a hundred and fifty years together—of an Establishment whose thorough independence in matters ecclesiastical the State recognised ; and thrice in the hands of Erastianized corporations, that bartered away their spiritual liberties for bread.—*January* 22, 1845.

TRINITY COLLEGE CHURCH

VERSUS

BURNS' MONUMENT.

THE wanderings of the Virgin's house at Loretto from its old Judæan site, until at length, after crossing many a land and sea, it settled down where it now stands, form the subject of a curious Romish legend, which devout Catholics in Italy are still trying to believe ; and the restless voyagings of St Cuthbert in his stone-coffin in quest of a suitable sepulchre, which for long years the over-particular saint failed to find, were once devoutly credited in the neighbourhood of Coldingham and Lindisferne.   But there was palpable myth in both cases; and the history of the Trinity College Church of Edinburgh, since it was pulled down a few years ago by the North British Railway Company, throws, we think, a flood of light on the origin of both stories.   It was not, as the legend bears, the Virgin's house,—a clumsy erection of stone and lime,— that went a-travelling of itself over the isles of Greece and the upper reaches of the Mediterranean ; nor yet did the stone coffin of St Cuthbert launch spontaneously upon the Tweed, as was reported, and float from Melrose to Tilmouth.   Both legends only body forth the many vexed discussions that took place regarding house and coffin in the Established Presbyteries and Town Councils of those early days, after a Jerusalem Aqueduct Company had purchased the site of the building and pulled it down, and a sanitary commission, in-

stituted by the old Saxon Wigamote, to inquire into the state
of the intramural cemeteries of the kingdom, had broken up
the saint's tomb, and carried his coffin outside the church-door.
The various stages at which both house and coffin are said to
have rested for a while, in reality only intimate the various
stages of the long discussion which took place regarding them,
and the many new sites suggested for their accommodation.
Nay, we are not sure whether the history of the Trinity College Church, since its demolition, if erected into a myth on
this obvious principle, would not make a better legend than
either of them.   Future ages may perhaps tell, should Pusey-
ism be destined to realize all its hopes in Britain, that when
religion was at its lowest ebb in Scotland, a wicked railway
company having resolved on demolishing, for their own secular ends, the church of the Holy Trinity, founded by the devout Mary of Guelders, the outraged building transported
itself in a single night to a rocky platform beside the Calton
stairs; that, however, after baiting for a while on its proud
perch, it then removed, first to the head of the Waverley
Bridge, then to a humble site at the side of the old Nor' Loch,
then to a corner of Ireland's wood-yard, and, finally, that,
returning to a shelf of the Calton, a little lower in place than
the one it had first selected, it demolished at one fell blow
the monument of a profligate poet, and, squatting itself down
on its site, remained there till this day.   There would, of
course, be no want of evidence, framed on the principle of Mr
Newman and his coadjutors, to make good the miracle.   The
mere probabilities would, of course, be found registering a
large balance in its favour; while, as real evidence, it could
be shown from the portfolios of the antiquaries, that while

there existed many prints and drawings that represented the building on its original and final sites, there existed at least one rare print, a tinted lithograph, which exhibited it resting on that earliest of the intermediate stages which was situated beside the Calton stairs.

In all seriousness, however, we cannot help thinking that the majority of our Town Council, consisting though it does of sensible and excellent men, has, in its previous decisions regarding this building, committed a mistake. It seems to have forgotten things that ought to have been remembered, and to have remembered things that ought to have been forgotten, and to have arrived at a conclusion, in consequence, that, if persisted in, must have the effect of placing it in a state of collision with all our better judges of the æsthetic on the one hand, and all the admirers of our great national poet on the other. But, as no overt act has yet been committed, we fain hope that the respectable men who constitute the slender majority in the case may yet see the propriety of re-siling from a position which cannot fail to expose them to much disagreeable animadversion and comment. Even re-garded as a simple economic question, it does look somewhat strange that, with many suitable sites at their eommand which would cost them nothing, the Town Council should have at length selected a site already occupied by an ornamental build-ing, that cannot be removed under an expense of nearly eighteen hundred pounds. Franklin's whistle was no doubt a very excellent whistle ;—we are assured on his own unex-ceptionable authority, that it made noise enough to disturb the whole house ; but then Franklin tells us also that he paid a great deal too much money for it ; and even admitting,—

what such judges of the æsthetic as Harvey and Macculloch
will to a certainty not admit,—that the site of the Burns
Monument is a site better by a barely perceptible shade for
the Trinity Church than any other that could be selected,
really eighteen hundred pounds is a large price for a barely
perceptible shade.   It is a large price for a mere whistle, especially, too, as undoubted judges of such articles say it is a
whistle that won't blow.   Further, the claim of the Trinity
College Church,—not as a church, be it remarked, but regarded simply as a piece of architecture,—to dispossess of its
site the monument of Scotland's greatest poet, is not a claim
—Scotchmen being the judges—that will be very readily recognised.   If in reality a serious and weighty claim, it ought,
of course, to be urged as a matter of principle at all hazards,
and against all the men of taste and genius in the kingdom ;
but not being a matter of principle, but of taste merely, we
question whether it would be prudent or advisable to urge it
in the form it must to a certainty assume,—viz., the claim of
a building that has not a single association connected with
it worth a farthing, to dispossess of its well-selected site the
monument of a poet more dear, with all his faults, to the
Scottish people, than any other his country ever produced.
The case is one of collision ; and as no person alleges that the
site of the monument is not a very suitable one for *it*, it re-
solves itself into the simple question, what are the claims of
the Trinity College building, whether æsthetic or otherwise,
to dispossess of its modest and proper site the monument of
the national poet ?

It must tell in behalf of the old building, in such an inquiry, that there exists at the present time such a rage for

the mediæval as existed up to the middle of the last century in favour of hooped petticoats and high head-dresses. And unquestionably a Gothic *interior*, independently of any existing prejudice in behalf of the site as a whole, is one of the noblest architectural ideas which man, in his pursuit of the æsthetic, has yet devised. But a Gothic *exterior* is a much humbler effort of mind, even when at its best,—even in a York or Strasburg Cathedral; and in the less happy instances it is a meagre, poverty-stricken thing. The interior embodies a natural idea,—the idea of a noble grove, with its colossal trunks twisted like the great chestnuts, or grooved, rodded, and clustered, like massive beeches and huge elms, and that emulates, in its fretted groins and interlacing ribs, the thickly woven branches that spread overhead. But the Gothic exterior embodies no such natural idea;—it is often a mere barn-like case for the stony grove within: and the old architects, as if sensible of this inferiority, often showed their art by concealing it in woods and hollows, over which a well-proportioned spire, pointing like a finger heavenwards, and worthy of being looked at, might be seen representing the entire building. And when the hollow was very deep, or the wood well grown, the exterior betrayed less than the ordinary care, and the architect concentrated himself on the interior almost exclusively. Such was peculiarly the case with the old Trinity Church, "besyde Edinburgh." Placed in a deep valley, almost within the shadow of a great precipice that overlooked its highest pinnacle, and surrounded, at the time of its erection, by a thick wood, it could be but imperfectly seen from any quarter; and so the architect devoted himself chiefly to the inside of the building, and produced one of the most delicate morsels of interior architecture to be found in this part of Scotland.   Its exterior, however, was greatly less to be admired, even where finished.   Its flying buttresses were squat and ungraceful, its walls low, and none of its windows or outer doorways very fine.   Unluckily, too, from the death of its foundress, some of the parts most essential to its general proportions were left unbuilt.   A squat, awkward-looking gable, serrated by its lines of crow-steps, took the place of a central tower or spire ; and where the nave should have joined on to the choir, there rose a flat wall of coarse rubble-work, perforated by a wretched window, that resembled a great eylet-hole, and that was flanked by a lesser eylet-hole on each side.   Where the nave itself should have been, there remained a blank ; and, seen on this side from a point of view which the architect could never have contemplated, —that furnished by the North Bridge,—the church of the Holy Trinity was, without exception, the ugliest building in Edinburgh.   It had less the look of an ecclesiastical edifice than of a cartwright's shop,—of a shop with three wheels hung upon the walls,—a big one and two little ones,—as a sign of what might be procured from the mechanic inside ; and was, in short, homeliness and misproportion themselves thrown into the architectural form.   The only sort of place in which the Trinity Church could be re-erected, either in accordance with the original design of the architect, or with due consideration of its actually unfinished condition, would be a place where it could be as well hidden as it was of old, ere the North Bridge laid open its posterior deformities to the gaze of the public, and where the visitor, after a sudden introduction to its completed eastern end, with its not unhandsome porch, curiously roofed with stone, would be at once ushered into its exquisite interior, so calm and solemn, with its lofty aisle, its rich groining, and its finely proportioned doorways. Even in Gothic buildings of greater exterior pretensions than the Trinity Church, the effect of a sudden introduction of this kind to what is best in them is very striking. The old parish church of Stratford-on-Avon is, even externally, an eminently handsome building, and, when seen outside the town, to which it is attached, looks well on every side. The passage to it from the street, however,—that street in which the " New Place," Shakspeare's residence, was situated,—is through so thick a grove of limes, that one can scarce catch in the passage a glimpse of the building ; and so it is to the noble interior, with its fine proportions and dim religious light, that the visitor is first introduced. We were scarce ever more strongly impressed than when, passing through the chequered passage of delicate green, with the sunlight playing in through the leaves, we were at once ushered into that awful interior, and saw the simple monument of the poet of greatest soul which the world had ever produced, glistening in the pale light upon the wall. And we doubt not that, amid the bosky hollows at the foot of the Calton, on its northern side, such a place of concealment might be found for the Trinity Church. The young wood in that quarter is thriving, and promises to be thick and tall.

In these remarks we have dealt with the question at issue simply as one of taste. The question, however, has as certainly an ecclesiastical as an æsthetic aspect. The parish attached to the Trinity Church is one of the most destitute in Edinburgh, and one of the most devoid of religions ordinances.

In passing through the Canongate, countrywards, on a Sabbath afternoon, we have seen more of the people who never attend any church lounging at the close-heads, than would have filled the church of the Holy Trinity thrice over. But not such the character of the locality in which it is proposed to re-erect it. The inhabitants of Regent and Carlton Terraces belong mainly to the upper ranks; the people of Norton Place and Comely Green, to the middle classes. They are church-goers already; and a new church in the district would be of no use to them, and of no moral effect on the community at large. We have, we confess, our quarrel with the Establishment. But we would ill like to thwart it did we see it setting itself in all earnestness to the recovery of the lapsed classes. It is only contemptible when, as in this instance, we find it running away from its proper scene of duty, though at the same time arrogating to itself the name of the "Church of the poor and the forgotten;" and planting itself down— on so-called æsthetic principles as false in taste as in morals —where there is no use for it whatever.

The claims of the Trinity Church to dispossess the Burns Monument of the site secured to it by many years of possession, is of course a different question from any of those to which we have already referred. We think the church can have no such claim. The ground fairly granted to a public monument ought to remain for ever after the property of the public, and this altogether irrespective of any change which may take place in opinion regarding the character of the man to whom it was erected. No one can have formed a lower estimate of Robert Burns than we ourselves have done of Charles II., of "glorious memory;" and yet, when, some years ago, the horse and man of Parliament Square were taken down, and a report went abroad that they were not to be re-erected, we felt as if an important historic document had been destroyed, and that Edinburgh had one point less of interest than before.   And the Burns Monument, regarded simply as a fact, should be at least equally sacred.   It is a greatly more wonderful fact than the statue of Charles. It is a fact which the American poet Hallec, on his visit to this country, viewed in the proper light :—

> " I've stood beside the cottage bed,
>   Where the bard-peasant first drew breath ;
> A straw-thatch'd roof above his head,
>   A straw-wrought couch beneath.
>
> And I have stood beside the pile,—
>   His monument,—that tells to heaven
> The homage of earth's proudest isle
>   To that bard-peasant given."

Yes ; a very strange fact, worthy of all due consideration ; worthy, too, of being carefully preserved, were it but for its curious *documentary* character.   Farther, it is also a noticeable fact, that all the men of genius who have lived since the days of the indomitable peasant have regarded his memory with the deepest and tenderest sympathy,—that they have found profounder meanings in his writings, and nobler traits in his character, than ordinary men ; for while ordinary men seemed to see but his specks and spans, as if they looked at the luminary through eyes naturally smoked and darkened, the higher intellects see but the all-enveloping blaze of his glorious genius. But perhaps their *morale* may have been at fault ?   That craves reflection.   We know that the pious Montgomery ranked among the fervent admirers of Burns ; and we have seen the face of the saintly Chalmers glow with delight as he pronounced one of his soul-stirring lines.   No one can defend all that the poet did or said.   True, his frailties have been somewhat severely dealt with.   He was, with all his faults, a greatly better man than either of his two greatest contemporaries.   He did not drink half so hard as William Pitt; and yet respectable people toast the memory of the " Heaven-born Minister," without making any allusion whatever to the four bottles of port that he used to put under his belt of an evening; and while he was certainly not more licentious or less sober than Charles James Fox, he was beyond comparison a more honest man ; for he was no gambler, and paid all his just debts, and would have died rather than fabricate the mean lie which deprived an honourable lady of her moral status as the wife of a British prince.   But it would be idle to represent Burns as other than an imperfect character.   His own honest pen gives the lie to the unwise friends of his memory who take up a position so untenable :—

> " The poor inhabitant below,
>   Was quick to learn and wise to know,
>   And keenly felt the social glow
>   And softer flame,
>   But thoughtless follies laid him low,
>   And stained his name."

Nor can it be denied that some of his writings have done harm.   It seems, however, to be a law of Providence that the earth-stains which pollute the fountains of genius should be deposited by the stream in its course, and that the living waters should at length run clear.   And it has been so with

the poetry of Burns.   It it not by his worse, but by his better
writings, that he is now remembered,—by his songs, unri-
valled in the literature of the world ; and by those undying
pieces, such as the " Cottar's Saturday Night," so rich in
character and manner, and in high moral sentiment withal,
that are destined to

> " Be known, perchance, when Scotland is no more,
>   And tell the tale of what she was before."

And if his writings have done harm, let us not forget that
they have also done no little good.   Robert Burns was the
man who first taught the Scottish people to stand erect.   Let
us not be blind to the great national faults, and only lynx-
eyed to the faults of the great national poet.   A mean and
creeping subserviency to the great,—a getting up " to be
hanged in order to please the laird,"—was the master fault
of the Scotch people; and a century of persecution had failed
to wean them of it.   That part of the General Epistle of
James which treats of " respect of persons," and the undue
partiality shown to men with " gold rings and goodly ap-
parel," might have been more appropriately addressed to the
Scotch, even after the rich had " oppressed" and drawn them
"before the judgment-seat," and "blasphemed the Holy Name,"
than to almost any other people of Europe.   But the independent peasant who, in the most trying circumstances, never bent
himself before the worthless wealthy or the titled great, and
who, in his ever-living strains, asserted the dignity of manhood, taught them another lesson, and they have learned it.
Yes; the Scottish people have lost the habitual stoop, and
now stand erect; and all honour, say we, to the *reformer*
who, more than any other, effected the change.   His life,

as certainly as his works, were effectual in producing it; and, had it accomplished nothing else, it would not, with all its errors and shortcomings, have been spent in vain.

> " Through care and pain, and want and woe,
>   With wounds which only death could heal,
>   Tortures the poor alone can know,
>   The proud alone can feel,
>   He kept his honesty and truth,
>   His independent tongue and pen,
>   And moved, in manhood and in youth,
>   Pride of his brother men.
>
> " Strong sense, deep feeling, passions strong,
>   A hate of tyrant and of knave,
>   A love of right, a scorn of wrong,
>   Of coward and of slave,
>   A leal warm heart, a spirit high,
>   That could not fear and would not bow,
>   Were written in his manly eye,
>   And on his manly brow.
>
> " Praise to the bard,—his songs are driven
>   Like flower-seeds on the wild winds strewn,
>   Where'er beneath the sky of heaven
>   The birds of fame are flown.
>   Praise to the man ; a nation stood
>   Beside his coffin with wet eyes,—
>   Her brave, her beautiful, her good,—
>   As when a loved one dies.
>
> " And still, as on his funeral day,
>   Men stand his cold earth-couch around,
>   With the mute feelings that we pay
>   To consecrated ground.
>   And consecrated ground it is,
>   The last, the hallow'd home of one
>   Who lives upon all memories,
>   Though with the buried gone."

THE FUNERAL OF CHALMERS.

DUST to dust ;—the grave now holds all that was mortal of Thomas Chalmers. Never before did we witness such a funeral ; nay, never before, in at least the memory of man, did *Scotland* witness such a funeral. Greatness of the mere extrinsic type can always command a showy pageant ; but mere extrinsic greatness never yet succeeded in purchasing the tears of a people ; and the spectacle of yesterday,—in which the trappings of grief, worn not as idle signs, but as the representatives of a real sorrow, were borne by well-nigh half the population of the metropolis, and blackened the public ways for furlong after furlong, and mile after mile,—was such as Scotland has rarely witnessed, and which mere rank or wealth, when at the highest or the fullest, were never yet able to buy. It was a solemn tribute spontaneously paid to departed goodness and greatness by the public mind.

Dr Chalmers had, we understand, expressed a wish to be buried in the lately opened cemetery at Grange, situated on the pleasant rising ground—once, we believe, a portion of the old Boroughmoor—about a quarter of a mile south of the Meadows, and little more than half a mile from the Doctor's favourite residence at Morningside. It is a singularly beautiful spot, surrounded on all sides by green fields, and on the south and west by lines of well-grown forest trees, that must have seen at least their century. And, sweeping downwards on every side,—towards the Grange House and Morningside

on the south and west, and towards Newington and the
Meadows on the east and north,—it commands within its
range of prospect every more striking feature of the scenery
for which Edinburgh and its neighbourhood are so remarkable.   The purple Pentlands, piled up, as seen from this point
of view, over the nearer Braid Hills and the Hill of Blackford, look down upon it on the one hand; the colossal Arthur Seat, just in the point of view where the lion-like con-
tour of the eminence is most complete, seems sentinelling it
on the other; the flatter lines of the landscape, roughened
with wood, and dotted over with buildings reduced in the
distance to mere speck-like points, present here and there,
in comparatively prominent relief, their bolder objects,—
here Liberton, with its church and tower,—there the rising ground of Craigmillar, with its ancient ruin,—yonder,
amid the tall trees, the Gothic chapel of St Catherine;
while along the long-descending ridge, bearing its picturesque
bravery of spires and monuments, and guarded by its veteran
castle at the one termination, and the tall escarpment of
Salisbury Crags on the other, stands the proud city, with
its smoke-wreath resting over it.   We had at one time half-
wished that Chalmers should have been buried in the Greyfriars,—with the Hendersons and M'Cries of our ecclesiastical, and the Robertsons and Mackenzies of our literary, history,—where the Church made its greatest and most imposing stand against the Erastian encroachments of the secular
arm, and where the dust of so many of the martyrs lie.   But
we recognise as more appropriate the choice which selected
the virgin soil of this new locality, whose main associations are
with the sublime of nature,—with the unnarrowed expanse

of the heavens above, and the plains and hills, the woods and fields, that give variety to the wide tract of earth, below. Chalmers, like all the truly great, may be said rather to have created than to have belonged to an era. Influenced by the past, like all men, he was yet less influenced by it in its immediate connection with his own Church and country, than any of our other great ecclesiastical leaders since the days of Knox. He could feel the poetry of the times of the Covenant, and sympathise with the Christian men who died in behalf of the rights and liberties of their Church,—rights and liberties identical, in those ages, with the cause of religion itself; but in looking for his patterns and examples, he did what was done by all our first Reformers,—passed over those uninspired times, on which we are perhaps too apt to linger, impressed rather by the scarce wholesome admiration of what our fathers did for God, than for what God did for them; and rested his whole mind on that more wonderful time when the adorable Redeemer walked our earth in the flesh, and fallible men, inspired by the Spirit, gave infallible testimony regarding Him.

The day was one of those gloomy days not unfrequent in early summer, which steep the landscape in a sombre, neutral tint of gray,—a sort of diluted gloom; and volumes of mist, unvariegated, blank, and diffuse of outline, flew low athwart the hills, or lay folded on the distant horizon. A chill breeze from the east murmured drearily through the trees that line the cemetery on the south and west, and rustled amid the low ornamental shrubs that vary and adorn its surface. We felt as if the garish sunshine would have associated ill with the occasion. A continuous range of burial vaults, elevated some twenty feet over the level, with a screen of Gothic architecture in front, fenced by a parapet, and laid out into a broad roadway atop, runs all along the cemetery from side to side, and was covered at an early hour by many thousand spectators, mostly well-dressed females.   All the neighbouring roads, with the various streets through which the procession passed, from Morningside on to Lauriston, and from Lauriston to the burying-ground,—a distance, by this circuitous route, of considerably more than two miles,—were lined thick with people.   We are confident we rather under-estimate than exaggerate their numbers when we state, that the spectators of the funeral must have rather exceeded than fallen short of a hundred thousand persons.   As the procession approached, the shops on both sides, with scarce any exceptions, were shut up, and business suspended.   There was no part of the street or road through which it passed sufficiently open, or nearly so, to give a view of the whole.   The spectator merely saw file after file pass by in what seemed endless succession.   In the cemetery, which is of great extent, the whole was at once seen for the first time, and the appearance was that of an army.   The figures dwindled in the distance, in receding towards the open grave along the long winding walk, as in those magnificent pictures of Martin in which even the littleness of men is made to enhance the greatness of their works and the array of their aggregated numbers. And still the open gateway continued to give ingress to the dingy, living tide, that seemed to flow unceasingly inwards, like some perennial stream that disembogues its waters into a lake.   The party-coloured thousands on the eminence above, all in silence, and many of them in tears,—the far-stretching lines of the mourners below,—the effect, amid the general black, of the scarlet cloaks of the magistracy, for the magistrates of Edinburgh, with much good taste and feeling, had come in their robes of office, and attended by their officials and insignia, to manifest their spontaneous respect for the memory of the greatest of their countrymen,—the slow, measured tramp, that, with the rustle of the breeze, formed the only sounds audible in so vast an assemblage,—all conspired to compose a scene solemn and impressive in the highest degree, and of which the recollection will long survive in the memory of the spectators. There was a moral sublimity in the spectacle. It spoke, more emphatically than by words, of the dignity of intrinsic excellence, and of the height to which a true man may attain. It was the dust of a Presbyterian minister which the coffin contained; and yet they were burying him amid the tears of a nation, and with more than kingly honours.

Churches long bear the impress lent them by the character of their founders. The Puritanism of New England has not yet wholly resigned the stamp imprinted on it by the Pilgrim Fathers; and Wesleyism in the Old Connection still exhibits not a few of the distinctive personal peculiarities of John Wesley. That theory of Hume regarding the formation of national character, which traces the leading moral and mental features of a people to the individual traits, caught up through the imitative faculty by admiring followers, which marked their first heroes, statesmen, and legislators, is doubtless over-stretched. And yet it does seem to explain, in part, how at least Churches very various often in their character, independently of doctrine, should be marked, even when drawing their membership from among the same people, by distinctive peculiarities.   There are Scotch Quakers as certainly as Scotch Presbyterians ; and the one body has as invariably borne, since its first beginnings, the impress of the passive, pacific Penn, as the other, in all its history, that of the war-like Knox,—he who bore the sword before George Wishart, prepared to defend against all assailants, however armed with mere legal authority, or formidable from their numbers, the preacher of the true evangel.   Could we wish aught better to the Free Church of Scotland than that it should bear the im-press of Chalmers,—the simplicity, backed by the wisdom,—the quiet gentleness, united to the extraordinary power,—the catholic tolerance, that looked to the "root of the mat-ter" in its dealing with other Churches, and was satisfied if it but found it joined to the honest zeal that would sacrifice all rather than yield up even one solitary truth in connection with its own,—above all, the unceasing interest in the eco-nomic, the physical, the mental improvement of the species, that diverted or misdirected, no, not for one moment, as is so frequently the case with the mere temporal philanthropist, —an intense love of souls, and the consequent labours for their salvation ?   We have seen many dissertative remarks on the character of Chalmers, but never yet a single remark on what has ever appeared to us as its most wonderful fea-ture.   Men are so constituted, not only in the average, but in even very high specimens, that the existence among them of two great parties,—the movement party and the stationary one,—seems inevitable.   There would be no progress with-out the impetus of the one, and no stability without the weight of the other.   In the working of the vessel, whether that of Church or State, the instinct of the one party leads it to busy itself with the hoisting of the sails, and that of the other with the laying in of the ballast. Now, it was peculiarly extraordinary in Chalmers, that he was not of either, but of both parties,—at once far in advance of the movement men, and firmest among the most firm of the stationary,—at once a promulgator of *new* truths, which in a better age than the present the world will gladly reduce to practice, and a determined conservator of *old* truths, and of what is truly good in the old state of things. Men being what they are, party seems inevitable; and yet how vast the waste of exertion which it occasions! In a world of Chalmerses there would be no party, and no need for it. The progress of the species, owing to the more complete construction of the intellectual machine, would go on steadily and safely without the drag.

Were we asked to give in one word the main characteristic of the present age, that one word would be "MOTION." We are living fast as a nation : the railways of the country are typical of its general career. There is as large an amount of change condensed in a few years of the present as in centuries of the past. Where are the old parties of the country ? Vanished during the last two twelvemonths. There is scarce an institution of the empire, secular or ecclesiastical, that has not wholly altered its character since the death of George IV. We have seen the cycle of the two previous centuries repeated during the last twenty years ; and the Free Church need scarce expect wholly to escape the influence of the time. It was with direct reference to this state of things that we have often felt the presence of Chalmers among us to be so peculiarly valuable. With greatly more energy than any other man of the body, he had also greatly more of the *vis inertiæ* that withstands the influence of a current from without. He formed, in one important phase of his character, a great immoveable anchor, that moored the vessel of the Free Church right over the Disruption ; and, now that he is gone, there must be sedulous watch kept, lest, yielding to the insidious tendencies of the time, we drift away. Washington Irvine has compared some of our great writers whose works have fixed the language, to huge trees flourishing beside the banks of a river, that cast out an immense extent of closely reticulated rootage, and thus preserve around them the loose soil, which, save for the protection they afford, would be washed out by the hollowing eddies, and swept to the sea. The illustration, in another and different application, brings out our idea of one of the great characteristics of Chalmers. He formed such a tree, and secured the institution in which he had taken deep root, and which sheltered under his shadow, against the disintegrating wear of the current. But the stately oak has fallen in its place ; and it were well surely that, fully aware of what his presence did for us, and of the peculiar dangers to which we are exposed now that he is away, we should be taking note of our true position, and of the means by which it may best be retained. There is still strong help in the God which he served, and potency and wisdom in the doctrines which he asserted, and the principles which he illustrated and maintained.—*June* 5, 1847.

ST MARGARET'S WELL.

THE differences which exist among men in matters of pure taste have long since become proverbial. The most disputatious among us soon arrive at an agreement respecting all that can be measured, weighed, or counted. No one contends that the pound Scots is equal to the pound sterling, or that the English mile is of such ample measure as the Scotch one, even when the latter is divested of the "*bittock.*" And though there was some dispute a few years ago regarding the comparative heights of Ben Macdhui and Ben Nevis, and though the old traveller William Lithgow was severe, about two centuries earlier, on "the ignorant presumption of blind cosmographers, who in their maps made England longer than Scotland," both points have since been very satisfactorily settled, the one by the Government surveyors, the other by those very cosmographers who, with all their blindness, have made it, we think, sufficiently apparent that the said William was literally *magnifying* his country when he described it as "outstripping the southern one in length by a hundred and twenty miles." In matters of taste, however, we have no such standard for settling a difference as that furnished by the balance or the measuring chain. It used to be disputed, in the early days of the writer, whether Byron or Sir Walter Scott was the greater genius; but we must confess that we failed to see the dispute very satisfactorily settled, even on the occasions on which we ourselves took a part in it. And as for those controversies respecting the merits of rival preachers, into which attached members of their congregations sometimes enter, we know not that we ever yet saw one of them settled, with the full agreement of the contending parties, after the same manner. The respective altitudes of Ben Nevis and Ben Macdhui were soon determined; but when did the people of the church in Crown Court, London, ever agree with the people of any other church in the world in their estimate of the altitudes of the Rev. Dr Cumming? We know not, however, a finer illustration of the great uncertainty of the standard of taste than the one unintentionally furnished us by Hume in his well-known essay on the subject. After professing to show that philosophy and common sense are alike hostile to the idea of an absolute standard for the determination of either real beauty or real deformity, he goes on to say, that "though this axiom, by passing into a proverb, seems to have attained the sanction of common sense, there is certainly a species of common sense which opposes it,—at least serves to modify and restrain it." "Whoever," he adds, "would assert an equality of genius and eloquence between Bunyan and Addison, would be thought to defend no less an extravagance than if he had maintained a molehill to be as high as Teneriffe, or a pond as extensive as the ocean." Alas! did ever hapless critic fall upon so unlucky an illustration before? Poor Bunyan,—though Cowper, Johnson, and Franklin, were all secretly admiring him at the time,—was greatly at a discount when Hume wrote; nor was the philosophic sceptic, with his cold, meagre fancy, and his exquisitely clear though decidedly Frenchified English, fitted, either by nature or education, rightly to appreciate for himself one of the purest Saxon styles Englishman had ever written, and one of the most vigorous imaginations man had ever possessed; and so, in setting off the merits of Addison,—a writer that lay more within the range of his appreciation,—he could bethink him, in an unlucky hour, of no fitter foil than Bunyan. It would be, of course, wholly idle to remark at this time of day, that, though Addison was a tasteful allegorist, neither the "Vision of Marraton" nor the "Vision of Mirza" at all equal in impressiveness or sustained effect the allegories of the two Pilgrims, Christian and his wife, or even that of the Holy War; or that the style of either the "Dialogues on Medals," or of the "Travels in Italy," with all its fresh and easy flow, is superior to that of the "Pilgrim's Progress." And yet, though at this time of day it must be wholly unnecessary to argue the point, we cannot deny ourselves the pleasure of quoting, as a set-off against the estimate of Hume, the essentially just criticism of Macaulay on both the style and the inventive powers of Bunyan. "We are not afraid to say," remarks the juster critic, "that though there were many clever men in England during the latter half of the seventeenth century, there were only two minds which possessed the imaginative faculty in a very eminent degree. One of these minds produced the 'Paradise Lost,' the other the 'Pilgrim's Progress.'" And not less decided is the critic's estimate of the style which Hume so depreciated. "The style of Bunyan," he says, "is delightful to every reader, and invaluable as a study to every person who wishes to obtain a wide command over the English language. The vocabulary is the vocabulary of the common people. There is not an expression, if we except a few technical terms of theology, which would puzzle the rudest peasant. We have observed several pages which do not contain a single word of more than two syllables; yet no writer has said more exactly what he meant to say. For magnificence, for pathos, for vehement exhortation, for subtile disquisition,—for every purpose of the poet, the orator, and the divine,—this homely dialect,—the dialect of plain working-men,—was perfectly sufficient. There is no book in our literature on which we would so readily stake the fame of the old unpolluted English language,—no book which shows so well how rich that language is in its own proper wealth, and how little it has been improved by all that it has borrowed." Such is the estimate of Macaulay, as opposed to that of Hume. Nor can we doubt that it is now generally received as the correct one. And yet, who can doubt that it serves to enhance the value of the illustration of the elder historian and critic, as an excellent though unintentional piece of evidence respecting his first proposition,—the non-existence of an absolute standard of taste? For assuredly, did there exist such an absolute standard, Hume would never have made choice of Bunyan as a foil to set off the peculiar excellencies of Addison either as a writer of English or as an allegorist.

Our introduction is rather a lengthened one, regarded as simply an apology for what is to follow,—a question of pure taste, on which we ask our Edinburgh readers to decide. There has been, however, not a little discussion of late years in the Scottish capital on matters of this nature. It has been discussed, for instance, whether the Queen's Park should be laid out with trees, or left in its present comparative nakedness; after what style the Meadows ought to be improved; where the most suitable site is to be found for the old church

of Mary of Guelders; and whether the new Exhibition Buildings should have been erected on the Mound, where they at
present stand, or elsewhere. And we believe that on at least
all the points already settled,—for the old Trinity Church
still wanders, like that of Loretto of old, in quest of a resting-
place,—the decisions, notwithstanding the want of an absolute standard to decide by, have been sound and good. And
now for the special point of vertu on which we are desirous
the Edinburgh public should arrive at a decision. They are
acquainted with the forlorn little village of Restalrig, in the
midst of its mud flats and fetid meadows, and which has so
greatly changed its character for the worse since the drainage of Edinburgh has been changed, in the course of modern
improvement, so very much for the better. The time is
comparatively not remote since the flat valley in which it
lies was traversed by a small clear brook, that, rising in the
Hunter's Bog, and receiving minute accessions in its course
from two very celebrated saints' wells, St Anthony's and St
Margaret's, found its way to the sea, after sweeping past the
old ruinous church, through the arid but fragrant wastes of
the Figget Whins. Even so late as 1790, when the now
gloomy mansion-house of Marionville, in its immediate neighbourhood, was the scene of the gayest private theatricals perhaps in Britain, and ere its possessor had gained for himself
the name of the " Fortunate Duellist," and become one of the
most unhappy of men, Restalrig was an eminently pleasant
suburban village, surrounded by rich gardens and cheerful
fields. At an earlier time,—not greatly earlier, however,
than the first beginnings of the Reformation,—it more than
equalled the town of Leith in importance; and at an after

time, its magnificent church, on which successive kings had
lavished their gifts, had become such a receptacle of imagery,
that the Reformers, finding themselves unable to purge it,
had to order its demolition.   In a greatly earlier age, when
all that existed of Edinburgh was but a rude hill-fort, perched
on a rock that rose from amid a wooded waste, glittering with
blue lochans, Restalrig had its chapel erected over the tomb
of a female saint, who died there in the fourth century, and
by whose relics miracles used to be wrought.   It was famous,
too, for its holy well, dedicated centuries ago to St Margaret,
and the haunt for ages of many a pilgrim.   But evil times
began to rise on the village.   First, the General Assembly of
1560 ordered that its magnificent church should, as a "monument of idolatry, be utterly casten down and destroyed."   And
about eleven years after, when Kirkcaldy of Grange held the
Castle of Edinburgh for the Queen, the Port of the Nether
Bow was built with a portion of the materials derived from
it.   The village which, during the siege of Leith under the
regency of Mary of Guise, had accommodated no small portion of the English army, gradually dwindled away; but it
was not until about the beginning of the present century that
the amenities of the place began to be destroyed.   Lying in
a prolongation of the valley which not only carries off, as has
been said, the wholesome drainage of the Arthur Seat group
of hills, with their pleasant springs and runnels, but also
drainage of a very different kind,—that of by much the larger
part of the Old Town of Edinburgh,—it has been inundated,
from the copious introduction of water into the city, and the
substitution of effective drains for the old practice which
Samuel Johnson, during his visit, "nosed in the dark," by a

river of liquid manure, which, by being spread out, on the irrigating principle, on both sides of it, has encircled it with fetid and pestilential meadows. It has, in fine, become a place of mud and manure.

But other evils have overtaken the village, which, though they have militated sadly against its ancient associations, are not altogether of so unmixed a nature. We formed our first acquaintance with it rather more than thirty years ago. It was at that time a place of great resort for its tea-gardens, and, though the foul-water meadows had begun to encroach on its amenities, had many pleasant and interesting points. We still remember the interest it excited when, on strolling one day into its church-yard, we unexpectedly saw in front of the ruins, the humble tombstone of " Henry Brougham, Esq. of Brougham Hall,"—the father of the distinguished states-man ; and on an older tomb immediately beside it, the name of a family dear to every admirer of the Covenanters,—that of the Johnstons of Warriston. There, too, in an ancient vault,—an exquisite piece of Gothic architecture of the middle English style, and curiously covered atop by a thicket of slanted yews,—we recognised the old burial-place of the Logans of Restalrig. It still contained at the time the tombstone of a Lady Logan of Restalrig who died in 1596,—only four years previous to the Gowrie conspiracy ; and it seems to have been from its damp, dark mould, that the skeleton of Logan him-self was exhumed, some six or eight twelvemonths after, to take its place at the bar of the Privy Council, and to have sentence of forfeiture and infamy passed against it, for the share taken by the living man in that mysterious transac-tion. But what we deemed the most interesting relict in the village or its neighbourhood was to be found a few hundred yards to the west, beside the broken pathway which at that time winded between the hamlet and the Abbey Hill. It was one of the two saints' wells to which we have already referred,—that of St Margaret. An exquisite piece of old architecture rose over a hexagonal cell, groined in the corners, and with a central pillar rising from amid the pellucid water, and which furnished a resting-place to the massive ribs that bent over it. No record fixed the age of the erection: it was palpably not older than at least the earlier eras of the pointed style,—for such was the form of its curiously involved arches; and yet such was its antiquity, that the ornate tomb of the Logans,—an erection of mayhap the times of James III.,—has been pronounced by the authorities a palpable imitation of it. Directly over the mossy dome in which the erection terminated atop, there rose an alder tree, gnarled and old; but when we first saw it, in the clear sunshine of a delicious morning in early summer, thickly speckled with its broad umbelliferous blossoms, it formed a not unpleasant object; while a little beyond there stood a small picturesque cottage, humble and not very tidy, but altogether such a one as the youthful limner would have chosen for a first sketch. Occupying a slope, too, the corner in which cottage and well were situated had escaped at least the immediate contamination, if not the unsightly neighbourhood, of the fetid meadows and foul water. But another, and at this time wholly unexpected, enemy was at hand. The North British Railway now runs at some little distance above the saint's well; and well and railway might have continued to exist harmoniously together; but unluckily the sloping bank was marked out for a station, and the foundations of a great building, designed for a sort of general workshop, were laid down on the site of the spring. The picturesque cottage was pulled down, the old gnarled tree grubbed up, and the workmen were proceeding to raze the little Gothic erection that had protected the water for more than six centuries, when they were arrested by an interdict. A sort of compromise was effected: the great building was erected on the purposed site; but there was a sort of open drain left under its foundations, to communicate between the well and the public road; and such of the curious as have zeal enough to enter a repulsive-looking hole, little more than four feet in height,—to descend by a few rude steps,—to wade through a gloomy passage floored with ordure, and charged with an atmosphere somewhat resembling that which reeks over a dunghill in a warm day,—may still find, just where daylight fails, the saint's spring welling up in darkness and disgrace under its canopy of ribbed stone. Had it been utterly destroyed, it would have existed as at least an agreeable recollection; whereas not a single association can be connected with it in its present condition that is not unpleasing.

Let us now state our question. We have said that two saints' wells sent their waters to swell the little brook which, in the better days of the village, found its way to the sea through the flat valley of Restalrig. The fate of one of these we have just related. The other, situated about three quarters of a mile higher up the valley, still comes gushing to the light from its hill-side, as free and pure as when the saint first took it under his patronage, or as when, at a later period, a power vastly greater than his rendered it classic, by giving it an abiding name in Scottish song. We of course refer to St Anthony's well,—so well known in all its striking features to at least our Edinburgh readers, many of whom may have never heard of the other, and whose name must be familiar over the world to all acquainted with our ballad literature. The picturesque ruins of St Anthony's chapel,—classical also from their introduction into song and legend,—in especial from the prominence assigned to them as one of the features of the trysting scene in the "Heart of Mid-Lothian,"—rises immediately above, and would surely harmonize well with the introduction into the scene of one ruin more. And why not set free the prisoned building that now lies in darkness behind its vestibule of dung at St Margaret's, and place it over the spring of St Anthony? Not only would it furnish a new point of interest to the Park, already so rich in these, but it would serve also to keep even St Margaret's itself more in remembrance than it can at present be, in its sunk and degraded condition. Of its interest as a piece of architecture, independent of its great antiquity, the reader may be enabled to judge from the following description by a very competent authority,—Dr Daniel Wilson, author of " The Pre-historic Annals of Scotland " :—

" Not far from the ancient collegiate church of Restalrig," he says, in his ' Memorials of Edinburgh,' " on the old road to Holyrood Abbey, is the beautiful Gothic well dedicated to St Margaret, the patron saint of Scotland. An octagonal [hexagonal] building rises internally to the height of about four and a half feet of plain ashlar work, with a stone ledge and seat running round seven [five] of the sides, while the eighth [sixth] is occupied by a pointed arch, which forms the entrance to the well. From the centre of the water, which fills the whole area of the building, pure as in the days of the pious Queen, a decorated pillar rises to the same height as the walls, with grotesque gurgoils, from which the water has originally been made to flow. Above the spring is a beautiful groined roof, presenting, with the ribs that rise from corresponding corbels at each of eight [six] angles of the building, a singularly rich effect when illuminated by the reflected light from the water below. A few years since, this curious fountain stood by the side of the ancient and little-frequented cross-road leading from the Abbey Hill to the village of Restalrig. A fine old alder tree, with its knotted and furrowed branches, spread a luxuriant covering over its grass-grown top ; and a rustic little thatched cottage stood in front of it; forming altogether a most attractive object of antiquarian pilgrimage. But alas !"

It would be surely worth while bringing such a curiosity to the open day and the fresh air, were it but again to see the dancing sunlight reflected from the water on the richly retted roof, gray with the lichens of many centuries.—*November* 10, 1855.

GEOLOGY OF THE BASS.

THE BASS IN ITS FORTIFIED STATE IN 1690.

1. The Bastion, having Thomas Hog's Cell on the left.   2. The Crane.   3. West Turret.   4. Governor's House.
5. On the east, the Prison and Soldiers' Barracks ; on the west, ditto, containing Blackadder's Cell.
6. East Turret.   7. St Baldred's Chapel, afterwards the Powder Magazine.   8. Garden.

GEOLOGY OF THE BASS.

"THERE are a small knot of us," said a literary friend, addressing the writer one evening about four months ago, "getting up what will, I daresay, be a rather curious volume on the Bass; and to-morrow we visit the rock in a body, to procure materials. Professor John Fleming undertakes the zoology of the work; Professor Balfour its botany; Professor Thomas M'Crie the historical portion, civil and ecclesiastical; Professor M'Crie's friend, Mr James Anderson, a learned Covenanter, grapples with the biographies of what are termed the Bass Martyrs; while your humble servant conducts the business part of the concern, and in his capacity of purveyor-general waits on you. Our to-morrow's expedition still lacks a geologist, and our literary speculation some one learned enough in pre-Adamite history to contribute the portion of the work analogous to that earlier part of the Welsh genealogy which preceded the famous note,—'N.B. About this time the world was created.' Professor M'Crie goes no higher than the days of St Baldred the Culdee, who died on the Bass some time early in the seventh century, and was interred entire in three several burying-grounds at once.   Will you not go with us to-morrow, and contribute to our book the geologic history of the island, from its first appearance, or before, down to the times of St Baldred ?"

"I spent a day on the Bass some four or five summers ago," I replied, "and saw, I believe, almost the little all to be seen on it by the geologist.   It consists of one huge mass of homogeneous trap, scarce more varied in its texture than a piece of cast-metal ; and what would you have me to say about a mass of homogeneous trap ?"

"Anything or everything," was the rejoinder.   "Dr Mantell writes an ingenious little book on a flint pebble scarcely larger than a hen's egg.   You may easily write at least *part* of a little book on a magnificent mass of rock, loftier by a deal than the dome of St Paul's, and a full mile in circumference.   At all events, come with us ; and if you do not find much to say about the rock itself, you can eke out your description by notices of the geology of the adjacent coast, and here and there stick in an occasional episode, commemorative of whatever adventures may befall us by the way.   We regard it as one of the essential requisites of our little volume that all its science be considerably diluted with gossip."

I was unlucky enough to miss making one in next day's party, all through lack of a railway bill.   And yet, convinced that the poet Grey was in the right in deeming "a remark made on the spot worth a cart-load of recollection," I could not set myself to write the geology of the Bass with aught approaching to comfort, without having first renewed with the rock the acquaintance broken off for years. But engagements interfered, and weeks and months slipped away, and summer passed into autumn, and autumn into winter ; and yet the Bass, inaccessible at times during the boisterous and gloomy season of the year which had now set in for weeks together, was still unvisited. I had fixed on one leisure day as convenient for the journey, and it rose foul with rain. I had selected another, and there came on during the night a storm from the sea, that sent up the white waves a full hundred feet against the eastern precipices of the island, and bathed the old rampart walls in spray. I staked my last chance on yet a third leisure day ; and, though far advanced in November, the morning broke clear and bright as a morning in May. Half an hour after sunrise I was awaiting the downward train at the Portobello station. There blew a breeze from the west, just strong enough, though it scarce waved the withered grass on the slopes below, to set the wires of the electric telegraph a-vibrating overhead, and they rung sonorous and clear in the quiet of the morning, like the strings of some gigantic musical instrument. How many thousand passengers must have hurried along the rails during the last twelvemonth, their ears so filled by the grinding noises of the wheels and the snorting of the engine, as never to have discovered that each stretch from post to post of the wires that accompany them throughout their journey forms a great Æolian harp, full, when the wind blows, of all rich tones, from those of the murmurs of myriads of bees collecting honey-dew among the leaves of a forest, to those of the howlings of the night hurricane amid the open turrets and deserted corridors of some haunted castle. I bethought me,—as the train,

P

half-enveloped in smoke and steam, came rushing up, with shriek and groan, and the melody above, wild yet singularly pleasing, was lost in the din,—of Wordsworth's fine lines on "the voice of Tendency," and found that they had become suddenly linked in my mind with a new association :—

> " The mighty stream of TENDENCY
>   Utters, for elevation of our thought,
>   A clear sonorous voice, inaudible
>   To the vast multitude, whose doom it is
>   To throng the clamorous highways of the world."

The Ediuburgh reader must have often marked the tract of comparatively level ground which intervenes between Arthur Seat and the Pentlands on the one hand, and those heights beyond Tranent on the other that merge into the Lammermoor Hills on the south, and piece on to the trap eminences of Haddington and North Berwick on the east. It furnishes no prominent feature on which the eye can repose. Nay, from this circumstance, though occupying a large portion of the area of the landscape, we find that an elegant poet, the "Delta" of "Blackwood's Magazine," wholly omits it in his description of the scene in which it occurs :—

> " Traced like a map, the landscape lies
>   In cultured beauty, stretching wide ;
> There Pentland's green acclivities,—
>   There ocean, with its azure tide,—
> There Arthur Seat, and, gleaming through
> Thy southern wing, Dun-Edin blue !
> While in the orient, Lammer's daughters,—
>   A distant giant range,—are seen ;
>   North Berwick Law, with cone of green,
> And Bass amid the waters."

The natural objects enumerated here, of course omitting the ocean, are the imposing eminences that form the opposite shores of the middle expanse,—Arthur Seat and the Pentlands on the one hand, and the Lammermoors, North Berwick Law, and the Bass, on the other. And the parts of the Frith opposite these boldly-featured regions partake strikingly of their character. The middle space that fronts the flat district ashore does not present a single island; whereas directly opposite the upper tract of hill and valley, we find numerous hill-tops rising above the water, and forming the islands of Inchkeith, Inchcolm, Inchgarvie, Inchmykrie, Carcraig, and Cramond; while opposite the lower tract we find another scene of half-submerged hills existing as the islets of Eyebroughy, Fidra, the Lamb, Craigleith, the Bass, and the May. Now, this inconspicuous flat space between, which leaves the sea so open to the mariner, and the land so free to the plough, and over which the first twelve miles of my journey along the rails lay this morning, forms the eastern coal-deposit, or *basin*, of the Lothians. The traveller may distinguish, on either hand, from the windows of his carriage, the numerous workings that stud the surface, by their tall brick chimneys and the smoke of their engines; and mark the frequent train sweeping by, laden with coals for the distant city. To conceive of the deposit in its character as a basin, one has to become acquainted with not merely those external features of the country to which I have adverted, but also with the internal arrangement of its strata. Standing on the banks of a Highland lake of profound depth, such as Loch Ness, or the upper portion of Loch Lomond, one can easily conceive of the rocky hollow in which the waters are contained, as a vast bowl or basin, and this altogether irrespective of the form of the sub-aerial portion of the valley that rises over the surface. We can conceive of the rocky hollow occupied by the lake, as a true basin, even should it occur in the middle of so flat a moor, that in winter, when the water is frozen over, and a snow-storm lies deep on the earth, the surface of moor and lake presented one continuous plain. We can conceive of a steep sloping side trending into a rocky bottom many fathoms below; then the opposite side rising in an angle equally steep; and, last of all, the horizontal line of ice or water stretching across the abyss, like the string across the curve formed by a bow bent tight by the archer. The Coal Measures of the Lothians represent pretty nearly such a lake; and their shores,—though, unlike those of the lake of my illustration, sufficiently bold to strike the eye as the leading features of the landscape in which they are included,—bear no comparison in height to the profound depth of the submerged portion at their feet. The ancient strata trend downwards in a steep angle from their sides, to the depth of at least three thousand feet, and then, flattening in the centre of the lake into a curved bottom, rise against the opposite eminences in an angle equally steep. Were the Coal Measures to be removed from that deep basin of the more ancient rocks in which they lie, there would intervene between Arthur Seat and the Pentlands on the west, and the Garlton Hills and Gullan Point on the east, the profoundest valley in Scotland,—a valley considerably more profound than Corriskin, Glen Nevis, or Glencoe. The twelve miles of railway which intervene between Piershill Barracks and the Garlton Hills may be regarded as a sort of suspension bridge stretched over the vast gulf; and the profound depth below is occupied by one hundred and seventy beds of shale, sandstone, coal, and clay, ranged in long irregular curves, that lie parallel to the bottom, and of which no fewer than thirty-three are seams of coal. And over all, as their proper covering, like the stratum of ice and snow spread over the surface of the Highland lake of my illustration, lie the boulder and brick clays, beds of sand and gravel, and the vegetable mould.

On reaching the station-house at Drem, I transferred myself from the railway vehicle to an omnibus that plies between the station and North Berwick; and we drove across the country. A coach-top is not quite the place from which the geology of a district may be most carefully studied; and yet it has its advantages too. There cannot be a better point of observation from which to acquaint one's self with what may be termed the geological physiognomy of a country. One sees, besides, of what materials the walls that line the sides of the way are composed; and they almost always furnish their modicum of evidence regarding the prevailing rocks. When speeding along the railway over the Coal Measures, the traveller finds that the fences are constructed of sandstone; whereas in the district across which the omnibus here conveys him he sees that they are almost all built of trap. And with this piece of evidence the features of the surrounding landscape entirely harmonize. The general surface of the country is soft and rich; but abrupt rocks,—the broken bones of the land,—here and there stick out high over the surface, as if to mark the wounds and fractures of ancient conflict. There are the Garlton Hills behind; a long ridge of feldspar porphyry rises immediately on the left; on the right the greenstone eminence on which the old Castle of Dirleton is built ascends abruptly from beside the smooth area of one of the loveliest, most English-looking villages in Scotland ; northwards, encircled by the sea, we may descry the precipitous trap islets of Fidra, the Lamb, and Craigleith ; several inland crags, more in the foreground, and half-hidden in wood, stud the sandy champaign which here lines the coast ; while on the east, immensely more huge than the hugest of the Egyptian pyramids, and, as seen from this point, scarce less regularly pyramidal in its outline, towards the noble monarch of the scene,—

" North Berwick Law, with cone of green."

In passing the ancient Castle of Dirleton, which, like the Castles of Dunbar, Edinburgh, Stirling, and Dumbarton, owed its degree of impregnability as a stronghold mainly to its abrupt trap-rock, and which stood siege against the English in the days of Edward I., it occurred to me as not a little curious, that the early geological history of a district should so often seem typical of its subsequent civil history. If a country's geological history was very disturbed,—if the trap-rocks broke out from below, and tilted up its strata in a thousand abrupt angles, steep precipices, and yawning chasms,—the chance is as ten to one that there succeeded, when man came upon the scene, a history, scarce less disturbed, of fierce wars, protracted sieges, and desperate battles. The stormy morning, during which merely the angry elements contend, is succeeded in almost every instance by a stormy day, maddened by the turmoil of human passion. A moment's farther cogitation, while it greatly dissipated the mystery, served to show through what immense periods mere physical causes may continue to operate with moral effect; and how, in the purposes of Him who saw the end from the beginning, a scene of fiery confusion,—of roaring waves and heaving earthquakes,—of ascending hills and deepening valleys,—may have been closely associated with the right development, and ultimate dignity and happiness, of the yet unborn moral agent of creation,—responsible man. It is amid these centres of geologic disturbance, the natural strongholds of the earth, that the true battles of the race,—the battles of civilization and civil liberty,—have been successfully maintained by handfuls of hardy men, against the despot-led myriads of the plains. The reader, in glancing over a map of Europe and the countries adjacent, on which the mountain groupes are marked, will at once perceive that Greece and the Holy Land, Scotland and the Swiss Cantons, formed centres of great Plutonic disturbance of this character. They had each their geologic tremors and perturbations,—their protracted periods of eruption and earthquake,—long ere their analogous civil history, with its ages of convulsion and revolution, in which man was the agent, had yet commenced its course. And, indirectly at least, the disturbed civil history was, in each instance, a consequence of the disturbed geologic one.

While pursuing the idea, a sudden turning of the road brought me full in view of the Bass, looming tall and stately through a faint gray haze, that had dropped its veil of thin gauze over the stern features of the rock. But the Bass though one of the Plutonic strongholds of the earth, and certainly not the least impregnable among the number, has, so far as the policy and character of its old masters are exhibited in the record, no very ennobling history. It has been strong chiefly on the side of the despot and the tyrant. Its name appears in our earlier literature only to be associated with lying legends and false miracles. Then, after forming for centuries the site of a stronghold little remarkable in the annals of the country, save that the unfortunate James I. took sail from it for France previous to his long captivity in England, the rock was converted into a State prison, at a time when to worship God agreeably to the dictates of conscience was a grave State offence. And so its dungeons came to be filled with not a few of the country's best men. At a still later period, it held out for James VII., and was the last spot in Great Britain that recognised as legitimate the event which placed the Constitution of the empire on its present happy basis. And then, for a time, it became a haunt of lawless pirates, the dread of defenceless fishermen and the honest trader. How reconcile with so disreputable a history the feelings of respect and veneration with which the old rock is so frequently surveyed and so extensively associated ? Johnson, in his singularly vigorous and manly poem, which poets, such as Sir Walter Scott, have so greatly admired, but which mere critics have censured as non-poetical, speaks of a virtue "sovereign o'er *transmuted* ill." Virtue *does* possess a transmutative power. The death of patriots and heroes under the hands of public executioners confers honour on scaffolds and gibbets ; the prison-cells of martyrs and confessors breathe forth recollections of the endurance of the persecuted, that absorb all those harsher associations which link on to the memory of the persecutor. Nay, even instruments of fierce torture come to be regarded less as the repulsive mementoes of a ruthless cruelty, than as the valued relics of a high heroism. And hence the interest that attaches to the Bass.

It is now many years since I gazed on this rock for the first time from the Frith beyond ; but the recollection of the emotions which it excited is still fresh. Some of its more celebrated sufferers came from the immediate neighbourhood of the locality in which I passed my childhood and boyhood, with my first years of labour,—a little northern oasis, in which, during the times of the persecution of Charles II. and his brother, Presbyterianism was as strong and vital as in any district of the south or west ; and the "echoes of their fame,"—to employ the language of Wordsworth,—"ring through" that part of "Scotland to this hour." In the quarry in which I first became acquainted with severe toil, and an observer of geological phenomena, I used to know when it was time to cease from my labours for the day, by marking the evening sun resting over the high-lying farm-house of Brea,—the little patrimony from which one of the captives of the Bass—Fraser—derived his title. And from the grassy knoll above the hollow I could see the parish churches of two of its other more noted captives,—M'Gilligen of Alness and Hog of Kiltearn. Hence many an imagination about the rocky Bass, with its high-lying walks and dizzy precipices, had filled my mind long ere I had seen it. I have now before me, among the jottings of an old journal, a brief record of the feelings with which I first surveyed it from the deck of a sailing vessel ; nor, though the passage does smack, I find, of the enthusiasm of early youth, am I greatly ashamed of it. "We are bearing up the Frith in gallant style, within two miles of the shore, and shall in a few hours, if the breeze fail not, be within sight of Edinburgh. Yonder is the Bass, rising like an immense tower out of the sea. Times have changed since the excellent of the earth were condemned by the unjust and the dissolute to wear out life on that solitary rock. My eyes fill as I gaze on it! The persecutors have gone to their place : the last vial has long since been poured out on the heads of the infatuated race who, in their short-sighted policy, would fain have rendered men faithful to their Princes by making them untrue to their God. But the noble constancy of the persecuted, the high fortitude of the martyr, still live. There is a halo encirling the brow of that rugged rock ; and from many a solitary grave, and many a lonely battle-field, there come voices and thunderings like those which issued of old from within the cloud, that tell us how this world, with all its little interests, must pass away, but that for those who fight the good fight, and keep the faith, there is a rest that is eternal."

It is not uninstructive to remark, from facts and feelings such as these,—and the instances on record are very great,—how much more permanently *good* connects itself with matter, in the associations of the human mind, than *evil.* The wickedness of the wicked cannot so infeoff itself,—if one may so speak, in even their contrivances of most diabolical design,—screws, and boots, and thumbkins, dolorous dungeons, and scaffolds hung round with the insignia of disgrace,—but that the virtues of their victims seize hold upon them, and so entirely appropriate them in the recollection of future generations, that the claim of the original possessor is lost. What a striking comment on the sacred text, "The memory of the just is blessed: but the name of the wicked shall rot!" It seems to throw a gleam of light, too, athwart a deeply mysterious subject. It was a greatly worse time than the present in this country, when the dungeons of yonder rock were crowded with the country's most conscientious men. And yet how intense the interest with which we look back upon these times, and on the rock itself, as a sort of stepping-stone by which to ascend to their scenes of ready sacrifice, firm endurance, and high resolve; and how very poor would not the national history become, were all its records of resembling purport and character to be blotted out! The evil of the past has served but to enhance its good. May there not be a time coming when the just made perfect shall look back upon all ill, moral and physical, with a similar feeling; when the tree of the knowledge of *good* and *evil* shall grow once more beside the tree of life in the Paradise of God, but when its fruit, rendered wholesome by the transmutative power, shall be the subject of no punitive prohibition; and when the world which we inhabit, wrapped round with holiest associations, as once the dungeon-house and scaffold of a Divine Sufferer, shall be regarded—disreputable as we may now deem its annals—with reverence and respect, as the *Bass* of the universe, and its history be deemed perhaps the most precious record in the archives of heaven?

I found a friend waiting me at North Berwick,* who kindly accompanied me in my exploratory ramble along the shore, and who, as his acquaintance with the district was greatly more minute than mine, enabled me to economize much time.

* James Cook, Esq., one of her Majesty's Heralds.

We passed eastwards under the cliffs, and soon found ourselves on the prevailing trap-tuff of the district,—a curiously compounded rock, evidently of Plutonic origin, and yet as regularly stratified as almost any rock belonging to the Neptunean series. The body of the tuff consists of loosely aggregated grains, in some of the beds larger, in some more minute, of the various trap-rocks and minerals, such as green-earth, wacke, a finely levigated basalt, and decomposed greenstone; and, enclosed in this yielding matrix, there lie fragments of the harder traps, some sharp and angular, others water-worn and round, that vary in size from a hazelnut to a hogshead. It encloses also occasional fragments of the aqueous rocks,— here a mass of red sandstone, there a block of lime. There occasionally occur in it, too, viewed over large areas, trap and sedimentary rocks of vast size, beds of the aqueous series many hundred feet in extent, and masses of the Plutonic, that exist as tall precipices or extensive skerries; but *they*, of course, can be regarded as no part of the tuff. As might be premised from its incoherent texture, we find it to be an exceedingly yielding rock. Wherever the lofty line of rampart which it here presents to the coast encroaches on the sea, we perceive that, hollowed beneath by the dash of the waves, it exhibits ranges of bold over-beetling precipices; while, wherever it retires, we discover that it has weathered down into steep green slopes, with here and there some of the harder masses which it encloses sticking picturesquely through. The enigma that most imperatively demands being read in the case of this rock is the union of sedimentary arrangement with Plutonic materials; nor does it seem a riddle particularly difficult of solution.

In the works of the Abbe Spallanzani, a distinguished continental naturalist who flourished during the latter half of the last century, the reader may find an elaborate description of the volcano of Stromboli, one of the Lipari Islands. There are, it would seem, several respects in which this volcano furnishes peculiar facilities to the observer. It occurs, not on the apex, but on the side, of a mountain ; and is so entirely commanded, in consequence, by the heights which rise over it, that the visitor, if the necessary courage be not wanting, may approach so as to look down into the boiling depths of the crater. Unlike most other volcanoes, it is in a state of perpetual activity ; and, what is of still more importance for our present purpose, it rises so immediately over the sea, that no inconsiderable portion of the calcined or molten matter which it has been ejecting day by day, and hour by hour, for at least the last two thousand years, falls hissing into the water. The Plutonic agent gives up its charge direct into the hands of the sedimentary one. Spallanzani relates, in his lively description, how, venturing as near the perilous chasm as he at first deemed safe, he found the view not sufficiently commanding ; and how, looking round, "he perceived a small cavern hollowed in the rock, near the gulf of the volcano," which, "taking advantage of one of the short intervals between the eruptions," he was fortunate enough to gain. "And here," he says, "protected by the roof of the cavern, I could look down into the very bowels of the volcano, and Truth and Nature stood, as it were, unveiled before me." "I found the crater," he continues, "filled to a certain height with a liquid red-hot matter, resembling melted brass, which is the fluid lava. This lava appears to be agitated by two distinct motions : the one intestine, whirling, and tumultuous; the other that which impels it upwards. The liquid matter is raised sometimes with more, sometimes with less rapidity within the crater ; its superficies becomes inflated, and covered with large bubbles, some of which are several feet in diameter ; and when it has reached the distance of twenty-five or thirty feet from the upper edge, a sound is heard not unlike a short clap of thunder,—the bubbles presently burst, and at the same moment a portion of the lava, separated into a thousand pieces, is thrown up with indescribable swiftness, accompanied with a copious eruption of smoke, ashes, and sand.   After the explosion, the lava within the crater sinks, but soon again rises as before, and new tumors appear, which again burst, and produce new explosions."   "In the smaller and moderate ejections," he adds, "the stones, still so hot, that their redness, notwithstanding the light of the sun, is distinctly visible in the air, fall back into the crater, and, at their collision with the fluid lava, produce a sound similar to that of water struck by a number of staves ; but in the greater ejections, a considerable quantity always fall outside the crater's mouth ; and, bounding down the steep declivity, dash into the sea, giving, on entering the waves, that sharp hissing sound which in a lesser degree is produced by a bar of red-hot iron plunged by a smith into a trough of water.   The Abbe, on another occasion, approached, he tells us, the foot of the slop on its seaward side, and saw the "ignited stones" rolling down.   "The five sailors," he says, "who had charge of the boat in which I was, and some other natives of Stromboli who were with me, and whose occupation often brought them to that part of the sea, told me that the volcano might now be considered as very quiet; assuring me that in its greater fits of fury red-hot stones were frequently thrown to the distance of a mile from the shore, and that, consequently, at such times it was impossible to remain with a boat so near the mountain as we then were. And their assertion appeared to me sufficiently proved by a comparison of the size of the fragments thrown out in the explosions I now witnessed, with that of those which had been ejected in several former eruptions. The first (many of which had stopped at the bottom of the precipice) were not more than three feet in diameter; while many of the fragments thrown out at other times, of similar quality to them, and which lay in large heaps on the shore, were, some four, some five feet in diameter, and others even still larger." The tract of sea immediately beneath is much perplexed with currents, and exposed to storms —(the Lipari Isles, in mythologic history, formed the kingdom of old Æolus); and though, since the volcano existed in its active state, lava and ashes to the amount of many millions of cubical yards must have been cast out, and though at one time, about forty-four years previous to the date of Spallanzani's visit, it ejected "such an immense quantity of scoriæ, that it caused," to use the expression of his informants, "a dry place in the sea," the *debris* has been so diffused by the waves and tides, that there is a depth of about twenty fathoms found but a few hundred yards in front of the crater. The ejected materials are spread by the sedimentary agents over a large superficies. Now, in the semi-Neptunean, semi-Plutonic deposit of Stromboli, which is even now in the forming, we are presented with every condition

necessary. to the formation of such a deposit of stratified tuff
as that which composes so considerable a portion of the coast
of North Berwick. There is first the general matrix of
ashes, sand, and triturated lava, laid down in continuous
layers by the aqueous agent; then the embedded fragments
of the harder Plutonic rocks, varying in bulk from the size
of a pea up to blocks of more than five feet in diameter;
and, lastly, with the transporting agency of tides and waves
at command, the occasional introduction of fragments of sedimentary rock, either derived from strata broken up when
the volcano originally burst forth, or carried from a distance,
can be no very inexplicable enigma.

As we proceeded towards the cottages of the fishermen of
Canty Bay, where boat for the Bass is usually taken, I was
informed by my companion, that Dr Fleming, who had been
residing for several weeks during the previous summer at
North Berwick, had detected on the surfaces of the trap-
rocks near the harbour, unequivocal marks of the action of icebergs. He found exactly such grooves and furrows on these
rocks as had been found by Lyell on those of the coast of
Nova Scotia, where the producing cause is still at work, and
every scratch and line may be traced to the half-stranded
masses that, dimly seen during the tempests of the winter
gone by, had grated harshly along the skerries of the shore.
Certainly the associations of the geologist take a wide range,
—"from beds of raging fire, to starve in ice." The rocks
here, in their structure and composition, speak of Plutonic
convulsion and the fiery abyss; while the inscriptions on
their surfaces testify of a time when colossal icefloes, strand
ed upon our shores,

> " Lay dark and wild, beat with perpetual storms
> Of whirlwind and dire hail, which on firm land
> Thaw'd not, but gathered heap, and ruin seemed
> Of ancient pile ; all else deep snow and ice."

The Bass is perforated by a profound cavern, occasionally accessible at extreme ebb. We had purposed attempting its exploration ; and as the tide, though fast falling, still stood high on the beach, we whiled away an hour or two,—after first securing the services of the boatmen, awaiting the recession of the water,—in examining the coast still farther to the east, and in surveying the magnificent ruins of Tantallan. For at least several centuries the ancient edifice has been associated in a familiar proverb with the imposing islet opposite, as the subject of two impossibilities,—

> " Ding down Tantallan,—
> Mak' a brig to the Bass,"—

a half-stanza which served for ages to characterize the sort of achievements which cannot be achieved ; and which, according to an old military tradition, formed the burden of the " Scots March." Hamilton of Gilbertfield,—a name once familiar in Scotch poetry,—assures Allan Ramsay, in one of his metrical epistles, that

> " Nowther Hielanman nor Lawlan',
> In poetrie,
> But mocht as weel ding down Tantallan
> As match wi' thee."

But we live in times in which the family of the impossibles is fast becoming extinct. The Bass still remains unbridged

only because no one during the late railway mania chanced
to propose running a line in that direction : we have seen
the verse of Ramsay considerably more than matched by
poets, both of Highland and Lowland extraction ; and Time
is fast " dinging down" the stately towers of Tantallan. Addison, in his vision of the picture-gallery, could see among the
masterpieces of the dead painters only one artist at work,—
an old man with a solitary tuft of long hair upon his forehead, who wrought with a pencil so exceedingly minute, that
a thousand strokes produced scarce any visible impression,
and who, as a colourist, dealt chiefly in brown. I recognised
the same ancient gentleman seated high on the central tower
of Tantallan, engaged, apparently, in whetting a scythe on the
stonework of the edifice, and ever and anon blowing away
the detached particles of dust with his breath. He seemed
to be quite as leisurely now in his habits as when seen in the
days of Queen Anne among the pictures. But there was an
expression of wonderful power stamped on his calm, pale, pas-
sionless visage ; and when I saw the marvels which he had
accomplished in his quiet way,—how, after laying the doughty
Douglases on their back, he had broken down the drawbridge
of their impregnable stronghold, and half-filled up the moat,
and torn the iron gate of their dungeon off its hinges, and
laid corridor and gallery open to the winds of heaven,—and
how, still as unfatigued as if his tasks had but just begun, he
was going on in his work without rest or intermission,—I could
not avoid recognising him as one of the most formidable oppo-
nents, or most potent allies, that cause or party could possibly possess ; and felt that it betrayed nought approximating
to conceit in Sir Walter Scott, that he should have employed

so confidently, and on so many occasions, his favourite Spanish proverb,

" Time and *I,* gentlemen, against any *two."*

The Castle of Tantallan consists of three massive towers, united by two curtains of lofty rampart, that stretch across the neck of a small promontory of trap-tuff, hollowed into inaccessible precipices by the waves below. The entire fortalice consists of three sides of wall-like rock, and one side of rock-like wall. The edifice, if laid down elsewhere, would be simply a piece of detached masonry, that enclosed no area, and could be rendered subservient to no purpose of defence; and so it seems difficult to imagine a less fortunate conception regarding it than that of a local topographer, viz, that though at present "nearly insulated, it once stood at a considerable distance from the sea," and what is now the perpendicular cliff immediately behind "ended in a gentle slope, which extended greatly beyond the Bass." The stronghold, so situated, would be in exactly the circumstances of the old warrior in the ballad, who, setting his back to a dry-stone fence to defend himself against odds, found his rear laid hopelessly open by the demolition of the crazy erection behind. Change has not been quite so rapid in its march as the myth here would argue; and the geologist may find on these ruins, marks not only of its progress, but of the rate at which it goes on. The two curtains, with the eastern and western towers, are composed of a pale-coloured Old Red Sandstone, —in the main a durable stone, though some of the hewn surfaces have become hollowed, under the weathering influences, like pieces of honeycomb, and the "bloody heart" is falling away piecemeal from the armorial shield over the gateway. But the greater part of the central tower, evidently a later erection, is formed of a fine-grained trap-tuff; and with it the agencies of decomposition and decay have been working strange vagaries. The surfaces of the solid ashlar have re-treated at least half a foot from the original line; while the more durable cement in which they were embedded stands out around and over them in thin crusts, resembling hollow cowls projecting over wasted heads,—like, for instance, the becowled head of the spectre monk in the " Castle of Otranto." Now, this trap-tuff portion of the tower,—evidently no part of the original design, but a mere after-thought,—is in all pro-bability not older than the days of Archibald, sixth Earl of Angus, the nephew of the poet Gawin Douglas, and the step-father of James V., of whom it is known, that on his return from exile on the death of James, he greatly strengthened the edifice; and its state of keeping serves to show how much, when operating on such materials, the tear and wear of a few centuries may do. I bethought me, in front of the old wasted tower,—as I marked at my feet a fragment of dressed stone, which, covered up till very recently by the soil, still retained the marks of the tool, with all the original sharpness,—of the time-worn aspect exhibited by the more exposed slopes and precipices of the hills and mountains of our country, com-pared with the dressed and polished appearance which they so often present in those portions which a protecting cover of mould or clay has shielded from the disintegrating influences. Arthur Seat, with its worn and lichened precipices, shattered by the frosts and rains of many centuries, resembles the time-wasted tower; while the stretch of grooved and furrowed rock

on its southern flank, which the workmen engaged in forming
the Queen's Drive laid bare about two years ago, and which
seemed at the time as if it had been operated upon by some
powerful polishing machine only a day or two previous, represents the piece of disinterred stone, sharp from the chisel.
And in the case of both the tower and the hill, as in many
other matters, things are not what they appear to be.   The
hewn surface of the tower was a greatly more ancient surface
than the present one ; and it is but the more modern frontage
of Arthur Seat that presents the marks of a hoar antiquity ;
while its dressed and polished portions, which appear so modern, are portions of what is truly its old skin, not yet cast
off.   It was once all scratched and polished from base to summit, just as the wasted tower once exhibited, from basement
to battlement, the marks of the mallet; nay, all Scotland,
from the level of the sea to the height of fifteen hundred or
two thousand feet, seems to have been dressed after this mysterious style, as if scoured over its entire area on some general cleaning night.   But the central tower of Tantallan tells
us how and why it is that only on the less exposed portions
of the surface of the country need we look for evidence of this
strange scrubbing-bout.   It is only on the buried pieces of the
hewn work, if we may so speak, that we find the sharp markings of the tool.

The enclosed area of the fortress, cut off from the land by
the towers and their curtains, and surrounded seawards by a
line of inaccessible precipices, we find occupied by a range of
sorely-dilapidated buildings, that rise in rough-edged pictu-
resqueness on the west, immediately over the rock-edge, and
by a piece of rich garden-ground, fringed on the north and

east by thickets of stunted alder. The ruins and the ne-
glected garden are all that remain of the scene which Scott
has so well described in "Marmion" as a favourite haunt of
the Lady Clare :—

> " I said, Tantallan's dizzy steep
> Hung o'er the margin of the deep,
> And many a tower and rampart there
> Repelled the insult of the air ;
> Which, when the tempest vexed the sky,
> Half-breeze, half-spray, came whistling by ;
> Above the booming ocean leant
> The far-projecting battlement ;
> The billows burst in ceaseless flow,
> Deep on the precipice below ;
> And steepy rock and frantic tide
> Approach of human step defied."

A fine morning had matured into a lovely day. The sun
glanced bright on the deep green of the sea immediately beneath ; and the reflection went dancing in the calm, in wave-
lets of light, athwart the shaded faces of the precipices ; while
a short mile beyond, the noble Bass loomed tall in the offing,
half in light, half in shadow ; and, dimly discerned through
the slowly dissipating haze, in the background rose the rampart-like crags of the Isle of May. Nor was the framing of
the picture, as surveyed through one of the shattered openings of the edifice, without its share of picturesque beauty.
It consisted of fantastically piled stone, moulded of old by the
chisel, and now partially o'ershadowed by tufts of withered
grass and half-faded wallflower. Could the old stately lords
of the Castle have tasted, I asked myself, the poetry of a
scene which they must have so often surveyed ? And, as if

to rebuke the shallow petulance that would restrict whatever is exquisite in sentiment to one's own superficial times, that "noble lord, of Douglas blood," who "gave rude Scotland Virgil's page," and who must a thousand times have looked out upon the sublime features of the prospect from the very spot on which I now stood, seemed to raise his mitred front in the opening, and then, stalking by, tall and stately, to evanish amid the ruins. The "schot-wyndo" that he "un-schet ane litel on char," to look out upon the bleak winter morning which he so graphically describes in one of his prologues, may have been the identical shot-window through which, a moment before, I had cast a careless glance upon the sea ; and these were the vaulted passages through which he must have so often paced, ere the field of Flodden was stricken, calling up, as he himself expresses it, in a line which would have stamped him poet had he never written another,

" Gousty schaddois of eild and grisly deed."

I succeeded in scrambling up to a middle range of apartments that are hollowed in the thickness of the front rampart ; but there is an upper range, inaccessible without a ladder, which I failed in reaching, and which, if once attained, might be made good by five against five hundred any day. I was informed by my companion, that some four or five-and-thirty years ago, when he was a boy at school, this upper range was seized and garrisoned by a gang of mischievous thieves, headed by an old sailor, who had been wrecked shortly before on the rocky islet of Fidra, and had taken a fancy to the ancient ruin. They had constructed a ladder of ropes, which could be let down or drawn up at pleasure ;

and, sallying out, always in the night-time, they annoyed the country week after week by depredations on portable property of all kinds, especially provisions,—depredations which, though they always left mark enough behind them, never left quite enough to trace them by to the depredators. Sheep were carried off and slaughtered in the fields; the larders of gentlemen who, like all men of sense, valued good dinners, were broken into, and turkey and tongue extracted; bakers were robbed of their flour,—provision merchants of their hams; a vessel in the harbour, on the eve of sailing, was lightened of her sea-stock; one worthy burgher, much in the habit of examining objects in the distance, had his spy-glass stolen,—another was denuded of his clothes; the mansion-house of Seacliff was harried,—the farm-house of Scoughall plundered; and quiet men and respectable women grew nervous over three whole parishes, when they thought of the light-fingered invisibilities that wrought the mischief, and asked what was to come next. Some of the North Berwick fishermen had seen lights at night twinkling high amid the ruins from slit openings and shot-holes; but supernaturalities are all according to nature in connection with such ruins as Tantallan; and so the lights excited no suspicion. A Highlandman who had been sent by his master to plant ivy against the old walls had been pelted by an unseen hand with bits of lime; but he was by much too learned in such things not to know that it is fatal to blab regarding the liberties which the denizens of the spiritual world take with mortals; and so he wisely held his tongue. At length, however, just as the general dismay had reached its acme, the haunt of the thieves was discovered by some young girls, who, when employed in thinning turnips in the garden of the Castle, were startled by the apparition of a weather-beaten face, surmounted by a red Kilmarnock night-cap, gazing at them as intently from a window in the fourth storey of the edifice, as if the owner of the cap and face had been some second Christy of the Cleek, and longed to eat them. They fled, shrieking, along the identical passage through which the "good Lord Marmion" escaped the grim Douglas, when

> " The ponderous grate behind him rung ;"

the neighbourhood was raised, the hold stormed, and, after a desperate resistance, the old sailor captured ; and with his ultimate banishment by the magistracy the last incident in the history of Tantallan terminated. The earlier passages were of a more chivalric character ; and yet, when, on groping my way into the dungeon of the fortress,—a gloomy cell, nearly level with the moat outside,—I saw one narrow opening, through which I could discern only a minute patch of sky, rising slantwise in the ponderous wall to the surface, and another still narrower opening, through which I could discern only a minute patch of sea, slanting downwards into the solid rock,—when I had breathed for a few moments the dead stagnant air of the place, and marked the massive iron hinges of the door corroded into mere skeletons by the unwholesome damps,—when I had looked upon the naked walls, and the rubbish-covered floor, and the low-browed roof of dripping stone,—I deemed it a greatly better matter to be contemporary with low rogues, such as the sailor in the red Kilmarnock night-cap, than with high-spirited, mail-covered, steel-helmed robbers, such as those ancient lords of Tantallan who had kept the key of this dolorous dungeon, and could serve at will the unhappy captives which it had once contained, as one of them had served Maclellan, tutor of Bomby, in their dungeon at Thrieve.

We quitted the ruins, and returned to Canty Bay along the cliffs. There occur between the bay and the Castle, as if inlaid in the trap-tuff, two immense beds of the Old Red Sandstone of the district; while a third bed, of at least equal extent, occurs a few hundred yards to the east of the ruins, in the neighbourhood of the mansion-house of Seacliff. In a locality in which the surface has been so broken up that at least three-fourths of its present area is composed of the disturbing trap, and in which the old sedimentary rocks exist as mere insulated patches, there can of course be no satisfactory determination regarding the relations of strata. There are, however, various appearances which led me to believe that these beds occur, when in their proper place, deep in the Old Red, and that in their present position they lie not far from the ancient focus of disturbance. They exhibit—what is greatly more common towards the base than in the upper deposits of the system—a large amount of false stratification: they hold a middle place, in point of distance, between the last patches of the lower Coal Measures which appear on the coast of Dirleton to the west, and the first patches that appear on the coast of Dunbar on the east; while the lie of their *true* strata, not very greatly removed in some of the beds from the horizontal, indicates a nearly central application of the disturbing force. This last circumstance is not unworthy of notice. Insulated patches of stratified rock, so covered up by soil and diluvium that their relations cannot be traced, are often held to have escaped the disturbing influences if their strata but rest in the original horizontal line; whereas the horizontality of their position may be a consequence, not of the absence of disturbance, but merely of its focal proximity. Behemoth, rising amid a field of float-ice, may occasion considerable disturbance and derangement among the pieces that tilt up against his sides; but the pieces which he carries up on his back retain nearly their original position of undisturbed horizontality. I spent a day early in the autumn of the present year, in examining that junction, at Siccar Point, of the Old Red Conglomerate, with the still older slate-rocks and micaceous schists of the district, which Playfair, in his "Memoir of Hutton," has rendered classical; and found the principle to which I refer, of apparent non-disturbance immediately over the focus where the disturbance had been greatest, as finely illustrated by the section as at least any of the other phenomena which its appearances have been cited to substantiate.

I enjoyed on this occasion the companionship of the Rev. Mr Dodds of Belhaven, and found his intimate acquaintance with the district, and with geological fact in general, of great value. On passing along the railway to the east of the town, where the strata, exposed on each side by the excavation, exhibit those alternations of sandstone and shale so common in the Coal Measures, he informed me that at this point the workmen had found numerous fossils; and he afterwards kindly procured for me one of the specimens,—a block of indurated shale, largely charged with two well-known corals of the Carboniferous Limestone,—Cyathophyllum fungites and Tubipora radiatus. A full mile and a quarter from where the primary rock first appears, we saw decided marks of the disturbance which it occasioned.   The Old Red Sandstone, exhibited here in sections of enormous thickness, lies tilted up against it in an angle which heightens as we proceed, till it assumes, at the point of junction, a nearly vertical position. But the *focus* of disturbance once reached, the *marks* of disturbance cease ; and the occasional patches of the Old Red which here and there appear rest horizontally on the primary rock.   They are—to return to my illustration—the ice-fragments which, carried up on the broad back of Behemoth, rest on their original planes, while those that lean against his sides have been set steeply on edge.   The Siccar Point is hollowed into a wildly romantic cavern, open to the roll of the sea, and scooped almost exclusively out of an ancient bed of purplish-coloured clay-slate, raised, like the schist in which it is intercalated, in a nearly vertical angle, and which presents, in the weathering, a sort of fantastic fret-work, as if a fraternity of Chinese carvers had been at work on its sides for ages.   And, forming the roof of the cavern, and laid down as nicely horizontal on the sharp edges of the more ancient strata as if the levelling rule of the mason or carpenter had been employed in the work, we see stretching over-head the lowest bed of the Old Red Sandstone.   On this very point, with the noble cavern full in front, old Hutton stood and lectured ; and he had for his auditory Playfair and Sir James Hall.   But a description of the scene in Playfair's own words may at least serve to show how admirably these Huttonians of the last age could write as well as reason :—

" The ridge of the Lammermoor Hills, in the south of Scotland, consists," says the accomplished Professor, " of primary micaceous schistus, and extends from St Abb's Head westward, till it joins the metalliferous mountains about the sources of the Clyde. The sea-coast affords a transverse section of this Alpine tract at its eastern extremity, and exhibits the changes from the primary to the secondary strata, both on the south and on the north. Dr Hutton wished particularly to examine the latter of these; and on this occasion Sir James Hall and I had the pleasure to accompany him. We sailed in a boat from Dunglass on a day when the fineness of the weather permitted us to keep close to the foot of the rocks which line the shore in that quarter, directing our course southwards in search of the termination of the secondary strata. We made for a high rocky point or headland, the Siccar, near which, from our observations on shore, we knew that the object we were in search of was likely to be discovered. On landing at this point, we found that we actually trod on the primeval rock which forms alternately the base and the summit of the present land. It is here a micaceous schistus, in beds nearly vertical, highly indurated, and stretching from south-east to north-west. The surface of this rock runs, with a moderate ascent, from the level of low water at which we landed, nearly to that of high water, where the schistus has a thin covering of red horizontal sandstone laid over it; and this sandstone, at the distance of a few yards farther back, rises into a very high perpendicular cliff. Here, therefore, the immediate contact of the two rocks is not only visible, but is curiously dissected and laid open by the action of the waves. The rugged tops of the schistus are seen penetrating into the horizontal beds of sandstone; and the lowest of these last form a breccia containing fragments of schistus, some round and others angular, united by an arenaceous cement.

"Dr Hutton," continues the Professor, "was highly pleased with appearances that set in so clear a light the different formations of the parts which compose the exterior crust of the earth, and where all the circumstances were combined that could render the observation satisfactory and precise. On us, who saw these phenomena for the first time, the impression made will not easily be forgotten. The palpable evidence presented to us of one of the most extraordinary and important facts in the natural history of the earth, gave a reality and substance to those theoretical speculations which, however probable, had never till now been directly authenticated by the testimony of the senses. We often said to ourselves, What clearer evidence could we have had of the different formations of these rocks, and of the long interval which separated these formations, had we actually seen them emerging from the bosom of the deep? We felt ourselves necessarily carried back to the time when the schistus on which we stood was yet at the bottom of the sea, and when the sandstone before us was only beginning to be deposited, in the shape of sand or mud, from the waters of a superincumbent ocean. An epocha still more remote presented itself, when even the most ancient of these rocks, instead of standing upright in vertical beds, lay in horizontal planes at the bottom of the sea, and were not yet disturbed by that immeasurable force which has burst asunder the solid pavement of the globe. Revolutions still more remote appeared in the distance of this extraordinary perspective. The mind seemed to grow giddy by looking so far into the abyss of time; and while we listened with earnestness and admiration to the philosopher who was unfolding to us the order and series of these wonderful events, we became sensible how much farther reason may sometimes go than imagination can venture to follow.   As for the rest, we were truly fortunate in the course we had pursued in this excursion : a great number of other curious and important facts presented themselves; and we returned, having collected in one day more ample materials for future speculation than have sometimes resulted from years of diligent and laborious research."

On reaching Canty Bay, we found the boatmen in readiness; and, embarking for the Bass, rowed leisurely round the island.   What perhaps first strikes the eye in the structure of the precipices, as the boat sweeps outwards along the western side, is the number of vertical lines by which they are traversed.   No one would venture to describe the rock as columnar; and yet, like most of the trap-rocks,—like Salisbury Crags, for instance, or the Castle rock of Edinburgh, towards the south and west, or the basaltic summit of Arthur Seat,—the artist who set himself to transfer its likeness to paper or canvass would require to deal much more largely in upright strokes of the pencil than in strokes of any other kind.   A similar peculiarity may be observed in some of the primary districts.   The porphyritic precipices of Glencoe are barred along the course of the valley, on both sides, by strongly-marked vertical lines, that harmonize well with the sharp perpendicular peaks atop; and where the vertical lines and perpendicular peaks cease, whether at the upper or lower opening of the glen, the traveller may safely conclude that he has entered on a different formation.   As we pass seawards under the higher precipices of the Bass, the vertical lining takes a slightly outward cast; the rude

columns seem bent forward like the bayonet-armed muskets
of a foot-regiment placed in the proper angle for repelling
the charge of a troop of horse; and on the shelves formed by
the rude cross-jointing of these columns do the innumerable
birds that frequent the rock find the perilous mid-air platforms on which they rear their young.   At the time of my
former visit,—to borrow from old Dunbar,—

> " The air was dirkit with the fowlis,
>   That cam with yammeris and with youlis,
>   With shrykking, skreeking, skrymming scowlis,
>   And meikle noyis and showtes."

But all was silent to-day.   November, according to the quon-
dam missionary of St Kilda, is the "deadest month of the
year :" " the bulk of the fowls having deserted the coast,
leave the rocks black [*i. e.*, white] and dead."   I was not
sufficiently aware, during my previous visit, how very much
the birds add to the effect of the rock-scenery of the island.
The gannet measures from wing-tip to wing-tip full six feet;
the great black gull, five; the blue or herring gull, about four
feet nine inches; and, flying at all heights along the precipices, thick as motes in the sunbeam,—this one so immediately over head that the well-defined shadow which it casts
darkens half the yawl below,—that other well nigh four
hundred feet in the air, though still under the level of the
summit,—they serve, by their gradations of size, from where
they seem mere specks in the firmament, to where they exhibit, almost within staff-reach, their amplest development
of bulk, as objects to measure the altitudes by.   And these
altitudes appear considerably less when they are away.   But
an abrupt rock-tower, rising out of the sea to the height of

THE BASS ROCK IN 1847.

four hundred and twenty feet, must be always an imposing object, whatever its accompaniments, or let us measure it as we may.

> " Dread rock ! thy life is two eternities,—
> The last in air,—the former in the deep ;
> First with the whales,—last with the eagle skies.
> Drowned wast thou till an earthquake made the steep :
> Another cannot bow thy giant size !"

I was not fortunate enough to effect a landing in the great cavern by which the island is perforated : the tide had not fallen sufficiently low to permit the approach of the boat through the narrow opening to the beach within; and, pleasant as the day was, an incipient frost rendered it rather "a naughty one for swimming in."   But we approached as near as the strait vestibule—half blocked up by a rock that at every recession of the wave showed its pointed tusk above water—gave permission ; and I saw enough of the cave to enable me to conceive of its true character and formation. One of those *slicken*-sided lines of division so common in the trap-rocks runs across the island from east to west, cutting it into two unseparated parts, immediately under the foundations of the old chapel.   As is not uncommon along these lines, whether occasioned by the escape of vapours from below, or the introduction of moisture from above, the rock on both sides, so firm and unwasted elsewhere, is considerably decomposed ; and the sea, by incessantly charging direct in this softened line from the stormy east, has, in the lapse of ages, hollowed a passage for itself through.   A fine natural niche, a full hundred feet in height,—such a one, perhaps, as that which Wordsworth apostrophises in his "Sonnets on the River

Duddon,"—forms the opening of the cavern, the roof bristling high over-head with minute tufts of a beautiful rock-fern, the basement course, if I may so speak, roughened with brown algæ, and having the dark green sea for its floor. But the cavern beyond seems scarce worthy of such a gateway : the roof appears from this point to close in upon it ; and a projection from one of the sides completely shuts up its long vista to the sea and the daylight on the opposite side of the island. The height of this tunnel of nature's forming is about thirty feet throughout ; its length about a hundred and seventy yards. Not far from its western opening there occurs a beach of gravel, which, save when the waves run high during the flood of stream-tides, is rarely covered. Its middle space contains a dark pool, filled even at low ebb with from three to four feet water ; and an accumulation of rude boulders occupies the remaining portion of its length, a little within the eastern entrance. It is a dark and dreary recess, full of chill airs and dropping damps,—such a cavern as that into which the famous Sinbad the Sailor was lowered, at the command of his dear friend the king, when his wife had died, and, agreeably to the courtesy of the country, he had to be buried with her alive, in order to keep her company.

So quiet was this delicate winter day, as Gilbert White would term it, and so smooth the water, that we effected our landing on the Bass without a tithe of the risk or difficulty which the midsummer visitors of the rock have not unfrequently to encounter. The only landing-places, two in number, occur on a flat shelving point which forms the south-eastern termination of the island. Our boatmen selected on this occasion the landing-place in more immediate proximity with the fortress, as the better of the two ; and we found its superiority owing to the circumstance that it had been originally cut, at no inconsiderable expense of labour, into the living rock, here of so solid a consistence, that—to employ the words used by Sir Walter in describing a similar undertaking —"a labourer who wrought at the work might in the evening have carried home in his bonnet all the shivers which he had struck from the mass in the course of the day."

The flat point in which the landing-place is hollowed forms a lateral prolongation of the lowest of three shelves or platforms, into which, with precipitous cliffs between, the sloping surface of the island is divided ; and the upper part of this lowest shelf or platform, which rises in level as it sweeps from the eastern to the western precipices, is occupied by the ancient fortress. The stronghold was so designed, that a single stretch of wall built across the point, and at its one extremity joining on to the here inaccessible cliff which rises towards the second platform of the island, and terminating at its other extremity with the sheer rock-edge that descends perpendicularly into the sea, served to shut up the whole Bass. The entire platform somewhat resembles in shape a gigantic letter A,—the flat shelving point, with its landing-places, representing the lower part of the letter up to the transverse stroke ; the higher portion of the platform, occupied by the various buildings of the fortress, the part of the letter above the stroke ; and the single cross wall, made effective in shutting up so much, the transverse stroke itself. To this transverse rampart there joins on at right angles a longitudinal rampart,—a line, to follow up my peculiarly *literary* illustration, drawn from the middle of the cross stroke

of the A to the apex of the letter; or if the reader has been accustomed to disentangle and peruse those fantastic ciphers, curiously compounded of capital letters, which one so frequently finds inscribed on the mouldering tablets and storied lintels of ancient castles, he may conceive of it as a T reversed, inscribed within a greatly larger A, the central cross line of the cipher serving to form the transverse stroke of each of the component letters. And this longitudinal rampart, by running along the middle of the enclosed portion of the shelf, both served to front the sea with its tier of cannon for purposes of offence, and to protect defensively from distant cannonading the buildings which lie clustered behind. The whole fortalice, in short, may be conceived of, in the ground plan, as a gigantic letter T, for the A represents chiefly the ground on which it stands. And while any part of it might be battered from a distance, only the transverse portion of it could be approached by an enemy from the landing-places; the longitudinal portion, protected in front by inaccessible rocks, and in flank by the transverse wall, being as entirely included in the enclosed area outside its parapet as within.

All the doors of the deserted fortalice now lie open except one,—a door by which the tenant of the Bass fences against unauthorized visitors the upper part of the island, with its flocks of unfledged gannets and its sheep; and this door, as it occurs, not in the transverse wall, but at the top of a long ascending passage beyond, leaves the space in front of the longitudinal rampart as open to the vagrant foot as the shelving point in front of the transverse one. The door divides the island into two unequal parts,—a lower and upper; and I am thus particular in detailing the circumstance, as it serves to show on what slight and trivial causes the preservation or extinction of a vegetable species may sometimes depend. The sheep are restricted by the door to the upper division of the island; while two comparatively rare plants, indigenous to the place,—the sea-beet and the Bass mallow,—are found in only its lower division. The same door which protects the sheep from the lawless depredator has protected the two rare plants from the sheep, and so they continue to exist; while in several other islands of the Frith, in which they once found a habitat, but enjoyed the protection of no jealous door, they exist no longer. Even in the Bass they seem to be in considerable danger from the recent introduction of a colony of rabbits, that have already made themselves free of both the lower and upper divisions of the island, and that, by scooping the soil from under the mallows, and by nibbling off the reproductive germins of the beet, have of late very sensibly diminished the numbers of both. The beet plants, in especial, seemed to be at least thrice more numerous when I formerly visited the place than I found them now.

The rabbits, however, though no friends to the rare plants, nor yet to the ruins,—for, with their unsightly excavations, they have been working sad havoc among the parapets and slimmer walls,—did me some service as a sort of geological pioneers. They had been busily at work immediately under what I have described as the longitudinal wall of the fortress, where the tree-mallow grows thick and tall in a loose grayish-coloured soil, which may be now safely described as vegetable mould, but which existed a century and a half ago simply as the debris and exuviæ of the garrison. And their excavations here, from two to four feet in depth, serve to lay open to the visitor a formation of comparatively recent origin, the various remains of which, animal and vegetable, organic and artistic, all speak of man. The accumulation constitutes such a deposit as would surely be now and then unveiled by the explorer of the more ancient fossiliferous beds, had there existed a rational tool-making creature in the earlier ages of creation, or had man, as some writers fancy, been contemporary with all the geologic systems in succession.

It is not unusual to bestow a name on the subordinate beds of larger formations, from the more characteristic organisms which they contain. We have thus "*Coral* Rags," and "*Ichthyolitic* Beds," and "*Gryphite, Encrinal,* and *Pentamerous* Limestones;" and were we, on a similar principle of nomenclature, to bestow on this limited formation a name from the prevalent remains which it exhibits, we would have to term it the *Tobacco-pipe* deposit. It abounds in the decapitated stalks and broken bowls of tobacco-pipes, of antique form and massy proportions, any one of which would have furnished materials enough for the construction of two such pipes

"As smokers smoke in these degenerate days."

Assisted by my companion, I picked up in a few minutes the bowls of five of these memorials of bygone luxury, and the stalks of about twice as many more. Some of the stalks at their terminal points are well rounded, as if long in friendly contact with the teeth ; while their lack of wax or varnish shows that the art of glazing for an inch or two, to protect the lips from the fretting absorbescence of the pipe-clay, had yet to be invented. The bowls are all broken short at the neck,—evidence that the wasteful practice of knocking out the ashes, not, as was Uncle Toby's wont, against the thumb-nail, but against a hard stone, has been by no means confined to our own anti-economic age ; and most of them still bear the darkened stain of the tobacco. There are few of the heads of that head-taking-off century, not excepting the head of the Royal Martyr himself, in so excellent a state of keep-ing, or that still bear about them such unequivocal mark of what had most engaged them in their undetached condition, whether the Virginian weed, unlimited prerogative *de jure divino*, or the Canterburian ceremonies. The deposit in which they occur lies parallel to, and immediately in front, as has been said, of the longitudinal line of rampart, along which the sentinels must have paced frequent and oft, humming, during the midnight watch, some reckless old-world song,— " If ere I do well 'tis a wonder," or " Three bottles and a quart,"—and consoling themselves, as the keen sea-breeze whistled sharp and shrill through embrasure and shot-hole, with a whiff of tobacco. The night is drizzly and chill ; and yonder, tall in the fog, may be seen the grimly-moustached, triangular-capped, buff-belted, duffle-becoated scoundrel of a sentry pacing along the wall, and *crooning* an old drinking song as he goes. One pipe is already smoked out : he stops ; and, firmly holding the stalk of the implement at the neck, he taps the bowl against the edge of the parapet, in prepara-tion for another. It breaks short in his hand ; and, with a sudden oath, that forms a rather abrupt episode in the tune, and disturbs poor Mr Blackadder in his cell, he sends the bowl a-whizzing over the rampart, and the stalk straightway fol-lows it. And now, after a hundred and eighty years have come and gone, here is both bowl and stalk !   One English poet has written verses on the detached heel of an old shoe ; another on a rejected quid of tobacco divested of the juice. I do not see why a mutilated tobacco-pipe of the Bass should not make quite as good a subject as either.   Their abundance here serves to demonstrate that the unscrupulous soldiery of the times of Charles II. must have been not a little remarkable as a smoke-inhaling fraternity ; while the fact that a vicar of the neighbouring parish of Golyn was deposed by James VI. for the high crime of smoking tobacco, about half a century before, shows that smoke-inhaling could scarce have taken rank, in the times of James's grandson, among the very respectable accomplishments.   The weed, if not obnoxious to all the anathemas of the pedant monarch's "Counterblast," must have still been the subject of an appreciation at least as disparaging as that of Lamb's " Farewell :"—

> " Sooty retainer to the vine ;
> Bacchus' black servant, negro fine ;
> Sorcerer that mak'st us dote upon
> Thy begrimmed complexion ;
> And, for thy pernicious sake,
> More and greater oaths to break
> Than reclaimed lovers take * * *
> Stinkingest of the stinking kind ;
> Filth of the mouth, and fog of the mind ;
> Henbane, nightshade, both together,
> Hemlock aconite."

With the broken tobacco-pipes I found numerous fragments of beef and mutton bones, that still bore mark of the butcher's saw, blent with the frequent bones of birds, and fractured shells of the edible crab,—memorials, the two last, of contributions furnished by the islet itself to the wants of its garrison or the prisoners. I picked up, besides, a little bit of brass, the ornamental facing, apparently, of some piece of uniform; with several bits of iron, long since oxidized out of all shape, and stuck round with agglomerations of gravel and coal, and bits of decayed wood, representative, to the young geologist, of the components of some ancient conglomerate of the Devonian or Carboniferous period, bound together by a calcareous or metallic cement. My companion found, glittering among the debris, what at the first glance seemed to be a cluster of minute, well-formed pearls of great beauty and brilliancy, set in a little tablet; but the jewel turned out, on examination, to be merely the fragment of some highly ornamented apothecary's phial, embossed into semi-globular studs, that owed all their iridescence to the sorely decomposed state of the glass. Glass decomposes under the action of the elements,—like many of the trap-rocks, such as greenstone, basalt, and the claystones,—by splitting into layers parallel to the planes, or, as in this instance, to the curves, of the original mass; and the plane of each layer, under the same optical law that imparts iridescence to minute sheets of mica partially raised from the mass, reflects the prismatic colours. Hence the frequent gorgeousness of old stable and outhouse windows, little indebted to the art of the stainer, but left to the amateur pencillings of two greatly more delicate artists in this special department,—cobwebbed neglect and decomposing damp. When examined by the microscope, I found the studs of the Bass specimen presenting exactly the appearance of—what decomposing balls of greenstone have been so often compared to—many-coated

bulbous roots, such as that of the onion or lily. In greenstone the disintegrating substance is commonly iron ; in glass
it is the fixed salt, such as kelp or barilla, used as a flux in
fusing the stubborn silex; and the concentric disposition affected by both substances seems to be in part a consequence
of the homogeneity induced in the mass by the previous
fusion, through which the main agent in the decomposition,
whether moisture or air, is permitted to act equally all round
at equal depths from the surface,—a process with which the
disturbing lines of stratification in a sedimentary mass would
scarce fail to interfere. I saw a large cannon-shot, of rude
form, and much encased in rust, which had been laid bare by
the rabbits in this curious deposit a few weeks before. It
had lain sunk in the debris to the depth of about four feet,
immediately under a partial breach in the masonry where
the fortress had been battered from the sea ; and it had not
improbably dealt it a severe blow in the quarrel of William of
Nassau. But what I deemed perhaps the most curious remains in the heap were numerous splinters of black English
flint, that exactly resembled the rejectamenta of a gun-flint
maker's shop. In digging on, to ascertain, if possible, for
what purpose chips of black flint could have been brought to
the Bass, my companion disinterred a rude gun-flint,—exactly such a thing as I have seen a poverty-stricken north-
country poacher chip, at his leisure, for his fowling-piece, out
of a mass of agate or jasper. The matchlock had yielded its
place only a short time before, to the spring lock with its
hammer and flint; but a minute subdivision of labour had
not as yet, it would seem, separated the art of the gun-flint
maker into a distinct profession; and so, during their leisure

hours on the ramparts, the soldiers of the garrison had been in the practice of fashioning their flints for themselves, and of pitching the chips, with now and then an occasional abortion, such as the one we had just picked up, over the walls. There was laid open a good many years since, among the sand-hills of Findhorn, on the coast of Moray, the debris of a somewhat similar species of flint-work, blent, as in this instance, with a few of the half-finished implements that had been marred in the making; but the northern flint-manufactory had belonged to a greatly more ancient period than that of the musket or its spring lock. The half-finished implements found among the sand-hills were the flint-heads of arrows.

My description of the time-wasted remains of this little patch may be perhaps deemed too minute. I am desirous, however, for the special benefit of the uninitiated, to exhibit —deduced from a few familiar objects—the sort of circumstantial evidence on which, drawn from objects greatly less familiar, the geologist founds no inconsiderable proportion of his conclusions. He is much a reasoner in the inferential style, and expatiates largely on the deductive and the circumstantial. It is, besides, not unimportant to note, that wherever man has been long a dweller, he has left enduring traces behind him—indubitable marks—of his designing capacity, stamped upon metal or stone, stained into glass or earthenware, or baked into brick. In sauntering along the shore on either side of the Frith of Forth, one may know when one is passing the older towns, such as Leith, Musselburgh, or Prestonpans, without once raising an eye to mark the dwellings, simply by observing the altered appearance of the beach. Among the ordinary water-rolled pebbles, composed mostly of the trap and sandstone rocks of the district, there occur in great abundance, in the immediate neighbourhood of the houses, fragments of brick and tile, broken bits of pottery, pieces of fractured bottles and window-panes, and the scoriæ of glass-houses, iron-furnaces, and gas-works.   And certainly few of these remains can be deemed less fitted to contend, through greatly extended periods, with time and the decomposing elements, than the fish and ferns, the delicate shells and minute coralines, of the earlier geologic systems. Dr Keith found the fluted columns and sculptured capitals of the ancient cities of the Holy Land as fresh and unworn as if they had passed from under the tool but yesterday; and he recognised, in the enormous accumulations of hewn stone which in some localities load the surface far as the eye can reach, the ready-made materials with which, almost without sound of hammer or of saw, as during the erection of the temple of old, the dwellings of restored Judah may yet be built. The burnt bricks that coated the Birs Nimroud, probably the oldest ruin in the world, still retain, as sharply as when they were removed from the kiln in the days of the earlier Babylonian monarchs, their mysterious inscriptions ; and the polished granite of the sarcophagus of Cheops has not resigned, in the lapse of three thousand years, a single hieroglyphic. I have been told by a relative who fought in Egypt under Abercromby, that the soldiery, in digging one of their wells, passed for eight or ten feet through the debris of an ancient pottery, and that even the fragments at the bottom of the heap,—mayhap the accumulated breakage of centuries, in a manufactory of the times of Cleopatra or the Ptolemies,—retained their bits of pattern as freshly as if they had been moulded and broken scarce a month before. If in all the earlier geologic formations, from the Silurian to the Tertiary inclusive, we find no trace of a rational being possessed of such a control over inert matter as the idea of rationality necessarily involves, the antiquities of the older historic nations, and even the debris and rubbish of the more ancient towns of our own country, serve to show that it is not because the memorials of such a being would be either so few as to escape notice, or so fragile as to defy preservation. No sooner does man appear upon the scene as the last-born of creation, than, in that upper stratum of the earth's crust which represents what geologists term the recent period, we find abundant trace of him ; and deeply interesting, when presented in the geologic form, some of the more ancient of these traces are.

The recent deposit of the Bass is charged, as has been said, with numerous detached bones, mutilated by the butcher's saw. One of the most ancient fossils that testifies to the existence of man does so in a somewhat similar manner. It exhibits him as vested in an ability, possessed by none of the other carnivora, of facilitating the gratification of his appetites, or the supply of his wants, by the employment of cunningly-fashioned weapons of his own fabrication and design. In the upper drift of the province of Scania, in Sweden, there occur numerous bones of a gigantic animal of the ox family ; and on the skeleton of one of these, singular for its degree of entireness, an ancient hunter of the country seems to have left his mark. " A skeleton of the Bos Urus or Bos primigenius," says Sir Roderick Murchison, in his admirable paper on the Scandinavian Drift, " was extracted by Professor Nilsson from beneath ten feet of peat, near Ystadt, the horns of the animal having been found deeply buried in the subjacent blue clay on which the bog has accumulated. This specimen is not only most remarkable as being the only entire skeleton yet found of an animal whose bones occur in the ancient drift of the diluvium of many countries of Europe, as well as in Siberia (where it is the associate of the Mammoth and the Rhinoceros tichorhinus), but also as exhibiting upon the vertebral column a perforation which Nilsson has no doubt was inflicted by the stone-head of a javelin thrown by one of the aboriginal human inhabitants of Scania. By whatever instrument inflicted, this wound has its longest orifice on the anterior face of the first lumbar vertebra, and, diminishing gradually in size, has penetrated the second lumbar vertebra, and has even slightly injured the third. Occupying himself for many years in collecting all the utensils of the aborigines of his country, and in studying their uses, Professor Nilsson shows that the orifice in the vertebra of the specimen of Bos primigenius in question is so exactly fitted by one of the stone-headed javelins found in the neighbourhood, that no reasonable doubt can be entertained that the wound was inflicted by a human being. He does not think that the wound was mortal; but, on the contrary, he indicates, from the manner in which the bone seems afterwards to have cemented, that the creature lived two or three years after the infliction of a wound produced by the hurling of a javelin horizontally in the direction of the head, but which, missing the head, passed between the horns, and impinged on this projecting portion of the back."

I insist rather on the permanency of the works of men

than on that of the framework of their bodies,—rather on the broadly-marked traces which former generations have left behind them, in the ruins and debris of the extinct nations, than on the scarce less perfectly preserved human remains of ancient catacombs and sepulchres ; and I do so chiefly in reference to a strange suggestion, not greatly insisted upon in these days, but not without its portion of plausibility, and peculiarly adapted to appeal to the imagination.   It at least addressed itself very powerfully to mine, when first brought acquainted with it, many years ago, by a friend then studying at the University.   I had already begun to form my collection of Liasic fossils, and, much struck by the strangeness of their forms, was patiently waiting for some light respecting them, when my friend, who had seen a good many such in the College Museum, and had just returned home from his first year's course, informed me that they were regarded as belonging to a bygone creation, of which not so much as a single plant or animal continued to exist.   Nay, he had even heard it urged as not improbable, that the ancient world in which they had flourished and decayed,—a world greatly older than that beyond the Flood,—had been tenanted by rational, responsible beings, for whom, as for the race to which we ourselves belong, a resurrection and a day of final judgment had awaited.   But many thousands of years had elapsed since that day—emphatically the *last* to the pre-Adamite race, for whom it was appointed—had come and gone.   Of all the accountable creatures that had been summoned to its bar, bone had been gathered to its bone, so that not a vestige of the framework of their bodies occurred in the rocks or soils in which they had been originally inhumed ; and, in consequence, only the remains of their irresponsible contemporaries, the inferior animals, and those of the vegetable productions of their fields and forests, were now to be found. How strange the conception ! It filled my imagination for a time with visions of the remote past, instinct with a wild poetry, borrowed in part from such conceptions of the pre-Adamite kings, and the semi-material intelligences, their contemporaries, as one finds in Beckford's " Vatheck," or Moore's " Loves of the Angels;" and invested my fossil lignites and shells, through the influence of the associative faculty, with an obscure and terrible sublimity, that filled the whole mind. But there is not even a shadow of foundation for a conception so wild : on the contrary, the geologic evidence, whether primary and direct, or derivative and analogical, militates full against it.

I say derivative and analogical, as certainly as primary and direct. The rational, accountable creature of the present scene of things stands in his proper place on the apex of material animated being : he forms the terminal point of that pyramid, the condition of all whose components is vitality breathed into dust. At the ample base we recognise the lower forms of life,—shells, crustaceans, and zoophites ; a little higher up we find the vast family of the vertebrate inhabitants of the waters,—fish ; still higher up we see a distinct stage in the ascent occupied by birds and reptiles ; still higher up are ranged those important families of the mammaliferous quadrupeds described in Scripture as the " beasts of the field ;" and then, supreme over all, and pointing to heaven, we mark, on the cloud-enveloped summit of the pyramid, reasoning, responsible man. How incomplete would not the edifice seem,—a mere unfinished *frustrum*,—were the intermediate tiers to be struck away, and man to be placed in immediate juxtaposition with the fish ! Such, however, would be the place and relations of a rational, accountable being, during the vast divisions of the Palæozoic period. Or how incomplete even would not the edifice seem, were but the second tier,—that comprising the beasts of the field,—to be struck away, and man to be placed in immediate juxtaposition with the bird and the reptile ! And yet such would be the place and relations of a rational, accountable being, during the vast divisions of the Secondary period. It is not merely on the palpable incompleteness of the chain in either case, or on the enormous width of its gaps, that we would have to insist, but also on the positive helplessness of a rational creature so circumstanced. The moral agent of such a world would be the unheeded monarch of an ungovernable *canaille ;* and, lacking the higher order of subjects, from which alone his servants and ministers could be selected, he would lack also, in consequence, any profitable command over the lower. The mighty armies which he would be called on to command would, from the lack of subordinate officers, be mere mutinous mobs, with which no combined movement could be accomplished, or general achievement performed. The earth, as it existed in these earlier periods, could have been no home for man ; and with this conclusion the direct findings of the geologic record thoroughly agree. In the Palæozoic, the Secondary, and the earlier Tertiary formations, we discover no trace whatever of a reasoning creature, who could stamp the impress of his mind on inert matter. Ancient as is the earth which we inhabit, we seem to be in but the first beginnings of the moral government of God.

of Edinburgh stands is a clinkstone ; while the trap-rock of
lighter colour and larger grain, which forms the noble range
of trap precipices that sweep along the brow of Salisbury
Crags, is a greenstone.   The trap of the Bass seems to be
of an intermediate hybrid species : several of the fragments
which I detached from the rocks in the immediate neighbourhood of the landing-place,—conchoidal in their fracture, and
sprinkled over with minute needle-like crystals of feldspar,
that sparkle in a homogeneous base,—partake more of the
nature of clinkstone ; while in the upper and middle walks
of the island, where the stone is less conchoidal, and both
more persistently granular and the grains considerably larger,
it partakes more of the greenstone character.   But the entire
mass, whatever its minuter differences, is evidently one in its
components, and was all consolidated under the refrigerating
influences, at some points perhaps more, at others less slowly,
but in exactly the same set of circumstances.   It may be mentioned, however, in the passing, that none of the detached
fragments exhibit the peculiar globular structure so frequently
shown in weathering by the greenstone family ; nor, indeed,
do we find among the precipices of the island, save in the line
of the cave, marks of weathering of any kind.   The angles
stand out as sharp and unworn as if they had been first exposed to the atmosphere but yesterday ; and to this principle
of indestructibility, possessed in a high degree by all the
harder clinkstones, does the entire island owe its preservation in its imposing proportions and singular boldness of outline.   Had it been originally composed of such a yielding
tuff as that on which the fortress of Tantallan is erected, we
would now in vain seek its place amid the waters, or would

find it indicated merely by some low skerry, dangerous to the mariner at the fall of the tide.

The sloping acclivity of the Bass consists, as has been said, of three great steps or terraces, with steep belts of precipice rising between; and of these terraces, the lowest is occupied, as has been already shown, by the fortress, and furnishes, where it sinks slopingly towards the sea on the south-east, the two landing-places of the island. The middle terrace, situated exactly over the cave, and owing its origin apparently to the operations of the denuding agencies directed on the same great fissure out of which the perforation has been scooped, has furnished the site of the ancient chapel of the island; while the upper and largest terrace, lying but a single stage beneath the summit of the rock, we find laid out into a levelled rectangular enclosure, once a garden.

The chapel, though history has failed to note the date of its erection, bears unequivocal marks of being the oldest building on the island. A few sandstone rybats line one of the sides of the door; and there is a sandstone trough which may have once contained the holy water; but these merely indicate a comparatively recent reparation of the edifice,— probably not long anterior in date to the times of the Reformation. The older hewn work of the erection is wrought, not in sandstone, but in a characteristic well-marked claystone porphyry, occasionally seamed by minute veins of dull red jasper, which is still quarried for the purposes of the builder in the neighbourhood of Dirleton. Like most of the porphyries, it is a durable stone; but in this exposed locality the wear of many ages has told even on it; and it presents on the planes, once smoothed by the tool, a deeply fretted surface.

The compact earthy base has slowly yielded to the weather-ing influences, and the embedded crystals stand out over it in bold relief. The masonry, too, of the walls and gables speaks, like the wasted porphyry, of a remote age. In the rubble-work of the fortress below, though sufficiently rude, we inva-riably find two simple rules respected, an attention to which distinguishes, in the eye of the initiated, the work of the bred mason of at least the last four centuries, from that of the un-taught diker, or *cowan*, of the same period : the stones are placed invariably on their larger, not their lesser beds ; and each, though laid irregularly with respect to its neighbours, ranges level on at least its own bed. A ruler laid parallel to the line in which it rests would be found to lie parallel to the line of the horizon also. But in the rubble-work of the chapel above we find no such laws respected. The workmen by whom it was built, like the old Cyclopean builders of Sicily and Etruria, or the untaught burghers of Edinburgh, who turned out *en masse* to raise their city-wall in troublous times, had them not in their mind. And the characteristic is a very general one of the mason-work of our older and ruder chapels, —our *Culdee* chapels, as I may perhaps venture to term them. The stones rest on whatever beds chanced to fit, or in what-ever angle best suited the *lie* of the *course* immediately below.

The garden, surrounded by a ruinous wall, and a broad fringe of nettles, occupies, as has been said, the upper terrace of the island. When I had last seen it in the genial month of June 1842, it bore, among the long rank grass that marks the richness of its soil, its delicate sprinkling of " garden-flowers grown wild ;" but the pleasant " cherry trees," of the fruit of which" Mr Fraser of Brea " several times tasted," were no longer to be seen ; and now, overborne by the wintry influences, the flowers themselves had disappeared, and the area lay covered with a sallow carpeting of withered herbage. What is termed the well,—a deep square excavation near the middle of the enclosure,—I found full to overflowing with a brown turbid fluid, which gave honest information to the organs of smell that it was neither necessary nor advisable to consult regarding it those of taste. It had proved, I was informed by the boatmen, the grave of a hapless sheep during one of the snow-storms of last winter ; and a cold infusion of undressed mutton,—for the animal had been left to decay when it had fallen,—would form, I am afraid, but tolerable drinking, even with the benefit of the finest of water as a menstruum. The water of the Bass, however,—and I saw considerable accumulations of it in two other receptacles,— must be bad when at the best. Mr Fraser complains, in his Memoir, that in the winter time, when communication between the island and the mainland was cut off by the surf, the prisoners had not unfrequently, for lack of better, to drink " corrupted water, sprinkled over with a little oatmeal." The frequent rains,—for there is no true spring in the island,—in soaking downwards through the rich soil, fattened during a long series of years by the dung dropped on it by the birds, becomes a sort of dilute tincture of guano, which, however fitted for the support of vegetable existence, must be but little conducive to the welfare of animal life. And hence one of the characteristics indicated by the laird of Brea,—the Bass water is " corrupted water."

A pyramid of loose stones,—the work of some of the troops engaged in the great ordnance survey,—occupies the apex of the island.   One is sometimes inclined to regret that these conspicuous mementoes of an important national undertaking, which in the remoter and wilder regions of our country furnish so many central resting points, from which the eye, —to employ a phrase of Shenstone's,—"lets itself out on the surrounding landscape," should be of so temporary a character.   Placed, as most of them are, far out of reach of the levelling plough and harrow, and of the covetous dyke-builder, they would form, were they but constructed of stone and run lime, connecting links between the present and remotely future generations, that would be at least more honourable to the age of their erection than monuments raised to commemorate the ferocities of barbarous clan-battles, or the doubtful virtues of convenient statesmen, who got places for their dependents.   They might have their little tablets, too, commemorative, like those of the old Roman wall, of the laborious "*vexillarii*" who had erected them, and usefully illustrative, besides, of the comparative powers, in resisting disintegration, of the various serpentines, marbles, granites, and sandstones of the country.   The stony sentinel of the Bass,— for sentinel, at a little distance, it seems,—occupies, like many of its fellows over Scotland, what in the winter nights must be a supremely drear and lonely watching station,—quite the sort of place for the ghost of some old persecuting prison-captain to take its stand, what time the midnight moon looks out through rack and spray, and the shadow of the old chapel falls deep and black athwart the sward.   The island must have been less solitary a-nights than now, during at least the summer season, some sixty years ago, when, according to an account by Alexander Wilson, the well-known literary pedlar, the climbers resided permanently on the rock at breeding time, " in a little hut, in which liquor and bread and cheese were sold" for the " accommodation of chance visitors, and of the sportsmen who frequented the place for the diversion of shooting." Wilson, laden with pieces of muslin and of verse, and with the prospectus of his first publication in his pocket, journeyed along the coast in the autumn of 1789, to make a "bold push," as he somewhat quaintly informs the reader in his journal, " for the united interest of pack and poems,"—recording each night the observations and occurrences of the day. He had visited Canty—or, as he writes the word, *Comly*—Bay, where then, as now, "a few solitary fishers lived;" and was much struck with the appearance of the Bass,—" a large rock," he says, "rising out of the sea to the dreadful height of six hundred feet, giving the spectator an awful idea of its Almighty founder, who weigheth the mountains in scales, and the hills in a balance,—who by one word raised into existence this vast universe, with all these unwieldy rocks,—and who will, when his Almighty goodness shall think fit, with one word command them to their primitive nothing." But though he eagerly transferred to his journal all the information regarding the rock which he succeeded in collecting, he was unable, it would seem, to visit it: times were hard; and his list, both of sales and subscribers, low.

> " The poor pedlar failed to be favoured with sale,
> And they did not encourage the poet."

Wilson pointedly refers, in his journal, to the "prodigious number of solan geese that build among the cliffs of the rock." With what feelings, as he lay on the green bank ashore, did he survey the flocks wheeling and screaming around it, thick as midges over a woodland pool in midsummer,—now gleaming bright in the distance, as they presented their white backs to the sun,—anon disappearing for a moment, as they wheeled in airy evolution, and the shaded edges of their wings turned to the spectator! Did the pulses of the incipient Ornithologist beat any the quicker as he gazed on the living cloud? or did there arise within him a presentiment,—a sort of first glimmer,—of the happy enthusiasm which at an after period pervaded his whole mind, when, week after week, he lived in the wild forests of the West, or swept in his canoe over the breasts of mighty rivers for hundreds of miles, marking every beauty of form, every variety of note, every peculiarity of instinct, vested in the feathered creation, and laying in, fresh from nature, the materials of his magnificent descriptions? Had we met such a poor curious pedlar to-day, we would willingly have indulged him in a gratis voyage to the Bass, and charged the expense of his entertainment to the account of the forthcoming volume; but pedlars of the type of the Ornithologist are, I suspect, rare.   The last of the fraternity with whom I came in contact was a tall, corduroy-encased man, laden with japanned trays.   There was an idle report current at the time,—for our meeting occurred shortly after the Queen's first visit to Scotland,—that her Majesty purposed purchasing Craig-Millar Castle, and getting it fitted up into a royal residence; and as the castle, on its noble slope, with the blue Pentlands in the background, and Arthur Seat, half in shadow, half bronzed by the sun, full in front, formed our prospect at the time, the tall pedlar was amusing himself in loyally criticising the landscape on behalf of his

Sovereign. "Yes," he said, "there's a wheen bonny parks there, an' there's bonny bits of wud atween them ; but yonder's a curn of *reugh* hills; an' its an ugly rocky lump that Arthur Seat. Nae doubt the place is no a bad place; but it wad be a hantle prettier place for a Queen if we could but tak' awa the *coorse* Pentlands and the *reugh* Seat."

How vastly more strange and extravagant-looking truth is than fiction ! Our Edinburgh Reviewers deemed it one of the gravest among the many grave offences of Wordsworth, that he should have made the hero of the "Excursion" a pedlar. " What," they ask, "but the most wretched and provoking perversity of taste and judgment could induce any one to place his chosen advocate of wisdom and virtue in so absurd and fantastic a condition? Did Mr Wordsworth really imagine that his favourite doctrines were likely to gain anything in point of effect or authority by being put into the mouth of a person accustomed to higgle about tape or brass sleeve-buttons ? Or is it not plain that, independent of the ridicule and disgust which such a personification must give to many of his readers, its adoption exposes his work throughout to the charge of revolting incongruity and utter disregard of probability or nature ?" If the critics be thus severe on the mere choice of so humble a hero, what would they not have said had the poet ventured to represent his pedlar, not only as a wise and meditative man, but also as an accomplished writer, and a successful cultivator of natural science, —the author of a great national work, eloquent as that of Buffon, and incomparably more true in its facts and observations ! Nay, what would they have said if, rising to the extreme of extravagance, he had ventured to relate that the pedlar, having left the magnificent work unfinished at his death, an accomplished prince,—the nephew of by far the most puissant monarch of modern times,—took it up and completed it in a volume, bearing honourable reference and testimony, in almost every page, to the ability and singular faithfulness of his humbler predecessor the " Wanderer?"   And yet this strange story, so full of "revolting incongruity and utter disregard of probability and nature," would be exactly that of the Paisley pedlar, Alexander Wilson, the author of the "American Ornithology,"—a work completed by a fervent admirer of the pedlar's genius, Prince Charles Lucien Bonaparte. There are several passages in the journal kept by Wilson when he visited Canty Bay and its neighbourhood,—though he was a young man at the time, unpossessed of that mastery over the powers of thought and composition to which he afterwards attained,—that serve strikingly to remind one of the peculiar vein of observation and reflection developed in the Wanderer of the "Excursion."   The following incident, for instance, recorded during the evening on which he jotted down his remarks on the Bass, seems such a one as the humble hero of Wordsworth would have delighted to narrate.

He had passed on from Canty Bay to Tantallan, where he lingered long amid the broken walls and nodding arches. And then, "having sufficiently examined the ancient structure," he says, " I proceeded forwards, and arrived at a small village, where, the night coming on, I obtained lodgings in a little ale-house.   While I sat conversing with the landlord, he communicated to me the following incident, which had recently taken place in a family in the neighbourhood. About six months ago, the master of the house, who was by trade a fisher, fell sick, and continued in a lingering way until about three weeks ago, when distemper increased to that degree that all hopes of recovery were gone. In these circumstances he prepared himself for dissolution in a manner that became a Christian, and agreeably to the character he had all along been distinguished by when in health and vigour. Meanwhile, his wife, being pregnant, drew near the time of her delivery; and as the thought that he should not see his last child cost the poor man no small uneasiness, it became one of his fervent petitions to Heaven that he might be spared until after its birth. But his malady increased, and all his relations were called on to take their last farewell. While they stood around his bed, expecting his immediate departure, his wife was taken suddenly ill, and in less than hour was delivered of twins, which the dying man no sooner understood, than he made signs that the minister should be sent for, who accordingly in a short time came. He then attempted to rise in bed, but his strength was exhausted. Hereupon one of his daughters went into the bed behind him, and supported his hands until he held up both the children, first one and then the other. Then, kissing them both, he delivered them over to their mother, and, reclining his head softly on the pillow, expired." Such is one of the more characteristic passages in the prose "*Excursion*" of the pedlar Wilson. It forms, however, no part of the Geology of the Bass.

Let us now see whether we cannot form some consistent theory regarding the origin and early history of the rock. It occurs, as has been said, in a highly disturbed district, which extends on the west to Aberlady Bay, and on the east to near the ancient Castle of Dunbar, and includes in its stormy area by far the greater part of the parishes of White-kirk, Prestonkirk, North Berwick, Dirleton, and Athelstane-ford. The trap islands and skerries that lie on both sides parallel to the shore show that this Plutonic region does not, at least immediately, terminate with the coast-line ; while the Isle of May,—a vast mass of greenstone, lofty enough to raise its head above the profounder depths of the Frith beyond,— may be regarded as fairly indicating that, on the contrary, it stretches quite as far under the sea as into the interior of the country. And occupying nearly the centre of this disturbed district, like some undressed obelisk standing lichened and gray in the middle of some ancient battle-field, rises the tall column of the Bass. How account for its presence there ?

The thick of the battle between the Vulcanists and Nep-tuneans has always lain around elevations of this character : they have formed posts of vantage, for the possession of which the contending parties have struggled like the British and French forces at Waterloo round Hougoumont and La Haye Sainte ; but the wind of the commotion has been long since laid, and they may now be approached fearlessly and in safety. The Wernerians, some of whom could believe, about the be-ginning of the present century, that even obsidian and pumice were of "aquatic formation," regarded them as mere aqueous concretions, terminating abruptly below, without communica-tion with rocks of resembling character, and as similar in their origin to the hard insulated yolks which sometimes occur in beds of sandstone and of lime ; while the Huttonians held them, on the other hand, to be, like the lava of volcanoes, productions of the internal fire, and believed that they communicated in every instance with the abyss from which their substance was at first derived. Both parties, of course, agreed in recognising immense denudation as the agent which had scooped from around them the softer rocks, in which, according to the Wernerian, they had consolidated under the operations of some unknown chemistry; or whose rents and chasms, opened by the volcanic forces, had furnished, according to the Huttonian, the moulds in which they had been cast,—as an iron-founder casts his ponderous wheels, levers, and axles, in matrices of clay or sand, that communicate by sluice with the molten reservoir of the furnace. Let us take immense denudation, then, the work of tides and waves operating for myriads of ages, as an agent common to both parties. From where Edinburgh now stands, a huge dome of the Coal Measures, greatly loftier than the Pentlands, and that once connected the coal-field of Falkirk with that of Dalkeith, has been swept away by this tremendous power; while from the western districts of Ross, a deposition of the Old Red Sandstone, full three thousand feet in thickness, has in like manner been ground down, and the gneiss rocks on which it rested laid bare. And in the one district we find eminences of harder texture than the mass that had once enveloped them, —such as Arthur Seat, the Castle rock, Corstorphine Hill, and the Dalmahoy Crags,—standing up in high relief; and mountains such as Suil Veinn, Coul Beg, and Coul More, in the other.

> " Who was it scoop'd these stony waves ?
> Who scalp'd the brows of old Cairngorm,
> And dug these ever-yawning caves ?—
> 'Twas I, the Spirit of the storm."

And, scattered over the disturbed district of which the Bass occupies nearly the centre, we find resembling marks of vast denudation ; the Bass itself, the four adjoining islands, the Isle of May, the Garlton Hills near Haddington, and the Law of North Berwick, serving but in little part to indicate the height at which the enveloping material once stood.   These eminences compose, according to the poet, the stony waves of the locality, scooped out of the yielding mass by the "Spirit of the storm."

With the denuding agencies granted, then, by both parties, as a force operative in converting the inequalities in solidity of the rocks of the district into inequalities of level on its surface, let us next remark, that all the eminences thus scooped out are composed of hard trap ; while the reduced mass out of which they have been dug consists either of soft trap-tuff, or of stratified shales, sandstones, and limestones,—rocks these last which Wernerians and Huttonians alike recognise as of sedimentary origin.   From the section of the harder traps, exhibited on the general surface by the denuding forces, can we alone judge of their original forms as solid figures, or of that of the buried portions of them ; and the difficulty of determining from mere sections the form of even *regular* figures may serve to show how much uncertainty and doubt must always attend the attempt to determine from mere sections the form of *irregular* ones.   Let us suppose that a mass of black opaque glass, thickly charged with regularly-formed cones of white china,—cones described by angles of many various degrees of acuteness, and carelessly huddled together in every possible angle of inclination,—has been ground down to a considerable depth, as if by the denuding agencies, and then polished. In how many diverse figures of white would not the china cones be presented! There would be paraboles and hyperboles, circles, ellipses, and isosceles triangles; the circles would be of every variety of size; the angles of every degree of acuteness; the paraboles, hyperboles, and ellipses, of every proportion and form compatible with the integrity of these figures; and who, save the mathematician who had studied conics, could demonstrate that the one normal figure, of which all these numerous forms were sections, could be the cone, and the cone only? But if the embedded pieces of china were not of regular, but of irregular figures, their forms as solids could, from the sections laid open, be but conjectured, not demonstrated. Such, however, is the difficulty with which the geologist, whatever his school, has to contend, who studies by section the forms of the trap-rocks, enclosed in sedimentary or tuffaceous matrices; and, of course, great uncertainty must always attach to arguments, whether for the support or demolition of any theory, founded upon these doubtful forms. It may be received as a general principle, for instance, that dikes and veins of aqueous origin, filled by the ocean from above, will terminate beneath somewhat in a wedge-like fashion, or, at least, that they will terminate *beneath*, and will be open above; whereas, of veins or dikes of Plutonic origin, filled by injected matter from the abyss, it may be received as a general principle, that while they may in some cases terminate in a wedge-like form above, they will be always open below. And, accordingly, much has been built by the Huttonian on dikes open beneath, and much by the Wernerian on similar dikes shut beneath, and merely open a-top. But the section in such cases can convey but an inadequate and

T

doubtful idea of the enclosed mass, whether deposited from above, or injected from below ; and even *were* the idea adequate, and the form of the mass demonstrably ascertained, existing in many cases as a mere fragment which the denuding agent has spared, exceedingly little explanatory of its origin could with propriety be founded upon its form.   There exists, I doubt not, many a wedge-shaped bed of trap that has now no connection whatever with the abyssmal depths. It is demonstrable, however, that such trap-wedges, though as entirely insulated as yolks or concretions, may have been filled from beneath notwithstanding.   Let me attempt an illustration, which may serve also to exemplify my theory of the Bass.

Let us suppose, then, that where Edinburgh Castle now stands there yawned of old the crater of a volcano.   The molten lava boiled fiercely within the chasm ; the imprisoned gases struggled hard for egress ; ever and anon showers of ashes and fragments of stone were emitted, and in their descent fell all around, until at length a considerable hill of a true volcanic tuff came to be formed, adown which there rushed from time to time vast beds of molten matter, which, gradually cooling on the slopes, alternated, in the form of trap beds, with the tuff.   At length the base of the hill, ever widening by this process, came, in the lapse of seasons, to extend eastwards to what are now Salisbury Crags,—the Crags being, let us suppose, but a portion of the tuffaceous bottom, topped by one of the lava-beds that had issued from the central crater.   It will, of course, be at once seen that I am not dealing here with the actual theory of the Crags or Castle Hill : the actual theory the reader may find, if he wills, ingeniously and satisfactorily stated in Mr Maclaren's interesting "Sketches of the Geology of Fife and the Lothians." I am dealing, not with the actualities of the case, but, for the sake of illustration, with what demonstrably *might* have been. Let us suppose, farther, that in the lapse of ages this volcano had become extinct,—that the lava within had hardened in the crater, like a pillar of molten bronze in its mould,—and that then, through the gradual submergence of the land, the eminence had come to be exposed to the denuding powers of the great Gulf Stream setting in against it from the west, and the prolonged roll of the waves of the Atlantic, occasionally aggravated by tempest. At first the western base of the hill would begin to wear away, as the tides and billows chafed against the unsolid tuff, and the lava beds, deeply undermined, broke off in vast masses and tumbled down. Anon the solid central column, moulded in the crater, would be laid bare ; yet anon, thoroughly divested of its case, it would stand out as an insulated stack, with but the tail of softer matter behind it, which it had shielded from the denuding forces. At length, of the entire hill there would remain but the central column, greatly shortened in its altitude, like the trunk of a tree two-thirds cut down,—the ridge on which the more ancient part of the city now stands ; and a portion of the eastern base of the hill, represented by Salisbury Crags, bearing atop a wedge of trap, terminating, at what is called the Hunter's Bog, in a thin edge, and, though at one time connected with the insulated column, and by the column with the Plutonic depths below, now cut off by a wide chasm from both. And then, at this stage, through an upheaval of the land, let us suppose that the denuding agents had ceased to operate, and that the extinct volcano came to exist permanently as a truncated column of rock, and a detached dike of consolidated lava, open above and shut below,—the one admirably suited to form the site of an impregnable stronghold,—the other to furnish the foundation of a Wernerian argument conclusive regarding the aqueous origin of trap. The mode of insulation specified here is but one of many in which wedges and overlying masses of igneous rock, originally derived from the gulf beneath, may have come to exist in altogether as insulated a state as sedimentary beds or travelled boulders.

But the grand question at issue between the two schools of geology may now be regarded as finally settled ; and the trap-rocks, with the exception of the tuffs, in the composition and arrangement of which, as has been shown, both the aqueous and the Plutonic elements may have been operative, have been made over entire to the Huttonian. No man would venture at this time of day to stand up for the "aquatic formation" of obsidian or pumice ; and few indeed for the sedimentary origin of either the greenstone of Salisbury Crags or the hybrid clinkstone of the Bass. The volcanic districts have been explored, and the passage of the lavas into the traps carefully noted, with their resembling powers of disturbance when ejected into fissures or existing as dikes. The assistance of the chemist, too, has been called in : trap has been fused into a porous glass, and the glass again re-fused, by a slow process, into a basaltic crystallite, undistinguishable in some specimens from the original rock, or converted, by a process less leisurely, into a liver-like wacke ; and lava similarly treated has been made to yield a resembling glass in the first instance, and, as the experiment was conducted more or less slowly, an almost identical crystallite, or a liver-like wacke, in the second. The more ancient rocks have also been put to the question, and a primary hornblende converted in the crucible into an augitic basalt. The quality possessed by the traps of altering other rocks in immediate contact with them has also been examined, and similar alterations produced simply by the agency of heat and pressure. Coal in juxtaposition with a trap-dike has been found converted into coke, clay baked into lydian-stone or jasper, chalk fused into marble ; and what the igneous rock did of old in the bowels of the earth, the experimenter has succeeded in doing in his laboratory, with but heat, pressure, and time for his assistants. There are few points better established in the whole circle of geological science than the igneous origin of the trap-rocks.

The ponderous column of the Bass,—to sum up my theory in a few words,—is composed, as has been shown, of one of the harder and more solid of these igneous rocks. Rising near the centre of the disturbed district in which it occurs, it indicates, I am inclined to hold, the place of a great crater, at one time filled to the top with molten matter, which, when the fires beneath burnt low, gradually and slowly consolidated into crystallite as it cooled, until it became the unyielding rock which we now find it. The tuffaceous matrix in which it had been moulded, exposed to the denuding agencies, wore piecemeal away ; much even of the upper portion of the column itself may have disappeared ; and what remains, rising from the level of the sea-bottom below to the height of six hundred feet, may be regarded as the capital-divested top of some pillar of the desert, that, buried by the drifting sand,

> And bid,—though centuries toiled in vain,—
> Her thousandth Eden bloom again ;
> Or solve what eras, since the shock
> Of flood and flame, rived hill and rock,
> Have rolled,—to turn to flint and stone
> The bison's horn, the mammoth's bone !
> Embedded deep and dark they lie,
> 'Neath mountains heaped on mountains high,
> So long, their very race is spent,—
> They exist but in their monument.
> But who their mausoleum made ?
> Did earthquakes wield that mighty spade
> That renders all old Babel piled
> But the card-castle of a child ?
> Strange, that Creation can't afford
> Such pomp to shroud her sixth-day's lord,
> But gives each mean or monstrous thing
> That burial she denies her king.
> These are earth's secrets ; but to gain
> Those of the Deep *thou* rent in twain,
> 'Twere worth a dull eternity
> Of common life to question thee."

The curtain rises, and there spreads out a wide sea, limited, however, in its area by a dark fog that broods along the horizon, and enveloped, even where best seen, in a gray obscurity, like that of a misty morning in May an hour before the sun has risen. It is the ocean of our Scotch Grauwacke that rolls beneath and around us ; but regarding its inhabitants,—so exceedingly numerous and well-defined in the contemporary seas of what is now England,—we can do little more than guess. We know merely that it rolls its waves over a gray impalpable mud, to whose numerous folds it communicates in the shallows the characteristic ripple-markings ; that it possesses a chambered shell of the genus

Orthocera, with two or three obscure Brachiopods; and that the gray mud beneath abounds in some localities with a curious zoophite, akin to the existing sea-pens of our deep submarine hollows. The most abundant denizens of that twilight sea are creatures shaped like a quill, or rather communities of creatures,—for each quill is a little republic,—that enjoy their central shaft, with its stony axis, as common property, and have their rows of microscopic domiciles ranged in the filaments of the web. The light brightens over the wide expanse, and the fog rises; myriads of ages have passed by; the countless strata of the Grauwacke are already deposited; and we have entered on the eras of the Old Red Sandstone. That change has taken place, to the reality of which, as conclusively indicated in space, the judgment of Playfair could not refuse its assent, but with whose slow operations, as spread over time almost lengthened into eternity, his imagination failed to grapple. The perspective darkened as he looked along the long vista of the ages gone by, and left on his mind but a perplexing and shadowy idea of a dim platform of undefined boundary, on which chaotic revolutions of incalculable vastness were performed during periods of immeasurable extent. It does seem a strange fact, and yet the evidence of its reality as such is incontrovertible, that when the lower beds of the Old Red Sandstone were—to borrow from the philosopher—"only beginning to be deposited in the shape of mud or sand, from the waters of a superincumbent ocean," the Grauwacke on which they were thrown down was quite as old a looking rock as it is now, and that the numerous graptolites preserved in its strata existed at the time as but the dimly preserved fossils which we now see them,—miniature quills, with thickly serrated edges, drawn in glossy bitumen on a ground of gray.

With the beginnings of the Old Red Sandstone a slight change takes place in the colouring of the prospect. There is a flush of ochrey red over yonder shallow, where the wave beats on the ferruginous sand; the skerry beyond seems darkened with sea-weed; and though we are still, as before, out of sight of land, and so can know little regarding its productions, we may see a minute branch of club-moss floating past, and the trunk of some coniferous tree, and can, in conequence, at least determine that land there is. But mark how brightly the depths gleam with the mirror-like reflection of scales,—scales resplendent with enamel, that owe their name—*ganoid*, or glittering—to their brilliancy. How strangely uncouth the forms of these ancient denizens of the deep, and, in some instances, how monstrous their size! Yonder, swimming leisurely a few feet under the surface, as if watching the play of a distant shoal of diplopteri, is the ponderous asterolepis, —its glassy eyes set in their triangular sockets, as in some families of snakes, immediately over its mouth,—its head armed with a dermal covering of bone, from which a musket-bullet would rebound as from a stone-wall,—its body tiled over with oblong scales, delicately carved, like the inlaid mail of a warrior,—its jaws furnished with their outer tier of minute thickly-set fish-teeth, and their inner tier of reptile-teeth, greatly bulkier than those of the crocodile, and set at wide intervals, after the sauroid pattern. And yonder,—a member of the same family, of larger scale, and more squat, though somewhat less colossal in its proportions,—swims the strong holoptychius. The numerous flight sof pterichthyes, with their compact bodies, spread wings, and rudder-like tails, resemble flocks of submarine birds; the plated coccosteus and the broad glyptolepis flap heavily along the bottom; crowds of minute cheiracanthi, with all their various congeners, bristling with spines, and poised on membranaceous, scale-covered fins, dart hither, thither, and athwart, in the green stratum above; while, dimly seen, a huge crustacean creeps slowly over the ribbed sand beneath. But ages and centuries pass in quick succession, as the waves roll along the surface,—species and genera pass away, families become extinct, races perish; the rocks of the Old Red Sandstone, holding in their stony folds their numerous strange organisms, are all laid down, as those of the Grauwacke had been previously deposited; and the scene changes as the unsummed periods of the system reach their close.

There is a further increase in the light as the day advances, and the sun climbs the steep of heaven; but the fogs of morning still hang their dense folds on the horizon. We shall look out for the land when the mist rises;—it cannot now be far distant. The brown eddies of a freshet circle past, restricted, as where vast rivers mingle with the ocean, to an upper layer of sea; and broken reeds, withered ferns, the cones of the Lycopodiaceæ, and of trees of the Araucarian family, float outwards in the current, thick and frequent as the spoils of the great Mississippi in the course of the voyager, when he has come within half a day's sail of the shores of the delta. But our view is still restricted, as heretofore, to a wide tract of sea,—now whitened, where the frequent flats and banks rise within a few fathoms of the surface, by innumerable beds of shells, reefs of corals, and forests of Crinoidea. Here the water seems all a-glow with the brilliant colours of the living polypi that tenant the calcareous cells,—green, scarlet, and blue, yellow and purple : we seem as if looking down on gorgeous parterres, submerged when in full blow, or, through the dew-bedimmed panes of a greenhouse, on the magnificent heaths, geraniums, and cacti of the warmer latitudes, when richest in flower. Yonder there lie vast argosies of snowy Terebratula, each fast anchored to the rocky bottom by the fleshy cable that stretches from the circular dead eye in its umbone, like the mooring chain from the prow of a galley; while directly over them, vibrating in the tide, stretches the marble-like petals of the stone lily. The surface is ploughed by the numerous sailing shells of the period,—the huge orthocera, and the whorled nautilacea and goniatite. And fish abound as before, though the races are all different. We may mark the smaller varieties in play over the coral beds,—the lively palæoniscus, that so resembles a gold-fish cased in bone,—and the squat deeply-bodied amblypterus, with its nicely fretted scales and plates, and its strongly rayed fins. The gyracanthis, with its massy spine carved as elaborately as the 'prentice pillar in Roslin, swims through the profounder depths, uncertain in outline, like a moving cloud by night; while the better defined megalichthys, with its coat of bright quadrangular scales, and its closely-jointed and finely-punctulated helmet of enamelled bone, glides vigorously along yonder submarine field of Crinoidea, and the slim stony arms and tall columnar stems, brushed by its fins, bend, as it passes, like a swathe of tall grass swept by a sudden breeze. We are full in the middle of the era of the Carboniferous Limestone. And some of us may be rendered both wiser and humbler, mayhap, by noting a simple fact or two directly connected with this formation, ere the curtain drop over it.

We have already marked in our survey numerous beds of shells, glimmering pale through the shallows ;—here argosies of Terebratula anchored to the rocks beneath,—there fleets of chambered nautilaceæ, careering along the surface of the waters above. But it is chiefly on the fixed shells,—the numerous bivalves of the profounder depths,—that I would now ask the reader to concentrate his attention. They belong, in large proportion, to a class imperfectly represented in the existing seas, and which had comparatively few representatives during even the Secondary periods, rich as these were in molluscs of high development ; though, during the great Palæozoic division, their vast abundance formed one of the most remarkable characteristics of the period. Of this class (the Brachiopoda of the modern naturalist), many hundred species have already been determined in the older rocks of our island ; while, as living inhabitants of the seas which encircle it, Dr Fleming, in his " British Animals," enumerates but *four* species ; and none of these—such is their rarity—the greater part of my readers ever saw.* These Brachiopoda, of which in the Carboniferous Limestone there existed the numerous families of the Terebratula, the Spirifer, and the Productus, were in all their species bivalves of an exceedingly helpless class. The valves, instead of being united, as in the cockle, mussel, pecten, and oyster, by strong elastic hinges, were merely sewed together, if I may so speak, by bundles of un-

* TEREBRATULA *cranium,* T. *psittacea,* T. *aurita,* and CRISPUS *anomalus.*

elastic fleshy fibres ; and the opening of the lips a very little apart,—so simple and facile a movement to the ordinary bivalve,—was to the Brachiopod an achievement feebly accomplished through the agency of an operose and complex machinery. To compensate, however, for the defect, the creatures were furnished on both sides the mouth with numerous *cilia*, or hair-like appendages, through the rapid vibratory movements of which they could produce minute currents in the water, and thus bring into the interior of their shells, between lips raised but a line apart, the numerous particles of organic matter floating around them which constituted their proper food. They resembled in their mode of living rather the orders below them,—radiata such as the Actinea, or zoophytes such as the Tubulariadæ,—than true molluscs. But there are no mistakes in the work of the Divine Mechanician : in the absence of an elastic hinge, the minute *cilia* performed their part ; and so, throughout the vast periods of the Palæozoic division, the helpless Brachiopoda continued to exist in vastly greater numbers than any of their contemporaries.

Now, it is a curious circumstance, that Paley, when adducing, in his " Natural Theology," some of the marks of design so apparent in the hinge of bivalves, such as the cockle and oyster, misses by far the most important point exhibited in its construction, and so converts his bivalves into poor helpless Brachiopoda, unfurnished with the compensatory *cilia*. It is further curious that, in the elaborate edition of the "Theology," jointly published by Lord Brougham and Sir Charles Bell, though there be a neat wood-cut of the Venus-heart cockle given to illustrate their author's idea, the omitted point is not noticed. "In the bivalve order of shell-fish," says the Archdeacon,—"cockles, mussels, oysters, &c.—what contrivance can be so simple or so clear as the insertion at the back of a tough tendinous substance, that becomes at once the *ligament* which binds the two shells together, and the *hinge* upon which they open and shut?" Most true! the inserted cartilage is both ligament and hinge; but even some of the helpless Brachiopoda have, in the one insertion at their back, both ligament and hinge, and are helpless Brachiopoda notwithstanding; whereas the cockle, oyster, mussel, and all bivalves of their order, can do what the Brachiopoda cannot,—open their shells with great promptitude; and at least a few of them can, like the pecten, dart edgeways through the water, like missiles thrown by the hand, simply by the rapid shutting of their valves again. These have been described as the butterflies of the sea. Whence comes this opening power, which Paley's description so evidently does not involve? The power of opening the human palm resides in the muscles on the back of the fore-arm; the power of shutting it, in the muscles in the front of the fore-arm, directly opposite. These last—the muscles operative in shutting the palm—are in the cockle, and all other bivalves of its class, represented by the adductor muscles; but what represents in the shell those antagonist muscles by which the palm is opened? The bivalve, from its peculiar construction, can have no antagonist muscles; its little circle of life is bounded by the lips of the two valves; and as the proper place of the antagonist muscles would be of necessity on the outside of the shell, far beyond that circle of vitality, antagonist muscles it cannot possibly possess; and yet, whenever the creature wills it, the work of the missing muscles is promptly performed.   Now, mark how this happens.   The cartilage inserted at the back is, according to Paley, at once the *ligament* which binds the two shells together, and the *hinge* upon which they open and shut; but it is yet something more,—it is a powerful *spring*, compressed, and, if I may use the phrase, "set on full cock," by the strain of the adductor muscles ; and no sooner is that strain relaxed than up flies the valve,—like some ingeniously contrived trap-door, when one releases the steel-spring,—in obedience to the mechanical force locked up for use in the powerfully elastic bit of cartilage, that without derangement or confusion serves so many various purposes.   Sir Godfrey Kneller is said to have remarked, in the plenitude of his conceit, that if God Almighty had taken *his* advice on some important points of contrivance, matters would probably have been better on the whole ; and the saying is recorded as characteristic of the irreverent vanity of the artist.   Alas, poor addle-headed coxcomb !   Paley and his two editors,—men of high standing compared with Sir Godfrey,—could not have been entrusted, it would seem, by the great First Designer with the construction of even the hinge of a bivalve.   The cockles, oysters, pectens, and mussels, hinged by them, would be all helpless Brachiopoda, with not only no spring in their hinges, but also unfurnished with the compensatory apparatus within, and would, in consequence, become extinct in a week.   Is there no lesson here ?

But, lo ! the mist rises, and slowly dissipates in the sun ; and yonder, scarce half a mile away, is the land,—a low swampy shore, covered by a rank vegetation.   Thickets of tall plants, of strange form and singular luxuriance, droop over the coast-edge into the sea, like those mangrove jungles of Southern America that bear on their branches crops of oysters. There are reeds, with their light coronals of spiky leaves radiating from their numerous joints, that rival the masts of vessels in size,—ferns, whose magnificent fronds overshadow half a rood of surface, that attain to the bulk and height of forest trees,—club-mosses, tall as Norwegian pines, —and strangely-carved, cacti-looking, leaf-covered trunks, bulky as the body of a man. Nor is there any lack of true trees, that resemble those of the existing period, as exhibited in the southern hemisphere,—stately araucarians, that lift their proud heads a hundred feet over the soil,—and spiky pines, that raise their taper-trunks and cone-covered boughs to a scarce lower elevation. And yonder green and level land, dank with steaming vapour, and where the golden light streams through long bosky vistas, crowded with prodigies of the vegetable kingdom,—Sigillaria, Favularia, and Ulodendra,—is the land of the Coal Measures.

Three of the great geologic periods, comprising almost the whole of the Palæozoic division, have already gone by ; and yet the history of the Bass as an igneous rock is still to begin. But we have at least laid down the groundwork of the surrounding landscape. And be it remembered, that all these scenes, however much they may seem the work of fancy, were realities connected with the laying of these deep foundations,—realities which might have been as certainly witnessed from the point in space now occupied by the rude crowning pyramid of the Bass, had there been a human eye to look abroad, or a human sensorium to receive the im-

U

pressions which it conveyed, as the scene furnished by the lovely sunset of this evening. Sir Roderick Murchison, in his magnificent "Silurian System," has given the example of rendering landscapes according to their real outlines, but coloured according to the tints of the geologic map ; and the practice possesses the advantage of making the diverse features of the various formations address themselves with peculiar emphasis to the eye. Were the real landscape which the summit of the Bass commands to be so coloured, we would see its wide area composed of characteristic representatives of each of the three systems whose successive depositions we have described. The distant promontory to the east, on which Fast Castle stands, with the hills in the interior that sweep along the entire background of the prospect, would bear the deep purple tinge appropriated by the geologist to the Grauwacke. Leaning at their feet, from the Siccar Point to Gifford, and from Gifford to Fala, besides abutting on the sea in insulated patches,—as at North Berwick, Canty Bay, Tantallan, Seacliff, and Belhaven,—we would next see, spread over a large space in the scene, the deep chocolate tint assigned, not unappropriately, to the Old Red. From Cockburnspath to Dunbar on the one hand, and from Aberlady Bay to Arthur Seat on the other, the landscape would exhibit the cold gray hue of the Coal Measures, here and there mottled with the light azure that distinguishes in the map the Carboniferous Limestone : while the trap eminences, with the tuff of the opposite shore, and the island mass at our feet, would flame in the deep crimson of the geologic colourist, as if the igneous rocks of which they are composed still retained the red heat of their molten condition. Such would be the conventional colouring of the landscape ; vast tracts of purple, of chocolate, of gray, and of blue, would indicate the proportional space occupied in its area by the three great systems that have furnished us with a picture a-piece ; and what we have now to conjure up,—the platform of the stage being fairly erected, and its various coverings laid down,—is the scene illustrative of the origin and upheaval of the various trap-rocks that have come to form the bolder features of the prospect,—among the rest, supreme in the centre of the disturbed district, the stately column of the Bass.

The land of the Coal Measures has again disappeared ; and a shoreless but shallow ocean, much vexed by currents, and often lashed by tempest, spreads out around, as during the earlier periods. But there are more deeply-seated heavings that proceed from the centre of the immediate area over which we stand, than ever yet owed their origin to storm or tide. Ever and anon waves of dizzy altitude roll outwards towards the horizon, as if raised by the fall of some such vast pebble as the blind Cyclops sent whizzing through the air after the galley of Ulysses, when

> " The whole sea shook, and refluent beat the shore."

We may hear, too, deep from the abyss, the growlings, as of a subterranean thunder, loud enough to drown the nearer sounds of both wave and current. And now, as the huge kraken lifts its enormous back over the waves, the solid strata beneath rise from the bottom in a flat dome, crusted with shells and corals, and dark with algæ. The billows roll back, —the bared strata heave, and crack, and sever,—a dense smouldering vapour issues from the opening rents and fissures; and now the stony pavement is torn abruptly asunder, like some mildewed curtain seized rudely by the hand,—a broad sheet of flame mounts sudden as lightning through the opening, a thousand fathoms into the sky,—

> " Infuriate molten rocks and flaming globes,
>   Mount high above the clouds,"—

and the volcano is begun.　Meanwhile, the whole region around, far as the eye can reach, heaves wildly in the throes of Plutonic convulsion.　Above many a rising shallow, the sea boils and roars, as amid the skerries of some rocky bay open to the unbroken roll of the ocean in a time of tempest; the platform of sedimentary rock over an area of many square miles is fractured, like the ice of some Highland tarn during a hasty spring thaw that swells every mountain streamlet into a river; waves of translation, produced at once in numerous centres by the sudden upheaval of the bottom, meet and conflict under canopies of smoke and ashes; the light thickens as the reek ascends; and, amid the loud patter of the ejected stones and pumice, as they descend upon the sea,—the roaring of the flames,—the rending of rocks,—the dash of waves, —and the hollow internal grumblings of earthquakes,—dark night comes down upon the deep.　Vastly extended periods pass away; there are alternate pauses and paroxysms of convulsion; and ere the Plutonic agencies, worn out in the struggle, are laid fairly asleep, and the curtain again rises, the entire scene is changed.　Of the old sedimentary rocks, there remain in a wide tract only a few insulated beds, half-buried in enormous accumulations of volcanic debris,—debris stratified by the waves, and consolidated into a tolerably adhesive tuff by the superincumbent pressure, and here traversed by long dikes of basalt, and there overlaid by ponderous beds of greenstone. The Bass towers before us as a tall conical hill, deeply indented atop by the now silent crater,—its slopes formed of loose ashes and rude fragments of ejected rock, and with the flush of sulphur, here of a deep red, there of a golden yellow, still bright on its sides.

Let us rightly conceive of the hill in this, the last of the bygone aspects. Nearly two centuries ago there was a large tract of land covered over, in the north of Scotland, by blown sand; and among the other interred objects,—such as human dwellings, sheep and cattlefolds, gateways, and the fences of fields and gardens,—there were several orchard trees, enveloped in the dry deluge, and buried up. Of one of these it is said that the upper branches projected for several years from the top of the pyramidal hillock that had formed around it, and that they continued to produce in their season a few stunted leaves, with here and there a sickly blossom; but the branches at length dried up and disappeared, and for more than a century there were scarce any of the inhabitants of the neighbouring district who seemed to know what it was the conical hill contained. And then the prevailing winds, that had so long before covered up the orchard tree, began to scoop out the sides of its arenaceous tumulus, and to lay bare twig and branch, and at length the trunk itself; but the rotting damps, operating on the wood in a state of close seclusion from the air, had wrought their natural work; and as the tumulus crumbled away, the twigs and boughs, with the upper portion of the trunk, crumbled away also; till at length, when the entire enveloping material was removed, there remained of the tree but an upright stump, that rose a few feet over the soil. Now, the conical envelop or tumulus of debris and ashes which at this stage composes the exterior covering of the Bass resembles exactly that which surrounded, in the buried barony of Cubin, the orchard tree; while its stony centre of trap, moulded in the tubular crater, with its various branch-like arms bent earthwards, like those of the weeping ash,—the remains of eruptive currents flowing outwards and downwards,—represent the tree itself. The denuding agent is not, as in the sandy wastes of Moray, the keen dry wind of the west, but the slow wear, prolonged through many ages, of waves and currents. The sloping sides crumble down, —the stony branches fall, undermined, into the tide, and are swept away,—until at length, as in the orchard-tree of my illustration, there remains but an abrupt and broken stump, —the ancient storm-worn island of the Bass.

The enormous amount of denudation which the theories of the geologist demand, however consonant with his observations of fact, may well startle the uninitiated. The Lower Coal Measures appear on three sides of this disturbed district : they may be traced, as has been shown, in the immediate neighbourhood of Dunbar to the east ; they occur at Abbey Toll, near Haddington, on the south ; and they extend a little beyond Aberlady Bay on the west; while the sedimentary rocks that appear in the centre of the area, directly opposite the Bass, belong, as has also been shown, to an inferior member of the Old Red Sandstone. The surrounding Coal Measures form the edges of a broken dome, that, upheaved originally by the volcanic forces, as a bubble in a crucible of boiling sulphur is inflated and upheaved by the imprisoned gas, has been ground down, as it rose, by the denuding agencies, until in the centre of the area the Lower Old Red rocks have been laid bare. And so immense was the dome, though, of course, destroyed piecemeal as it rose,—as a log in a saw-mill is cut piecemeal by being gradually impelled on the saw,—that immediately over the Bass it would have now risen, had it been suffered to mount unworn and unbroken, to an altitude scarce inferior to that of Ben Nevis or Ben Macdhui. In this region of birds,—dwellers on the dizzy cliff,—no bird soars half so high as the imaginary dotted line some three or four thousand feet over the level, at which, save for the wear of the waves when the volcanic agencies were propelling the surface upwards, the higher layers of the Coal Measures would now have stood. Denudation to an extent equally great has taken place immediately over the site of the city of Edinburgh. Lunardi, in his balloon, never reached the point, high over our towers and spires, at which, save for the waste of ocean, the upper coal-seams would at this moment have lain. There are various localities in Scotland in which the loss of surface must have been greater still; and fancy, overborne by visions of waste and attrition on a scale so gigantic, can scarce take the conception in ; far less can the mind, when unassisted by auxiliary facts, receive it as a reality. Viewed, however, in connection with the vast periods which have intervened since the last of these denuded rocks were formed, —and be it remembered, that immediately after their formation denudation may have begun,—viewed, too, in connection with that work of deposition which has been going on during these periods elsewhere, and with the self-evident truth that, mainly from the wear of the older rocks have the materials of the newer been derived,—it grows into credibility, and takes its place among kindred wonders, simply as one of the facts of a class.   During the *denudation*, to the depth of three or four thousand feet, of the tract of country where the capital of Scotland now stands, a *deposition* to a vastly greater depth was taking place in the tract of country occupied by the capital of England.   Nor does it seem in any degree more strange that the rocks in the one locality should have been ground down from the red sandstones of Roslin to the calciferous beds which underlie the Mountain Limestone, than that strata should have been laid over strata in the other, from the Triasic group to the Oolite, and from the Oolite to the London Clay.   Had there not been immense waste and attrition among the Primary and Palæozoic rocks, there could have been no Secondary formations, and no Tertiary system.

My history speeds on to its conclusion.   We dimly descry, amid fog and darkness, yet one scene more.   There has been a change in the atmosphere; and the roar of flame and the hollow voice of earthquake are succeeded by the howling of wintry tempests and the crash of icebergs.   Wandering fragments of the northern winter, bulky as hills, go careering over the submerged land, grinding down its softer rocks and shales into clay, leaving inscribed their long streaks and furrows on its traps and its limestones, and thickly strewing the surface of one district with the detached ruins of another. To this last of the geologic revolutions the deep grooves and furrows of the rocks in the immediate neighbourhood of North Berwick belong, with the immense boulders of travelled rock which one occasionally sees in the interior on moors and hill-sides, or standing out along the sea-coast, disinterred by the waves from amid their banks of gravel or clay. But this last scene in the series I find drawn to my hand, though for another purpose, by the poet who produced the " Ancient Mariner :"— ·

> " Anon there come both mist and snow,
>   And it grows wondrous cold ;
> And ice mast-high comes floating by,
>   As green as emerald.
>
> And through the drifts the snowy cliffs
>   Do send a dismal sheen ;
> Nor shapes of men nor beasts we ken ;—
>   The ice is all between.
>
> The ice is here, the ice is there,
>   The ice is all around ;
> It cracks and growls, and roars and howls,
>   Like noises in a swound."

But the day breaks, and the storm ceases, and the submerged land lifts up its head over the sea ; and the Bass, in the fair morn of the existing creation, looms tall and high to the new-risen sun,—then, as now,

> " An island salt and bare,
> The haunt of seals and orcs, and sea-mews' clang."

THE END.

EDINBURGH : PRINTED BY MILLER & FAIRLY.

CATALOGUE OF
POPULAR AND STANDARD BOOKS

PUBLISHED BY

WILLIAM P. NIMMO,

EDINBURGH,

AND SOLD BY ALL BOOKSELLERS.

A SUPERB GIFT-BOOK.

The 'Edina' Burns.

JUST READY,

Beautifully printed on the finest toned paper, and elegantly bound in cloth extra, gilt edges, price One Guinea; or Turkey morocco extra, price Two Guineas; or in clan tartan enamelled, with photograph of the Poet, price Two Guineas,

A HANDSOME DRAWING-ROOM EDITION OF

THE POEMS AND SONGS

OF

ROBERT BURNS.

WITH ORIGINAL ILLUSTRATIONS BY THE MOST DISTINGUISHED SCOTTISH ARTISTS.

The 'EDINA' EDITION of BURNS contains Sixty-four entirely Original Illustrations, drawn expressly for it; and the names of the Artists who have kindly given their assistance—comprising several of the most distinguished members of the Royal Scottish Academy —are a sufficient guarantee that they are executed in the highest style of art. The engraving of the Illustrations is executed by Mr. R. PATERSON; and the volume is printed by Mr. R. CLARK, Edinburgh.

3.69.

NIMMO'S
LARGE PRINT UNABRIDGED
LIBRARY EDITION OF THE BRITISH POETS.
FROM CHAUCER TO COWPER.

In Forty-eight Vols. Demy 8vo, Pica Type, Superfine Paper, Elegant
Binding, price 4s. each Volume.

The Text edited by CHARLES COWDEN CLARKE.

With Authentic Portraits engraved on Steel.

The following Works are comprised in the Series :—

	Vols.		Vols.
WYATT,	1	CHURCHILL,	1
SPENSER,	5	BEATTIE, BLAIR, FALCONER,	1
SHAKESPEARE, SURREY,	1		
HERBERT,	1	BURNS,	2
WALLER, DENHAM,	1	COWPER,	2
MILTON,	2	BOWLES,	2
BUTLER,	2	SCOTT,	3
DRYDEN,	2	CHAUCER'S CANTERBURY TALES,	3
PRIOR,	1		
THOMSON,	1	CRAWSHAW, QUARLES' EMBLEMS,	1
JOHNSON, PARNELL, GRAY, SMOLLETT,	1	ADDISON, GAY'S FABLES, SOMERVILLE'S CHASE,	1
POPE,	2	YOUNG'S NIGHT THOUGHTS,	1
SHENSTONE,	1	PERCY'S RELIQUES OF ANCIENT ENGLISH POETRY,	3
AKENSIDE,	1		
GOLDSMITH, COLLINS, T. WARTON,	1	SPECIMENS, WITH LIVES OF THE LESS KNOWN BRITISH POETS,	3
ARMSTRONG, DYER, GREEN,	1	H. K. WHITE AND J. GRAHAME'S POETICAL WORKS,	1

Any of the Works may be had separately, price 4s. each Volume.

NIMMO'S 'CARMINE' GIFT-BOOKS.
NEW AND CHEAPER EDITIONS.

I.
Small 4to, beautifully printed within red lines on superior paper, handsomely bound in cloth extra, bevelled boards, gilt edges, price 7s. 6d.,

ROSES AND HOLLY:
A Gift-Book for all the Year.

With Original Illustrations by eminent Artists.

'This is really a collection of art and literary gems—the prettiest book, take it all in all, that we have seen this season.'—*Illustrated Times.*

II.
Uniform with the above, price 7s. 6d.,

PEN AND PENCIL PICTURES FROM THE POETS.
Choicely Illustrated.

III.
Uniform with the above, price 7s. 6d.,

GEMS OF LITERATURE:
ELEGANT, RARE, AND SUGGESTIVE.
With superb Illustrations.

'For really luxurious books, Nimmo's "Pen and Pencil Pictures from the Poets" and "Gems of Literature" may be well recommended. They are luxurious in the binding, in the print, in the engravings, and in the paper.'—*Morning Post.*

IV.
Uniform with the above, price 7s. 6d.,

THE BOOK OF ELEGANT EXTRACTS.
Profusely Illustrated by the most eminent Artists.

V.
Uniform with the above, price 7s. 6d.,

THE GOLDEN GIFT.
A BOOK FOR THE YOUNG.
Profusely Illustrated with Original Engravings on Wood by eminent Artists.

HUGH MILLER'S WORKS.

CHEAP POPULAR EDITIONS,

In crown 8vo, cloth extra, price 5s. each.

I.
Thirteenth Edition.

My Schools and Schoolmasters; or, The Story of my Education.

'A story which we have read with pleasure, and shall treasure up in memory for the sake of the manly career narrated, and the glances at old-world manners and distant scenes afforded us by the way.'—*Athenæum.*

A cheaper edition of 'My Schools and Schoolmasters' is also published, bound in limp cloth, price 2s. 6d.

II.
Thirty-fourth Thousand.

The Testimony of the Rocks; or, Geology in its Bearings on the Two Theologies, Natural and Revealed. *Profusely Illustrated.*

'The most remarkable work of perhaps the most remarkable man of the age. . . . A magnificent epic, and the Principia of Geology.'—*British and Foreign Evangelical Review.*

III.
Ninth Edition.

The Cruise of the Betsey; or, A Summer Ramble among the Fossiliferous Deposits of the Hebrides. With Rambles of a Geologist; or Ten Thousand Miles over the Fossiliferous Deposits of Scotland.

IV.

Sketch-Book of Popular Geology: Being a Series of Lectures delivered before the Philosophical Institution of Edinburgh. With an Introductory Preface, giving a Resumé of the Progress of Geological Science within the last Two Years. By Mrs. MILLER.

V.
Ninth Edition.

First Impressions of England and its People.

'This is precisely the kind of book we should have looked for from the author of the "Old Red Sandstone." Straightforward and earnest in style, rich and varied in matter, these "First Impressions" will add another laurel to the wreath which Mr. Miller has already won for himself.'—*Westminster Review.*

A cheaper edition of 'First Impressions of England' is also published, bound in limp cloth, price 2s. 6d.

HUGH MILLER'S WORKS.

CHEAP POPULAR EDITIONS,

In crown 8vo, cloth extra, price 5s. each.

VI.
Ninth Edition.

Scenes and Legends of the North of Scotland;
Or, The Traditional History of Cromarty.

'A very pleasing and interesting book. The style has a purity and elegance which remind one of Irving, or of Irving's master, Goldsmith.' —*Spectator.*

VII.
Eleventh Edition.

The Old Red Sandstone; or, New Walks in
an Old Field. *Profusely Illustrated.*

'In Mr. Miller's charming little work will be found a very graphic description of the Old Red Fishes. I know not a more fascinating volume on any branch of British Geology.'—*Mantell's Medals of Creation.*

VIII.
Fourth Edition.

The Headship of Christ and the Rights of
the Christian People. With Preface by PETER BAYNE, A.M.

IX.
Tenth Edition.

Footprints of the Creator; or, The Asterolepis
of Stromness. With Preface and Notes by Mrs. MILLER, and a Biographical Sketch by Professor AGASSIZ. *Profusely Illustrated.*

'Mr. Miller has brought his subject to the point at which science in its onward progress now lands.'—AGASSIZ. *From Preface to American Edition of the 'Footprints.'*

X.
Third Edition.

Tales and Sketches. Edited, with a Preface,
by Mrs. MILLER.

XI.
Third Edition.

Essays: Historical and Biographical, Political
and Social, Literary and Scientific.

XII.
Second Edition.

Edinburgh and its Neighbourhood, Geological
and Historical. With the GEOLOGY OF THE BASS ROCK.

A New Work by Ascott R. Hope.

In crown 8vo, elegantly bound, cloth extra, price 6s.; or gilt edges and sides, 6s. 6d.,

STORIES OF SCHOOL LIFE.

By Ascott R. Hope,

Author of ' A Book about Boys,' ' A Book about Dominies,' etc. etc.

Crown 4to, cloth extra, gilt edges, price 6s.,

THE NATIONAL MELODIST.

Two Hundred Standard Songs, with Symphonies and Accompaniments for the Pianoforte.

Edited by J. C. Kieser.

Demy 4to, cloth extra, gilt edges, price 3s. 6d.,

THE SCOTTISH MELODIST.

Forty-Eight Scottish Songs and Ballads, with Symphonies and Accompaniments for the Pianoforte.

Edited by J. C. Kieser.

The above two volumes are very excellent Collections of First-class Music. The arrangements and accompaniments, as the name of the Editor will sufficiently testify, are admirable. They form handsome and suitable presentation volumes.

Demy 8vo, cloth, price 10s. 6d.,

JAMIESON'S
SCOTTISH DICTIONARY.

Abridged from the Dictionary and Supplement (in 4 vols. 4to), by John Johnstone. An entirely new Edition, Revised and Enlarged, by John Longmuir, A.M., LL.D., formerly Lecturer in King's College and University, Aberdeen.

NIMMO'S
LIBRARY EDITION OF STANDARD WORKS,

𝔚𝔢𝔩𝔩 𝔞𝔡𝔞𝔭𝔱𝔢𝔡 𝔣𝔬𝔯 𝔓𝔯𝔦𝔷𝔢𝔰 𝔦𝔫 𝔘𝔭𝔭𝔢𝔯 ℭ𝔩𝔞𝔰𝔰𝔢𝔰 𝔞𝔫𝔡 𝔥𝔦𝔤𝔥 𝔖𝔠𝔥𝔬𝔬𝔩𝔰.

In large Demy 8vo, with Steel Portrait and Vignette, handsomely
bound in cloth extra, in a new style, price 5s. each.

I.
THE COMPLETE WORKS OF WILLIAM SHAKE-SPEARE.

II.
THE COMPLETE POETI-CAL AND PROSE WORKS OF ROBERT BURNS.

III.
THE MISCELLANEOUS WORKS OF OLIVER GOLDSMITH.

IV.
THE POETICAL WORKS OF LORD BYRON.

V.
JOSEPHUS: The Whole Works of FLAVIUS JOSEPHUS, the Jewish Historian.

VI.
THE ARABIAN NIGHTS' ENTERTAINMENTS.

VII.
THE WORKS OF JONA-THAN SWIFT, D.D. Carefully selected, with Life of the Author, and original and authentic Notes.

VIII.
THE WORKS OF DANIEL DEFOE. Carefully selected from the most authentic sources; with Life of the Author.

Four Volumes, Crown 8vo, cloth, price 18s.,

THE PEOPLE'S EDITION OF
TYTLER'S HISTORY OF SCOTLAND.

'The most brilliant age of Scotland is fortunate in having found a historian whose sound judgment is accompanied by a graceful liveliness of imagination. We venture to predict that this book will soon become, and long remain, the standard History of Scotland.'—*Quarterly Review.*

'An accurate, well-digested, well-written History; evincing deliberation, research, judgment, and fidelity.'—*Scotsman.*

'The tenor of the work in general reflects the highest honour on Mr. Tytler's talents and industry.'—*Sir Walter Scott.*

'The want of a complete History of Scotland has been long felt; and from the specimen which the volume before us gives of the author's talents and capacity for the task he has undertaken, it may be reasonably inferred that the deficiency will be very ably supplied. The descriptions of the battles are concise, but full of spirit. The events are themselves of the most romantic kind, and are detailed in a very picturesque and forcible style.'—*Times.*

NIMMO'S POPULAR EDITION OF THE WORKS OF THE POET.

In fcap. 8vo, printed on toned paper, elegantly bound in cloth extra, gilt edges, price 3s. 6d. each; or in morocco antique, price 6s. 6d. each. Each Volume contains a Memoir, and is illustrated with a Portrait of the Author, engraved on Steel, and numerous full-page Illustrations on Wood, from designs by eminent Artists.

I.
Longfellow's Poetical Works.

II.
Scott's Poetical Works.

III.
Byron's Poetical Works.

IV.
Moore's Poetical Works.

V.
Wordsworth's Poetical Works.

VI.
Cowper's Poetical Works.

VII.
Milton's Poetical Works.

VIII.
Thomson's Poetical Works.

IX.
Beattie and Goldsmith's Poetical Works.

X.
Pope's Poetical Works.

XI.
Burns's Poetical Works.

XII.
The Casquet of Gems.
A Volume of Choice Selections from the Works of the Poets.

XIII.
The Book of Humorous Poetry.

XIV.
Ballads: Scottish and English.

*** This Series of Books, from the very superior manner in which it is produced, is at once the cheapest and handsomest edition of the Poets in the market. The volumes form elegant and appropriate presents as School Prizes and Gift-Books, either in cloth or morocco.

'They are a marvel of cheapness, some of the volumes extending to as many as 700, and even 900, pages, printed on toned paper in a beautifully clear type. Add to this, that they are profusely illustrated with wood engravings, are elegantly and tastefully bound, and that they are published at 3s. 6d. each, and our recommendation of them is complete.'—*Scotsman.*

UNIFORM WITH

NIMMO'S POPULAR EDITION OF THE WORKS OF THE POETS.

I.
The Complete Works of Shakespeare.

With Biographical Sketch by MARY COWDEN CLARKE. Two Volumes, price 3s. 6d. each.

II.
The Arabian Nights' Entertainments.

With One Hundred Illustrations on Wood. Two Volumes, price 3s. 6d. each.

III.
Bunyan's Pilgrim's Progress & Holy War.

Complete in One Volume.

IV.
Lives of the British Poets:

Biographies of the most eminent British Poets, with Specimens of their Writings. Twelve Portraits on Steel, and Twelve Full-page Illustrations.

V.
The Prose Works of Robert Burns.

Correspondence complete, Remarks on Scottish Song, Letters to Clarinda, Commonplace Books, etc. etc.

Second Edition, Crown 8vo, cloth extra, price 3s. 6d.,

FAMILY PRAYERS FOR FIVE WEEKS,

WITH PRAYERS FOR SPECIAL OCCASIONS, AND A TABLE FOR READING THE HOLY SCRIPTURES THROUGHOUT THE YEAR.

BY WILLIAM WILSON, MINISTER OF KIPPEN.

'This is an excellent compendium of family prayers. It will be found invaluable to parents and heads of families. The prayers are short, well expressed, and the book as a whole does the author great credit.'—*Perth Advertiser.*

'Thoroughly evangelical and devotional in spirit, beautifully simple and scriptural in expression, and remarkably free from repetition or verbosity, these prayers are admirably adapted either for family use or for private reading.'—*Kelso Chronicle.*

NIMMO'S PRESENTATION SERIES OF STANDARD WORKS.

In small Crown 8vo, printed on toned paper, bound in cloth extra, gilt
edges, bevelled boards, with Portrait engraved on Steel,
price 3s. 6d. each.

I.
WISDOM, WIT, AND ALLEGORY.
Selected from 'The Spectator.'

II.
BENJAMIN FRANKLIN:
A BIOGRAPHY.

III.
THE WORLD'S WAY:
LAYS OF LIFE AND LABOUR.

IV.
TRAVELS IN AFRICA.
THE LIFE AND TRAVELS OF
MUNGO PARK.

V.
WALLACE,
THE HERO OF SCOTLAND:
A BIOGRAPHY.

VI.
EPOCH MEN,
AND THE RESULTS OF THEIR
LIVES.

VII.
THE MIRROR OF CHARACTER.
SELECTED FROM THE WRITINGS OF
OVERBURY, EARLE,
AND BUTLER.

VIII.
MEN OF HISTORY.
By Eminent Writers.

IX.
OLD WORLD WORTHIES;
OR, CLASSICAL BIOGRAPHY.
SELECTED FROM
PLUTARCH'S LIVES.

X.
THE MAN OF BUSINESS
Considered in Six Aspects.
A BOOK FOR YOUNG MEN.

XI.
WOMEN OF HISTORY.
By Eminent Writers.

XII.
THE
IMPROVEMENT OF THE MIND.
By Isaac Watts.

XIII.
TALES OF OLD ENGLISH LIFE;
OR, PICTURES OF THE PERIODS.
By W. F. Collier, LL.D.

*** This elegant and useful Series of Books has been specially
prepared for School and College Prizes: they are, however, equally
suitable for General Presentation. In selecting the works for this
Series, the aim of the publisher has been to produce books of a perma-
nent value, interesting in manner and instructive in matter—books that
youth will read eagerly and with profit, and which will be found equally
attractive in after life.

NIMMO'S HALF-CROWN REWARD BOOKS.

Extra Foolscap 8vo, cloth elegant, gilt edges, Illustrated,
price 2s. 6d. each.

I.

Memorable Wars of Scotland.

BY
PATRICK FRASER TYTLER, F.R.S.E.,
Author of 'History of Scotland,' etc.

II.

Seeing the World:

A Young Sailor's Own Story.
BY CHARLES NORDHOFF,
Author of 'The Young Man-of-
War's Man.'

III.

The Martyr Missionary:

Five Years in China.
BY REV. CHARLES P. BUSH, M.A.

IV.

My New Home:

A Woman's Diary.
By the Author of 'Win and
Wear,' etc.

V.

Home Heroines:

Tales for Girls.
BY T. S. ARTHUR,
Author of ' Life's Crosses,'
'Orange Blossoms,' etc.

VI.

Lessons from Women's Lives.

BY SARAH J. HALE.

NIMMO'S FAVOURITE GIFT-BOOKS.

In small 8vo, Illustrated, printed on toned paper, richly bound in cloth
and gold and gilt edges, with new and original Frontispiece,
printed in colours by KRONHEIM, price 2s. 6d. each.

I.

The Vicar of Wakefield.

Poems and Essays.
BY OLIVER GOLDSMITH.

II.

Bunyan's Pilgrim's Progress.

III.

The Life and Adventures of Robinson Crusoe.

IV.

Æsop's Fables,

With Instructive Applications.
BY DR. CROXALL.

V.

The History of Sandford and Merton.

VI.

Evenings at Home;

Or, The Juvenile Budget Opened.

*** The above are very elegant and remarkably cheap editions of
these old favourite Works.

NIMMO'S SIXPENNY JUVENILE BOOKS.

Demy 18mo, Illustrated, handsomely bound in cloth, gilt side, gilt edges, price 6d. each.

I.
Pearls for Little People.

II.
Great Lessons for Little People.

III.
Reason in Rhyme:
A Poetry Book for the Young.

IV.
Æsop's Little Fable Book.

V.
Grapes from the Great Vine.

VI.
The Pot of Gold.

VII.
Story Pictures from the Bible.

VIII.
The Tables of Stone:
Illustrations of the Commandments.

IX.
Ways of Doing Good.

X.
Stories about our Dogs.
By HARRIET BEECHER STOWE.

XI.
The Red-Winged Goose.

XII.
The Hermit of the Hills.

NIMMO'S FOURPENNY JUVENILE BOOKS.

The above Series of Books are also done up in elegant Enamelled Paper Covers, beautifully printed in Colours, price 4d. each.

₊ The distinctive features of the New Series of Sixpenny and One Shilling Juvenile Books are: The Subjects of each Volume have been selected with a due regard to Instruction and Entertainment; they are well printed on fine paper, in a superior manner; the Shilling Series is Illustrated with Frontispieces printed in Colours; the Sixpenny Series has beautiful Engravings; and they are elegantly bound.

Third Edition, Crown 8vo, cloth extra, price 3s. 6d.,

A BOOK ABOUT DOMINIES:

BEING THE REFLECTIONS AND RECOLLECTIONS OF A MEMBER OF THE PROFESSION.

By ASCOTT R. HOPE, Author of 'A Book about Boys,' etc.

Bell's Weekly Messenger.
'A more sensible book than this about boys has rarely been written, for it enters practically into all the particulars which have to be encountered amongst "the young ideas" who have to be trained for life, and are too often marred by the educational means adopted for their early mental development. The writer is evidently one of the Arnold school—that "prince of schoolmasters"—who did more for the formation of the character of his pupils than any man that ever lived.'

NIMMO'S SUNDAY SCHOOL REWARD BOOKS.

Fcap. 8vo, cloth extra, gilt edges, Illustrated, price 1s. 6d. each.

I.
Bible Blessings.
By Rev. Richard Newton,
Author of 'The Best Things,' 'The Safe Compass,' 'The King's Highway,' etc.

II.
One Hour a Week:
Fifty-two Bible Lessons for the Young.
By the Author of 'Jesus on Earth.'

III.
The Best Things.
By Rev. Richard Newton.

IV.
Grace Harvey and her Cousins.
By the Author of 'Douglas Farm.'

V.
Lessons from Rose Hill;
AND
Little Nannette.

VI.
Great and Good Women:
Biographies for Girls.
By Lydia H. Sigourney.

VII.
At Home and Abroad; or,
Uncle William's Adventures.

VIII.
The Kind Governess; or,
How to Make Home Happy.

NIMMO'S ONE SHILLING JUVENILE BOOKS.

Foolscap 8vo, Coloured Frontispieces, handsomely bound in cloth, Illuminated, price 1s. each.

I.
Four Little People and their Friends.

II.
Elizabeth;
Or, The Exiles of Siberia.

III.
Paul and Virginia.

IV.
Little Threads:
Tangle Thread, Golden Thread, Silver Thread.

V.
Benjamin Franklin:
A Biography for Boys.

VI.
Barton Todd.

VII.
The Perils of Greatness; or,
The Story of Alexander Menzikoff.

VIII.
Little Crowns, and How to Win them.

IX.
Great Riches:
Nelly Rivers' Story.

X.
The Right Way, and the Contrast.

XI.
The Daisy's First Winter,
And other Stories.

XII.
The Man of the Mountain.

NIMMO'S TWO SHILLING REWARD BOOKS.

Foolscap 8vo, Illustrated, elegantly bound in cloth extra, bevelled boards, gilt back and side, gilt edges, price 2s. each.

I.

The Far North:
Explorations in the Arctic Regions.
By ELISHA KENT KANE, M.D., Commander second 'Grinnell' Expedition in search of Sir John Franklin.

II.

The Young Men of the Bible:
A Series of Papers, Biographical and Suggestive.
By REV. JOSEPH A. COLLIER.

III.

The Blade and the Ear:
A Book for Young Men.

IV.

Monarchs of Ocean:
Narratives of Maritime Discovery and Progress.

V.

Life's Crosses, and How to Meet them.
By T. S. ARTHUR,
Author of 'Anna Lee,' 'Orange Blossoms,' etc.

VI.

A Father's Legacy to his Daughters; etc.
A Book for Young Women.
By DR. GREGORY.

VII.

Great Men of European History.
By DAVID PRYDE, M.A.

NIMMO'S EIGHTEENPENNY REWARD BOOKS.

Demy 18mo, Illustrated, cloth extra, gilt edges, price 1s. 6d. each.

I.

The Vicar of Wakefield.
Poems and Essays.

II.

Æsop's Fables,
With Instructive Applications.

III.

Bunyan's Pilgrim's Progress.

IV.

The Young Man-of-War's Man.

V.

The Treasury of Anecdote:
Moral and Religious.

VI.

The Boy's Own Workshop.
By JACOB ABBOTT.

VII.

The Life and Adventures of Robinson Crusoe.

VIII.

The History of Sandford and Merton.

IX.

Evenings at Home.

X.

Unexpected Pleasures.
By MRS. GEORGE CUPPLES, Author of 'The Little Captain,' etc.

*** The above Series of elegant and useful books are specially prepared for the entertainment and instruction of young persons.

NIMMO'S POCKET TREASURIES.

Miniature 4to, beautifully bound in cloth extra, gilt edges,
price 1s. 6d. each.

I.

A Treasury of Table Talk.

II.

Epigrams and Literary Follies.

III.

A Treasury of Poetic Gems.

IV.

The Table Talk of Samuel Johnson, LL.D.

V.

Gleanings from the Comedies of Shakespeare.

VI.

Beauties of the British Dramatists.

'A charming little Series, well edited and printed. More thoroughly readable little books it would be hard to find; there is no padding in them, all is epigram, point, poetry, or sound common sense.'—*Publisher's Circular.*

Crown 8vo, cloth extra, price 6s.,

WAYSIDE THOUGHTS OF A PROFESSOR:

BEING A SERIES OF DESULTORY ESSAYS ON EDUCATION.

By D'ARCY WENTWORTH THOMPSON,
Professor of Greek, Queen's College, Galway; Author of 'Day Dreams of a Schoolmaster;' 'Sales Attici,' etc. etc.

CONTENTS.

Introductory.
School Memories.
College Memories.
A Teacher's Experiences.
Our Home Civilisation.
What is a Schoolmaster?

Youth and College.
Boyhood and School.
Childhood and the Nursery.
Girlhood, Womanhood, and Home.
All Work and no Play.
Manhood and the World.

Crown 8vo, cloth extra, price 6s.,

LAST LEAVES:

SKETCHES AND CRITICISMS.

By ALEXANDER SMITH,
Author of 'Life Drama,' 'Dreamthorpe,' etc. etc.

Edited, with a Memoir, by PATRICK PROCTOR ALEXANDER, M.A.,
Author of 'Mill and Carlyle,' etc. etc.

NIMMO'S POPULAR RELIGIOUS GIFT-BOOKS.

18mo, finely printed on toned paper, handsomely bound in cloth extra,
bevelled boards, gilt edges, price 1s. 6d. each.

I.

Across the River: Twelve Views of Heaven.
By NORMAN MACLEOD, D.D.; R. W. HAMILTON, D.D.; ROBERT S.
CANDLISH, D.D.; JAMES HAMILTON, D.D.; etc. etc. etc.
'A more charming little work has rarely fallen under our notice, or one that
will more faithfully direct the steps to that better land it should be the aim of all
to seek.'—*Bell's Messenger.*

II.

Emblems of Jesus; or, Illustrations of
Emmanuel's Character and Work.

III.

Life Thoughts of Eminent Christians.

IV.

Comfort for the Desponding; or, Words to
Soothe and Cheer Troubled Hearts.

V.

The Chastening of Love; or, Words of Con-
solation to the Christian Mourner. By JOSEPH PARKER, D.D.,
Manchester.

VI.

The Cedar Christian. By the Rev. Theodore
L. CUYLER.

VII.

Consolation for Christian Mothers bereaved
OF LITTLE CHILDREN. By A FRIEND OF MOURNERS.

VIII.

The Orphan; or, Words of Comfort for the
Fatherless and Motherless.

IX.

Gladdening Streams; or, The Waters of the
Sanctuary. A Book for Fragments of Time on each Lord's Day
of the Year.

X.

Spirit of the Old Divines.

XI.

Choice Gleanings from Sacred Writers.

XII.

Direction in Prayer. By Peter Grant, D.D.,
Author of 'Emblems of Jesus,' etc.

XIII.

Scripture Imagery. By Peter Grant, D.D.,
Author of 'Emblems of Jesus,' etc.

Popular Works by the Author of 'Heaven our Home.'

—o—

I.

ONE HUNDREDTH THOUSAND.

Crown 8vo, cloth antique, price 3s. 6d.,

HEAVEN OUR HOME.

'The author of the volume before us endeavours to describe what heaven is, as shown by the light of reason and Scripture; and we promise the reader many charming pictures of heavenly bliss, founded upon undeniable authority, and described with the pen of a dramatist, which cannot fail to elevate the soul as well as to delight the imagination. . . . . . Part Second proves, in a manner as beautiful as it is convincing, the DOCTRINE OF THE RECOGNITION OF FRIENDS IN HEAVEN,—a subject of which the author makes much, introducing many touching scenes of Scripture celebrities meeting in heaven and discoursing of their experience on earth. Part Third DEMONSTRATES THE INTEREST WHICH THOSE IN HEAVEN FEEL IN EARTH, AND PROVES, WITH REMARKABLE CLEARNESS, THAT SUCH AN INTEREST EXISTS NOT ONLY WITH THE ALMIGHTY AND AMONG THE ANGELS, BUT ALSO AMONG THE SPIRITS OF DEPARTED FRIENDS. We unhesitatingly give our opinion that this volume is one of the most delightful productions of a religious character which has appeared for some time; and we would desire to see it pass into extensive circulation.'—*Glasgow Herald.*

A Cheap Edition of

HEAVEN OUR HOME,

In crown 8vo, cloth limp, price 1s. 6d., is also published.

II.

TWENTY-NINTH THOUSAND.

Crown 8vo, cloth antique, price 3s. 6d.,

MEET FOR HEAVEN.

'The author, in his or her former work, "Heaven our Home," portrayed a SOCIAL HEAVEN, WHERE SCATTERED FAMILIES MEET AT LAST IN LOVING INTERCOURSE AND IN POSSESSION OF PERFECT RECOGNITION, to spend a never-ending eternity of peace and love. In the present work the individual state of the children of God is attempted to be unfolded, and more especially the state of probation which is set apart for them on earth to fit and prepare erring mortals for the society of the saints . . . . The work, as a whole, displays an originality of conception, a flow of language, and a closeness of reasoning rarely found in religious publications. . . . . The author combats the pleasing and generally accepted belief, that DEATH WILL EFFECT AN ENTIRE CHANGE ON THE SPIRITUAL CONDITION OF OUR SOULS, and that all who enter into bliss will be placed on a common level.'— *Glasgow Herald.*

A Cheap Edition of

MEET FOR HEAVEN,

In crown 8vo, cloth limp, price 1s. 6d., is also published.

Works by the Author of 'Heaven our Home'—*continued*.

III.
TWENTY-FIRST THOUSAND.
Crown 8vo, cloth antique, price 3s. 6d.,
LIFE IN HEAVEN.

THERE, FAITH IS CHANGED INTO SIGHT, AND HOPE IS PASSED INTO BLISSFUL FRUITION.

'This is certainly one of the most remarkable works which have been issued from the press during the present generation; and we have no doubt it will prove as acceptable to the public as the two attractive volumes to which it forms an appropriate and beautiful sequel.'—*Cheltenham Journal.*

'We think this work well calculated to remove many erroneous ideas respecting our future state, and to put before its readers such an idea of the reality of our existence there, as may tend to make a future world more desirable and more sought for than it is at present.'—*Cambridge University Chronicle.*

'This, like its companion works, "Heaven our Home," and "Meet for Heaven," needs no adventitious circumstances, no prestige of literary renown, to recommend it to the consideration of the reading public, and, like its predecessors, will no doubt circulate by tens of thousands throughout the land.'—*Glasgow Examiner.*

A Cheap Edition of
LIFE IN HEAVEN,
In crown 8vo, cloth limp, price 1s. 6d., is also published.

IV.
SEVENTH THOUSAND.
Crown 8vo, cloth antique, price 3s. 6d.,
CHRIST'S TRANSFIGURATION;
OR, TABOR'S TEACHINGS.

'The work opens up to view a heaven to be prized, and a home to be sought for, and presents it in a cheerful and attractive aspect. The beauty and elegance of the language adds grace and dignity to the subject, and will tend to secure to it the passport to public favour so deservedly merited and obtained by the author's former productions.'—*Montrose Standard.*

'A careful reading of this volume will add immensely to the interest of the New Testament narrative of the Transfiguration, and so far will greatly promote our personal interest in the will of God as revealed in his word.'—*Wesleyan Times.*

A Cheap Edition of
CHRIST'S TRANSFIGURATION,
In crown 8vo, cloth limp, price 1s. 6d., is also published.

*** Aggregate Sale of the above Popular Works, 157,000 copies. In addition to this, they have been reprinted and extensively circulated in America.

Uniform with 'Heaven our Home.'

Third Edition, just ready, price 3s. 6d.,

THE SPIRIT DISEMBODIED.

*WHEN WE DIE WE DO NOT FALL ASLEEP:
WE ONLY CHANGE OUR PLACE.*

BY HERBERT BROUGHTON.

OPINIONS OF THE PRESS.

'This book will be read by thousands. It treats on all-important subjects in a simple and attractive style.'—*Chronicle.*

'This is a book of very considerable merit, and destined, ere long, to attract attention in the literary world. The subject of which it treats is one of surpassing interest.'—*Berwick Warder.*

'This is a remarkable work, and well worth the study of all inquiring minds.'—*Renfrew Independent.*

'The last chapter supplies us with a few more instances of the deaths of pious men, in proof that angels do attend the deathbed scenes of the saints of God, to carry the disembodied spirit to heaven.'—*Pall Mall Gazette.*

'The author shows as conclusively as it can be shown, not only that the soul is an immortal part of our being, but that there are mysterious links connecting us with those we love on earth, and that when "clothed upon" with immortality, we shall "recognise each other and be together in eternity." '—*Exeter Post.*

'We think the author has satisfactorily demonstrated both the immortality of man, and also that the spirit lives in a condition of conscious existence after death. His chapter on the recognition of friends in heaven, proves that point in a convincing manner. His narratives of the triumphant deathbeds, and the celestial visions of many departed saints, will be prized by not a few readers.'—*Dundee Courier.*

NIMMO'S
HANDY BOOKS OF USEFUL KNOWLEDGE.

Foolscap 8vo, uniformly bound in cloth extra.

· PRICE ONE SHILLING EACH.

——o——

I.
THE EARTH'S CRUST.

A Handy Outline of Geology. With numerous Illustrations. Third Edition. By DAVID PAGE, LL.D., F.R.S.E., F.G.S., Author of 'Text-Books of Geology and Physical Geography,' etc.

'Such a work as this was much wanted,—a work giving in clear and intelligible outline the leading facts of the science, without amplification or irksome details. It is admirable in arrangement, and clear, easy, and at the same time forcible, in style. It will lead, we hope, to the introduction of geology into many schools that have neither time nor room for the study of large treatises.'—*The Museum.*

II.
POULTRY AS A MEAT SUPPLY:

Being Hints to Henwives how to Rear and Manage Poultry Economically and Profitably. Fourth Edition. By the Author of 'The Poultry Kalendar.'

'The Author's excellent aim is to teach henwives how to make the poultry-yard a profitable as well as pleasant pursuit, and to popularize poultry-rearing among the rural population generally.'—*The Globe.*

III.
HOW TO BECOME A SUCCESSFUL ENGINEER:

Being Hints to Youths intending to adopt the Profession. Third Edition. By BERNARD STUART, Engineer.

'Parents and guardians, with youths under their charge destined for the profession, as well as youths themselves, who intend to adopt it, will do well to study and obey the plain curriculum in this little book. Its doctrine will, we hesitate not to say, if practised, tend to fill the ranks of the profession with men conscious of the heavy responsibilities placed in their charge.'—*Practical Mechanic's Journal.*

IV. ·
RATIONAL COOKERY:

Cookery made Practical and Economical, in connection with the Chemistry of Food. Fifth Edition. By HARTELAW REID.

'A thousand times more useful as a marriage-gift than the usual gewgaw presents, would be this very simple manual for the daily guidance of the youthful bride in one of her most important domestic duties.'—*Glasgow Citizen.*

NIMMO'S
HANDY BOOKS OF USEFUL KNOWLEDGE—
Continued.

V.
EUROPEAN HISTORY:

In a Series of Biographies, from the Beginning of the Christian Era till the Present Time.　Second Edition.　By DAVID PRYDE, M.A.

'It is published with a view to the teaching of the history of Europe since the Christian era by the biographic method, recommended by Mr. Carlyle as the only proper method of teaching history. The style of the book is clear, elegant, and terse. The biographies are well, and, for the most part, graphically told.'—*The Scotsman.*

VI.
DOMESTIC MEDICINE:

Plain and Brief Directions for the Treatment requisite before Advice can be obtained.　Second Edition.　By OFFLEY BOHUN SHORE, Doctor of Medicine of the University of Edinburgh, etc. etc. etc.

'This is one of the medicine books that ought to be published. It is from the pen of Dr. Shore, an eminent physician, and it is dedicated, by permission, to Sir James Y. Simpson, Bart., one of the first physicians of the age.'—*The Standard.*

VII.
DOMESTIC MANAGEMENT:

Hints on the Training and Treatment of Children and Servants. By MRS. CHARLES DOIG.

'This is an excellent book of its kind, a handbook to family life which will do much towards promoting comfort and happiness.'—*The Spectator.*

VIII.
FREE-HAND DRAWING:

A Guide to Ornamental, Figure, and Landscape Drawing.　By an ART STUDENT, Author of 'Ornamental and Figure Drawing.' Profusely Illustrated.

'This is an excellent and thoroughly practical guide to ornamental, figure, and landscape drawing. Beginners could not make a better start than with this capital little book.'—*Morning Star.*

IX.
THE METALS USED IN CONSTRUCTION:

Iron, Steel, Bessemer Metal, etc. etc.　By FRANCIS HERBERT JOYNSON. Illustrated.

'In the interests of practical science, we are bound to notice this work; and to those who wish further information, we should say, buy it; and the outlay, we honestly believe, will be considered a shilling well spent.'—*Scientific Review.*

OTHER VOLUMES IN PREPARATION.

Popular Religious Works.

SUITABLE FOR PRESENTATION.

———o———

I.

Foolscap 8vo, handsomely bound in cloth extra, antique,
price 2s. 6d.,

CHRISTIAN COMFORT.

BY THE AUTHOR OF 'EMBLEMS OF JESUS.'

'There is a fitness and adaptability in this book for the purpose it
seeks to accomplish, which will most surely secure for it a wide and
general acceptance, not only in the home circle, but wherever suffering
may be found, whether mental, spiritual, or physical.'—*Wesleyan Times.*

———

II.

By the same Author, uniform in style and price,

LIGHT ON THE GRAVE.

'This is a book for the mourner, and one full of consolation. Even
a heathen poet could say, "*Non omnis moriar;*" and the object of this
book is to show how little of the good man can die, and how thoroughly
the sting of death, deprived of its poison, may be extracted. It is the
work of one who has apparently suffered, and obviously reflected much;
and, having traversed the vale of weeping, offers himself for a guide
to the spots where the springs of comfort flow, and where the sob passes
into the song. . . . . The form and elegance of the book, we must add,
make it peculiarly suitable as a gift.'—*Daily Review.*

———

III.

Uniform in style and price,

GLIMPSES OF THE CELESTIAL CITY,
AND GUIDE TO THE INHERITANCE.

With Introduction by the
REV. JOHN MACFARLANE, LL.D.,
CLAPHAM, LONDON.

———

Second Edition, enlarged, price 3s., richly bound,

STORY OF THE KINGS OF JUDAH AND ISRAEL.

WRITTEN FOR CHILDREN.

By A. O. B.

Illustrated with Full-page Engravings and Map.

NIMMO'S
Series of Commonplace Books.

Small 4to, elegantly printed on superfine toned paper, and richly bound in cloth and gold and gilt edges, price 2s. 6d. each.

I.

BOOKS AND AUTHORS.
CURIOUS FACTS AND CHARACTERISTIC SKETCHES.

II.

LAW AND LAWYERS.
CURIOUS FACTS AND CHARACTERISTIC SKETCHES.

III.

ART AND ARTISTS.
CURIOUS FACTS AND CHARACTERISTIC SKETCHES.

IV.

INVENTION AND DISCOVERY.
CURIOUS FACTS AND CHARACTERISTIC SKETCHES.

V.

OMENS AND SUPERSTITIONS.
CURIOUS FACTS AND ILLUSTRATIVE SKETCHES.

VI.

CLERGYMEN AND DOCTORS.
CURIOUS FACTS AND CHARACTERISTIC SKETCHES.

'This series seems well adapted to answer the end proposed by the publisher—that of providing, in a handy form, a compendium of wise and witty sayings, choice anecdotes, and memorable facts.'—*The Bookseller.*

Crown 8vo, handsomely bound, price 5s.,

THE YOUNG SHETLANDER,
Or,

SHADOW OVER THE SUNSHINE:
BEING LIFE AND LETTERS OF THOMAS EDMONSTON, Naturalist on board H.M.S. 'Herald.'

EDITED BY HIS MOTHER.

Just published, Crown 8vo, cloth extra, price 3s. 6d., Second Edition,

A BOOK ABOUT BOYS.
BY ASCOTT R. HOPE,
Author of 'A Book about Dominies.'